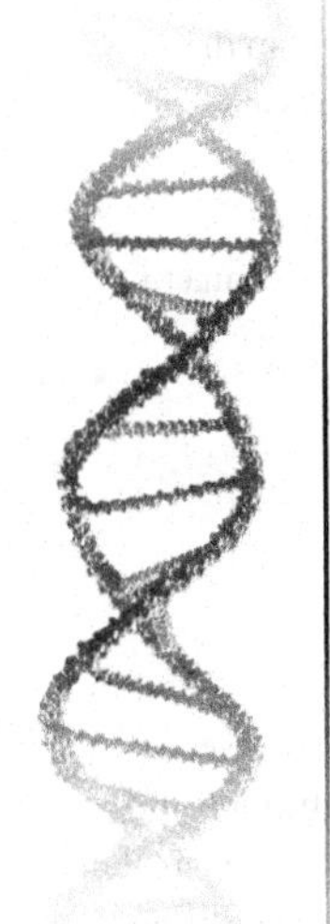

Michael Crowe

Tales of the NEPHILIM

TALES OF THE NEPHILIM

iUniverse books may be ordered through booksellers or by contacting:

iUniverse
1663 Liberty Drive
Bloomington, IN 47403
www.iuniverse.com
1-800-Authors (1-800-288-4677)

ISBN: 978-1-5320-0445-2 (sc)
ISBN: 978-1-5320-0446-9 (e)

Print information available on the last page.

iUniverse rev. date: 08/02/2016

a timeline science fiction story about
eggmen emeralds and alien DNA

Contents

Eggmen and Emeralds

a time-line science fiction story.
three generations of the Browning family

First Generation

"The Gentiles tried to confound the followers of the prophet, after they tarred and feathered him in Missouri and murdered him in Illinois. The Lehmanites and the Sons of Seth came to our aid, by the glory of God, even though we had slandered them and the nation of the Latter Day Saints was arisen."

Aenas Enoch Browning The story of how I got rich.

My folks come from so far back in the bush I am sure that they never even suspected that there was a second word for asshole. I am the eldest and every body knows I am a lot like him, like Daddy I mean. Especially as we both play guitar and all. In fact, I can imitate his guitar playing and his lyrics dead exactly and his voice as well. It was fun when we were growing up for me to imitate his hymns in front of the other kids with some of the lyrics switched around for our enjoyment. I am still in mortal danger of singing about shepherds embracing their sheep n the wrong company, due to having sung the corrupt versions far more often as a kid, than the approved hymn.

New Zion is the best place possible ever to grow up and I reckon that just through luck I got the best possible raising you could have there. First of , I got my first real gun when I was eight so I could take over a chore which ma didn't relish. She hated having to rush out on the back porch and fire at whatever was at the chickens. So I got to do it. I even got to put some food on the table. Another grand thing about where we lived on New Zion was it was wild and warm enough all year. An eight year old boys dream. Shoes weren't such a bad idea in the winter months, but they weren't absolutely necessary either, and many boys feet were like blocks of wood.

It was a wonderful place to camp out with fire-flies and big frog legs roasting on the fire. When I was young before daddy got somewhat successful, we lived upriver beyond the wire but when I was ten we got a farm. It had all the things mom had never had. Toilets, baths, washing machines, vehicles , telephones, tooth brushes, toilet paper, and razors. No, I am joking again, and at the expense of a wonderful lady. The extent of mom's upriver upbringing is a family joke and has kind of in a way, rendered her forever goofy and way too appreciative of things like toasters, metal stove , lamps and furniture.

Any way, my ma was his first wife. Daddy's I mean. She was a widow and a barren widow at that. She was thirty or so and had been married to an old man for fourteen years when he kicked the bucket at eighty . Then daddy sang his way into her life. Daddy can sing a widow off her stool and have her flopping around on the ground. I've seen him do it, hundreds of times. I guess he was about twenty. It would have been a bit scandalous. The widows aren't really supposed to knock off the young bucks. Everybody expects them to marry men in their thirties who have acquired some substance and the ability to consider a first wife. But ma didn't, she drug him to the altar. And then quick as she could she promoted his career as a hymn singer and preacher.

It seems to me, I didn't mention that mom has religion really bad. It's a funny kind of religion, but I wont get into that. At any rate she promoted him in her religious circle and got him married off a couple more times to widows younger and richer than herself.

It helped appearances. For the first time in her life she had material comforts. As first wife, she is also queen of all she surveys. Yup, New Zion is a great place to grow a boy up but it is a grim place to hit sixteen.

At age sixteen high school ends and all the little sweeties you have been coveting are suddenly married to old hairy men, at least twice your age . It is a real bummer. It was going to be the telestial kingdoms for me. It at least sounded interesting. I had my pioneer suit and my off world i.d. tags with my picture on them . I was going logging. And when I next came home in years time I would still only be one third of the way to becoming an elder of the church and an elder was what I needed to be before I could finally return home to a land abounding in bouncy widows and maybe even, if I was rich enough ,some of that sweet young pussy which had been so cruelly stolen from my own latter teenage years . It wasn't a bad system . Kind of like having a party and saying that the one who stays awake latest gets all the women . But it was hard to be sixteen.

Dad came home from choir work in New Vaundoo to see me off. He spent the entire weekend at our little house on the farm with my ma and my little sister and me. Usually ma makes sure he is scrupulously fair about sharing up his time with his other wives and other kids. I know its because he loved me and I also know that its because he knew that the position of any sixteen year old boy in our society was a pretty rough one. He had been there himself before me after all .

Mormons don't drink, however ma made potions and elixirs which more than made up for the lack and she dosed daddy up good every time she had him under her wing. Not to mean that she neglected to dose and potion herself either . In fact everyone who lived under her roof got dosed elixered and potioned on a regular basis. And on this particular evening with me leaving, ma had foisted a particularly large array of botanicals on me to preserve my health and I guess hers and daddy's too as they drank them along with me.

Daddy and I sang 'tempted and tried', 'that lonesome valley', 'You are my sunshine' till ma fell off her stool and flopped around crying on the floor and siss and I had to beat a retreat. I snagged a bottle of botanicals on the way out despite my sisters scowl.

Did I mention that siss is religious too? She is just as goofy as ma and with half the excuse. But with me going in the morning, I was determined to talk her up as best I could. She is my full sister after all and she also remembers when the family was just the four of us not the twenty some of the present day but I guess I shouldn't have snagged the bottle in front of her because she got all in a huff in her goody goody way.

I ended up dragging the bottle and my guitar off to the barn where I sang late until the botanicals finally curdled my stomach and I puked and end up giving myself a pretty rough body to have to inhabit at lift off the next morning. Romans are lousy loggers. I would imagine that that is because is nothing much left to log on any of their home worlds On time lines where Rome continued to be more or less successful the twelfth century saw space flight. Even on analog worlds where Constantinople was founded and the empire was halved beggaring Rome and leaving it to be sacked Rome was still in space early on, It appears to be

Justinians empire being humbled by plague, which constitutes a deeper divide with space flight becoming much less likely on time lines where the plague occurred. .

There has been industry on the Roman home worlds for a long time. I heard their worlds described as being like 'a carpet that has been walked on too much' Oh hell, they are o.k. Loggers, if you let them have lasers and the shops to back them up but how a technology can reach space flight and time line travel without inventing the chain saw is more than I can imagine. At any rate its lucky for us as I found logging for the Romans to be not that bad.

The world itself was not that different from what the New Zions were like when the Mormons first got to them a bunch of years back Lots of big reptiles and dinosaurs about and few mammals and chosen that way for the same reason In their relations between mankind and viruses and bacteria unfamiliarity breeds ineptitude and the less similar mankind is to their customary hosts the better it is for us. If you were going to found a colony on an alternate earth like us Mormons ,or even just drop in for a nice light snack as the Romans mostly did it was best not to have to deal with more nasty diseases than necessary.

Besides, dinosaurs and most reptiles taste like chicken Even goannas taste like chicken and I hate goannas. One of them ate my dog and another of them ate my granny and if you was here and you was to let on you thought that was funny I would bust every tooth out of your mouth. She was a real nice old dog. Goannas are a bloody drag way worse than dinosaurs. For one thing they are cold blooded. This means they have about a twelfth the calorie needs of a similar four hundred pound critter such as a dino .

If you will think about this for a minute you will realize that this means that there can be about fourteen times as many of them in any given locale than there would be of a warm blooded critter, hiding patiently for days behind most every big rock But they have other horrible attributes other than abundance. They drip poison drool constantly, well its not actually "poison" its more like a bacterial promoting ooze which facilitates bites becoming gangrenous. Their strategy is to wait in ambush behind a rock and then to run out and bite you. Presumably afterward your wound rapidly festers and when you begin to stink up the neighborhood every body close by enough to join the fun comes around to kill and eat you. I absolutely loathe them. Dinosaurs by contrast aren't so bad. For one thing they aren't ambush predators so they aren't always hanging about waiting to jump out at you Anyway from the point of view of l wild life for my sixteen year old self it was a pretty interesting world You might think that seeing a hundred and fifty foot crocodile couldn't be that much different from the thirty footers upriver from new Vaundoo but I will guarantee you that this is not the case.

A real big croc is an event of nature. I got to watch one snap up herbivores crossing a river on migration they say that particular critter only gets to eat once a year. I saw lots of other really neat stuff. The work itself was also pretty interesting to do, but the camp itself was a bit of a heart breaker. I had chose this job because of the better pay scale without giving too much thought to why it paid better. It was pretty much a kind of isolation pay. In most cases our lumber camp would be located close to some other Roman operation such as a mining camp and would provide the logging incidental to its needs. This meant there was a town and lots of amenities fairly close by.

The camp however, which I had chosen logged high class lumber to be shipped off world and was the reason for the Roman presence on this world The several hundred occupants of my world for the next two years were the exclusively male and exclusively Mormon occupants of the logging camp. It was a kind of spiritual Hell to which I only gradually became immune. It was a teetotalling camp with no ma there to feed me potions. It was a killer for my musical spirit as well because I found that most Mormons found music to be sinful unless you used the word Jesus for every third lyric and I couldn't find the privacy even to play my guitar on my off hours.

I did hear however, hours of tall tales about all the goings on of all these various loggers in other camps they had been in where there were Roman towns nearby. It sounded absolutely enthralling. There were lots of facilities for us young pioneers' to better ourselves while we whiled away our twenty years of celibacy.

And one thing I recognize of as being of worth in me which I acquired in this camp, as well as a certain hardness of spirit which I still rely on, was the ability to speak Roman. I took it on as a pledge to myself and learned it in the evenings. Commercial Roman 101 made a big difference I wasn't expecting months down the line. I got to bid on a different job than setting chokers and I got the bid. I had been working on the logs all day and I was glad to see the ground. when setting chokers the choker men and the rigging slinger move about upon a jumble of previously felled trees downed one on top of the other like pick up sticks the boots have spikes set within them and are specialized for this purpose] It had been a regular type day. Me and the other chokerman being worked like a pair of horses.

The chokerman's job generally entails a seven minute run and a three minute opportunity to rest repeated all day long. The rest is mostly spent panting for breath and gobbling huckleberries by the quart, as they grow up abundantly between the fallen corpses of the larger trees. It's a bitch but really cool in its way.

It can also make all forms of more sedentary work look pretty, bloody good. There was a bid board up outside our 'dry' room where we changed up after work. I had sort of noticed for a while, that one of the postings wasn't being bid on too fast. After only a year and a half in the saddle I didn't have the seniority to bid on anything better so I never paid it much attention until one of the boys read it out loud in my presence.

It turned out to bid for this posting a person needed commercial roman 101 which apparently wasn't that common. I got the job.

A project clerk is an assistant to the superintendent but he is very far from being an assistant 'super' nevertheless most superintendents spent their first days as project clerks and while not management itself it was nevertheless the lowest rung on the management ladder , unless you hired straight on out of higher school with an engineering degree. My new boss fit the last description . He was one of those short men who are most at ease in a situation where they are constantly allowed to exert authority and dominance over those around them. It is not an endearing tendency, but useful and to be looked for in anyone functioning as a "straw boss'. Our first conversation was pretty unpleasant. He told me the first thing he needed to establish was how stupid I was. Actually he pronounced it shtupid,.

He asked me half a dozen questions and fired some roman at me. I did allright on the roman but drew a blank on all six questions. He had a rather awed look o his face and said slowly and in a not unfriendly fashion " Oh, you are very shtupid. No matter, Don't worry. I won't fire you. I can do all of the work which needs intelligence." It wasn't a great way to start but I soon got used to the are you shtupid stuff. He would say it half a dozen times a day and expect me to nod or say yup. I soon got not to mind too much because Eddie Doom {that was his name} was a pretty interesting guy and I liked talking to him . It also, I am afraid, soon seemed to me to be just a pretty accurate rendition of the truth. I had never met anyone with a real education before ,[beyond how to log, or build rifles in a machine shop I mean.} I had taken my history lessons from a preacher who was right up on his Shadrac, Neeshack and Abendigo but kind of ignorant of the last couple of thousand years. To put it bluntly I knew nearly Dick about nearly everything and I was beginning to be conscious of it.

I was Eddie Doom's shadow and because I was his shadow he demanded that I be respected insisting that I also be called sir even though it made me squirm with embarrassment. He also bullied the canteen staff into providing me with food in our quarters although I didn't really rate it. He was kindly, in fact once he realized I was curious about the greater world he once told me that he reckoned he would have been shtupid too if he hadnt' been raised in a civilized place. On the not so good side as he was my boss, once he had decided to improve me he could do things like order me to read the "rise and fall of the roman empire by Gibbon' for several hours a day and then gleefully hold me to it. All in all it was good for me and Eddie himself had a Hell of a lot of fun proving how shtupid I still was by asking questions and laughing like Hell at my answers.

We didn't have much real work to do. The camp was being wrapped up and moved to a new world. Our job was to hang out to the end after the rest of the crew left and make sure none of our company's equipment was left behind and to make sure that all of our cut wood got taken, as it would be no skin off the nose of the roman transport crew if a whole bay full of our cut floating timber got left behind.

After the logging crew left it was to be just Eddie and I and the Romans on the planet possibly for quite a long time . I noticed hm sizing me up a little more than usual the first day after the crew left and I also noticed that he had hardly asked me if I was shtupid except once or twice almost in spite of himself all day long. It seemed as if he was going through some sort of sea change in his opinion of me. It made me edgy a little bit to have him be so nice . He had always had some weird foreign ways about him , admiring my body and wishing that he had been blessed with so much raw material when he had almost been a youth wrestling champion, and admiring the purity of my essence as how I wasn't yet "polluted" by women (I hated him going on about that one) also while I was pretty sure he just wanted to demonstrate wrestling takedowns and he was damned good at them, when he did so .

I was always prone to a silly notion that he just might end up putting his hand on my leg. He sometimes made me as nervous as a dog shitting razor blades. I actually hate all wrestling like Hell and avoided really hard hearing about all his college experiences as wrestling runner up which inevitably ended up with a demonstration of what really should have happened with me suddenly wrestled to the floor and pinned as a stand in for his former opponent. When he started , during the first day we were alone without other members of our own company around , to tell me that he had decided to take me into his confidence about a secret vice he had, I felt so nervous that I got a stutter back which I haven't suffered from since I was seven years old.

II was really, really, glad when he pulled out a bottle of whiskey instead of his dick. The poor benighted foreign bastard was just hot to trot for a bottle and a game of cards and afraid I would rat. I myself was about as dry as an old boot so Eddie and I brought our relationship to a new height. We got drunk together and I lost miserably time after time as I learned to play poker proving repeatedly to Eddies delight just how "shtupid" I was.

That evening, Eddie got around to telling me that he had decided I could hitch my caboose to his train if I wanted to. Up until now our association had been intended to end with lift off but Eddie told me that if I wanted I could follow him on to his next project. Oh he made sure that he told me he still thought I was shtupid but he said that he had decided that he trusted me and that I tried hard and that these things were more important. He also told me about emeralds and about what our next posting was to be. It sounded exciting .

There are basically two types of postings as I mentioned before. There are those like my last one. It had been a straight one company logging show where we had cut high class timber to be shipped directly off world. Nobody around but us Mormon men or there are multi -company shows where a big company such as a mining company is joined in an endeavour by many others and a town is built.

In this case it was to be an emerald deposit and our company was supplying the timber for the houses, buildings, sluices and all the rest of it. What I cared about was we would be logging twenty miles away from a Roman town which at least theoretically a person could figure must have at least some real girls in it. The absence of female voices in my life was a real killer at the time and I felt it like a physical pain. What Eddie cared about was the emeralds. Eddie said the word emeralds the way a hungry man says smoked salmon with the syllables getting wetter and more lugubrious to the end as the saliva increases in the mouth.

I owe a lot to Eddie Doom and its sad to me how he got ate later on so perhaps knowing that you can understand easier the warmth I feel towards a basically unpleasant sociopathic individual. First off, without him, I wouldn't have known about a hundred or so of the words which I have used in this past narrative and I would have substituted aint for isn't', will not, 'wont, am not, are not and several other contractions that this most useful of words successfully replaces. I would also probably have included the word ' finda' a contraction of 'fixing to', quite a few times and several other words that Eddie claims aren't even actually English.

Once Eddie Doom had decided I was to be his protégé he became a dedicated teacher although not a very nice one and drove me to study with insults and threats. He didn't really have to drive very hard. He just always acted that way any way because he liked to. I hadnt' realized before that I really was stupid, but once it seemed incontrovertibly proven by Eddie.

"Yes. I was shtupid", I was young enough that I suddenly had a deep desire to change myself and become aware of the world . I read every book he downloaded for me and read it as fast as I could and asked for another. After a couple of months the tone of his insults changed and I could tell that he actually was proud of me.

After mentioning that Eddie eventually got ate, I guess I should switch forward as fast as I can to when that happened for the benefit of the readers so I will try to wrap up the remaining year and a bit that Eddie and I spent together as fast as possible.

In truth nothing much happened except In my head. Eddie and I waited with him worrying and obsessing that he might lose his plum contract and obsessing as well about all the ways that emerald mining was more likely to make fortunes for small fry. He was right of course. Diamonds come from kimberlite pipes beneath the surface and the miners are very thoroughly deprived of their finds as they reach the surface. Gold and silver mining are worse as the metals are derived from ores which must be subjected to industrial processes before they give up the treasure. Your average miner never even sees a piece of the gold he produced in his working life.

Emeralds are different. Emeralds are potholed. They are dug or washed from deposits of sometimes mostly loose earth near the surface. But there is more to their accessibility than that. There is little more random occurrence in this world than the annual choice of the route of some rivers. And while the Romans could pick with exactitude earths in which veins of gold would run in exactly the same place. With Emeralds it was a little bit more random as they are only rarely found in the veins in which they were made and most often in alluvial sands or gravels .. . Generally only the biggest surest claims were staked by the mother company and they would let lots of gyppo outfits or potholers come along to share the expenses and the risks of finding the emeralds whose location was less certain. This, as Eddie was constantly telling me, was a recipe where quite a number of emeralds could end up in astute private hands.

Finally a big industrial ship came by and picked up the remaining Romans and the rest of our wood and let us know that our own pickup for us our boomboats and our handful of buildings, packed full of company valuables not to be left behind, was only two weeks away.. of these 'buildings' one , was a storage container packed full of toilet paper and another a welding shop.

I was to be glad of both of these later on. All our 'buildings' were on the same model , although of various sizes they were actually standardized containers for roman inter-At first glance they looked like a bunch of common white trailers and actually they functioned more or less well that way. They were, however fashioned of half inch thick steel and rested on thick rubber skids. They had airlocks which were left unused while the trailers were on the ground to prevent damage to their seals and a "common door" which had seen use this last ten years on this planet but had recently been welded shut. They had been checked out and held pressure just fine. That was good as me and Eddie were about to entrust our lives to one of them.

Roman ships aren't really ships at all. At least the big ones fur shipping aren't. There is no shell , just a mess of girders . They are a lot more like a cross between a Rubriks cube and a Pezz candy dispenser. When a steel container such as the one containing the toilet paper or the one containing me and Eddie is zapped up off the planet to appear directly in front of the roman ship. The ship grips it with electro- magnets and feeds it into a slot in its belly to be further moved about by magnets to an appropriate spot within the cube .

At any given moment of your journey your container is surrounded by steel girders and vacuum. If you want lunch or air pressure you have to bring it yourself. I wasn't looking forward to the lift off. Just being discombooberated and recombooberated a couple of times is a drag let alone the trip itself but when the time came I was very ready to go.

There is something incredibly spooky about being the only two human beings on a planet. Suddenly the thought of being marooned forever with Eddie Doom entered my life as a nightmare possibility. I had a weird dream that we had been marooned and Eddie wanted us to keep the human race going and I was unable to find it anywhere in the company rule book to prove to him that one of us was supposed to be a woman. I got so worried about being abandoned that I mentally estimated the worth of all the boom boats and cranes etc, that were left to be picked to reassure myself that the company couldn't just dump us there. And then all of a sudden I got scared to go out in the bush beyond the wire. I know a lot of people are afraid of the bush (Eddie for example) but I was from New Zion and I have always loved nature.

The whole last three years I had been on Earth X as I called it to myself (it didn't really have a name) I had spent at least a day or so each week just wandering around in the bush with my Browning Auto Five looking for something to shoot and cook on a little fire and I hadn't got ate yet myself], but suddenly the bush out beyond the wire looked foreboding as Hell and I quit going out.

When lift off day came Eddie wasn't in the most cheerful frame of mind. A week before he had exercised his self control and sworn off what had seemed an ever increasing and more constant bender. He gave up the booze.. He had carefully searched our office and quarters for any bottles, bottle caps or anything else which could leave us open to administrative punishment . On lift off day he wasn't exactly seeing snakes and goblins but he wasn't the calmest individual either. We strapped ourselves down in our lift off couches and listened to the hum of the air scrubbers in the closet.

Everything went well for many hours of weightlessness until right before we expected to be diss- and recombooberated again, when there was a blackout of the lights and our container was hit and rung like a bell by some big chunk of metal being slammed against it. When the lights went on Eddies face was ashen white and he looked like he had even peed his pants a bit. The next ten minutes however went as they should and we were jostled about while we were maneuvered within the cube by magnets and then finally popped out into space where we could be kerschnacked down to the planet's surface

I was the first up and over to open the port. It wasn't the waist high grass that gave me my first clue that something was going on [although that probably should have, as it was unusual for a prepared drop off area] It was the three foot tall pile of dino dung three feet in front of our front door. It had that particular twist to it like soft ice cream which sometimes distinguishes predator poop from other poop. What I first noticed and focused in on to the exclusion of all else was the steam rising from it. I backed straight backwards through the open doorway saying something to Eddie about what I was doing and I headed out of the lift off chamber into our regular office to get my gun.

You know, I aint sure in retrospect that I warned Eddie, or at least that I warned him well enough, and I guess I might always feel somewhat guilty about it , as I do at this moment. Anyway, Eddie muttered something about me being stupid and went wandering the Hell out there when he shouldn't have and when I got back with my gun and stuck my head out of our office a great big motherfucker T Rex was already walking off eating him like a cob of corn. It was a grotesque picture. Those little forearms which t -rexes have were holding him almost daintily . It was already all over for Eddie. His head had been popped or bitten off. Seeing as Eddie was already dead I didn't even think of firing at a critter that size with a shotgun. I just watched it wander off along the river where in the distance I could see many other containers like ours winking consecutively into existence.

Now I know it was a bug attack which caused the explosion, but at the time we didn't think of that . When you are transporting containers for a hundred or so small mining out fits any one of which might have become overly casual in its explosive handling and storage there are too many mundane reasons for sudden big bangs.

Besides back then nobody much new that the bugs were a threat. Oh I had read about them alright. I knew that somewhere really far away in terms of the alternate earths that the species to have achieved space flight other than our own were social insects. But that was all I knew about them, so we had no reason to bring them to mind now.

We all just thought that some asshole had stored his explosives badly, blown a corner off the ship, and caused it to settle into the wrong groove and deposit us in the right place on slightly the wrong world. There was nobody else here. I was especially alone as our whole crew had arrived on the earlier ship and set up a camp a upriver. The plan had been for the second ship with half the people on it, to arrive on a world where there were already Perimeter wires set up to keep out the critters as well as nice big piles of lumber ready for building the town and hydrogen generators set up for the equipment. They were somewhere or at least somewhen else. We were marooned

There aint no flies on the Romans when it comes to whipping up a town site. There were no big piles of lumber waiting and even no chainsaws but the machine shops turned out a few thousand nice axe heads and pretty soon the Romans had a old-timey looking town built next to the river. All out of pecker poles, log cabin style. Each cabin or other building was built close close but not quite attached to the steel shipping container which was the center of each little lot. The question was what to do next.

We weren't entirely unprepared. As I hinted at before, the Romans don't often find reasons to actually colonize new worlds. However just their lifestyle tends to sprout colonies the way a dog drops fleas. We certainly weren't the first ship to end up somewhen else.

They had rules when large numbers of people went from place to place. We had silos full of grain to last years and there was a beacon blaring on the ship and, even if we weren't picked back up within a couple of years, as the odds apparently said we would be, we had specials containers full of seeds and even of domestic animals and other critters frozen rock solid live. which we might want to introduce on our world if we got our act together enough to do so.

But in the beginning nobody here was thinking of trying to move in. They were thinking of emeralds. They had even managed to find a bunch. I am going to admit to it now and then try to repress it for the rest of this narrative. I too love emeralds.

I caught the bug from Eddie. When I say the word my mouth comes up all succulent and a beautiful green light suffuses my consciousness. But did you know that they aren't all green? Look at a ruby lately ? I doubt it because there aint really no such thing. Look at the royal rubies of England , they is one kind of red rock while somewhere else a ruby s a different rock. They aren't all even just corundum or spinel

There is no science to it. Its like "cod" fish. which more or less just means any of a bunch of unrelated fish with nice white tasty flesh. Well we had some ruby emeralds . Lovely pink and red ones that look like candy and seem to stay cool in your hand a long time like ice. Its easy to day dream about emeralds, there are just so many nice things about them. They even make me lose my train of thought. Where was I? Oh yes, None of the people were thinking about being on the planet a long time but only of the work in front of us to mine emeralds without any of our heavy machinery.

All of our mobile machinery and all of our pumps ran on hydrogen. The hydrogen generators were somewhen else having been set up by an earlier more specialized crew. There was good logic to it but in this instance it wasn't working out too good. I guess maybe the roman shops could have built them in a bunch of years but I seriously don't know for sure .To see all that machinery lying there, unusable made me ache for the technology back home.

Mormons on New Zion grow lots of corn. If you can build a still you can run our equipment. But there was no sense bragging about our equipment . I had a fleet of boom boats a convenient half mile from the river and no way to pull the trailers and not a single chainsaw in any of our containers. I was out of the logging business. I became a combination traveling minstrel and toilet paper salesman. It was the best time of my life so far. The town itself had free electric power and there was lots of food and booze about. There was actually a festive excited attitude all about the place. Most of this crew had been together with the town in exactly this same grid for the previous ten years on an analog planet not so far down the line and many of them had seen the planet before it.

If you like to look at women, being a toilet paper salesman is a great job to have. I had about a zillion rolls and probably could have sold them off in bulk but they weren't really mine and at first when we were all expecting to be back in contact with our companies really soon, I didn't want to end up with a bill for them. Besides it didn't suit my purpose. What I wanted was to be able to go down town somewhere and have an excuse to sit and fool around with my guitar while I looked at women and girls. I had been deprived -- over a thousand days without the sound of a woman's voice. I didn't expect to touch them and I didn't care what they did . I just wanted to watch them walk around and listen to them talk. I was goofy as all get out. It took me a couple of months to get over it and notice some of the other things that were going on around me.

Such as the logging. The demand for wood was still really high due to all the sluice works and other general building going on on all the claims which had sprung up along the river, but two months down the line they were still using axes. Now I am not suggesting that they should have been able to whip chain saws up out of nowhere, although I privately figure maybe Mormons could have done so, but to my mind they hadn't just slipped a single rung down the technological ladder but several .

By slipping from chainsaws to axes they missed what would have been the achievements of the nineteenth century on the Mormon home planets. No Peeveys and no cross cuts. Both of which were invented in the eighteen seventies to deal with the newly available large timbers of the west coast. The Romans were all the way back with Paul Bunyan and his blue ox but without the ox. I got into the welding room back of our offices and made six cross cuts and a dozen peeveys. I also hacked away at a few of our logging blocks in order to make them accept lighter tackle and welded a couple of them together to make the top double block of a typical block purchase arrangement. I am sure I don't need to explain block purchase to you as anybody who can read must likely know all about it.

Telling it makes it sound easy but it wasn't, First off for a variety of reasons to do with the shape and needed hardness of the tines I couldn't figure out how to make a real cross cut but I figured out a way to make an unreasonable facsimile. I had quite a collection of circular saw blades but no equipment to drive them with. I had the idea of just hacking off sections of tines from them with a cutting torch. And then electro -welding the sections onto the bottom of a long fourteen inch sheet of quarter inch steel plate. I had to double the blade sections in width as they were onlyone eigth but the final product looked like it would cut.

It had one large difference from a regular crosscut. The marvel of a crosscut is that its unique cutting service allows it to cut both when pushed and pulled My saws were only fifty percent that effective as the tines from a circular saw cut in only one direction . I made six of them. As it turned out they still cut like a hot damn and a bit of oil poured in the kerf helped the "dry" return . They were heavy as Hell but with several men to handle them that was alright because weight of blade increases speed of cut. The marvel of a saw versus an axe is it directs the human energy towards a very thin strategically placed kerf in the wood, where as an axe works at a tree with the same sophistication as a beaver and requires the removal of hundreds of times more wood. Also axes just don't work on trees more than two axe handles wide . In a forest like this that meant the Romans were only cutting a third of the lumber and being forced to ignore the rest even when it was quite close to town.

A year before I would probably have taken my good idea to the shop foreman of one of the roman machine shops and been satisfied with a pat on the head. After a year of reading and of exposure to Eddies get rich scheming I had become far more devious. I wrapped the saws up carefully so no one could really get a look at them on the way out of town and I chose a spot to log that was unnecessarily way far up the river from a logging point of view but which would allow me to keep my operation unobserved until I was ready to float a boom down to town. I figured I needed four men to a saw I needed a crew of about twenty men, but who I trusted next was the most crucial point in my plan. I decided to go slow and think about it.

Mrs. O. was my landlady. She was one of those ladies I really like. Kind of hard and crunchy on the outside and soft and chewy on the inside, as my dad would have said. She was pretty old, she must have been nearly thirty.

I had quit bunking down in Eddie and my office . It was comfortable enough, but it was outside the perimeter with the other industrial containers and made for a sketchy walk home late at night as far as maybe getting ate was concerned. Mrs. O. was real strict and kept a very proper house on account of having two wonderful daughters about eight and ten years old, Gabrielle and Veronique .

I ate with the family. I had finally gotten comfortable in the language and although I still made plenty of mistakes which set the little girls laughing at least I generally, now knew what was funny. There had been weeks earlier when just the prospect of trying to speak roman all day had made my head hurt when I woke up in the morning but I had studied hard alone in my office and practiced hard with the people I met selling bum wipe and I had gotten past it. Mrs. O was kind of beautiful. She had her full dark hair tied back severely and wore eyeglasses that looked picked to intimidate as well as clothes with no frivolousness about them at all, but her voice was warm. You could sense that her harsh demeanour was an conscious effort on her part to whip some less civilized part of herself into submission. She was also built like a brick shit house. She made me stutter sometimes on account of I couldn't help having thoughts about her.

In fact one time she came into the kitchen where I was sitting late at night to deal with some small thing and she had her hair down, her glasses off and her night clothes on. It had hit me just as bad as if she had walked in with her shirt off. I stuttered so badly that she immediately and intuitively understood my problem . She turned red but then there was a real long count before she turned and fled the room. She never mentioned it in the morning but my secret life ached with what ifs for weeks afterward . Anyway, I decided to ask advice of my landlady.

Mrs. O. was a teacher. She taught a class of mostly young girls. I heard about them some over the supper table but never met them. Mrs. O. was also a widow . Gabrielle and Veronique's dad had met a very young sad death trying to do a re-drill of a hole which had not been entirely cleaned out after the last attempt. His drill hit a stick of nilite with a cap in it and he got killed. It happens all the time.

I heard about it individually from all three of them at different times and I was glad I had learned from my dad being a preacher how to deal with grieving folk . Especially females. It had happened a couple of years ago. Its hard to keep to the thread of the story about how I got rich when I have to tell you at least somewhat about the people I met and interacted with while I was in the process of having done so and it was Mrs. O. as much as Eddie who was responsible for my good fortune .

At any rate, I explained my whole situation to Mrs. O. about how I had a technical innovation which I thought could bring in a lot more lumber, but which was so easy to imitate, I didn't want to hire just any logging crew to walk off with my secrets. I needed a weeks hard work with a crew in secrecy and get a boom together and then a chance to bargain with the bigwigs for an exclusive right to log in return for my cheap logs. I was going to borrow some of Eddies clothes and pass myself off as a boss.

Mrs. O. thought my problems over really hard and then came back with a bunch of unexpected a questions about what the dangers and benefits would be to my helpers. Then she got me the High school football team. She said she knew the coach and something in the way she said 'knew' made me look at her suddenly, causing her to blush and leave the table. Mrs. O. was full of surprises

You know that old story about Tom Sawyer making fence painting look fun? Well, I didn't even have to work at it . To these boys the prospect of knocking over tall trees seemed as appealing as any sort of vandalism or hooliganism. They were all for it. Football teams are made up of competitive individuals, anyway and the prospect of outdoing the three hundred or so other men in the forest didn't hurt a bit. I had ten guys and I promised each one ten percent of the value of the timber we cut and let them know that that was what I was doing. I hoped to take my cut on the next round. When I had half a dozen teams cutting.They were ready to log.

As you must have guessed everything worked out Jim Dandy and two weeks later I was a bigshot with fifty guys in the bush and plenty of company script stuffing the drawers in Eddies desk. Two weeks after that with the use of some machine shops and skilled workers I turned out some real cross cuts and halved again production. The next few months were probably the most contented our little community had. The Romans build really fine aqua-ducts and sluice ways, if you give them some decent lumber.

The whole community took it upon themselves to wrest those emeralds out of the soil even if not one piece of our mobile equipment ever moved a foot. The main claim was right behind our camp in a four hundred high cliff that stretched along the river for a number of miles. It was an emerald rich pegmatite, the earthy, top most decomposed layer, of which the big company had meant to mine it with water from the river pumped up for the purpose. No hydrogen, no pumps.

Instead they built a five mile long sluice way with my nice wide boards. It diverted water from further up the stream before it hit a series of waterfalls which brought it down to its present course. It worked like a garden hose on fresh dog shit. They were getting the emeralds. The potholers were doing their thing as well and there was the definite feeling of a boom in town with lots of booze being drunk and stores being stripped of luxury goods as prices escalated[although the big company in its wisdom still gave out power and sold food at it's un-inflated price.

I still didn't personally get to see any emeralds but I was rich in company script and didn't give a damn. Besides, I had just seen the girl that I was sure I wanted to marry. Then the beacon went out. A chill swept through our little community. Without a beacon our pickup likelihood switched from within a year or two to within a generation or two. Maybe. If we had known that the bugs had followed the beacon in and were up above nibbling away on our ship we would have been scared shitless, but thankfully we had no idea anything like that was going on and were spared the worry.

Suddenly, sluicing for emeralds was passé and everyone except the big company switched to thinking about freeholds and crops in the ground,. After a couple more months even the big company gave up on the emeralds as well and put its energies elsewhere. Suddenly emeralds started turning up in my cashbox in a spiral of ever decreasing worth. The price of my wood stayed steady. Eddie taught me when to hold them and when to fold them. I took every emerald I was offered and still managed to pay my crews in script. In the end I had bags of them. I still keep enough around so that I can lock myself in a room and just dribble them through my fingers and go 'wa ha ha ha wahahhaha' over and over again louder and louder. But I wasn't going to get into that too much.

It would cut a long story too short to just say that, yes we did get rescued fairly soon and yes I did end up with bags and bags and bags of emeralds . So I won't do it I am going to go back to where I first set my eyes on Tess. I knew I wanted to marry her as soon as I first saw her.

I didn't know how I could have not seen her before with just our population of a couple of thousand. I reckoned that if I had seen her before it must have been with her yellow hair covered and I hadn't singled her out. It was her hair which first made my throat catch. From a distance she could have been my sister or my mom or any of those pretty girls from school back home. I guess some of you who is familiar with Italians might be wondering why blonde hair is so rare amongst Romans. Well to put it in a nutshel , the Romans mixed all the races of their world together and blenderized them about a thousand years ago and blonde hair is about as rare as extra ribs.

So Tess stood out when she first came running out on the playing field. Here I have to make a short embarrassing admission. I, Aenas Enoch Browning, admit to having escorted my landlady's two young daughters to their ball game once a week, solely so that I could recline in a nearby field and pretend to read a book when truly my eyes were actually glued over the rim of the aforesaid book and watching a much older group of girls throwing the pigskin around.

It was the highpoint of my week. When Tess came bounding out on the playing field with her blonde hair flying about and her knockers bobbing around. My heart just about stopped and my bottom lip started to tremble. I wanted her to marry me. I wanted her to be my bride. I wanted every sugary sweet and sappy thing every man has ever wanted for a woman. So I started off by stalking her.

Pretty soon my stalking had enabled me to suddenly appear at the pump several times to offer to carry her water at just the right moment to save her old dad the trouble of carrying it and although the old man always declined the offer and refused to wax friendly, I could see by her parting glances that she appreciated my efforts.

This was occurring at about the moment in the life of our little colony, where the fact that the beacon was no longer calling rescuers to us was starting to 'set in' as they say back home. Emerald mining was losing its allure and most folks including me were starting to think about a freehold and doing some farming. I wanted to try farming corn . I needed a wife and as so far as I had known I was the only Mormon in the bunch I had reckoned I was going to have to get used to foreign food.

Then Tess came along to play a game of ball with the Roman girls and my whole life changed. I found that Tess lived with an old man of at least fifty with a big grizzled grey beard, who I was sure must be her dad, in a medium size container with a small machine shop and a store. It was the kind of outfit which would be let down on an outpost world for a month or two and then got lifted off to another. He had a big sign out front. "Warren Jeff Young. Gunsmith, Gun seller , Specializing in used military rifles from the Mormon earths." He was an entrepreneur.

Romans make lousy guns for much the same reason as they are lousy loggers. Oh don't get me wrong. They make great weapons. They have outfits that will strike you at a thousand yards and with the turning of a little knob they can decide whether to tickle your fancy or turn you to toast. But if you shoot at a dinosaur with an outfit like that you will probably make him run over and stamp on you really hard. Big game needs a weapon that blows a whole and the Roman projectile throwers are kind of polly wolly crappy.

I found reasons to visit their (Tess and her daddy's) shop , even buying expensive stuff that I didn't really need to demonstrate to the old boy that I was by the standards of the place a man of substance and maybe worthy enough to court his daughter, but he cut short any conversations I tried to start and began to look at me with real unfriendliness. I guessed I could see his point as I was fixing to deprive him of the person he must certainly love best. I never let his hostility get to me and always continued to treat him friendly and decent as I told myself that as I would have to learn to love him after I was married to his daughter there was no point in letting things get too out of hand with him no matter what the provocation.

And while things weren't going to good with the old man Tess had clearly begun to warm up to me on account of my insistence. I thought I could tell that she too wished that our lives would just give us some opportunity to be together which they hadn't so far. Events were to take a turn in our favor.

The first casualty of the beacons silence was the value of both emeralds and company script. The second was our civil peace. Our police force started free lancing. They weren't really police. That was part of the problem. They were more like goons. Most hamlets get by with a couple of cops but if your hamlet is composed with fifty percent of its population being single male miners, with a large disposable income, you require a different solution.

The most usual practice, in a lot of places. is to hire goons. Large tree trunk sized men with bulging forearms to patrol dormitory corridors in groups and nip incipient parties in the bud. They aren't really cops but in the small print of your agreement to reside in the dormitory or company lodgings is your agreements for the caterer or their agents to physically remove you and your belongings at any time .

The prerogative of their office is to enter by kicking down your door, It is after all actually 'their' door and they will just tell a maintenance guy to come over and fix it in the morning; a job he performs after dramatic entrances several times a week. Only the largest men are hired for this position and a platoon of goons is unmistakable. They aren't usually chosen for brains or moral character and their usual former careers are boxers, wrestlers or bouncers. We had thirty of them, huge big stupid buggers who had actually done their jobs fairly well up to date. After the beacon had stopped for a couple of months and their company script paychecks had become useless they decided to run the place on their own account. They began collecting for themselves in return for their protection which was mainly of course from themselves. They could probably have gotten away with it if they hadn't been so bloody stupid in the process of trying to sequester to themselves all of the spare, and not so spare, pussy. In the process, they managed to chase off a bunch of the youngest girls into the jungle (a story I will now tell in detail) and got themselves universally disliked and rapidly deposed.

It was a ball game like any other - hair flying and tits bouncing, with me perched up on a little hill not so far away trying to read my book or maybe I should say pretending to read it. I liked to be far enough away that I couldn't actually hear the horrible shrieks of girlish laughter. Tess had come and I could see her pa with a rifle up on another hilltop not far off keeping tabs on his little girl. With the beacon out, things had had an uncertain feeling of late.

It was a normal enough day and I didn't even notice it when a column of red suited figures with sidearms went walking by on the far side of the playing field. I did notice when a dozen of them came back half an hour later. They watched for maybe fifteen minutes and then began rounding up some of the older girls including my Tess and tying their hands. I was paralyzed. I was unarmed. I confess that at this point in my life I only thought of my gun in terms of food and hadn't paid much attention to the "Roman" politics of who I paid my cut to. Until they started to drag off my girl.

Tess' pa did better. He sat on his grassy knoll and picked up the Carcano he carried and plugged holes in the lot of them. It took him a while what with them trying to skitter off out of his sight but it was an open hillside and he was a good shot. They couldn't fight back much. They had really nasty sidearms that could quell or kill a crowd close up but the old man was just a tad out of range of their weapons and they however were just where he wanted them. The girls, every last one of them, spooked and ran, staying in a mob just within sight until a new platoon of redcoats appeared from town, headed in the direction of the firing at which point the girls melted into the bush.

When the old man and I met he handed me his rifle and said that I was young and spry I should run after the girls and round them up then take them to a safe compound on a claim he knew of outside the city. I was worried about what would happen to the old man when the other redcoats showed up in the next few minutes. He told me he had a good story worked out and to get the hell out of there, It was a good story. After I left he just told the redcoats that it was I who had done the killing. They had no trouble believing him whatsoever and for a while I would have been shot on sight but things changed fast.

I didn't take the girls to the place where the old man had told me. I took them out to my own first logging camp, now semi abandoned, ten miles further out. I could tell you I did this because it was a safer and better which it probably was, but by now you would know it was bullshit I am sure. I wanted a chance to be alone with Tess, to tell her how I felt. I wouldn't try to kiss her of course but at least I wanted to hear from her one time that I oughta keep on looking for her dad's permission. I got more than I bargained for.

It was a lovely walk out to my camp. I am overly used to critters and tend to filter them out of my narrative as I also am more used to trees lying down dead ready to be hauled away and seldom mention either variety. But for the roman girls it was a treat as they were townspeople. The forest we walked through was mostly Red Woods and Douglas Firs. Both species which had perfected their survival strategies in the presence of dinosaurs. Even on worlds where dinosaurs have been extinct for sixty million years like the human home-worlds. Douglas Firs still concentrate their growing tips a hundred feet in the air to avoid long- gone seventy foot tall dinos.

On this planet there were also flowering plants as there had been on the Zions but hadn't been on my last three year stint of logging. I had been glad to see them back. The girls picked a bunch and the day wasn't even without a bit more excitement. Usually, when I walk the bush, I walk slow and silent and smudge up often with burning sage so I don't smell so damned tasty. This time I had thirty noisy and possibly stinky females, with no sage on hand. It made for an especially eventful walk .

I shot a nice sized anaconda for the girls to look at before it ate one of us and an allosaur, who was trying to do the same thing. Then, when we arrived at the camp, I got a good fire going out front of the palisade. We watched what it attracted all evening with me shooting the nastier critters in safety from behind the palisade. That being the point of the exercise, as being it is way easier to shoot them then than in the morning as they would surely have hung around. I didn't lose a girl. Not even a little one. It was a very domestic evening but not very private With all the girls outdoing themselves in cooking fresh dino and snake with some of the preserves from the camp, Tess and I were always surrounded by the other girls. It didn't seem to bother Tess as the few times I tried to talk she just told me to wait until later. When bed time came and it was time for us to part I was pretty down cast.

Now I am not going to give you prurient bastards a account of me losing my cherry when Tess snuck into my tent an hour later. Or at least only a little bit. I had often been told by various preachers that women are born the vessels of sin but on that night it actually seemed to me to be proved so. Some of the things Tess thought of to do, I figured could only have been put into her head by her nature itself , as I figured as I sure would never have thought of them. I figured women must just be possessed of an innate erotic nature. It never even occurred to me that she just might have learned them somewhere else.

In the early morning when I finally had her to my own for the 'talk' that I needed to have. I told her not to worry that I was going to make things right by talking to her pa in the morning and asking for her hand in marriage. For a minute or even longer Tess just stared at me as if I had grown a second head,,as they say, and then she howled with laughter. Not a very pretty description but in this case quite apt. I have never been fond of the sound of womens' laughter for some reason. Even the giggling that groups of young girls commence when they walk near me discomfits me somehow and this was worse. When she stopped laughing she asked me how old I thought she was. And when I answered she said " just because I play ball with school girls doesn't mean I am a school girl and then after another pause she told me that Warren wasn't her father, he was her husband . And then. to quote her exactly, she said " Y'all better watch, he'll be finda' kill ya daid". I don't know why I didn't kick her out the next night. I have a low nature I guess.

I didn't stay an outlaw for long. As I mentioned before chasing off all the girls into the dino - filled bush really pissed off the natives and the column of red coated men left the next day on their regular tribute collection journey. A handful of natives, soon joined by others, decided to interfere with their return within the town perimeter by nipping at them with rifles as soon as they crossed the horizon. The redcoats decided , quite rightly, that the tactical advantage of those with rifles would be lost after dark and they decided to wait around until then . In the dark, they would try to try to approach within a distance to where their superior numbers and close country weaponry would prevail.

They decided to light a big fire and then wait it out for a few hours. It was a really bad idea. Fire attracts dinos like they say it does rhinoceri or or whatever they are called. I could pretty much just say that something came along in the night and ate them and stop there and I wouldn't be far wrong. They had various allosaurs. t-rexes and some ceratops to deal with, (they aren't carnivorous but they don't like fires either). Apparently, their fire was stomped out early on by something or somethings big and then for the rest of the night there were various versions of Custers last stand played out all over the place accompanied by the vain crackling of energy weapons and the honks of the enraged dinosaurs.

The next day there was a new regime in power and I was a hero. The relatives of girls who had been searching for us, found us and told me how it was my rebellion as well ; cause when every body had heard how I single- handed knocked off a dozen of them to save a bunch of their women I had been their inspiration to rebel. You cant argue with what everybody knows. I could have run for mayor. I didn't feel like running.

My poor little heart was broke and I was afraid that Warren Jeff Young was" fixin" to kill me "daid". I ran to the safety of Mrs. O'.s. When I came in the front door and she saw that I had brought her girls home safe to her she kissed me on the lips. She served wine with dinner that night and let her hair down. And she listened to Veroniques' story of how I had saved her from the giant snake and Gabrielle/s story of how when the allosaur attacked I had run out in front of all the girls so it would have eaten me if my shot hadn't killed it.

I didn't bother to try to tell her that anacondas aren't that dangerous when you know how to look out for them or that I hadn't really run out in front to make an offering of myself but just to get a good clear shot, without little girls running in front shrieking to distract me. It had been a big sucker and needed three steady shots. I knew I wasn't a hero but I had gotten fast used to basking in undeserved fame that I just let it ride. As I said earlier, I had just discovered I have a low side to my nature.

When Mrs. O. got out the wine with dinner I resolved to get out my guitar. I had my stutter back but its not so bad if I keep singing . After an hour or so she sent the very tired girls on up to bed and then the next time I paused in my guitar playing for a drink of wine she crawled straight up my leg. Pa would have been proud.

I sure never expected Tess to show up the next morning. I had thought for sure I would be clear and done with her a simple case of misunderstanding. Nothing that anyone would want to go on a confession jag to their husband about and get me killed over I hoped. I didn't even think she knew where I lived . And then she turned up the very next day before noon walking up our street. I was having a civilized cup of tea with Mrs, O in the kitchen when suddenly out the window I could see her coming from far down. I felt more nervous than I ever remember having felt before about potentially being in the same room with both Tess and Mrs. O (having boinked the both of them in the last three days) and told neither. Seeing as Mrs. O.s back was momentarily turned, I simply bolted from the kitchen and went to my room to bolt my door and stick my fingers in my ears. I let Mrs. O. face the caller.

A week later a Roman freighter pulled in and saved the lot of us, especially me. Warren Jeff Young and his wife Tess didn't choose to set down again with this mining outfit, but continued on until points unknown. It was weird to get my Mormon threads on again. I had kind of quit wearing them. I had to get all my emeralds together in small trunks of yew which I had whipped up in the sawmill for the purpose 'Wahahahah/ Wahahahahaha' with a bunch of pillow cases of company script in my and Eddies lockers.

For my own old logging company (I mean the one I used to work for not the one I put together which was of course now defunct) I left script to cover the steel and saw blades etc. that I had gone through. I rode to the next earth in the same chamber Eddie had walked out to die from and for the first and maybe the last time ever I kind of missed Eddie Doom – at least a little tiny bit.

As it turned out, I still had my job if I wanted it and since I needed a room I kept it for a bit. I guess I could mention in passing that I needed a room because Roman women seemed to be possessed of an exceedingly pragmatic nature. They don't treat all relationships which end up with two people humping as being preparatory to marriage. I guess the best way to explain it is that she just gave it to me for fun and leave it at that. In other words, Mrs. O. didn't want to marry me either. I think she had some old friggin gym teacher in mind. I had proposed, unsuccessfully to two women in ten days or less. I decided to really bite my tongue and try to give it a break for a while. I had to think about my future.

During its first week of reunification, the Roman town gave itself over to one long fiesta. The unusual nature of the last months had left a lot of the rubies and emeralds in hands they wouldn't usually grace. There were lots of reunions and not a few divorces when couples whose work had split them up for a supposed couple of weeks were reunited again after most of a year. I just mostly hung out and smelled the flowers. My new boss knew I was due to go back home from the telestial worlds and also knew I had been marooned, although not much about it.

He gave me a cabin of my own and thirty days of on planet recuperative leave until I lifted off. He was a "good shit" as they say. He pretty much just let me goof off and bide my time till I went home. I mostly just spent my time hanging out down town. The new town was a lot like the old, with most of the same people in much the same locales as it consisted of the same containers laid out in the same grid on much the same plain. But this time when we arrived there had been piles of saw milled lumber on every street corner and the town had gone up in a sixteenth the time and with a different face.

I hung out downtown drank wine, played guitar and ate foreign food, or hung out down by the river watching booms come down and joined the herd of town kids who converged on the river in the morning when the crocodile hooks were winched in with the four ton critters flopping about like trout in a boat. I knew my days in the town were numbered and yet I also knew that in some way I had not had my fill of it at all yet. I had, by chance gotten back in contact with a couple of the football players who had put in the weeks work for me early on. They were going off to school. They were going to study really neat subjects that I hadn't hardly even heard the names of. I wished I was going too, but I reckoned I had better go home.

I figured my dad to have been pretty bright, but whereas if he had been let to, [at a young age I mean], he would probably have read thousands of books, the way his life had actually taken him, it had only included a couple of books and he had read those thousands of times. It made him kind of dense. His beliefs were no longer shakeable. If you asked him about the broader ancient world , the parts which aren't actually directly covered in the bible or the book of Mormon, he would likely give you a story like this one about our family.

On a day long, long ago a child was born to the fairies. He was born in the morning , named at noon, and went in the evening to seek the daughter of the King of Missouri. Dunn was his name. Before he left his mother took a rod of enchantment and was about to give t it to him when she had a second thought . "Whatever am I doing!" she exclaimed "you are going to live amongst men and they would only steal it from you!" So she plunged it deep within him (without parting flesh) where it would be safe for all time and for all his sons. This rod of enchantment allows even outright lies to be believed by others as it gives the gift of persuasion.

Dunn was eager to arrive, so he took a mile at a jump and a hill at a leap until he arrived at the western ocean where he kicked a boat a mile out to sea and then jumped into it. It warn't long before he was at Missouri. He continued on as before skipping across vales and bounding hills over the land of Missouri until he came to the castle of the king. The king welcomed him because he could see that he was fairy born by the witches tit which he bore, and by some other attributes, but the king of Missouri was suspicious as the fairy people had never before wanted to take the wives of men so he asked his fairy visitor about himself. "His visitor explained that as how he had only been born in the morning named in the afternoon and sent that very same evening sent to seek his brides he really knew very little about himself .There were some giants troubling the land and the king decided to make use of his new visitor and test his strength before giving over his daughters so he sent Dunn to conquer the first giant. At this point the tale becomes about as repetitive as "the three little Pigs " and I will spare you some of it if I can.

Dunn approaches the castle of each giant and prevails upon the housekeeper to let him in . She does and a bit later when the giant arrives, hammering on the gate and making the castle ring like a bell, with a game bag full of dead men on his shoulder. He immediately smells his guest, clapping his hands together with glee and instructing his housekeeper to prepare some orange sauce for the nice fat fairy -- allowing as how the men he had snared could do with being aged a few days any ways.

At this point Dunn launches his argument and convinces the giant to believe that Dunn is his ally and has come to warn him of an impending invasion by the warriors of Missouri. The giant immediately believes him .It is Dunn's fairy mothers gift at work and feeds him up well and gives him lodging until morning. In the morning Dunn asks the giant for pay for his supposed good deed and the giant nonchalantly tells Dunn of a bag of gold under the bed and tells him to take his fill. At this point Dunn launches his mothers gift again and talks the giants into needing badly to visit their old tired mothers in the land of giants, far away . He suggests, before they go, that they store their most treasured possessions with him for safekeeping. The one giant is about to hand Dunn his magic fiddle when he has a second thought "Oh how silly of me"

he says "you live among men and they would only steal it from you" . So he plunges the fiddle into the center of Dunn's body without breaking ribs and leaves it there. "Now for you and your sons all instruments shall be magic".

The second giant is about to give Dunn a small vial of magic perfume which makes women love him when he exclaims out the same words "Oh my whatever was I thinking of doing…etc." and plunges it within Dunn's guts for safekeeping, exclaiming that from now on Dunn and all of his sons would be forever womens' first choices. The last giant deviates from the line a bit in that he has two favored possessions a cloth of plenty and a cloak of concealment which he tucks out of the way in the heroes ear and up his butt or someplace.

The problem with dad is that he really seriously believes this kind of shit. He thinks they are the gifts of the male line of our family. He thinks he is the hootchy kootchy man and he can tell it to you to make you believe it. He had been standing there with a bunch of other folks I didn't immediately recognize, when I got back home.

Did you ever hear one of those dislocated time stories where the Roman pilot is supposed to have been a little loose in the groove and left people a standing waiting to be met on worlds which are damned near exactly the same as the ones they belong on? Except that in this time line their parents have never met or perhaps their wife turns out to be married to their brother. I suppose it must have happened to some people. Anyway, for a minute I felt sure it was happening to me. There she was, my secret crush of all Grade Nine, a girl whose brassiere string I had once unhooked standing on the pavement with a toddler in her arms. Then I realized she was dad's new wife.

Boys will be boys. Surprisingly I didn't even feel choked. In fact over the past several weeks I had become positively averse to the idea of marriage. I guess I had finally figured out that in a world where milk was free you didn't really need to own a cow, as Eddie Doom had once very rudely put it. I rapidly resolved that I intended to leave New Zion fast and in an unmarried state. I had a secret fear of waking up "shtupid" once again. It could happen so easily. Dad was pretty "shtupid" and mom and siss as well, for that matter.

My little sweety from grade nine, who was dads eighth wife, looked easily "Shtupid" enough to cause us no end of trouble especially because of the way her breasts kept talking to me. I swear they would pick up and take notice whenever I came into a room and commence to trying to point at me whichever way she herself was attempting to look. You don't need to be a weatherman to know which way the wind blows.

I knew I needed to bolt from the moment I set foot back on the old Rock. I was lucky I had emeralds. I gave mom a bag and bought my way out. Dad was trickier he had a new son to brag about and etiquette pretty much demanded that he And I wander off somewhere and get drunk to which I was not really averse to even though I knew I would probably spend the whole evening saying "yup" "UHUH" and "oh for sure" to various propositions and stories of his which I actually felt to be entirely bogus.

It was just how it was with dad and me when he was drunk. Occasionally in the past if sis was in the room she would point out that no one was listening to his story but dad would always point at me and say "ass hole is" using my nickname like anybody else and I would never own up to not listening. I guessed I could handle one more round of it but I made sure I bought myself a ticket off planet just to hang onto and fondle as a talisman while I visited my family.

It did happen to me. Getting "shtupided up" I mean. Dad decided to let me in know the curse of the household. It was a follow up to the story of the 'brown man Dunn', as dad called him. One part of the curse of our family was that we seldom threw males that survived pregnancy to term. Most boy babies miscarried. Dad pointed out that amongst sixteen daughters he only had two sons and both of us bore the witches tit and other signs upon our body as did he himself.

For a moment I forgot myself and tried to explain that any gene which behaved as he said it did (going always and inevitably from father to son and nowhere else) would have to be carried on the y chromosome and that science had proved that the only thing carried on the y chromosome was hair in the ear. If you have hairy inner ears and your father or son doesn't perhaps you should think about it, otherwise not. It slowed him down for a second and gave him a bemused look but when he started in again after my interruption, in exactly the same place and manner, I resolved to keep quiet and not extend the discomfort of paying attention to bullshit.

Apparently according to Dad, all I have to do to avoid the worst part of the curse of the family, is never to marry the daughter of another man with a witches tit or the children will be an abomination. It was the way he said abomination like he was in the pulpit which made me stupid again. It hit me right between the eyes like a rod of enchantment and made me "Shtupid" with belief just like that.

I was so glad to get away that even the combooberations of lift off and arrival in Rome seemed not too bad. I am going to school now and writing this up is actually a part of my course and likely to count I guess for just a few percent of my total mark. I had best not let it grow too much larger. I followed my former employees to their school and paid for a curriculum suited to myself. I am, as it turns out, of a very curious turn of nature, While it would probably not bother some to have the parts nibbled of their ship by bugs, without hearing about them before or after I must know. I have also heard about the farthest regions of the alternate worlds where an asteroid did not graze earths moon and where some very curious beings gaze down from their station on the moon upon the earth.

We have sent envoys there . Mankind I mean. And their domesticated and much genetically modified descendants still populate the alternate earths near the border. The universe is a CURIOUS PLACE AND GETTING CURIOUSER BY THE MOMENT AS IT GROWS.

Aenas Browning University at Rome. The End.

Inter-Time Privateer
Ships Captain at Fifteen Years of Age
How I Got There

By Isiiah Browning

Second generation Browning family,

The day that was to change my life started off like most others. I was sent off by the ladies to bring daddy his porridge. The chore always falls to me on account of I have blonde hair like he used to and daddy always recognizes me right off the bat. When Daddy doesn't recognize someone coming up towards his porch, and that person isn't perhaps really obviously, a female, Daddy has a disconcerting habit of firing a couple of shots into the air until the approacher makes a bunch of noise and he does recognize him.

Daddy don't live in the compound with all his women. He says its on account of having all the commotion around makes it hard to shoot a critter from his rocking chair on the porch to cook for his dinner on a little fire outside like he always does. I am sure that might be part of it . He does enjoy being the bit of cheese in his own mousetrap. He considers near every animal on this planet to be cuddly compared to his home where tyrannosaurs or something similar were what you mostly had to shoot at.

Daddy doesn't actually have anything to do, what with having a hundred or so wives, and I don't know how many offspring to do stuff for him. So he spends his time on the porch waiting for stuff to sneak up on him, then he shoots it. For variety, he had his hut put overlooking the valley so he could fire on any air traffic going by. It is a pretty nifty set up. When traffic goes by in the valley he can actually fire on them from above from a little tree fort with a flight of stairs that he had built without the flyers being able to see anything but unbroken jungle .You can't mostly down a flyer with small arms fire but it makes them keep their distance and the presence of small arms in an area makes it less likely to be chosen for their next slave raid,

Daddy was a slave for a while, he ain't from around here. He is, as I mentioned. actually an off-worlder who got himself plopped in the bag and ended up a slave on the plantations for a while. They even castrated him like they do to all slaves, and by rights I shouldn't be here if it wasn't for the fact that he had one undescended testicle)(just like I do) and they missed it when the put the constrictor band on.

Nothing cheers up daddy more than being able to fire at a flyer. He was possibly beaming with joy on that particular morning, having just had the opportunity, a half an hour or so before. It had been an unusual craft; not just a plane from the town but a landing craft with off-world lines and to hear daddy tell it he figured he had downed the damn thing. It had come by close enough and slow enough with some crew out in the air on top, and when one of them had opened the port to reenter the ship, he had put a slug right down the hole. The effect had been fast. The ship had broken off its flight pattern and its automatics had come on . Daddy swore that the ship was presently just in sight, on the bald top of a butte towering empty above the plain.

I had a look with Daddy's glasses and sure enough I could see a glint of light just where he said it ought to be.

It warn't that far away as a bird flies but the the ground around here sort of folds into big clefts which would maybe double the distance, and I knew that there were a couple of raging rivers in the bottom of them. That wasn't the worst of our problems if we wanted to try and claim our prize. The miles of plain between here and there included several tribes at war with us, a couple of others who we used to be at war with us, and a couple of other groups of people beyond that who had come into the area recently, who we had never come into contact with much yet, but whom we could presume to be at war with until we met them officially and had a ceremony with them sometime and maybe decided the opposite.

I didn't rightly see how we were ever going to get Daddy's prize but he was for sure set on looking at it. Daddy was lamenting the loss of his old bunch. They had turned up in this valley maybe thirty years back. They limped in in a ship which had taken a shot right through the brain which never flew again and they had to go native. They were instantly demoted by the loss of their ship from outlaws with off-planet origins and pretensions, to a bunch of renegades who made the best of it and married in. For some reason of their own they Christened their new planet as "Dogpatch"

I think my daddy was a real good and blood thirsty pirate chief. Having had one of his nuts cut off had made him lose a little perspective and I think for a while he had fit right in with a rather rough crowd. Coming here to our land had changed him again. His partners had gone on as before, treating people with brutality, but daddy didn't. In the beginning he had built himself a little cabin like he said that his grand dad once had. He built himself a still, dusted off a guitar and played his grand daddy's music and tried to retire.

It turned out that in the whiskey bottle he found religion, and in his guitar he found a desire to change the world. He was singing that old song about how :"one day god was gonna cut them down" when the whiskey made him realize that retiring in material comfort wasn't what he ought to do. He figured God was asking his help. He headed out into the plains when the horse tribes were spilling out of the valleys. He brought a wagon full of bibles and rum, a few good rifles and his guitar, and set up a tent for a revival right in their path. When he had converted his first thousand or so heathen he brought them on home with him, and set up a new regime in our little town. Daddy's name was Aeneas Browning but nobody ever called Daddy by his name in my lifetime. He don't like it for some reason. He is either just called the old man, or the prophet. Some of the tribes call him Mosiach. I always just called him Daddy.

Now its true that Daddy had lots of wives, more so even than is common here. But that is just the way it was with my mom's people. I notice that lots of people think that one guy with all those women just cant be fair, but they just don't imagine how the system worked that's all. First off they don't realize some very basic facts . For example my granddad (moms side), held his position for all of three years before a leopard ate him . His next in line, his paternal younger brother lasted about a year before a leopard ate him, too. Average tenure over the years is maybe four or five years at most in the top job . The job description after all, mainly entails shepherding groups of women and kids around, and being willing when the necessity arises, attack big cats with a sharp stick while everybody else runs away screaming.

On the day in question before I had ever had a single wife, I was watching my daddy carefully. I guess I never explained that I knew my daddy much better than you would think I would given the number of kids he had and the fact that I was not one of the first so I guess I might as well explain that now, Daddy said I was his true son, and the only son that he had sired. He could tell for certain this was true, as I carried the mark of the beast upon my body, as he did himself: a 'witch's tit', (just a little part of an extra nipple) as he called it, hairy inner ears, and an undescended testicle. Seeing as I am writing this for family or for history or maybe both I am trying to throw aside the conventions with which we protect our family stories. It feels unusual to do so and gives me pause sometimes to be so candid.

I figured he was nuts. Nuttier than a fruit cake, as they say. I was treated differently. As I was the only son that he recognized, I knew Daddy pretty good, and I knew all the ins and outs of what he was muttering about him and his old bunch. It was sad to see the old decrepit bastard looking so defeated. It seemed to him that twenty or thirty years ago before he got religion and fell out with his crew; he would have been able to snatch the prize just like " that there", Or maybe he was just bummed by being so old and maybe so drunken. It is hard to say what he really thought of that week, while sat and drank in his comfy chair, and looked out at her with the glasses (the ship I mean). He was bummed and I could tell.

I was kind of bummed as well. The next week at school really dragged ass, but before I can make you understand my small story I guess I had better explain what my corner of the probability incline was all about. I guess even people on the New Zions more or less understand the general scheme of things, but I will rough it out some anyways.

Prof says that history is a little too close to religion, so it gets lied about a lot. I aint quite so sure of what he means by that, but I know the prof is a smart man and here is the history of our neck of the woods, as he himself taught it to me. First off, we aint Roman, or at least Daddy and a bunch of the guys with him weren't. They was from New Zion. Now a good number of you Romans may be saying where the Hell is that? Well look in your textbooks, I can't schpiel out everything.

New Zions have people on them that speak a language called English, and they are one of half a dozen johnny- come- latelies who managed to make the jump across the time lines, and spewed out mini diasporas until the main roman lines noticed them and filled them in on the "house rules". A distinction of the world I was born on is that it was an edge world. The edge is those time lines next door to our probability where the menace seems to be stirring, bug Zones and nicely gardened planets with strange masters. I didn't know it growing up, but that's where we were, in a zone where the empire proper didn't want to venture. We were too close to time lines with domesticated, genetically altered, peoples and too close to the bugs too. Prof says we are hiding in the dark. I once asked the prof what animal he figured humans most resembled. I had been fresh from a sojourn with the horse people, where we had all taken our totems and I was more than a little disappointed and confused when the prof said cockroaches, but he said that was the best analogy he could come up with.

Cockroaches have a couple of desires. One is to constantly seek surfaces which touches both the top and bottom of their bodies at the same time. They love cracks. Well we are kind of like that. We love time cracks. It appears the others don't. Bugs inhabit the system and aliens send ships to the stars. We know that much, but they don't or at least didn't, jump from time line to time line. They are either in a time line, or not, dependent on the logic of that time line itself. Is that clear? Anywhere men have blundered into a time line where they encountered bugs or aliens they were mostly either ate or enslaved depending. So far so good? Prof says things have been changing the last couple of centuries. Bugs have spawned from time line to time line at least once or twice, and the garden planets have replaced some of the more remote roman worlds. Well I have to try to zero this thing in on my own experiences so hear goes.

The name of my home town is Tomahawk. It is situated at the door to the highlands in dense forest at the beginning of a deep fissure down to a river below. For the best part of two housand years since people found the copper seam and then later the coal, it has been a foundry. We make whiskey, arrow heads and tomahawks, and since pa and his bunch got here, we also make crappy single shot rifles-any caliber. We sell them to the tribes. We have kind of an ideal hidden location as a foundry. We are well hidden . A big building anywhere on the planet may be destroyed just as a matter of principal by the plantation owner, and any big agricultural community will be slave raided and dispersed.

They want a nice uncivilized hinterland to mine slaves from, and not much else. Tomahawk is a fairly hard nut to crack, and besides from a satellite photo we cant be seen. The forest is our friend, The foundry itself is at the bottom of the gorge by the river, and any nosy- parkers close enough to see the foundry, are also low enough to be fired on from the ridges above, and not fired on by daddy's muskets either.

When Daddy's old ship limped in she was chock full of all kinds of useful items. The forest is full of much of what we eat, but the arrow heads rum and rifles we make bring us lots of trade from the wild people in their little villages in the plains below, and even directly from civilization by way of the big river.

Tomahawk has had several changes of dynasty in the years of its existence, mostly repeats on what daddy and his bunch did. One bunch of outlaws with ships and modern weapons or another took over the joint to raid plunder and smuggle from, until they either left of their own accord, or ran out of ammunition and spare parts and were forced to go native. Tomahawk was quite separate in language and culture from the tribes who brushed against it from all sides. The Roman it spoke wasn't all that different from what Daddy had us taught in school but the religion was something else. When daddy came down off the mountain he put an end to it.

It would be catering to an unhealthy interest and disloyal to my home town to give you too big an account of these things; which are all in the past anyway, but I will give you the short list. Human sacrifices, burning of widows, witch hunts and immolations. and the use of bits of the human body, parted with in the most agony possible as good luck charms and in magic rituals (dicks, hands and whole human skins were very popular). They were " fucked up". As pa put it. They also kept slaves. Now we are a democracy and we follow the rules daddy brought down off the mountain with him. We are Mormons.

As I was saying, the next week at school really dragged ass. Every day I would take daddy up his porridge and whatever other juicy tidbits the ladies had gathered up for him, Then I would head on down to the school in the valley. I noticed that his glasses were still sitting out on a rock with a view, and when I had a look myself each morning you could still see the glint on the edge of the craft, daddy himself wasn't up to much talking. I could see his copper still had been seeing some use ,and one morning I even came upon him passed out on the ground not too far from his still . From how comfy he was setup, it looked like he had run out of all the botanicals he had actually brewed up, and he had been lying underneath the still to catch the drops an as they came out.

I figgered he was going through a bad patch. I hoped he didn't get ate. I could feel for him, my own life was going through a bad patch as well. Fifteen years old is both pretty old and pretty young at the same time. All my grass brothers my own age were going through their coming of age ceremonies and taking on the chores of men with their ma's people, but I didn't have any people to speak of in that sense.

Ma was dead, and her tribe wasn't close by. She hadn't been a local. I guess she was more like a gift you would say from a visiting tribe. And she hadn't lasted long. A leopard ate her a really long painful time ago. I told you pa figures I am his only son, and all the rest are just grass sons. He could well be right, and he says he knows he is right.

Mloko is my grass brother for sure, no real relation what so ever. When his mom married my pa he came along for the ride. He is about one year older than me . He don't like me much. We are too close for that somehow, and ever since I saved his life two summers ago when I took my first hair, and heavily indebted his honor to me, he has liked me even less. I don't always understand what motivates tribes people all that well. My moms blood not withstanding, I wasn't raised by them all that much. If somebody had saved my ass, I figure I would be indebted to the guy but Mloko doesn't see it that way.

Several of his tribal age mates, and others of my grass brothers, had watched it happen. I guess I had better explain that grass brothers [and sisters] are what happens when you keep on donating some old fart like my dad wives by the fives and tens. It is no shame on my dad. The shamed ones are the men who cannot claim their biological sons and get their due as fathers, That is how the horse tribes tribes look on it anyway. Daddy mostly got wives as a part of the politics of this place. When my daddy took his religion to the tribes around he had been more or less obligated to take wives from them, really quite a few, as usually one girl from any new tribe wouldn't want to come along alone so he often got half a dozen sisters or cousins at a time, and then he got a whole bunch more when he occupied tomahawk and set up his law. I don't mean to say my dads marriages were a sham . He took each and every new wife dead seriously . It was his religious obligation, and it was also probably fun , I am related by blood through my dad to hundreds of people in this little town. Daughters grandkids and great grand kids of my My name is Isiiah and since I was little my daddy has told me my purpose in life was to take over from him in teaching a lesson to the people. My daddy wants me to teach the people that god wants mercy and not sacrifice. Being the only acknowledged son of a prophet was part of why I was having such a drag time. Dads old bunch just called me Ishy for short.

As to dads old bunch where would I start to tell you about them? I guess I could tell you about their boat. She was called the 'Wild Thing', and I know her well because she forms the core of the school I go to. Another thing I could tell you about them is they aint called the "old bunch". Uncle John says I make them sound like a bunch of fierce old codgers, when they was actually quite young back then. They called themselves the Wild bunch. They didn't crash land the "Wild Thing" or anything haywire like that..They just brought her into the canyon and put her down careful, expecting a repair and off again, and ended up staying the rest of their lives.

She couldn't be fixed. It wasn't an entirely unprepared for development however ,and the people on board when she landed had pretty much everything they needed to take over the town and live out their lives in comfort. But the "devil wouldn't let them" or so my daddy tells it. It had been his ship, and I think he was one crazy one nutted blood thirsty pirate chief, but there was always a bit of the freedom fighter and a bit of Robin Hood mixed in. Men were worth money, and the ship he had stole was rigged for slaving , but he wouldn't touch the trade even though it was legal., He specialized in "wild cultivated botanicals" as he ungrammatically called them, by which he meant drugs grown off the main plantations which definitely was illegal. . Anyways , daddy eventually got stuck here ,and led a religious revival which is still going on. I knew all about it , and to me it was just boring old hat, It went like this. " Pa had retired but his crew had misbehaved, and in general got involved with the worst of the town element, so daddy came back down from the hills saved the world etc. etc. blah blah" or at least thats about how I felt about it back then .

I had way bigger and more important fish to fry, Mloko was being prepared for his future duties as a husband by various designated women of his tribe , I, however ,it seemed, could not get laid for the first time to save my bloody life. The first problem was that on account of dear old pa, I was related to just a about every local woman I got to know, grand daughters of his mostly but some daughters and great grand daughters, too. In other words, I had way too many sisters and nieces great grand nieces of his to keep track of as well and in addition, Daddy had been helping me out with it, by instilling a dread in the abomination which would result if I had sex with any woman descended from a man with a witches tit in me since I was five years old . Thanks dad. He also taught sermons about it to everybody else including just about every girl I knew in church .Everybody knew that as well as being a probable messiah. I was the potential carrier of an abomination. A sexually connected abomination.. Have you ever noticed how nuttiness is infectious?. I have to mention that nobody else in the old bunch not the professor or uncle John or any of the rest of them believe any of dads theories about himself and me, the hootchy kootchy man, elf blood , alien DNA, or any of his talk of abominations or anything else. They think my daddy is entirely nuts too just like I do. The problem is that about a thousand other people all around here including everybody my own age [except Mloko of course] refer to me as the chosen one even in their casual conversation. People come up to me in the street sometimes and want to anoint my feet with oil. My dad is the prophet and when he dies I am supposed to be the head of the church I will be the amazing; "Son of Prophet:" It is a real pain in the ass.

I decided to take my problems to uncle John. Over the years I have taken a lot of problems to uncle John , like two three years ago ,when Mloko and I started to not get along, and other less personal stuff such as just trying to get a handle on the nature of things.

Uncle John was a smart man and educated too. He could have stayed at home and done well and never heard the sound of a slave ship recall beacon. But he hadn't , curiosity and the devil had led him into the fringe and he had been a full fledged slave ship captain with a lovely little slave ship until daddy had cut it in half one day, and killed all of Uncle Johns companions, They didn't kill uncle John on account of his blonde hair. Daddy was always in search of his lost roots, so he collected blonde haired people. There weren't too many of his kind around. Mostly they didn't turn out to be from the new Zions anyways, but he struck gold in Uncle John. He not only knew what the Church of Latter Day Saints was. He was also Daddy's elder in the church, It saved his neck. Daddy was usually kind of harsh with slavers. After uncle John repented and got washed in the blood of the lamb again, dad took him on as first mate in the botanicals business.

Its real easy for me to picture my uncle John sitting in his grog shop being king of all he surveyed except of course for his wife. He was a man of 'singular' attributes he used to say. He had just one leg, just one eye and just one wife. His lady, Meg had always been one of my favorite moms, she was a big dark lady of a racial type you don't see on that world, and John had brought her there with him. They spoke English at home, just like daddy and a few others of his old bunch, and their kids.

For most people, English was the language of the holy book and the holy music, and every body learned it in school along with standard roman, for some reason, that I of course had never thought to ask about, they had no kids.

I figure I might have spent even moretime at Uncle John's bar if daddy hadn't said not, not that he personally had much intention of raising me full time. He was way too tied up in being a prophet, having visions, and getting dead drunk with his still, when nobody was watching, in his little cabin up on the hill. Besides, he had way too many wives he had to concentrateon getting to know, in his holy duties, to have much room for anything else. Such as me. Whenever I really wanted to understand the world I would go talk to Uncle John As I say that I realize that it aint really fair not to mention the Prof as being an even more major source of who I am .

He taught me music, but the Prof's view on things was always pretty cosmic. He had been on sabbatical from a university, when he had the bad luck to be scooped by slavers and sent to this plantation world, He had been a slave and lost his nuts. He had a reason to take a cosmic view, but it made him a bit hard to talk to about my little problems. Uncle John was way better.

When I got to Uncle Johns bar he could see right off that I was glum, and after Meg finished stuffing me at supper time he took me down into the bar with him to tend to the evening crowd. He had his special table up and away from the rest on a little mezzanine where he could both see all that was going on in his inn , and still keep a little removed from the merry makers. He brought the two of us a hot toddy ,with mine artfully concealed in a clay bowl like they served soup in, just in case Meg should happen to come into the bar and glance in our direction.. The hot spicy liquid had a magic effect as it went down my throat and the place felt so homey I felt good for the first time in a week or so. Uncle john took his time to talk and we both sat back enjoying the roman guitar playing with its castanets When Uncle John finally broke his peace it was to ask me if Mloko had been riding me, or if I had managed to get myself switched by the lay brothers again. Well both those things had happened recently.

Mloko had even invented a new pet name for me. He called me the chosen one just like lots of people did, but he used his own language in which chosen one usually referred to a sweet little virgin girl who had been promised to be married. He thought it was a hell of joke, as did a bunch of the other boys in the class, including both the boys with tribal affiliations who understood the joke right off, and the town kids who had to have it explained to them. It was looking to become my new nickname, and I wasn't too pleased about it. But that wasn't what I wanted to talk to Uncle John about, I wanted to know what he thought of the ship parked on a ridge , who did he figure was on it? What were the people like? Did he think there was maybe anyway I could contact them and get the HELL away from Tomahawk and my fate as "boy prophet" I guess you might wonder why I had much of an idea that there was an outside world that I might want to go to, but it was one of the little peculiarities of our little town was that we were cybernetically connected with the outer universe. The wild thing had full computer hookups and communications. We could surf the net in school . Theoretically,we could even send out going traffic from the Wild Thing itself if we wanted to, but we didn't as that could bring us nosey parkers with guns, I had a pretty good education. I knew that outside the fringe there were normal places with universities and schools , I took in a bit of their world on sitcoms and adventure shows we watched daily. I wanted really badly to get the hell out.

Uncle John was plenty interested in the ship when he heard about it, asking where away it had landed, and fetching a map especially spryly for a man with a peg leg. He calmed down considerably when he discovered exactly where I had placed it. He started to explain to me that while it might seem close, it was through impossibly dense and hostile country. He started to explain about how when any townspeople left our immediate area, they did so as part of a tribal entourage, and under their protection, and all about the warring tribes between here and there.

When he realized by the look on my face that I knew all of that, he left off talking and said "It might as well be on Mars son,." then left it at that. I didn't keep on talking about it ,as I had a secret plan which was forming in my head, instead I just let the matter drop. Uncle John looked relieved at first, but Uncle John is a good judge of men, and after a few minutes he commenced to giving me long hard quiet looks once again ,finally saying "You aint thinking of trying to make it there by yourself are you ?" It had ceased being a question before it was half out of his mouth. He paused for a second and then said "you know that the odds are you wont make it, and that even if you do those people probably can't or won't help you.".

I just shrugged and didn't answer in my best fifteen year old fashion. He let the conversation drop. Later on, after I had hugged meg and was about to depart, he said to Meg "there were some leopard pugs outside town today, dear, I hope you don't mind if I send Bobo to walk the boy home?" It had been a long time since I had needed Bobo to walk me home to my room where I boarded at the school, so Meg was a bit surprised, but she went along with Uncle John without a fuss .

It reminded me of being a little kid again, to be walking back to my room at the school with Bobo shuffling along at my side. Bobo is a Little Person. Not the feral kind that live in the forests all over this world, but a store bought factory delivered little person, He was some kind of special purpose model a lot more beefy than the little people of the forest, and maybe not as bright. John had got a hold of him young and raised him. Raising a little person aint like raising a dog but it aint like raising a regular human child either. Somewhere in between I guess.

Bobo was devoted to Uncle John and Meg but he liked me real well too. Some of you might be scratching your heads and wondering what the hell are little people, as I know they don't allow them on the urban worlds. Well, little people are what your books refer to as "constructs", you use them on your outer planets and your food is mostly grown by them. But I want to tell you, calling them 'constructs' a lie. They are human beings, just dumbed-up and smalled-down in size, and with a couple of extra chromosomes thrown in so they can't interbreed with regular human beings. Removing the genes for most of the speech center made a real big difference. They were genetically engineered to be our slaves, and they are the slave population most places except on backwaters like Dogpatch where it is still easier just to catch and enslave regular garden variety human beings.

I didn't expect to see Bobo curled up under the porch the next morning, as normally he would have gone back to Uncle John's. There he was, all curled up like a dog with his head next to his ass, a big furry lump of bad smelling little person. He wouldn't shoot off home when I told him too, but stood his ground It was clear Bobo wasn't going to leave anytime soon. He liked to please Johnny, and a walk up country where he might be able to kill something and eat it raw and squirming was Bobo's favorite thing in the world. I figured uncle John had told him to hang out with me as maybe I was going down country.

It looked like I had a constant companion for the next few days until Bobo forgot about his mission. Uncle John was a tricky old bastard. It looked like my trip to the ship wasn't going to be entirely alone. I thought long and hard about who I could tell I was leaving, and came up with a couple I had to tell. .I intended to see Dad one more time, ask him a few hard questions and then book. I didn't need much of a kit, as the weather was warm, and there was plenty of food around at this time of year. It wasn't going to be a matter of finding food in the wilderness, but a matter of not providing a little extra for some carnivore with my own mortal coil or more likely getting shot or plugged full of arrows or spears. .

I hiked on up the hill to dads ladies compound to pick up dads porridge and bits ,and then hiked on further up towards dads cabin, It was a beautiful sort of morning with the sun still not shining down in our valley and the air cool although a few miles away out on the savannah you could use a rock out in the sun to cook food on. There wasnt much stirring , although bobo managed to see something and knock it off with one of the little football shaped rocks he carried. After a bunch of squeaking and commotion in the bushes Bobo came back with his mouth crammed full and a little tail hanging out of his mouth, Bobo had bad manners but at least he was easy to please. We were just about up at dads cabin when I saw the hyena shit. We have a saying around here for when a conclusion is is obvious . The people say " Well if an old lady is missing and the hyena shits white hairs....." I really didn't expect to find him when I got up there and I was right I did not find him.

There were plenty of tell tale signs all about to show what had happened. Leopard pugs all about and a wet scuffed up area on the ground that Bobo had his nose snarffled into figuring it all out. There was a clear drag path to the edge of the ridge where the leopard had drug something heavy over the side. I tried without success to dissuade Bobo from following the path down the side, because I didn't want him to fetch back any bits. Daddy's fate was clear. There was a half finished bottle of store-bought rum sitting on his observation rock, next to his spy glasses, with a glass next to that brim full. There was an empty bottle on the ground next to his comfy chair. That was a lot of whiskey even for daddy.

I wasn't all that happy with Bobo a minute later when he returned carrying pop's skull with about six inches of spine still attached.. Luckily it wasn't all that gory, having been broken and emptied, and then worked on by ants until it shone. You couldn't have boiled it any whiter and cleaner. I set the skull down on the rock next to the glasses and sat down in Daddy's comfy chair, checked his mug of rum for bugs, and then had a sip, I gave the glass to Bobo, and pulled the bottle closer to myself, and had a long red hot draw from it as I looked out upon the view.

There was a lot of weather about, although not near us. There was a storm dancing around some buttes in the middle distance ,with lightening dancing around the rocky knob where it stuck up out of the trees ,and a giant black evil looking halo of cloud in the sky above it. We were situated on a ledge maybe 3000 feet up on a plateau and we could see straight down to the flat savannah which separated us from some buttes in the area which also arose to the height of the plateau we were on. There were some clouds around the rocky knob further off where the ship had been sitting as well, although not as dense as around the butte that was getting the pounding. I sat with daddy's spy glasses in my lap waiting for my chance to have one more look at the ship before I gathered up myself and headed off towards it. I don't suppose that there was any doubt in my mind that the ship would still be sitting there, so when the clouds blew away for a moment and I saw no sign of a glint on its rocky knob I was just blown away. The rock was just as bare as it had been all my life before last week. The bird had flown. I was doomed.

Well I guess you all might be wondering what exactly I found so bad about finding myself to be the son of a prophet and the head of a community and a religion. Well frankly there was a whole bunch wrong with it, but now I will tell you just a few of my biggest beefs to give you an idea. To begin with Dad had to make a few minor changes in the religion he inherited from his own dad when he set it up here on Dogpatch .

The change he made which concerned me most was in the marriage laws. In order to get along with the present institutions of the people he decided it wouldn't matter much if wives were inherited.[Not your own mom of course, but the rest of them] I know it wasn't that way back on the New Zions. I have read up on the subject quite extensively. I knew it wasn't fair, right, or even decent, but on that morning I had just inherited a hundred or so wives, lots were more than twice my age some of them more than triple it and several of them four times it. I had inherited every possibly stinky; hairy ,scary one of them and there was nowhere to run to.

Me and Bobo sat there staring out at the weather playing out in front of us, as Dad used to do, and we drank his liquor. His half bottle was done in no time, and I pulled the cork from another bottle in daddy's six-pack of whiskey and we drank it too. Bobo was a good drinking companion for my present mood, and sat there listening to me without saying a damned thing. With a glass in his hand and his old mans face framed in white whiskers he didn't look half as dumb as I knew he was, so I talked to him at length about my troubles, not caring that he didn't really understand zip , A troop of monkeys passed over us in the trees above, and I shot a couple of them with the piece that Daddy kept sitting by his rock . I lit a little fire and put them on to roast whole on the grill and in the early evening me and Bobo had grilled monkey along with the porridge and bits I had brought up for dad and then we went into dads cabin, and after I played a few sad songs on dads guitar we went to sleep.

I woke up early the next morning with my head pounding and a sense of defeat. As soon as I stood up the closeness of the place and the sudden movement as well as dads skull sitting on the table made me queasy as Hell ,so I pushed the door open in a hurry and busted out in case I was gonna hurl. It was a beautiful day in paradise outside, full sun in most places with big blue butterflies dodging about. You could smell their perfume as they flew by, and their color of blue was so bright they appeared to have lights within them. All their dodging about made me feel unsteady on my feet.

A humming bird flew abruptly up to me hovered in the hair nest to my head and flew away, or at least I was pretty sure one did. Sometimes a real bad hangover has you feeling like you are being buzzed by troops of humming birds when there are none around. I was in bad shape. Paradise felt horribly intrusive. I pissed like a racehorse {as daddy always put it], over the edge of the ravine, and made my way to daddy's comfy chair by his look out spot, with its extra six pack of rum bottles still sitting there and threw myself down. I knew daddy always fixed a hangover up really fast with a little hair of the dog, so I tried to do the same, but the mere act of holding a glass of rum near enough to me that I could see and smell it ,set off a seething and loathing which it is pretty hard to describe if you haven't been there.

Bobo looked pretty low himself ,only pulling himself far enough from the house that he could lie down hard in a nice dusty spot and roll around. I sat there in f daddy's chair trying to pull myself together and gazing out at the view without seeing it for several minutes without realizing that there was a familiar glint of reflected sunlight on the top of a butte in front of my eyes. It wasn't the far off slope which the craft had been perched on this last ten days ,but a much nearer one at perhaps half the distance. I grabbed the glasses and had a look, It stood out much clearer this time.

I could see the ship its shape now and even make outs its registration and markings. It was sitting right on top of the butte which had taken the pounding from the storm the day before.

I Hadn't been able to see her for the cloud. I sat up and started thinking hard.

The first thing that struck me was that my plan of yesterday which had been to just sneak off was no damned good somehow. It just warn't the right thing to do. Plus now there was no chance of anybody ratting me out to my pa and having him stop me. I had to say goodbye face to face to Aunt Meg, the professor, and most of all to Mloko my former bosom buddy and present day nemesis, even if took me a little bit of extra time. Besides, Uncle John was a smart individual, and I realized I would be a fool not to ask his advice. Before I left the cabin I took the time to return once more into daddy's cabin and to think about him for a moment.

There was a table in the corner where daddy used to write way back when. I opened the drawer and there right on the top was a little book with my name on it. I took the book a pair of pistols which dad had made hiself years back, and looked about for anything else I could take. There wasn't a bloody thing. I took my daddy's skull from the table and set it on the mantle, then I said goodbye to my daddy and closed the door.

Uncle John's place was hopping. He was up on the mezzanine using his dagger to carve a set of interlocking rings out of hardwood. With the rifle he used as a crutch leaning up against the wall beside him. It had been modified a bit with a regular cane bottom, and rubber end, having been inserted in what once was the bayonet holder, and by having had a metal framework suitable for a crutch support replace the wooden handle. He kept it loaded and nobody liked to get John upset, as he waved it around a lot when he was pissed off ,which made everyone else in the room pretty edgy.

Uncle John didn't look too cheerful today, although he was plainly glad to see me. I sat down opposite him, and he ordered me a drink in a soup cup as he always did, and covertly directed my attention to a group of men in the far corner of his establishment.

They weren't from Tomahawk, and they weren't tribesmen either. They had come up the river on the plains below in a boat, and had made their way up to Tomahawk. ostensibly to trade . " There is trouble there Johnny" he said, giving a nod in their direction. " Days on a ship, and up the dusty valley, and they aren't thirsty enough to drink. Something stinks little Ishey, something stinks".

John kept on muttering in a low voice as much to himself as to me. I looked across the busy bar past where a party of tribesmen were drinking to the alcoves at the back. There were six or eight big hard men with a sameness in their demeanor. " they look like soldiers to me Ishey. Do you see the fellow on the right? The others bring his food to him, and he drinks when the others don't. I would say he was the officer. They could be soldiers Ishey, here to check the place out,. Or just maybe they are an independent posse staying sober because they are about to take away my money tonight.".

I could see a decision pass across his mind, and he finished up by saying to me "I think they need a little rest and relaxation". He waved a signal to the bar maid who went into the kitchen to fetch Meg. When Meg arrived John sat her ample ass on his lap and jollied her up. It was how he liked to be, but it also gave him the chance to talk to her quietly about the men ay the far side of the bar. It took him a minute to catch her attention, as her gaze had wandered to my "soup" bowl which I had neglected to hide. I saw her give me a hard look and stash the thought, away for further comment later on.

Uncle John confided his suspicions to his wife and suggested to her with a wink that yonder soldiers looked like they needed a bit of rest. Then he said to her, "not in the booze this time, the most of them aren't drinking" and gave her a wink. Ten minutes later I saw Meg approach the men and fed them their dinner. Twenty minutes after that every single on one of them passed out stone cold on the floor.

Ten minutes later beyond that Uncle John's staff had them manacled and wheel-barrowed off to his dungeon so he could have a little talk with them later. Once the immediate business had been looked after Uncle John perked up and ordered us both some extra supper and asked what I had been up to.

When I told Uncle John about Daddy's demise, he looked cheerful and relieved more than anything else, although he tried to cover it up pretty good- out of respect for me. When I told him that the flyer had picked up and landed again half as far away as it had been he was very interested. When I told him I could make out her name and numbers on the hull, he sat straight up, and for a second his genial mask slipped and I could see some hard calculating going on beneath the surface. His smile soon resumed, and he called the girl and gave instructions for our food to be wrapped up to go, and for his palanquin crew to be roused up.

Uncle John gets about pretty good on his own in his establishment. He has a few little holes drilled in his hardwood floors, which fit the end of his peg leg so he can be solid in his favorite perches,. But when it comes to getting about around town, he gets hisself carried.

We were headed to the school, or more properly to the part of it which was the Wild Thing, daddy's ship. Uncle John had the idea that now he knew their name and numbers he could find out what kind of ship they were, and maybe even rouse them over the radio. He cleared off a big table in the com room and unwrapped my food and laid it out for me telling me just to sit down and have my 'chippies' while he tried to see what he could do. I was fifteen and Uncle John customarily talked to me like I was nine, but I figured his heart was in the right place so I let it go, and sat back and ate while he worked, eating the pile of chips and the variety of breaded deep fried little critters which were served with it .

Uncle John fired up the computers and dialed up the pile of data. John had a habit of muttering quite a bit, so he kept me informed of what he was up to, without talking to me directly. He fed the flyers name and numbers into the computer ship and it spat out a bunch of information right promptly which produced a smile of satisfaction from Uncle John and the comment that she couldn't be a navy ship as her info wasn't even encrypted.

Pretty soon he looked up and muttered geological survey and wondered out loud what was she doing down on the planet? Geological survey work could usually be done from space. He answered the question for himself by suggesting that they had been after a bit of wild honey to bring home. By which I figured he meant a batch of "wild crafted off plantation botanicals" as Daddy used to call the drugs they bought and sold when he flew the Wild Thing. The next thing Uncle Johnny had a look at was her armament and concluded out loud that they probably hadn't much on board besides ceremonial swords and pistols for the officers.

He dialed up some of the info on the 'Etruscan Princess', that was the flyer's name into the corner of the screen where he could save it to refer to while he made the call. He then sat back for a minute and said to himself " well who should we be then? Who would they trust?" He looked me directly in the eyes and said "Ishey I cant just tell them I am first mate Johnny Jackson of the privateer the 'Wild Thing' now can I?"

He sat quietly for a few minutes with the wheels grinding in his brain. We can't be navy, because if they have been up to no good they won't reply. We cant be a research vessel, because I couldn't keep up the "parlay" good enough with real scientists. which these may be, Unless maybe? He hesitated for a moment, then said "yup we are a research vessel but the vehicle itself is in orbit presently on its way out of this probability, and I will be the officer in charge of an engineering detail left behind. O.K. that's it, we are a crew of diamond drillers left behind for a month while our ship heads home. Now which ship then?".

Saying this he dived back into the search until he had a likely candidate to impersonate. He had the ships crew lists and specs in front of him on the screen. O.K. Johnny here we go. Uncle John clearly enjoyed this activity and for a moment I had the feeling he had done it all before. He pressed the broadcast button and spoke into the mike calling out The Etruscan Princess by her call signs which he had obtained in his research. He followed it up by identifying himself as a major Gaius in charge of an engineering unit. And gave his own I.D. numbers. My jaw had dropped when Uncle Jack had begun parleying in perfect crisp roman just like that used on the urban worlds.

Uncle John was good, He had hit the repeat button and his words had wrung out three or four times over the airwaves. A breathless and rather young voice came to us over the speakers. It was a lieutenant on board the Etruscan Princess, who quickly schpieled out how they had taken a stray shot through some of their equipment and how later on all three of the superior officers had failed to come back from walks which hadn't been meant to take them more than a few hundred yards from the ship. The lieutenant was clearly spooked and the voice had more than a little panic in it.

Uncle John has a way with people. He can make his voice get all gravelly and soothing, and he soon had the Lieutenant eating out of his hand. He asked him if he had an accurate account of just what the stray shot had busted and what part they needed to order in. And told him that as our supply ship was still in the system preparing for a probability jump. He would be able to radio a list of the parts out to them and have them brought back when she returned in a month.

The young voice on the other end sure sounded thankful to my Uncle John, in fact we could hear his voice breaking and he sounded pretty near ready to cry. He finished up his requisition list to uncle John by beginning to give the coordinates of his position. This had Uncle John back on the airwaves pretty fast, ordering him to shut up and chewing him out, reminding him that this wasn't a secure planet and that if he gave out his coordinates he would have unfriendly visitors down his throat before my uncle could possibly get to him.

The young lieutenant gulped a couple of times so loudly we could hear it over the air and said to my Uncle "Sorry sir. What do you figure we should do?"

My Uncle finally smiled and relaxed. He winked at me before continuing in his best crisp Roman, "Lieutenant we have you in sight. If you just stay there we will send some one local who can guide you in where we are, if that is what you would like to do. We have a bit of a hidey hole here It is probably better than sitting out in the open like a sitting duck as you are at present."

The lieutenant started talking about how he couldn't leave on account of his missing officers but Uncle John said he thought perhaps we could help him find his officers on account of our good relations with the natives in the area. It was another lie. That tore it. The young man's mind was made up, especially on account of Uncle told him that our land party probably wouldn't get there for at least ten days anyways, and if his officers hadn't made it back under their own steam by then it wasn't likely that they ever would.

Uncle John flipped the machine off and sat down beside me opening up his pack of chips and critters and cracking a beer for the two of us. He was cheerful as all get out.

Now I am not dense enough not to have noticed a few things that didn't seem to fit; namely, where was the Etruscan Princes's part going to come from and what was Uncle John so goddamned cheerful about. I decided the best idea wasn't to dissemble, but to take it on. I thought about how Daddy would have done it and gave it a try.

I gruffed up my voice and instead of calling him unka Jack I addressed him as "Johnny Jack " as my father did and just ordered him to spill the beans, Uncle John choked on his critters and spun to face me. After he finished coughing up the bits, he got control of himself and said" well little Ishey you sure gave me a turn for a moment it was just like having your old daddy standing there again." I didn't say anything but continued giving him a hard look. I could see the wheels whirring in his brain. I didn't want to give him the time to get too inventive.

He continued, "Well Ishey, we sure enough do have their part. All they lost was their spatial coordinator and a spatial coordinator is exactly what you have your beer bottle sitting on at this moment." It seemed that it was true and he was so willing to talk about it that I immediately dropped the topic, and asked him directly what it was that had made him so cheerful.

His answer rang true." I think I have figured out a way to come with you, Ishey. Me and Meg are going to get the Hell off of Dogpatch." He laid out a plan to me about how him and Meg were going to assume some different identities, and ship off with me. He said he didn't have all the pieces sorted out yet of how we were going to get all the things to happen just right. He sensed that there had to be a way to spin the tangled web he had just wove, into something that resembled Uncle Jack saving the Etruscan Princess from a trap laid for her by the dastardly Johnny Jack and the Wild Bunch who had been posing as drilling crew and trying to entrap the Princess.

I could see it working, and I began to relax as John spun on as how he figured how he could not only save the Etruscan bitch and get a free ride off the planet, but also a heroes welcome to boot, when we got to the core worlds. He said it didn't pain him at all to double cross all the rest of the wild bunch, as they were bad characters one and all, and hadn't probably really repented when my dad got religion and spared their lives. Besides, he said, "the Etruscan Princess is a tiny ship and when they hijacked her, there wouldn't be room for more than a dozen crew anyways, and that fact would most likely start a war fighting over the spots.

It sounded like he was laying it on a mite thick, but I figured he must have a guilty conscience to deal with and was trying to justify his actions to himself and not to me .So I let it go. I had one Hell of a journey to prepare for, and because the young lieutenant wasn't going to fly off with the princess I had more time to prepare for it than I would have had before. After Uncle John went on home I went straight to my room on the far side of the school, where the other boys boarded, and I lived pretty much full time.

There weren't any other boys around on this particular night, as it was a big holiday coming and every body had headed home. I tried to think out my plans but I soon realized that what I needed was a big long sleep in my own bed. It might be a long. while or maybe never, before I saw it again. I settled in and went out deep in just a few seconds.

When I woke up Uncle John was at my door with some stuff he thought might be useful. There was a sub-machine gun and some bandoliers that must have come into this valley with the Wild thing. It still had quite a bit of grease on it and had clearly just been dug out of its crate. There was also a hand held tracking device which would let me know where I was even in dense bush. There was also a Bobo-sized pack sack, which I noticed was stuffed with hand grenades.

There was way too much stuff, but I was glad to pick through it. Uncle John had been about to leave again, when I saw him thinking hard on something, and turn back. He called me over and began to take off his jewelry and lay it down upon the table. I opened my mouth to protest, when he told me to just shut up and take a closer look. The two rings which he took off the middle fingers of each hand turned out to have a little trick. If you turned the signet around a little needle protruded from the front, Uncle John pointed out the little needle muttering "poison, enough to kill a man or a leopard outright, and to make anything larger lose its interest in you."

The big gem on the gold chain which he took from a pretty box, turned out to be a small explosive with a timer. Uncle John was full of tricks. He had a look at the pistols I was taking of Dad's and instead suggested a couple of Derringers, only three inches or so long which he produced from one of his pockets. He shook my hand and walked out the door turning one last time as he did so to say " Ishey if I aint here when you get back it will be on account of Meg having shot me dead for letting you try this."

He appeared dead serious and kind of worried. So I thanked him again for his efforts and he finally shoved off. I spent the next hour picking and choosing and getting my kit together while I simultaneously fretted about the prof not being in his quarters at the back, as I really wanted to see him before I left, but he never arrived, so eventually, I just left him a note on his dresser telling him my plans and thanking him for educating me and raising me at least fifty percent as well. It seemed a cheap way to sneak out on a fine old man but I didn't see a choice. I had finally got my kit together and was about to put the pack on Bobo and go seek out Mloko when he popped around the corner into the school itself.

He looked like he had been crying and then said to me in English, " Dads dead , I guess you heard?" And then from some sore spot down inside him he squeaked out in a breaking voice."He always liked you best"

It was true, and I didn't know what to reply to it. When I was saved from having to say anything by Mloko suddenly taking in how I was dressed, and the sub-machine gun slung over my shoulder. " Holy Moses Isiiah what are you up to?" he said in very surprised voice. I took in two things right away. Mloko was using English to talk to me, and he was using my real name not one of his pet nicknames. Mloko spoke English as well as I did, and standard Roman too, for that matter, but a couple of years back he had started only talking to me in the Romish dialect which was the tribes tongue, and he had quit using my real name. It seemed that now dad was dead I might have my buddy back.

I filled Mloko in on the flyer and its location, and what Uncle John and I intended to do about it, while Mloko cooed and clucked over the big gun. In the tribes, a gun like that would be worth a fortune, and not just in money, but in prestige and esteem. However after about five minutes of fussing about with it he tossed it on a sofa in the corner and said "too bad we cant take it" I damned near started crying. It looked like I had my big brother back.

Mloko started off by rejecting just about everything I had collected to take with me, except the g.p.s. the hand grenades and a couple of wicked looking knives he said were too cool to leave behind, as well as the derringers ,which he said the same thing about. To replace the submachine gun, he had me fetch an itsy bitsy monkey rifle which pa had made me for one Christmas when I was about seven years old. I

t weighed about four pounds and a hundred rounds of ammo didn't fill a cup, and it had a sweet little silencer built permanently into the barrel. With it you could easily shoot one monkey after another without sending the pack racing off unless one of the monkeys made a lot of noise in dieing. I suddenly had a memory of how good it had felt when my dad had handed it over and then, unbidden. I had another little flash of how my older brother Mloko had admired it, and how dad had given him absolutely 'dick' for Christmas that very same year. Even though he had to come over to Mloko's moms to give it to me, as I was more or less living there back then. My daddy was like that, kind of an asshole in some ways. Mloko also rejected Bobo as a traveling companion, and had me trick him into my room and lock him in, where he moaned, hopelessly, suddenly, well aware that we were going for a walk without him,

I don't know about other earths, but although Dogpatch seems awfully fair when you look upon it. It seems to have more than its share of foul tricks. Here is a partial list. In the jungle lowlands if you drink the water from a stream with your mouth like a deer, or even with your hands like a man, there is a critter resting on the bottom which senses your warmth ,and rises towards you, trying to get itself drunk so it can live in your liver. In the plains, if you drink water directly from a river without somehow filtering it first there is a tiny crustacean which you may ingest that harbors a worm which may grow up to six feet long within the muscles of the human body, and there is yet another little critter which inhabits snails in sluggish water in the plains, and also infests the human body, often seething within the still living eyes of its host. You don't even need to eat or drink that one, or the hookworms either, as they just bore in through your skin, A fifth denizen of the water is a parasite which when drunk causes blockages which make a mans nuts swell up so big he needs a wheelbarrow to carry them --no that is not a joke. That ain't all. Its just all I feel like telling you about right now,

When Mloko and I left the school buildings beside the ship a couple of his tribal age mates got up from a spot of shade under a tree where they had been waiting for us and walked with us as we followed Tomahawk's little river where it fell down out of our gorge to join in the big gentle river on the plains. As we walked Mloko was explaining to his buds the quest we were on, and how it would make us the stuff of legends, and how they would tell tales of our bravery around the fires for years to come. As he talked I had a sudden remembering, of how brave and adventurous my older brother was, and also how rash, dangerous and down right haywire.

I suddenly remembered that all of my near death encounters to date, had been in his company. One of Mloko's buds wasn't having any of it. He was a big fellow. He looked a bit older than either of us. After listening for a few minutes he suggested that anyone trying to cross the plain right now, was going to end up dead right fast, and that it was just plain a bad idea that he wasn't gonna contribute to. To hear it put out just like that, by a fella who should know, set me back a piece. It didn't even slow Mloko down. He colored up right off the bat, and said that he knew that to be true, and the plane wasn't what we were about. We were taking the big river. And sure enough when the trail forked leading to Mloko's tribe's camp, we took the other fork that led on down to the big river and we set up a little camp along the side of it not so far from the factors buildings, where we conducted our trad

Now for you to have a real idea what we were about, I guess I need to give a little geography lesson. Where Tomahawk was located was on the edge of a massive plateau maybe thousands of square miles or so big. Down below us was a plain with a big river lying alongside it, where many rivers gushed down to join it from our plateau through gorges and valleys The one where Tomahawk was located was kind of flat tor a gorge, and kind of precipitous for a valley. The big river wound around for some thousand miles upriver from us sometimes radically changing its direction and running for hundreds of miles south while on the other side of a mountain. Relatively close by, it was engaged in running hundreds of miles north.

It had pretty much made up its mind by the time it got to Tomahawk. From there it ran relatively straight the few hundred miles to the sea. I said relatively straight, by which I mean that it was straighter than a corkscrew but not quite as straight as a rainbow,.

The part Mloko wanted us to traverse was loopy as a piece of spaghetti ,and would turn a sixty mile trek across a plain into a couple of hundred mile journey. The plateau we were on ended abruptly at the plain and yet there were bits of it dribbling on out into the plain in the form of buttes that suddenly rose up with mesas on top. Some were little and some huge and running for ten or twenty miles covered in just the same jungle as the plateau we were on. Our destination was the big knob with the glint on it, which arose from one of these jungle covered mesas in the distance.

To hear Mloko tell it that evening as we sat around the fire, it was our only choice that wasn't certain suicide. It sounded to me like maybe 'damned near, but not quite' certain suicide, but I held my tongue. Mloko didn't really know a damned thing about the river, but he and all his buds thought the plains were deadly to attempt to ride across right now. I am sure they were right and I realized from their talk that if Mloko hadn't turned up to change my plans tomorrow, or the next day would probably have been the last days of my life.

What Mloko had in mind was to take a canoe and hook a couple of outriggers to it and then to artfully decorate the outriggers with branches affixed just so so that our craft would resemble a tree top merrily floating downstream in the middle of the river. We would float downstream until the river made a cross country run near the mesa we wanted to climb and we would cross the relatively small area of open land to the base of the mesa and head on up.

News of Mloko's quest spread fast, and the next day our camp was full of Mlokos age mates bringing in stuff they thought might help us ,and helping Mloko to put together our outrigger. To begin with they fashioned us a dugout without touching up and finishing the outside of the hull. They left it as nature had made her ,all covered in bark to enhance our disguise. By dusk the outriggers were on her and she was full of our gear and ready to push off in the morning. As we sat around the fire that night Mloko was jubilant while most of his buddies were quiet and somber and I was just plain scared shit-less.

In the local legends the Big river was the home of the devil. Satan lived on the bottom of the river. It is no wonder that the river had a bad rap among Mloko's people. It did nothing for them, but as it cut through their territory it created a highway a highway for intrusions from outside such as slavers and it was a dangerous pestilential place as well, on account of its fever carrying mosquitoes ,its giant crocodiles and snakes, and its voracious flesh devouring little fishes. Satan was said to be a huge crocodile that migrated up the river yearly in search for females and ate sixty or eighty people each year on his migration. Dad said the critter was real, but it warn't Satan..

Mloko'speople were horsemen. They were rulers of the wild horseless people on the plains, but they did not live with them. The problem with the plains from Mloko's peoples point of view, was a little biting fly they called the horse killer. Six months of the year a horse on the plains was a dead horse. The bite of the fly could sometimes give a man a fever but it killed a horse every time. Once a year they came billowing up and drove Mloko's people out. The horse people ran to the edge of the plateau and up the gorges and valleys lke the one Tomahawk was in, until they were high enough that the flies didn't come, and spent their time there until six months later they could erupt onto the plains again.

Mloko didn't know dick about the river, but he warn't scared and the thought that he was coming with me cheered me up for half that sleepless night. The second half of the night I had some different insights which mostly focused on the thought that every one of those near death experiences which I mentioned earlier, had also been a near death experience for Mloko as well as me..

What would I feel like if Mloko got knocked off? He had nothing personal in this game. He loved this world and had no desire to leave it. He also wasn't contributing any special expertise, as he knew nothing about the river and probably lots less about the jungle highlands than I did, on account of where we respectively had spent most of our time. I started to think of my dead daddy and what he would have said.

He said to me, clear as if I could hear it, "You have only one conscience. Don't break it because you cant fix it." Just before dawn I slid out into the bush for a piss, and then with a clear sense of conviction I walked down to the shore got into the dugout and shoved her off. Mloko was going to resume hating my guts pretty fast I figured.

The dawn broke on a beautiful day on the river. It was the kind of day when you might think that Dogpatch was a pretty wonderful planet. There were millions of pink birdies, and hundreds of blue red or emerald green ones. I had taken my craft out dead center of the river, where the little habitations of the people on the edge could no longer be made out, but the occasional plume of smoke said I wasn't alone in the world. The world was going by at the pace of a rather fast walk. I was warm and comfy and I had lots of of shade for later in the day.

I realized one more time, that my brother was a pretty smart hombre. There was lots of good grub ,and skin bags full of cool clear water right alongside me, with lots more stuff in the outriggers. I got out my little monkey gun, and every time I saw a double pair of eyes poking up above the water to have a look at me I fired and tried to take one of them out. It was a lazy sort of day but I had no trouble trying to stay awake.

By the afternoon I was pretty happy about my situations in so far as the daylight hours were concerned, but I became increasingly concerned about what to do at night. There was still plenty and enough smoke showing up here and there on the shore to convince me that I shouldn't go anywhere near it. There were occasional tiny uninhabited islands here and there which I passed throughout the day and I began to hope that on one would present itself around evening. The other two alternatives, that of trying to keep afloat and bombing along blindly, or of looking for shelter on an inhabited shore, both sounded pretty sketchy. I lucked out. A suitable shaggy little island came into view and I tied up on the ass end of her and fell fast asleep in my comfy little space.

I woke up in the morning feeling like king of all I surveyed. The river was majestic and wild, and there was no smoke in site on either shore. I seemed to be moving into a less inhabited area . I rummaged around a bit out on the pontoons for some good grub and stood up in the bow of the boat to piss . It hadn't made a sound in coming, but suddenly the foreparts of a big vessel began to take shape not a hundred feet from me as it passed the island I was anchored at the bottom of. I dived back into my bushes ,and watched as she passed me by.

I could read the features of all who passed me by. The brutal features, the gentle features and the shocked and hopeless ones. It was a raft of saleable logs doubling as a slave ship taking the long voyage down river to the plantations. If I had been facing another direction to relieve myself the " tonton macoutes" would surely have seen me and popped me in the bag. I sat and ate my breakfast I no longer felt like king of all I surveyed Not even a little bit.

It was another utterly beautiful day and by noon I was somewhat bucked up in spirit and by early afternoon pretty confident one more time. I hadn't seen smoke on the shore for a long time and there were enough islands that I felt sure of snagging one. Sure enough ,a little island turned up just when I wanted one that evening and I tied alongside. This time I took quite a bit more care to pick a spot where I blended in than I had the night before. I was making pretty good time. I had no idea of the exact miles covered but I had no need to know, for from the river I could easily see both the plateau I was leaving behind and the butte I was heading towards, although at this point it appeared that the river was running away from rather than towards my destination, I knew that somewhere ahead this would change.

I passed a couple more days like this with everything running like clockwork and little islands turning up just in time for me to snag onto at dusk. On the fifth day things began to get different , for one thing the channel of the river became much narrower ,and the banks much closer to me ,and in addition smoke from fires became plentiful again and I began to see other craft than my own upon the river. To top it off there was no island to pull in along side of towards dusk, so in the darkening night I had to take my craft into a former loop of the river as deep as I could. I tied her up in a pond that I found at the other end, up by a nice clear mound which I found there . It seemed out of the way ,and deep enough hid, but here was a foul stink about the place, and an entirely gloomy feel. It started out as the worst night of my trip and rapidly got worse.

I had tied up in the near dark, which had rapidly become complete, and as I decided there could likely be no humans nearby in so horrible a spot as this, I decided to risk a light while I got my sleeping gear together. I rustled up a bit of food.

I had become absorbed in my own little world when I casually shone the torch at the water under the boat beside me and saw her looking up. There was a girl under the water next to the boat staring straight up with her mouth and eyes wide open. She was moving in little fits and starts. A closer look showed that there was only half a girl in the water beside me, and the movement was because many small crocodiles and some fish were nibbling away at her. I shone my torch around and found many other corpses (or parts thereof) also in perpetual motion and also hundreds of small beady pairs of eyes looking straight at me. I was in a crocodiles combo larder and nursery.

Crocodiles kill lots of large critters that they aren't equipped to polish off right away, their answer is to drag them off to a special place to leave to soften up. Kind of like squirrels store nuts. Crocodiles also protect their young. There was no chance of pulling out of that spot, so I spent the whole night perched with a grenade in my hand investigating every noise with my torch. Mama never came back but it was the worst night of my life before or since.

I was back out on the river before dawn was even close to breaking, and as the miles passed I became more and more concerned about the traffic I was seeing, and also about the turn that the weather was taking for the worse. You may be wondering why I was so paranoid about running into anybody whatsoever, but that was the nature of Dogpatch, and especially of the river.

About the only enterprise which wasn't downright prohibited was slave trading, and a bit of raw material extraction. This particular river was the highway which most of the slaves were brought down to this particular river basin full of plantations. It had little slaver forts all along its length ,whose posses ravaged the simple people of the hinterland behind them. Just about by definition, anybody who lived along this river, anywhere along its length was a bad person, and even if I ran into a good one, how good was he? My ass was good money to the next boat going by. Nope, the river wasn't a good place to try making friends. As it turns out, the bad weather probably saved my ass, as I passed by the most populated places during weather that no sensible person would go out on a boat in, or even perhaps go outside.

I had watched the weather building up in the last few days. For a while storms had danced around the butte which was to be our eventual destination. In the farthest distance, I had been able to see a deepening blackness. When the river finally passed its farthest wandering and began to head back to the butte again we started to head right towards the stormy weather. It looked as though the big thunderhead way off in the plains was reaching a black cats paw right towards us. Soon the weather worsened, the skies got cloudy, and I lost my cosmic viewpoint. The storm was coming upon us.

There was no warning when we came upon the plantation. I had intended to get in a half an hour more travel and then pull off into the jungle somewhere to wait out the storm, when there suddenly there was no jungle to pull into. Both shores of the all too near shore were cleared to the waters edge and the land behind the was full in crops. This was unexpected and very bad. We had expected only wild country here. Clearly the plantation culture had made a jump.

Where there were plantations there were flyers and motorboats, and binoculars and rifles, that could shoot farther than a couple of hundred yards with great accuracy.

As the course of the river had narrowed over the last days we had commenced to race compared to our early lazy pace, and as the storm closed in I commenced to pass many boats sitting at the shore; and others just being driven up on it, for the moment there wasn't hell of a lot of wind. Hailstones of gradually increasing size began to fall and the temperature dropped from tropical to freezing in minutes. My boat was soon full up with hail. I still had free board so I did nothing about it, and continued to head downstream with a tarp over my body to deflect the two inch hail stones which I was being pelted with. It warn't long before the hail let up and the wind began to grow.

Have you ever seen a twister? I have seen lots of the from up on Dads perch and been close to a couple others. This one wasn't anything out of the ordinary as twisters go, in fact it seemed downright Jolly and frolicsome, as it danced about maybe a half mile inland and paralleled our course, pretty much keeping up with us.

Sometimes it would seem to lose interest in the river and dance away inland, and then it would remember its interest and catch back up again. When it got closer I could see the swath it cut through trees and buildings and for a while watched a boat it picked up get carried aloft for the better part of ten minutes before being discarded for a new toy. It had a crown of lightening around its brow and occasionally it seemed to think about killing me personally, I could almost hear it thinking "I see that boy over there hiding. I think I will go and kill him" and it would begin to wander my way only to be distracted by a boat or barn that it suddenly preferred to lift up. In the end it didn't kill me, but it covered me in the best white camouflage and kept the people inside and off the river all through the day, while I passed the biggest patch of civilization I had ever laid eyes on,

I saw lots of stuff I had never seen before, except on cyber. There were cars and trucks and buildings and parked flyers of all sorts. It was very educational. I was glad when the river finally widened out and started to look wilder again, As dusk was coming in, I snagged another island and emptied out my boat of its load of hailstones

The next morning it was a tropical paradise once more ,and the mesa that was my destination was getting closer and huger in the process. The side I was looking at was all cliffs, but on the far side where the river ran closest I knew it was a gentle 3000 foot climb. I started to think about how I was going to manage it.

I was never alone on my boat for very long, and although the bad weather seemed to have emptied it [except maybe for snakes] , I soon had some parrots sitting on the fronds beside and above me, and a matched pair of turtles who sat next to each other as if they were in love on one of my pontoons. Occasionally as we drifted along I would have to fire at a pair of eyes too close, and too intent, but I felt I had kind of got the hang of the thing.

Every crocodile came close swimming right up visible, so I had a long chance to see them coming, They didn't mostly try their underwater sneaking up tricks until the last couple of hundred yards, and even then just about every one came up for a long hard last look about a hundred feet away before actually making their attack. I reckon they could smell me hidden in the bushes but couldn't quite scope it out visually. It really wasn't a problem, you just had to keep an eye out and have lots of bullets. Night times were sketchier but I had been lucky, and I had hand grenades. Hand grenades can be ideal for night time camping. One morning I noticed that the leaves along the shoreline were changing color as some knew tree began to predominate..

You know what scares me more than crocodiles? Its tigers. Tigers scare the shit right out of me. Not that I had ever seen many of them. The prof says it is natural that they do. They are our natural predators; they are our ancestral primate eaters. Way more of your living breathing ancestors got drug away by tigers than was ever killed by cars or bullets or leopards. They are primate specialists. Orange and red are naturally scary colors to humans, on account of tigers are mostly orange-red. If you play a recording of a tiger's growl it quickens the heart beat of all primates, including people,and critters that don't know tigers exist.

Now you notice I am not speaking of all big cats. Leopards and lions are kind of adaptable eaters and I am careful of them too, but it doesn't make my heart race just to look at them. I have seen plenty of lions and sabre-tooths as well, which are actually quite a big bigger than tigers and maybe you might think to be more scary looking as well, with their huge teeth and all. These critters are just as dangerous maybe, but something in my genes, and also in everybody elses' genes makes tigers the scariest thing on the planet. . I just hate the bastards. When I pulled in closer to shore to see what the new pattern of vegetation was [on account of that I would soon be hiking through it]. I was pretty displeased. The newcomer trees were mangroves. I just hate mangrove swamp. It is usually right thick with tigers. As the river broadened out it was becoming more rich with islands for me to tie onto. I tied off on the next one that came along although it was only early afternoon and sat back to think about it.

I could see the butte not so far away, and there was a long root of higher ridge land that stretched my way. On top of it I could see the reassuring color of the highland vegetation I was used to, not so many miles away. Going any further towards the back side of the mountain seemed like a really bad idea all of a sudden. Already I would have quite a few miles of who knows how hard slogging before I got to the ridge. I had about decided to cut my camouflage off the boat and dodge back upstream a ways to find a place with more open going , when the first of a series of canoes suddenly appeared and passed me much too closely. I abandoned my idea and cut loose allowing the current to drive me into the shore and under the mangroves.

I have to admit I was pretty much in a panic. It wasn't early in the day; and the idea of spending the night anywhere in this lowland jungle wasn't an option. If a tiger didn't find me and eat me during the night ,I would surely be dead of fright in the morning anyways, the only reassuring thing about my situation was the hand grenades

A tiger swamp is an unhealthy place to be. You remember that little list of parasites I told you about before? Well they were the mountains and the plains parasites, the swamp has a whole list all its own. Some of them you might call "tigers little helpers".

There is a worm which is accustomed to inhabiting two different species of mammals at different times during its long complicated life cycle. One of its hosts is a meat eater which acquires the parasite from the meat of its prey. The worm treats carnivores differently from herbivores because it is in its best interest not to much diminish the tigers vitality. It establishes a long term infestation in the tigers bowels feasting off the tigers food rather than the tiger itself, all the while giving off millions of tiny eggs in the tiger poop. If a human catches the worm from eating meat with cysts within it , the worm assumes we are tigers , invades our intestines , and begins a long term but relatively benign infection. If, however, a human ingests the parasite from dirty grass or water, the parasite assumes we are a herbivore. In the herbivore the worm has a different strategy. Its can only propagate its kind if this particular herbivore gets ate by a tiger, so it sets out to increase the likelihood of this happening by infecting the muscles and organs, especially the brain, with inch long little wormies. This makes the herbivore inept and much more likely to be eaten.

There was tiger shit all over the forest I was walking through. I made sure I only ate fruit from the trees and nothing from the ground. I certainly didn't drink the water. I was dealing with mosquitoes as well. Mosquitoes carry malaria. The tribes deal with bugs, and with de-stinking themselves for forest travel by covering themselves with grease in which mint and garlic have been cooked. I was covered in it one quarter inch thick. It wasn't too reassuring really, as although I no longer smelled especially like a primate, in my own mind, I seemed to smell exactly like the delicious roast with the garlic and mint sauce which we had eaten at Christmas. I know that is a demented little thought, but I couldn't seemed to shake it.

I had much too heavy a pack, but it lightened up fast. Every time I came to a particularly dense and scary spot I would toss off a hand grenade, and see if anything bolted for cover. I was paying especially close attention to a nasty looking little patch of bush by the trail side, but when I tossed the grenade into it a tiger broke cover from right behind me ,rather than in front of me, and ran off into the bush. It was the only one I saw. As I said there is nothing more reassuring than a pile of hand grenades for certain ventures. I finally made the ridge as the lights were going out. I got out my hammock climbed a tree and set it up and went to sleep.

I awoke with the familiar highland trees around me which I had grown up, with and instantly felt more relaxed. I figured that as I climbed higher I would soon be past the bugs as well. There was still the occasional pile of tiger shit to terrify me, but there was starting to be a lot more plain old leopard shit around. I had just started to pretty well relax when something came up that I didn't like at all. I hit a trail. A well used human trail, and it went the same way as I wanted to.

When I hit a muddy patch from the rains I was able to see tracks, and .the topmost layer was all covered in tracks going the same way I was. There were definitely people above me somewhere, and at least half a dozen of them too, by the look of things. I didn't have any choice really, but to follow the trail ,and as I did I kept on the lookout for any tell tale bits of garbage which might let me know what sort of folks I was dealing with. I found the sort I was really hoping not to. Civilized packaging and a couple of empty rifle cartridges. If they had guns I was really going to have to watch my ass.

I wondered what the party ahead was up to and I hoped it wasn't because some sharp eye down below had noticed the flyer up on the knob. It seemed unlikely that it had been seen from below , as I myself had been unable to make it out since leaving dads eyrie.

I figured it out a while later. they were collecting Schmoo plants. Dads bunch call them that, but the tribesmen call them the leopards friend, or corpse plant. They are a kind of mushroom. They grow to various sizes depending on the corpse underneath them and they can be huge. They look rather like a loaf of bread and taste not too differently and they have little cups within their surface, with which are filled with what a might as well be called honey. They are also shot through with a psychoactive chemical and some others which inhibit thirst and hunger. If you eat a little bit, you will feel very lethargic and wonderfully content and happy. What the mushroom is hoping, is that you will hang out by its side until you die, or more likely, until something comes along and eats you, ripping you to shreds in the process and leaving little bits around for the plant to colonize. It can smell corpses and puffs out clouds of spores when it smells something ripe.

Monkeys love corpse plant. If they find only small ones it does them no harm but if there are too many small ones. Or maybe, if the monkey finds a great big one, then it lies around stoned until it gets ripped up, and then the mushrooms may get to eat bits of monkey. Even when the plants are quite tiny there is often a mouse or two hanging out quite near to the shroom, enthralled in the cycle of eating sugar water loaded with drugs and then lying around stoned. The larger plants capture monkeys and the biggest have been known to capture unwary or very desperate human beings. When one of its slaves dies, the plant colonizes the corpse. There is often one old worn out plant in the center of a ring of its progeny, each one marking the spot where someone, or some critter, or part thereof, laid .

The mushrooms are worth money dried, and apparently the party ahead of me was nothing but mushroom pickers. Unfortunately, they appeared to be well armed ones, with close ties to 'snivelization' as Pa used to call it. I was glad of one thing, as I saw no sign of dogs I would likely be able to hide quite close to them without discovery. When dark came I I went just off the path and hung my hammock high up in a tree above a nice big frond .

I woke up in the morning with voices more or less right beneath me. They were speaking a dialect of roman which wasn't particularly intelligible to me , although I got the gist. They were teasing a prisoner and telling him how good his hands were going to taste cooked. (Did I mention cannibalism before? Its another one of the local vices that Dad expects me to fight against). I could see them quite clearly, but they could not see me whatsoever at all, which was a very satisfying way for it to be. The tormentors were a couple of the types that pop up around civilization on this planet. Slave raiding is in peoples blood around here, just like cannibalism and all the rest of it, but the proximity of snivelization makes it all way worse, if only for the way more efficient weapons which are entered into the mix. These boys were a posse. They had a permit to buy goods and sell slaves in town. They had pretty good equipment. They were also wild as the planet itself and liked to eat "long pork". They were telling a young fellow about my age, how good his hands were going to taste cooked. They said that they would feed him some, so he could see for himself They were only in my range and hearing for a moment, and then they were gone onto the other side of many folds in the terrain.

They were followed up by ten more much like the first. All were carrying bags of corpse plant. I figured it was the whole crew heading back to town and finally getting the Hell out of my way so I could get forward faster without constantly thinking about maybe running into a bunch of Skinnys.

I waited half an hour after I saw the last of them before I unslung my hammock and climbed down the hundred feet out of the tree and continued on my way up the spur of the ridge towards my destination. I made good time finally, and triumphantly laid myself out on the ridge that night under the sky with no trees above. Soon I would be able to make the knob where I hoped the craft still sat.

I felt like a king again, and as I lay there at night I found myself thinking about how good it would be to tell the story of my journey to Mloko and the professor. The first sign of a fly in the ointment was when I realized I was intending on leaving out the part about the cannibals and their captive. I don't know why it is, but my conscience gains a lot of strength in the middle of a pitch black night, but by dawn it still hadn't wrestled me into going back to help the kid. I just wasn't going to do it .

Then one more thought came across my mind. Just who was the bloody kid anyways? Where had they found him? There were clearly no other folks up here but the flyer's crew. Was he the same junior lieutenant we had talked to on the phone? Was I about to abandon my only pilot? It all of a sudden seemed totally likely to me that this was the case. I was going to find the flyer emptied of personnel and I myself could not personally fly it.

My story in the eyes of Mloko, not that he would be likely ever to hear it, would be that I had failed to be sufficiently valorous. I had failed to attack slavers and cannibals when and where I recognized them, even though dad had made the tribes around him promise to do just that. I would die a failure whom Mloko would have been ashamed of.

I decided I was going to take scalps . I found myself humming dads old favorite song as I raced down the path the next morning . It's a real old favorite of mine too, called "someday gods gonna cut em down" Maybe you know it .

It was kind of a turkey shoot. They were just making their way in single file down a path carrying heavy loads and taking no precautions whatsoever; not even mostly trying to stay together. They had also been sampling their wares. I shot every one I came across in the back with my quiet little rifle, cut his throat for good measure and lifted his hair.

There were still half a dozen up front when night came. They stopped to set up camp. I climbed up a tree and watched them freak out as their stragglers never did show up for supper. By their talk, they weren't very concerned about human enemies. They figured I was one of Satan's little helpers. In the end they decided to make things a lot easier, by barricading themselves in for the night behind a rock and leaving the boy tethered out for the devil to eat.

Along about the very center of the night I wandered over and tossed two grenades behind the rock and then took out my knife and walked over to cut the boy loose. I wasn't expecting him to scratch my face, poke me in the eye and head butt me. I had to catch him and beat on him a bunch, and eventually even tie a thong onto him while we had our first conversations as the dawn was coming up.

It wasn't really hard to do. He was built pretty slight and awkward and you could tell just by the way he had grown he had never done any hard work. On closer examination he wasn't nearly as young as I had first taken him to be. He even had long fingernails. I wasn't too impressed. You would think that because I was able to establish right away that he was from the flyer and that I was the self same 'scout' who was supposed to guide him in for repairs, that he would have been thinking good things about me.

This apparently was not the case. I guess seeing as our relationship started off in a bad way with my first scaring, and then thumping, the shit out of him, and then leading him around on a little tether for half of a day, this wasn't too surprising. Still, I was disappointed. He was kind of near me in age and could have been a really useful friend

During our first conversation Jack was pretty skeptical of my authenticity, and finally asked me why it was that, although I spoke standard off-world roman, I was naked, covered in stinky grease and had the hair of half a dozen human beings tied to my belt and quite a bit of caked blood all over my left leg where they had dripped.

For some reason I couldn't right off think of a good reason for this, or at least one that I could explain to him. After a few minutes of silence on my part, Jack pointed out a particularly frizzy pelt and said. "He was a really nice man, he gave me water". For some I reason I was on the defensive and said "yeah really nice for a cannibal."

Jack's reply was sudden and sharp. "He was not a cannibal. He told me so. He was a Hindu and a vegetarian. He told me he wouldn't eat me when the others did. You killed a Hindu holy man."

I lost the moral high ground pretty fast. I ended up by making a stupid remark about "Hindus taking more care who they go camping with". I lost the argument. I kind of lost every argument me and Jack engaged I in and I was unable to raise my status in his mind one iota, especially after I got us lost.

Jack had been moaning and complaining for a couple of days that he thought I was heading in the wrong direction. I just ignored him on account of his being so lame about everything and because there really wasn't any arguing with the the G.P.S. no matter which way jack actually thought he had come.

When we finally got a look at the craft she was in plain sight only about a mile or two away on the other side of a gorge about 3000 feet deep. We were going to have to backtrack many, many, many miles. About ten minutes later when Jack was carping at me with I-told-you-so's, I accidentally knocked the G.P.S. over the edge. I would have swore by the look on Jack's face that it made him happy, just because it proved me to be a klutz, even if it cost our lives.

Me and Jack were developing a strange relationship. I kept telling him to quit his complaining and buck up and be a man. Jack would turn to me and say I was "oh so stupid, So very, very stupid" and then talk on to himself in a lingo that wasn't Roman, maybe Greek, while giving me very harsh looks. We weren't having fun.

Then, as I said, I got us lost. We wandered on to the wrong side of one of the many ridges and followed the wrong ridge up. We got to the knob all right, but nowhere near the craft ,and no idea where away we might find the bloody thing. We had to backtrack once again. We were more or less entirely lost . By this time we had no supplies left and I kept us alive by bush craft alone. Jack tried to get himself ate, tromped, or poisoned by such a series of animals it would be tedious to relate, if it hadn't after awhile quenched his contempt for me when I rescued him for at least the eighth or ninth time. I am, I admit, exaggerating, but it felt more or less like that. As time went on I gradually ended up vindicated. When I finally got us to the flyer, we were actually getting along pretty decent. I was even getting kind of proud of Jack. Learning to eat raw animals - and like them - can entail a pretty stiff learning curve.

When we finally spotted the Etruscan Princess, she was a little below us and about a mile away, but what caught our eyes just as much was one of those tiny little perfectly clear lakes that you find in the highlands. Unlike all the water down below they are perfectly all right to drink or to swim in. Neither of us had been bathed for weeks, and we each had our quarter inch of lemon grass scented grease, which we were a tad tired of applying each morning on account of it being rancid and all.

We were walking straight forward to jump in when Jack said to me one more time. "You so stupid. Would you like to know why you are so stupid.?" I sure didn't, and I had hoped we were past this kind of question, but I was raised polite, and said "O.K. let me have it."

Jack walked to the edge of the rock, and began removing the overalls he had had on for the last umpteen days while facing the water. When Jack had shucked his top and was unzipping his bottoms he turned around to face me and said "I think you are very stupid Isiiah, for thinking that I am a boy."

Then she stood in front of me naked and tremendously interesting looking, before turning around and diving into the lake. As pa used to say " I didn't know whether to shit or wind my wristwatch". I guess I had been thrown off by the coverall uniform, the shaved head, the unibrow and the hairy legs, but she didn't look whatsoever like a boy with her clothes off. Kind of an ugly little puppy though, if the truth be told, and I am not sure I should be telling it.

Me and Jaquelline got our relationship sorted out over the next few days we spent alone on board the princess. Jaquelline wanted to look for her dad. He was Captain Roussopoulos and she was Lieutenant Roussopoulos, the same that I had listened to over the radio, He had gone missing on their second day on this rock and his two next most senior officers had disappeared a few days later while supposedly just walking nearby. Then a few days after that, she herself had been popped in the bag by the cabouters, who luckily had not seen the ship, or been sophisticated enough to infer its existence.

There were no ratings on board . She had been left alone . I was into looking for them her dad and the other officers. I noticed that now I found Jaquelline to be such an interesting person. I didn't care all that much what we did, or where we went, as long as I got to be able to--- Well you know what I mean. She was my first girlfriend.

So we were gonna go look for her dad. It seemed like as good a quest as any, Just me and her back into the jungles to eat barbecued monkey and hang out together. I was all for it. I didn't think there was much chance that her dad was alive, or if so, much chance that we could find him or anything like that. What I was mostly envisioning was lots of sex in a jungle setting. Not that I wasn't expecting to look real hard or anything. It was just what I had in mind for our free time.

As it turns out, it wasn't all that hard to solve the mysteries, I had seen a fair bit of the sign of little people about. I was used to noticing such things as they were around quite a bit in the woodlands on the plateau above Tomahawk. They were way down on a persons list of dangers. Sure you could die in a hail of rocks, but it wasn't likely.

Up at his place Pa left them out presents, which he said favorably disposed them, and they left him gifts in return. They liked tiny bits of metal like old nails that they whetted sharp, and fragments of glass and things of that nature. Most other things including food they wouldn't touch. They had a reputation in some legends of having occasionally helped stranded people find their way home. I was skeptical as a bunch of other legends concerned people just about to get home when they were killed by a hail of rocks . Around pa's place, where they hadn't been hunted for decades, and they had been somewhat buttered up, you could even sometimes approach them. Me and pa had done it, I reckoned to try it again.

There was some unneeded glass on board the Princess that I smashed into shards for presents, and I commandeered every knife and small metal piece which I could find and put an edge on it. Pretty soon I had a whack of first rate presents for little people and I started salting the forest with them.

Now when I start talking about little people I don't want you to start imagining apes, They are way different. An ape can't throw worth a damn, and cant be taught to do so. It seems to me that our use of language isn't what separates us from the apes. It is way more important to be able to hit a bunny with rock than to be able to sit around and cook it and brag about it after. The ability to throw a rock accurately and intentionally cause damage to another animal with it is one Hell of a skill. Compared to walking up and hitting said animal with the rock held in your hand. Or maybe hitting it with your fist there is nearly zero risk. A troop of humans can throw rocks toward a dangerous animal such as a leopard, and drive its from its kill with arguably less danger than a lion can kill a tiny gazelle ,as there is always a possibility that the tiny gazelle hoof may kick the lion in the eye, or an antelopes hoof break his jaw. An attack with a thrown rock is nearly risk free compared to the strategies of most any animal. It was our best trick for hundreds of thousands of years. Cooking and yakking about it have been overrated. Besides some apes have better memories than we do and memory is the better half of intelligence.

Little people specialize in ripping off leopards. Leopards are good killers but at the best of times have trouble holding onto their meat. They are driven off by lions and hyenas mostly, out on the plains at least , but in the highlands the little people fill the niche. They let the leopard eat for a while ,so he doesn't argue too much, and then they drive him off with rocks, or sometimes they find the leopard kills up in trees, and get them down with poles. It is a good gig. They also drive off the hyenas as much as possible ,which is all right with me as hyenas are never popular.

As it turned out pops was easy to find. Little people are smart in their own way and I am sure they knew that the gray haired big person living with the baboon troop wasn't in his natural element and me laying out a bunch of presents was probably a dead giveaway that I was looking for something myself. They delivered him the next morning, the quicker to be rid of us I am sure. Pops was in rough shape. He stunk and he had fleas, parasites, and fever, and also he seemed a little nuts but he was alive.

He had wondered off and got lost, which I can guarantee is a really easy thing to do. He had no equipment and only a pistol. Hanging out with a baboon troop had been a really sensible thing to do. Every night baboons go somewhere safe and this lot climbed a ledge on a rock face each night. Pops had followed. them up and in the daytime he stayed on the edge of the troop and followed them to where the grub was.

His first night out had given him the idea that anything just out wandering about gets ate. He had a few little problems ,such as he seemed to have picked up a few involuntary grimaces and growls from hanging out with low company for weeks, but he was o.k.

The officers weren't that hard to find either. There was a really good bunch of corpse plant about a half mile from the ship. It was the kind of vigorous patch which happens when leopards rip something up into lots of big bits and there are no hyenas around to clean up. I kicked the fungus off some rounded humps and found the skulls. I doubt that they were into the nectar. Leopards are dangerous enough all by themselves, and any corpse in this forest was likely to receive the spores. I popped the skulls in a sac and brought them back to the captain.

I was a hero. The captain idolized me and Jaquelline thought I was pretty good as well. We were in radio contact with Uncle John and everything was going swell. We were set to leave the next morning and we had put together a picnic with really lots of good food which were were going to eat up at the little lake which I mentioned before. Everything would have been perfect if I hadn't noticed when we went in for a swim that pops had a witches tit. It wasn't identical to mine but daddy had never said that there were exceptions or anything. It ruined my night.

I was a hero again the next morning for the flight across the plain. I was a hero right up to the point where we pulled into the gorge and parked on a big x limed out on the ground for us. I stopped being a hero when one of the Wild Things big guns which had been hidden on a hill side chewed the tail end of our ship right off. Jaquelline was looking at me with with looks which could kill and Captain Roussopoulos had a really hurt expression all over his face, when the radio started spewing out Uncle John's voice. Captain Roussopoulos motioned to me to communicate if I wished, so I flipped the switch and was about to give Uncle John an earful when he told me to hold my horses if I valued his life and my own and not to say another word over an open mike. He wanted Captain Roussopoulos permission to come aboard his ship and talk things over. Captain Roussopoulos readily gave it of course, and Uncle John came on board for a parlay.

Uncle John is one Hell of a good talker. I guess he ran an inn for way more years of his life than he ever as a pirate captain, and he had the gift of making men relax. He treated Captain

Roussoppulos with the utmost respect, just as if he hadn't just had the tail of his ship shot off, and pretty soon the two of them hit it off really well. I guess it aint so strange, as they was both ex captains, and civilized men as well, who had gone to universities and such. As soon as Uncle John had made sure Captain Roussopoulos wasn't fixing to shoot him with his pistol ,he ordered out for food and drink. Mounds of it. As we ate Uncle John explained there had been a little change of plan.

They weren't gonna fix the Etruscan Princess. They were going to repair the Wild Thing. He explained as how he didn't want Captain Roussopoulos thinking he was the kind of man either to have arranged a double cross. He explained as how his original intention had been bring aboard the part Roussopoulos needed and then lamb out of there with him, but his plan had been foiled by a little mistake on my part.

I choked on my chips when everybody turned at the table to have a have a little look at me. Johnny spoke to me directly for the first time, " Ishey didn't you think about what would happen if our little plan concerning the Princess warnt kept a secret? And what might happen if you left some little notes around? N" " I allowed as I never t had thought about it all that much" by which I actually meant not at all. I suddenly felt not only less like a hero but also dead dense as well. Uncle John went back to talking to the table at large . Taking my part and making excuses for me as I was just a lad, and saying it just plain wasn't my fault that I had acted in such a stupid way.

He wanted Captain Roussopoulos to understand just what forces were at play, but he wanted to say right off why he was so interested in filling the captain in on such events. He wanted him as mate, and he wanted his help to get the Wild Thing into the air. Captain Roussopoulos perked right up. It wasn't long before they excused themselves from us and wandered off to look at schematics of the two ships on the screen and think about repairs. I was a little nervous about being left alone with Jaquelline. I was not only not a hero and had been proved kind of dense, but the topic which I wanted to talk about wasn't all that pleasant either.

I had spent the night before trying to remember all I could about "abominations". As far as I recollected abominations had no arms or legs but they had some kind of super powers, and they weren't human as we usually use the term. They also weren't exactly individual persons. If there was more than one of them was about they kind of fused together mentally like wet candy left in a bag. And oh yeah, they were a little bit of alien engineering in an attempt to improve the human race. Or maybe it was fairy blood or both. I couldn't remember or perhaps never knew how dad claimed to have come across these bits of information

Me and Jaquelline had sex maybe forty times in two weeks. I was a bit afraid she was pregnant, I wasn't sure how to bring up the topic of abomination . As it turns out I didn't need to. As soon as Jaquelline got the gist I was concerned about pregnancy, she cut me short and explained that she had a birth control implant in her arm. She went on to explain that she, and her fiancee were responsible civilized people, and that she couldn't wait to get back to see him. It was more than I bargained for. She had that 'I hate you so much' look in her eyes again, so I decided to shut up, go to the cabin I had been given, and get some rest.

Uncle Johnny was blue eyed and chipper when he woke me up the next morning ,it seemed like things were going his way. Pops Roussopoulos was in like a dirty shirt. He was Mate. It wasn't a difficult conversion. Uncle Johnny had been right way back then, about it being unlikely the Etruscan Princess was supposed to be down on the planets surface at all. Roussopoulos had been picking up a "package" and had lost his ship. Back home he would be fried in a pan. Uncle John had been prepared to ask him to choose 'lead or gold' as they say, but the necessity hadn't even come close.

There was a big political meeting coming up that Uncle Johnny had to fill me in on, as he said that I had to play a part. He started off more in sorrow than in anger to tell me how things had turned for him after I left without mentioning to him that I had blabbed his plan all over . He said the first he had known anything was wrong , was when an extremely hard party consisting of all the old privateers and their sons and grandsons had turned up at his hotel to let him explain all about his plans to leave Dogpatch.

They had been about to hold his foot close to the fire when a much larger crowd of townspeople arrived who suspected My Uncle John and the Old bunch of having intended to steal the ship and pull the pin, which of course had been the general plan in one way or another. John is an awful good talker. He right away got up and began smooth talking the townspeople and taking the side of the crew, just as if they hadn't been about to toast his toes with the potbelly stove five minutes earlier. He talked their way out of it. It was just about the moment when the crew and the townspeople were reconciling their differences and deciding what to do with the ship when an even larger group yet, of suspicious tribesmen all armed had appeared who suspected the townspeople's intentions.

Uncle took over again,, and explained that the main intention s of the townspeople and of the original crew was to get off the planet to find good guns for the tribes to spread my daddy's gospel with, and he had the sense at that moment to order drinks for every man in the crowd.

As I told you Tomahawk was sort of a democracy, The kind that leaves blood on the floor. Uncle Johnny says Pirates and mercenaries invented democracy He says to read Xenophon. Anyways we have democracy. Anyone can vote in Tomahawk even Christian tribesmen, but there aren't usually many of them around.

This time was different. Mloko had been stirring them up. When I stole his boat he had just taken that as a sign from the spirits that he hadn't been meant to act in a surreptitious manner. He had filled a wagon with crates of whiskey and some bibles and had hit the plains to preach to the tribes just like pa had back in the beginning when he spread his religion all over the place around here. He took pop's skull in a sack and popped it up on a lectern he had set up in the front of the wagon, next to the fancy machine gun he had coveted, while he gave his sermons.

He told them I was coming back with a ship and I was going to fill the prophecy of my name by bringing them guns so they could teach the slavers and idolators that God wants mercy and not sacrifice. He had got himself elected war-chief of all ofthe previously warring tribes who occupied tomahawks front yard, They was all ostensibly Mormon and had been for years ,but had agreed to dissagree with one other, so they they could continue lifting hair from each other, and other important social pursuits which peace hindered, or at least that was how it had been up to this point. The way that Uncle John laid it out was that Mloko was really giving me a 'run for my money in the son of the prophet business' I was glad he was doing so good as I would be glad to give the part up if only I could."

Uncle John was dead serious about the guns. He had the business angle pretty well thunk out. He was particularly happy to have acquired Captain Roussopoulos and not just because he badly needed ships officers but also because Captain Roussopoulos possessed current information on where to take a package, and receive payment for it. It was intended to work something like this. The tribesmen collected the botanicals and we shipped out and sold them, taking the gold we received to somewhere else to buy arms and bring them back. Uncle John knew pretty nuch where he figured we ought to go for the guns. He figured the New Zions. Anywhere near "downtown"Rome was out of the question. In any reasonably well organized place we would be noticed and snapped up. We had to stay in the fringe which is precisely where the New Zions are located. Uncle Johnny is like me, in that we are both descended from folks who lived on the New Zions but got spewed out into the general roman Diaspora which is going on. We needed a friendly reception on the other end, so Uncle John figured on going right back where pa was from ,and explaining as how dads preaching was an "ongoing glorious phenomena on Dogpatch " He figured that might get us the friendly reception we needed.

Uncle John was certain I needed to attend the meeting that afternoon, and put a lot of effort into priming me for the part. The way he saw it there were three constituencies he had to please. First and most there were all the tribes people who had been spilling into town. They were mostly interested in guns and jihad and they liked me a lot. They even had new names for me and Mloko "He was "talks with dead people" and I was " burning spear". I just had to play the part of a zealot and froth at the mouth for five minutes or so.

Then there was the townspeople. They liked me too, but distrusted the old crew, and were afraid of the tribesmen . For them, John said I was to play up the significance of getting back into the contact with the religious folk and with civilization generally on dads old world. That left the crew themselves. Uncle Johnny said they didn't like me all that much, on account of my dad having taken such a religious turn and all, but Johnny said he pretty much had them all sewed up as they didn't have anywhere else to turn.

He had tried to convince them that I wasn't all that religious underneath it all. It sounded to me like he had it all in the bag, and I guess he thought so too because he was one jolly old elf all morning. The meeting went without a hitch. I didn't have to make any speeches, just stand beside Uncle John while he made them, and then yell and holler a bunch about how I agreed with him every time he winked at me. It went off without a hitch. Uncle John is one Hell of a good explainer and perhaps the best liar I ever met.

The Wild Thing wasn't about to fly too soon. She had sat for over thirty years and while the old bunch had kept up the pretense that they would be leaving soon for a decade or two, keeping the ship up and passing on their shipboard skills to their children , at some point they had lost faith, and she had become a bit dilapidated. There wasn't any problem with repairing the brain, I am sure Uncle John had that figured out before he ever allowed the Etruscan princess to be fired upon. It takes much the same equipment to sling a sugar cube from world to world as it does a ship, and the piece of The Wild Thing which originally took the bullet was a replaced in a day or two. It was every bloody other thing which had to be checked out. Relay switches which haven't been thrown for fifteen years tend to weld into place and brains which haven't been used for thirty years get even more cemented. Uncle John was on top of it all though, and along with First Mate Roussopoulos, as he was called, now was gradually putting the ship and the crew back into place. Me and Jaquelline had lots of time together but somehow suddenly neither of us wanted it. Jaquelline's dad had only one condition before he joined our merry crew. He wanted her well out of it and back at school. She was only a cadet and had a life she had planned ahead of her. Uncle Johnny had agreed, fast and the idea was that when we got back to New Zion she would ship out of there on a regular boat back to her old life.

She was going to downtown Roman Empire somewhere to a totally normal life. I envied the Hell out of her. She only stayed mad all the time for a week. We were both still bunking on the Etruscan princess but for different reasons. For her it was her ship and her home, but for me it was the only place where Uncle John and Pops Roussopoulos could shove me that I wasn't instantly at the center of a growing crowd. It was a real , real drag having people falling to the ground in front of me, and trying to anoint my feet and shit like that.

You want to know what happened to the third Imam? He ran for it. I guarantee you. It was heavy going so I mostly just hid out. It didn't take too long before Jacquelline figured out that her dad was a whole lot happier than she had expected him to be, and as she found that out and also that everyone was trying to get her home, I guess she started to like me again and we ended up talking quite a bit.

She was amazed to find out what my ambitions were. I pretty much wanted to go to a school that wasn't run by big dumb lay brothers with straps on a planet without slaves and slavers, but which had libraries and stores and all the interesting things which I knew existed elsewhere but not on Dogpatch. I also very much wanted not be the son of a prophet but just somebody regular, a college kid like she was for example. I hungered I for it just as bad as I had been hungering for pussy a month before. I guess up to this point Jaquelline had never seen my tender guitar playing side, only my stinky greased up scalp taking side. She fell for me all over again. I was kind of confused . I didn't ask about the fiancé. .

I found the time to read my daddy's journal which he had left me' and I will make sure it is published with these papers and available for you to read] but for now I will just tell you the bit you need to know. It was called "How I got rich" by Aeneas Browning which was my daddy's name, although he never used it after he took up the pirate trade ', It was just the story of how he grew up on New Zion , it having been writ down, when he was only a few years older than I was when I was reading it. I was amazed how much of his life was much like my own right down to having a crazy old man as a father who believed in abominations and stuff like that '. I never felt like I really knew him until I read it. He weren't so bad. I was also really interested to hear his account of his own home town, especially as we were heading there.

I also have to admit that I was very interested in the fact that he said he was rich, and also with how easy it was going to be to slip Jaquelline into a normal life from a place like the new Zions. You didn't even need a ship , to leave ,as a big container craft from the inner empire called regularly picking up passengers. I didn't even need to depend on daddy still being rich back in his hometown, as I had his personal chest anyways ,and it was stuffed with gold bars and gems and such. It seemed likely that if things worked out for us at all well on New Zion, I would have no trouble making the slip if Uncle John agreed to it, and I couldn't see why he would want to keep me on a cabin boy and cheering section once he had things so well under way.

Me and Jaquelline began to plan on it as if it was a done deal. I was really surprised at how Uncle Johnny behaved once he got wind of it. John was always one to hear a man out ,so he let me give all my desires and expectations, without hurrying me along or interrupting. When I finished up by saying that "I couldn't see what he would need with me as a cabin boy by then" He got a look of real wonder on his face and lapsed into the colloquial English of his home world. " Well Ishey, I never thought you were dense before this moment. What the Hell do you think all the bloody voting was about? You are not the fucking cabin boy on board this ship. You are the fucking captain of it, and No, you cannot jump the Goddamned ship." It was the first and only time My uncle ever talked angrily with me. I think he was just overawed and amazed at my denseness. He had a vein pulsing in his fore head and he even slammed the door on his way out. It looked like I had responsibilities after all.

Me and Jaquelline's relationship heated up considerably again. Something about the contrast between our noble love being torn apart by circumstance combined with what a slut she was going to feel like when she got to her boyfriend, seemed to be energizing her. It made the next few weeks when I couldn't get out and about a lot more fun.

The Wild Thing was gotten ready pretty quickly. everything which could be run and checked was seen to be working and pops old crew [and such stand ins and proteges, as they had been able to train] were ready to give it a try, We had a Hell of an unusual crew , insofar as each each of the interest groups in town had put as large a group as they could on board her. This was o.k., insofar as we could use the manpower during smash and grabs, but inconvenient insofar as the politicking going on. Uncle John figured that once we were up and away we would all pull together. We had lots of tribals all painted up with guns and hair hanging from their belts, but also as many religious townspeople on board as Uncle John could manage to attract to come with us.

He figured our reception on New Zion was likely to depend on how many people we could muster to walk off the ship clutching books of Mormon and wanting to talk about Jesus, He was dead on accurate.

We decided to check out our bread route. Pops Roussopoulos package drop off went without a hitch and we took our gold to New Zion. Now New Zion isn't a particular world [from the point of view of probabilities nowhere really is]. It is a bunch of colonies thrown out from the old earth by an ascendant Mormon state in North America. There a few wrinkles depending on which exact time line you mean. The mother time line is pretty much gobbled up by Rome these days as they believe in assimilating any time lines that achieve the technology to get off planet, but some of the Mormon colonies that shoved off before the Romans showed up have kept their old ways.

There are a bunch of colonies in the New Zions although each has a local name as well. "Bountiful New Zion", where Daddy was from, was a little out of step even by Mormon standards, although to tell you the truth, I never bothered to find out exactly how. Now I don't know why those old Mormons of the mother time line liked dinosaurs so much, but they planted the New Zions on worlds which are right thick with them. Maybe they didn't like the idea of things being too paradisiacal. Well anyways they aren't. You could risk it most places on Dogpatch with just rocks and spears (homesteading I mean), as long as there were enough of you, you could pretty much wander off anywhere on Dogpatch and make a pretty good go of it, People have. Not on the New Zions. The day any of those worlds, or even any little part of them lost the ability to make or otherwise acquire high quality guns, their end would only be a little while later as a patch of grease on some dino's jaw. Even after several centuries they are still very sparsely settled.

It only took me one walk in the bush to get lonesome for Dogpatch. Uncle John had the right idea how to make friends on Bountiful He had the ship loaded with ladies clutching bibles and books of Mormon. The ship had lots of room for people [she had been a slaver once]. He brought my daddy's choir ,and as many pretty little girls as he could manage, and when we landed by the town dad was from, he let them all march out babbling about Jesus and playing songs on guitars. We found out soon that Bountiful was willing to make another kind of trade. All the horny old men of substance about the place started marrying up our girls within a couple of weeks of our arriving, and let us know they would like us to take a whole load of excess young men off their hands to help us straighten things out on Dogpatch. It was a great deal.

We spent quite a while there, that first time, cementing relations while we polished up the Wild Thing and gave her maintenance. We had to wait for a freighter for some of our stuff. The town was pretty excited about our gold as well, and retooled a local machine shop to make us a bunch of the nicest rifles you can imagine. A funny thing (and a nice touch) is that they came with my name engraved on every one. Apparently an ancestor of mine was a famous gunsmith who had first made this rifle to fight the evil legions of the American state, like it says in the bible or somewhere, and the Mormons have been making it with his name on it ever since. Personally, I guess I have to say that my cup runneth over. I got married to a dozen of the nicest girls you ever laid on.

I got to know my granny. She was a funny little old crone and sure resembled my Daddy although not perhaps in the best ways. She brewed botanicals nonstop, and fired guns towards, if not at, strangers who she didn't recognize, coming up to her door. The bunch who took me off to meet her was a bit nervous, on account of she was really old and not terribly good at recognizing anybody anymore.

They needn't have worried as she only fired off a few shots and them not hardly towards us, before she saw me, dropped her gun, and started crying. She walked straight on up to me, and tore open my shirt and felt my witches tit before she hugged me and started calling out my daddy's name. I let her go on for quite a while, before I figured that I had to tell her that I wasn't her son come back to her, but when I started she suddenly dried her eyes with her hands, straightened herself up, and said ", I know you are not my son . But you are his son are you not?" after I allowed as how I was she said in a real tired out voice. 'Well I am glad you come home, let me show you to your room."

Well it wasn't what I had been expecting or planning. Somehow, somewhere, it hit such a nice gentle chord in me that I just walked in and sat down while she shooed all my companions away. I don't know if it came through in this narrative so far, but I was kind of short of parenting. Especially maybe of mothering. Oh, I had four or five moms all right, but they was all kind of borrowed, and I knew it. All of a sudden while this little old lady was pottering about her kitchen trying to find me some "Rickety Uncle" and make me a nice hot botanical, I realized that I liked her an awful lot.

Our integration on Bountiful wasn't totally without problems. There was a honeymoon period at first, until the powers that be on Bountiful, in the little town of Jeffville near where we had landed, noticed that their religion had gone through some changes in daddy's hands. They weren't at all happy that everybody referred to my pa as the prophet. According to their outlook, the "age of the prophets" was in the past and there weren't supposed to be any more. They were even less happy that I was regarded as "the chosen one".

All of a sudden there wasn't much doubt in some of their mind that we were heretics and that I deserved tarring and feathering at the very least. I didn't see it coming. I had been living with my granny for a few weeks. We had developed a routine her and I, in the evening we would sit back together in her living room sipping botanicals and she would pick my brains about pa. He had been her only boy child, and very well loved, and he had disappeared from her life forever at just twenty some years of age. I gave her my Daddy's journal and while we sat there in the evening I would answer questions, and tell her stories about pa and his life on Dogpatch. All in all it made her pretty happy to hear he had a real interesting life, as all these years she had imagined he came to his death at twenty years old.

We were just slipping into our routine of sipping and talking one evening, when there was a whole hullabaloo outside of horses being rode in and lots of shouts and hollering outside of our house. There was two parties of men outside. One was composed of some the important men of the town, with a bunch of excited hangers on. The other was composed of the folks from all the houses round about. Mostly granny's relations, and they were right outside the house having a really serious argument about me.

Granny stopped the arguing by walking out on her porch listening for a minute and then shooting a man who had been shouting loudly for me to be dragged out, right up and off the back of his horse with the twelve gauge, three and a half inch magnum , SSG. cartridge, semi automatic, seven shot critter gun which she always carried.

There was a moment of dead silence. Granny addressed the newcomers, apologizing as how she was an old lady and her finger had slipped. While she talked she kept her gun more or less focused on the group composed of the most important men about town. After apologizing for the death of their comrade, she he pointed her gun at half a dozen of the men individually, and invited them in for tea to talk things over. They had some choices, but they were too chicken to take them, and walked in quiet and meek as mice. A big rough looking- fellow and a few others tried to follow in behind , but granny shoved her gun barrel hard into the belly of the first one and walked him backwards out onto the porch. There was still a crowd of men up close to the porch filling granny's front yard.

She singled one out by name, pointed her gun at him, and told him that the broken branches under his horse were her 'Mrs. Bigelow Roses.' She allowed that it made her so upset to see her roses smashed up that it made her just tremble all over with the saddest feeling. The fact that she was trembling while holding a twelve gauge scatter gun loaded with S.S.G. (that she had just killed a man with) caused a general movement back and away from the immediate vicinity of her house. Away from the possibility of standing on her roses. Nothing causes a bunch of men to damp down their testosterone like an old lady with a shotgun. It holds out worse possibilities than being beat up by a girl. The crowd moved on away from the house content to let heir leaders sort it out.

It was all very civilized in granny's front room. Everyone of the gentlemen of substance whom she had invited in had a comfy chair, and they pretty soon they each had a cup of something hot in front of them. She had entertained all of them in this self same living room before, when they had come to ask a rich old widow for bucks for their church. She treated this meeting just the same.

First she picked on the fattest one of the bunch and made him take off his dirty boots and clean them up properly, while she handed out the cordials. The fire was warm and she made herself an ally in the first ten minutes by secretly slipping hard booze into the drink of an old codger with big white whiskers and a purple face, whom she knew often alternated his tea-totaling religion with his drinking bouts sometimes on the same day. She figured him to be as dry as a camels hoof, what with all the excitement, and his likely having had to hang about with a crew he couldn't sip in front of for a considerable time period. It was a jolly crew and nobody even seemed inclined to start talking first.

Granny laid her scatter gun against the chimney, and picked up her knitting to work on. She suddenly got all hunched over and old- looking while she worked just like a tiny very old lady. After a couple of minutes had passed she looked up again at their presence and appearing startled , said in a real tired ancient voice, " Oh my gentlemen I am getting so old, ... fer a moment I forgot you was all heah, (by which she meant "all here"). What is it about today? Do you need more funding for the choir? I had heard some of the ladies saying you might be coming on up here to talk about an organ?"

The old codger with the now red but formerly purple face was feeling the loquaciousness provided by several ounces of straight whiskey in front of a nice warm fire. He had a sparkle in his eye which let me know that he knew he wasn't dealing with a dumb old lady, but with one of the sharpest tools in the shed.

" Well Zenobia", he said pausing. It was her first name he was using. It hadn't ever occurred to me that she probably had one. "There has been some things being said about your son and your grand son here. People have said that they have been setting themselves up as false prophets and messiahs, and you know what the book says about Pretenders and Usurpers?"

I could see which way the wind blows. Me and Uncle John had some conversations on how this might come up some time, although I hadn't first expected to hear about it from a lynch mob. As part of being captain Uncle John has been giving me extensive lessons in how to explain things to people. He says you have to make sure you aren't afraid to scrape the bottom of the barrel. He also said that most really good explanations have a certain amount of lying in them. He says it is called diplomacy. I reckon he is right.

Now that the shooting and yelling had stopped it warn't that hard to put out the fire. I handled the part about Dad being a prophet first. I told them that Dad had never called hiself a prophet, (that was a lie.), and I added how, in fact, he abhorred the practice himself. (another lie). I also explained, how me being called "the chosen one wasn't a claim that I was to be the Savior of Mankind" (a definite third lie), but how it was that my daddy had always said I was the one who was chosen to lead the people back to the "True Untainted Religion" by making contact with the wise group of men who ran his home town of Jeffville, not so far from New Vaundoo where his daddy taught the choir on the on the planet Bountiful in the New Zions

I told them the reason I was there on their planet, was to listen to them, and that their decision on all things religious was just fine with me. It was like feeding warm milk to a cold kitty. Once I had their confidence and attention, I even brought up a few practices which I thought just needed their looking at first. They had never even heard about how Pa had changed things so he could allow wives to be inherited. All six condemned it as a heathen practice. They started talking among themselves about how they would set up an investigation and an instruction committee, and an information book for the folks on Dogpatch.

Bossing people around is just what folks like that most enjoy to do, so they were happy as pigs in shit when granny kicked them out. I was in like a dirty shirt. When I told Uncle John about it he said he was proud of my powers of explanation . Lying is an important skill.

Another big hitch in our integration was a while down the line, when they realized where we got our silver and gold from was. We were drug runners . It wasn't something they really wanted to know about, since by that time a good bit of our silver and gold was lining their pockets with more to come. I was glad I didn't have to handle this one, Uncle John was there to give the sermon.

We were at a meeting which had been called and facing a group which included all the merchants which we were dealing with, as well as the big wigs of the church. I knew that daddy referred to Uncle John as his elder in the church but I never knew that Uncle John had actually been a preacher. He had never been one much for religion on Dogpatch. Later on, I learned that the way he had got off to university, was by excelling in a religious school not much different from the ones right here. He clearly had this one all thought out ahead of time. He gave the standard sermon on Jesus advising his followers to pay taxes to the roman empire. You know the famous saying Jesus said " Give unto Caesar what is Caesar's. He gave the whole sermon just right just as everybody had heard a thousand times he even excited their awe for his knowledge by being able to quote a bit of Aramaic, "Deno de malkutho dino" he thundered at the room half a dozen times " The law of the land is our law" .

Twenty minutes into it he had never even mentioned us and our boat. I have to admit there was kind of a gaping hole in the middle of his sermon where he never actually explained how all the aforesaid was supposed to apply in any logical way to us, but apparently it didn't matter all that much. They wanted to believe that our money belonged in their pockets and that bit about "give unto Caesar what is Caesars" had a hell of a nice ring to it. He got us off the hook.

Now some of you may be wondering if this narrative is going to run on forever and include my whole bloody life. Well it aint. I had in mind to write a piece like my daddy's, on account of as it had been so wonderful for me and granny to find. Now I want to admit or rather to interpose that I am now covering the events of a certain year in what is now my youth. I will tell you all now that I am no longer young.

It ain't the beginning of the end or anything like that, but a I am sure it is at least the end of the beginning, I am forty years old and I have been ships captain for twenty five.. Most of what you have read I wrote years ago but I have taken it in hand today, to finish it off what I never writ then. before I windup my personal narrative of my fifteenth year and assuming my captaincy, I would like to give you a peek at what happened on Dogpatch and Bountiful over the last years.

It appears as if the combine which runs the plantations on Dogpatch isn't as mighty as we thought. Mloko and his buddies wiped out the plantation at the bend of the river the first year they had good guns. We all waited for retribution to come but there was nothing. A couple of years later he sent a flotilla of war canoes down the river to all the plantations of the delta and torched the lot. There are still plantations on Dogpatch. We can hear their radio traffic, and know their locations but they are not on our continent and don't seem to be interested in us .

The wild thing shot up a few flyers, who came to investigate, so I guess they know that they aren't just up against indigenous resistance over here, and they are willing to share the pie with our posse. There have been a few unexpected developments. Bountiful is emptying out. There are as many people born on Bountiful living on Dogpatch now, as there are on Bountiful itself.

There are probably a whole bunch of reasons for that, but the biggest one has got to be that nobody really likes dinosaurs. They are just one absolute drag from beginning to end . There is maybe nothing worse except goannas. I just hate goannas. And carnivorous plants, I hate them more than dinos too, but seeing as all these things all exist on Bountiful but not on Dogpatch they don't detract from my argument. Dogpatch has stores , and gun factories and all kinds of normal stuff now, and The wild Thing is no longer our only ship. I never made it to Rome or even got back to school. The old bunch is all dead except of course for Bobo.

What else can I tell you about historical stuff , before I finish off telling you about my own personal fifteenth summer? Not much I guess, so here I go on about myself again. Or at least I will after I tell you about my son. Just like I did and his grand daddy did, he got hisself preceded by a whole bunch of sisters. He also has a witch's tit, and like I was, he was probably raised with a bunch of scary boggledegook about witches' tits ,elves, aliens, armless legless Eggmen, faerry gifts, changelings, alien " ABOMINATIONS"; alien DNA; etcetera, but unlike me he got shipped off world to school to a normal environment before it messed up his brain too much. Or at least I hope so. I sent him to military school at Rome.

Before I diverge from my purpose and let this epistle get too broad. I figure I will let it get back to its original form as mostly just a letter to the family to match my daddy Aeneas Browning's letter on how he got rich. I like simple titles. I think I will just call this one, "Inter time privateer. How I became ships captain at fifteen. An account of how I got there by Isaiah Browning". But to finish off here, I am going back to to how things was after I slipped "back" into my room at granny's (Mrs. Zenobia Browning's) house.

At first my granny wasn't too interested in me as an individual. She was a loving mother whose only boy child had left home at sixteen and only returned once before disappearing forever, a few years later.

She was like a dry sponge for information. Each evening we would sit down drink tea and I would tell her stories about my dad. It wasn't all that easy to do since I kind of had to turn my head around in order to say so many positive things about him, when I hadn't been used to thinking much positive about him at all since I hit twelve years old. She was a needy old lady and very nice to me. I gave it my best shot even to the point of going to Uncle John and picking his brains about the parts of daddy's life I didn't know too well.

Living at her place was pretty nice most ways, and it also extricated me from the problem of me and Jaquelline's relationship. After a couple of weeks though, Granny had had enough, and one evening when I prepared for the inevitable, not too comfortable conversation, I started to bring up some bits I had retrieved from Uncle John. She smiled at me and told me that I had been a nice boy, but that we could quit talking about my daddy now. It took me a while before I figured I knew my granny well enough to know if I wanted to ask her her opinion on all that stuff about the witches tit and abominations, alien DNA, evil armless legless eggmen, and all the other crap which I had learned all my life and which had made courting so complicated for me, but I did finally bring it up. I asked her what she knew.

It wasn't a very auspicious tale, in that it was full of fairies and changelings, and stuff of that nature. I was a little bit surprised when aliens appeared to have nothing to do with it according to Granny . Granny had actually never managed to hear about aliens herself and denied their existence to begin with, and then after I argued with her some, she continued to insist that aliens, even if they existed, had nothing to do with this story, as my dad had originally been told it.

The story was called the 'Story of the Hootchy Kootchy Men'. Its basic premise was that the fairies had given a curse and a blessing to one lineage of men. Supposedly this happened back in the mythical land of Missouri, where the Mormons came from, and where the original gift was to a Melungeon whatever that is. In the original story the gift is the abilities to play music please women, and win disagreements.

We have what amounts to superior strength of mind, in some funny way. The peculiarities of our family are the witch's tit and the rest, and the curse is that if we inbreed we produce egg men who are nasty stuck together group intelligences. According to granny once one Eggman has been produced, all the male babies born of his lineage afterward, even men with two arms and legs, can come under his sway. The gestating babies don't really produce separate personalities, and when they open their eyes at birth the nasty Eggman from down the road looks out.

The more Eggmen are connected together the stronger the power becomes of the colony to enslave those of their own blood. Even those who are not descended from the bloodline are subject to pressure.

According to Granny, the legends say this has happened time and again on Bountiful, and the resulting communities have been thrown out of the covenant. The jungle had taken them back. It sounded so certainly like bullshit. I actually started to relax as she told it and began to appreciate it as a kind of ghost tale. I even smiled at an inappropriate place and got her temper up. I tried to explain my opinion and ended up mentioning that things probably looked a lot differently to her because she couldn't read. (female illiteracy happens quite a bit on Bountiful). It seemed to me because of the whole way it was told , to be certain to be a legend.

I was really surprised when My Granny said " What does reading have to do with it? Why don't you go look at the grave of the eggman which your greatgrandma killed and that of all his slaves, if you don't believe me"

She mentioned a location on the other side of the big town, New Vaundoo and up river about forty miles. It was where granny herself was from. From the way she told them, I had been sure all her stories referred to times in the remote past. It brought me up short to realize she was talking about happenings of only decades, rather than centuries ago.

The domination of this little community had supposedly begun in what Granny assured me was the usual way. An Eggman had been born despite the Mormons' careful attention to family histories, and the parents had hid, rather than destroyed it. Over the next decade a series of children born within the village to the close kin of the parents were not separate individuals. As well, the Egg boy began to slowly dominate the minds of adults who were closely related to him, while they dreamed. This was not noticed for many years, until it was too late . The village was lost .

Grandmas community had been just a few miles away. The remaining individuals of the stricken village arrived in her village. She knew absolutely all about it. It was known to be necessary to kill the egg man. There were too many related individuals all around and about who were susceptible . Nobody wanted to see an egg man staring up from their new born babies eyeballs, because he existed unbeknownst to them in some shack in the woods nearby. Eggmen were unpopular. They bred more of themselves. The Eggman had to go.

Now I ain't mentioned Jaquelline again up to this point, not because I was saving her for last, but I suppose because I would kind of preferred not to have to talk about her at all, I guess. Here goes anyways. I decided to lay the whole sordid story -- witch's tits, elves, fairies , the Eggman, alien DNA., hootchy kootchy men, Missouri and the Mellungeons -- in front of her, and just see what she made of it all.

Jaquelline was actually a pretty smart person. I know I described her as dumb and non agile etc. but her and my situations kind of reversed when we stopped living in the jungle. All of a sudden when it came to civilized living I was the lame, stupid one. There is really no other way to put it. I wasn't all that comfortable with the situation. She also, kind of, had an axe to grind. It was on account of how I had treated her, but I was also starting to suspect that maybe women generally have an axe to grind once you start fucking them. Anyway, that is way too cosmic for the present account, so suffice it to say that we weren't hanging out all that much, and I could see that we were both glad when I found a new crib at my granny's house.

As long as all we did, when we shared each others company, was to screw, things seemed to work out alright. We kept things like that for quite a while.

We waited for the Roman freighter which pulled in a couple of times a year to pull in and zap up a container load of passengers who were off to the telestial worlds and zap down the Wild Thing's refit materials

Every time I talked to Jaquelline for more than ten minutes, I would have to ask her the meaning of words that she used, and this time wasn't any different. The first stumbling block was "archeologist". Now there are one Hell of a lot of "ologists" out there, but since there had been none on Dogpatch, and possibly not more than a few on Bountiful, either, I hadn't paid all that much attention to the lot of them. Oh sure, I knew what a biologist was, or a geologist was. I aint stupid, but it's true I couldn't at the time have told an opthquamologist from an anthropoplogist

Anyway to cut a long story short, she wanted to dig the son of a bitch up. The frigging egg man I mean. The whole idea of robbing a grave, particularly this grave, got the little hairs on my neck standing right up. At first I thought I had misheard her, and then I nearly felt like crying when I realized she expected me to do it. I tried explaining to her as how I had never heard of grave robbing as being an allowed thing, or even a thing anybody ever thought of doing. Then I tried to explain to her that it wasn't just a matter of it not being socially acceptable. I allowed as how it could actually be downright dangerous on account of the spirits and the barrow wights and such, which could lay a curse of sickness or misfortune upon us.

That is when I learned my second new word of the day. It is called "superstition." Apparently, superstition is when you believe in the powers of spirits ------which you cant' see. To me this just sounded like plain old religion, and I told her so, which shut her up, but also made her angrier which didn't help. So of course, it ended with me agreeing to dig the s.o.b. up and carve a bit off of him for science.

I felt way better when Jaquelline said that she would at least come too. I loved to hear her talk science about the whole project and the pictures she dialed up for me of 'archeological digs' made me feel downright fearless about grave robbing, as long as she was around that is. It is a funny thing, but as soon as she weren't round about and I started thinking about our project, I started seeing it in terms of mouldy dead corpses that would either assume new life and wiggle around before my very eyes ,or lay silent deadly curses of misery and misfortune on me and my line.

Whenever Jaquelline talked about it, the whole operation seemed easy as pie, so I just generally tried to keep her talking I didn't even have to pay all that much attention for it to work just fine. She had a great idea right off that since the whole episode had happened only three quarters of a century ago we should have a look in old newspapers and see what they said. Five minutes later some old copies had dialed up just fine and we were having a look at the news of the New Vaundoo herald, as well as the Brigham Young Memorial Tribune, from seventy two years back, as well as links to various other articles concerning "Egg men going back two hundred years.

The one from the Brigham Young Memorial tribune was written by a preacher. It was a reprint of a Sunday sermon. It would have done Pa proud. The title was "abominations" and it spent a full four pages talking about sin without giving nearly no useful information at all. In fact, it topped my fear of spirits, the devil and damnation up to near panic levels, to the point I had to get Jaquelline chatting on about science, just to slow my heart beat.

The second article was better. It was called " Egg men empty gold field". It was written by someone called Billy Missouri, a financial correspondent. It was the closest to an intelligent independent account that we were going to find. It looked like a fair to middling sized gold grounds was in the process of quitting to be worked on account of " Eggmen", which the author was pointing out were not an actually scientifically attested occurrence.

City people who had their money resting on it weren't happy to lose it, and they maybe didn't believe in eggmen any more than Cabouters, Black peters, or Santa Claus. The author had done a round up on all the available data, {including the earlier links which I too had found }, and came up with a rather startling claim. He said that the eggmen maybe weren't imaginary,as most people probably believed, and that they weren't a fairy curse/blessing of the Mellungeons and the sons of Seth as the backwoods preachers taught either.

This fellow Billy Missouri had been educated in Roma somewhere and he pointed out that "The New Zions were all on the fringe, in a place considered too close to the aliens for the Roma themselves to consider colonizing. He thought that rather than a touch of the tar brush like the church thought, maybe what we were dealing with was a little touch of alien DNA . It wasn't a popular idea and it didn't send people rushing off to the gold fields too fast, either. A year or two ahead of this date, issues of the newspaper talk of the eggman's landing, and the little spur of a railroad that ran off it to the gold field and the little towns around it as being defunct. People put their energies elsewhere. Me and Jaquelline decided to take a run up there.

In some ways by then me and Jaquelline had what amounted to a pretty cool relationship--not that either of us was trying to head towards our being together after her freighter pulled into orbit. She was zapping up and moving out, no doubt about it, but we had been through some stuff together, and Bountiful itself pulled us together as we were both off-worlders here, without much in common with the people around us. A trip together off somewhere together to more or less just check out what Bountiful had to offer suddenly seemed pretty good to us. We decided right away that we weren't even going to dig up the stiff. It was to be an exploratory journey in the best sense. We could come back with a crew and shovels later if everything looked rosy.

The trip on up to New Vaundoo was interesting in itself, what with its square mile upon square mile of corn and cattle, all grown in the bend of a big river where critters couldn't get them, protected by lots of of men on horseback with rifles. Bountiful isn't what you would call a productive colony in the Rome sense. If it weren't for a dusty old treaty back when the Romans conferred some favors on the Mormons as they welcomed them into the Empire, which allowed that the Romans would service their present colonies, if the Mormons didn't spew out any more of them

Bountiful probably wouldn't have rated the freighter. But, seeing as it did rate a freighter, the Mormons weren't slow at making what they could off of it. There were other little colonies elsewhere, doing other things, but New Vaundoo and the towns around it produced mostly produced corn, gold and cattle. It was a pretty big place. Cancel that. For me at the time, coming from Tomahawk with a population of a couple thousand, to New Vaundoo with at least fifty thousand people, was more of a shock for me than I really would care to describe.

If you never looked at your first flush toilet at a near adult age, you won't catch what I am talking about anyway. Oh I had seen ships toilets before alright, but I guess I had never suspected that earth bound culture ever reached that high. Yes, it is true that I had a long drop toilet growing up, and no, that is not where I got my goddamned nickname, a detail which I am going to include at the end of this epistle for my own vanity's sake. For now, back to the narrative.

Me and Jaquelline was getting along pretty good. She used New Vaundoo to have some fun with me, and to say goodbye to me on what was as close as we could find to her turf. In other words, a civilized place. We ate food in restaurants, drank wine, and walked about the city, feeding popcorn to the budgies, pigeons, squirrels and cane rats. We walked about hand in hand and looked at stuff. If you hadn't known us, you would have thought we were falling in love, rather than just biding our time to get out of it.

I bought myself a new guitar and spent lots of time playing it while Jaquelline stared at me with a peculiar look on her face. I didn't ask her about it. Some things are better left unsaid. Sometimes she just looked like she wanted to marry me, but at other times she looked like maybe she was thinking about killing me and feeding me to her young. Women are peculiar, and no matter how many more I acquired they never got less so.

Once again, that is a bit off of the topic, which was as I recall the Eggman. He was, the old ladies said, responsible both for my intelligence, gift of persuasion, gift of music, etc. Or at least, one old lady did, my Grandma. She was reckoning to marry me off and had already begun investigating the lineages of a bunch of pretty young maids for me her 'very important rich son in law the Captain Isaiah Browning' as she called me.

Apparently the idea of marrying me in fast to a bunch of fine young girls of a traditional religious nature, was a popular idea among the religious powers as well, who were still a bit worried about my "chosen one" status. At any rate, by the time me and Jaquelline went for our trip they had been throwing pussy at me fast and furiously for around a month ,not that I got very close to any of it or anything. It was just a series of afternoon teas where girls were brought in to meet me kind of one by one to drink tea and chat for half an hour, and I was supposed to pick out a dozen or ten. There wasn't a witches tit t for at least three generations back in any of their families. Granny did the checking. I reckon I would have been a fool to say no.

Anyway, once again back to the Eggman or at least to Eggman's Landing. We tried to get up there, as it weren't far upriver on a map from the last inhabited town. On Dogpatch, you could travel a distance like that on any kind of small boat although you would have to take care, but the first thing I noticed on the dock in the rinky-dink town was that there were no small boats whatsoever. The critters were just too big, full fledged dinosaurs and their kin on dry land and in the water as well. Any boat under forty or so feet was liable to be outright picked up and shook. Larger boats were subject to being climbed up onto by critters near their own weight and capsized . All boats were well fitted out with gun towers from which gunfire could be directed at the decks to keep them clear.

We were pretty flush with cash. We could have hired something really big to carry us upriver to have a look at the landing, but we were able to establish pretty fast that a look would be all we would get anyway. Eggman's landing was all overgrown in the thickest sort of second growth as ever hid a nasty critter, and there would be no way at all for Jaquelline and I to follow up the railroad spur or do anything in the grown over town, even if we got there. Jaquelline was more unhappy with that than I was. The science looked interesting, and her attraction was lifelong to science.

I had mostly been whining about not being able to meet women, and seeing as my granny was proving so good at producing some really interesting ones, who were guaranteed abomination free, my own interest in digging up the egg man had fallen right off, in fact, although I didn't admit it I kind of wished I had never brought it up. When we got back from our trip to grandma's sleepy little town, we weren't expecting to find the fat in the fire but that was exactly what was going on.

Uncle John was dead, hair had been lifted, and relations between the crew of the Wild Thing and her neighbors was in deep disrepair. Most of the hard men who should have been aboard her were off freelancing, mostly storming the local jail.

Old Mr. Roussopoulos is awful good at running a ship, but I reckon he ain't ever killed anybody and don't want to try. He wasn't about to help me out. There was a lot of upset people asking me what to do. I figured the odds were pretty good that a bunch of Federales would arrive pretty soon ,while the ship was mostly undefended throw us all in jail or kill us, and then maybe after that they would ask all those hard questions about us that the local merchants and religious dudes had never felt like asking. It was time for a parlay. Things had gone to hell in a hand basket really really fast. It started with Old Uncle John getting hisself shot. It would never have happened if aunt Meg had been along but she warn't.

Uncle John had got hisself shot over a woman, a nice plump young wife of an old religious man, At this point Uncle Johns minions who was standing right there had shot the old codger. Finally my dead uncle's minions had got them selves enfilladed on the way out of town by a bunch of locals who disapproved of said religious old coot having been shot, especially by guys who weren't even locals, even if said old codger had been firing bullets in their direction. The legal aspect was kind of muddled right from the outset. The Sheriff had arrived in town and arrested a couple of my uncle's dudes, who were lying around wounded after the ambush, which killed most of them. He said they was "finda hang em ", by which they meant "fixin to" hang them.

Around about this time, the folks on the ship had got together and decided to forcibly retrieve said wounded comrades from the jail, before they was hung. This bunch finally got back the evening after my arrival with their object accomplished and proud of having lifted lots of hair in the process. From the point of view of me the 'commanding officer', the shit was hitting the fan.

I got on the phone to our closest contacts in town-- people like the merchants, the mayor and my gramma. I gave them a statement of our point of view to pass along. I told them that while the Captain (me) had been away, there had been some untoward events. These had led to a chain of things occurring that none of us wanted and that I had an excellent idea of how to resolve things (a lie, but a pretty good sounding one I thought). I also told them I would have the men whom they considered to be the main culprits locked up in the brig, if they gave me their names. I was pretty damned sure they wouldn't know any names, but it sounded awfully damned conciliatory. I told them I wanted them to send a delegation out to the ship to talk in the morning.

I knew they would come whether I asked them or not. In closing I asked if they would limit the size of their delegation so I didn't have any of my inexperienced heavy machine gunners get scared and jump the gun to thinking they was being bushwhacked ,and accidentally shoot the lot of them. I figgered they needed a little reminder that they, on their own a bunch of bumpkins from a horsey little town, could not really take the Wild Thing from us, should we choose to deny it. When we met in the morning it was clear that the shooting was over and the cleanup had begun.

There were two things in our favor. The first, was that while our boys had lifted five of their boys hair, including the sheriff , their boys had managed to knock off ten of our boys during their kamikaze-style frontal attack on the jail. According to local sentiment, the score was clear ten to five and the home town had won.

They seemed mostly interested that we wouldn't be sore losers than in further justice. The second thing in our favor, was that the whole thing had started on account of some hairy old religious dude shooting his young wife's sweetie.

The problem was that on Bountiful if you allowed stuff like that to be printed, there would be a story on the front of the local rag with the same sorts of headlines three times a year, so there was a general desire just to shut the thing up in its box and sit on it. Besides, it had seemed as if the law was probably mostly on our side until somebody shot the sheriff. Bountiful is a boisterous sort of place on an occasion. Pretty much none of the young men have wives. It must hurt. In the short term, we were off the hook.

I didn't feel sad when my Uncle John got knocked off . At he time I put it down to me maybe not being of a sentimental nature, or something, but with the benefit of time and an enlightening occurrence I was able to put it down to something else --dead clear insight, I am pretty sure Uncle, former captain Johnny Jacks was intending to knock me off. If there hadn't been all those bucks arrive outside my uncles bar, to interrupt his deliberations with his old pirate buddies, way back when, I figure I would have been dead soon after the Etruscan princess laid herself down . He warn't really my uncle . I was wrong to have been trusting him. I was lucky he got knocked off. If I had kept his little secret back on Dogpatch I would have died.

I hate hangings. I had seen plenty just growing up. Pa always had plenty of judging to do, so I probably saw more than I should have at a young age, which is probably what makes me more shy of them than I guess I ought to be. The part which got me most was all the kicking after they were hoisted up or the pony was slapped out, but after Uncle john was gone I had to stand up to the plate and do a real job as captain and hanging was part of the job. I just wasn't expecting it to come up in my first weeks work,

We weren't exactly unpopular around town, despite having knocked off the sheriff, his deputies, and the aforesaid old geezer. I was enforcing the law around the ship and keeping all our hard men at home until things cooled off, at least somewhat. One dead man pretty easily leads to another.

I had ideas to get my lot away from Jeffville, where they stirred up too much trouble, and off doing something useful. There was quite a few cultural differences between Bountiful and Dogpatch that caused no end of troubles. First off, on Bountiful, killing somebody was actually illegal, whereas on Dogpatch there wasn't a law or even a rule really. Like the pirate said , it was more in the neighborhood of a ' loose guideline'.

Tied in with this was the general matter of civility. On Dogpatch, everybody is polite. You get killed pretty fast if you aren't. On Bountiful, people expected to get liquored up and say whatever they want and not get worse than a punch in the nose for it.

Even the matter of liquor was more controversial than you would imagine, on two recognizably thirsty planets. In Tomahawk, where we had come from, pretty much everybody in Tomahawk who had a job got their wages paid in rum. You drank what you needed and took the rest to the factors forts down by the river and traded it off. Bountiful had a thing called "prohibition", although I don't suppose less booze got drunk on Bountiful, maybe it was even way more booze. If you wandered around with a bottle on Bountiful the religious cops would take it off you and put you in the pillory for a day.

It also didn't help our boys temperament that we had brought thirty nubile, sweet, young things to this planet who had got married in right fast, whereas my boys hadn't been in position to snap a bra strap for several months.

As well as the attrition to my boys through getting themselves hung, shot, or jailed, I also had another problem.

We was losing our crew to the problem of there being lots of good jobs roundabout, as most of the young men of Bountiful went off planet to work during their pussy-less twenties. My boys were wandering off and not coming back. You couldn't blame them. I wanted to do it myself. What I needed to do was to remove most of my men from the vicinity of the ship, and leave Pops Roussopolous with the men he wanted to do the refit, and get the rest of them the hell out of there.

I decided to take them gold digging, not that we needed the gold, as their was still a pile higher than my nose in the treasure room on board ship, but they didn't know that, nor was it their personal gold. You will notice that I said take them 'gold digging' not 'gold hunting'. There isn't much reason to hunt. The earths are pretty much geologically the same or at least the ones humans mess about on are, so if there was gold in a certain place on on one earth its almost sure to be there on another. New Vaundoo had been put where gold was known to be. Lots of it. You didn't have to find it, you just had just to pay for the maps and pay your cut to the government. I bought the maps and the title to the goldfields up the way from Eggman's Landing. I was even feeling optimistic and enjoying my new job until the hanging came up.

I don't think I see no reason to get into what the fella done. He probably wasn't a bad sort, just raised wrong. I never saw much devil worshiping around Tomahawk, probably mostly on account of who I am, but also cause Pa hung them pretty regular in the first days after taking over. I guess he thinned them out. It ain't really the prayers to the devil that bother me. If they prayed for good things I wouldn't much see the difference. The problem is the taking of body parts for magic and good luck rituals which are most effective ,if obtained while the victim is still alive and in great pain when the parts are taken.. Back in the old days, pretty near everybody kept a dried dick for good luck and buried the hands of a baby under the doorway of their house. They were nice people too, who wouldn't dream of cutting off a neighbors dick to keep for good luck, but would buy one all nice an pre-dried if if it was offered to them for sale and not even think at all about where it came from.

Pa's answer was to make them extremely bad luck. If you got caught with dried human skins, hands , dicks .pussy lips or a few other parts you got hung. Scalps didn't count..So this boy had to be hung. No, I don't know if he did the killing himself or anything else about it. All I knew, was that I was expected to hang him. Culturally I am a bit of a hybrid, as I am sure you will have noticed. In some ways, I had solved conflicts by just adopting one attitude or the other for myself, from the townsfolk or the tribes folk, depending on whichever seemed the most convenient to me.

So far I had only killed people as a tribesman would and I always took the hair so I could remember the man individually and get on the right side of his spirit after he was dead with ceremony. This was looking to be different. It gave me the willies. The way a tribes person looks at things, this was going to be a taboo killing. The spirit would haunt me. I had a couple of dreams about the feet kicking before we even hung him. I gave it a hard think how I could get right with his spirit, and came up with the idea of making sure he died fast, so then when it came to haunt me, I would have something to 'show for myself'. I couldn't just shoot him because it weren't the rule, so I had him long dropped, as I have every hanging since. Dangling is just plain cruel. I overdid the drop and seeing he was a big heavy man, his head popped off. That is how I got the name of 'Long Drop.'

It is funny, the sorts of the thing which can make a crew like its captain. Popping the head off also tends to lighten up what might be an over solemn moment.

Eggman's Landing turned out to be one Hell of an interesting experience. We lost disposable crew members by the threes and fours along the way, and turned a kind of motley bunch of men and an inexperienced captain, into a wild bunch that really worked together.

The first fella got snapped up not long after we was out of port. He had climbed up on some rigging maybe thirty or so feet above the water to relax and smoke a bowl full, and watch the world go by, when a head which appeared to be composed mostly of teeth, snaked out of the water on the end of a thirty or forty foot neck, plucked him off his perch without a sound and disappeared beneath the surface. It was utterly soundless and occurred in the space of several heart beats - right I front of all of us!

It is no easy feat to unload a boat of men and supplies if you can't go near the water. The captain of our board had his own crew aboard for just that purpose. They were composed of cutters, riggers, and shootists, and numbered about thirty men who were in charge of offloading the scow and establishing us a beach head so we wouldn't all get gobbled up the first night ashore. The gear they wore ranged from Davy Crocket to Paul Bunyan with the nicest collection of chainsaws and rifles you ever laid eyes on.

When the captain pulled our barge up along side the Eggman's Landing, these boys hit their chores at a run. They boat crew dropped down a pick while a thirty foot boat was gotten ready to drop in the water.Before they dropped the boat in the water, rifle men dropped perhaps a dozen grenades in a grid all around in the surrounding area and shot at a couple of large critters, which momentarily surfaced.

The boat was the slung into the water On its deck was its prize, a heavy block to be hung on a crag at the back of Eggman's Landing. Streaming out behind the boat was a light 'straw line' which would be used to draw the larger tackle cable through the block after it had been placed. We watched these boys hit the shore without incident with the gunmen going ahead and securing the place. The work crew manhandled the hundred pound iron block and its tackle up to its crag and secured it. It was a piece of cake. We could hear quite a bit of popping of their rifles, but they returned to shore in less than a day mission accomplished, with the end of the straw line in their hands.

When the captain attached the ends and pulled his craft taught with its anchor motor the line which ran through double drums of a donkey engine mounted on her deck was pulled taught and rose in the air from its attached tower to the crag a thousand or more feet back from the shore. People and supplies, mostly concrete blocks and railway ties and steels, could now be off loaded without coming anywhere near the water

The next morning the same bunch of men offloaded with the addition of cutter. My lot sat on deck and watched drinking the rum (of which I gave them a very measured amount). We had a beautiful view. It was a lot like watching a football game. For at least the first hour or so it seemed like the game was going heavily towards the invaders, trees were falling along the length of the line we had strung and pallets of cargo were dangling suspended and making their way to shore.

We heard a portable air horn go off on shore, from back in the woods somewhere It was a series of undifferentiated sharp dashes. It meant 'watch out Here come some big ones'. Immediately, every chainsaw in the placed was silent, and the donkey engine shut down so that it became very easy to hear the honking. They were really stupendous critters, mostly taller than the trees we were cutting. They were the usual predator model everyone associates with T. Rexs, a whole gaggle running along in a flock like chickens, and sure enough the third one to run into sight had a tiny little man gripped between his teeth.

The distance to the boat wasn't overlong so my boys were soon shooting as well, and the critters were pretty well instantly perforated and dropped on the ground as they entered our shooting gallery. A few minutes later, the same air horn blew an all clear signals and the chainsaws started up again. We was all very sad that afternoon when they hoisted that fellow who got bit back to the ship and I gave out a double of tot of rum as they brought him aboard to honor his bones.

My boys and me spent the next day working hard, unloading and setting concrete blocks. Houses made out of sticks such as two by fours, don't work out too well when there might be really big dinosaurs around. They are liable to sneak up to it in the night and kick it around like a chicken kicks a pile of leaves before picking out the good bits. Concrete blocks are the answer, especially when you pour cement in them as well. We worked our asses off building some of the best dinosaur resistant bunkers as had ever been built on the planet.

We were all tough guys from Dogpatch, supposedly, but the truth is we were all to a man scared shit-less of dinosaurs. It was actually a Hell of a lot of fun.

Our ambition was to follow the old railway spur up to the goldfield and to replace it. We were inexperienced , but it worked out well for us that we had one in front of us an example of how things had been solved by the guys three quarters of a century before. We had really good guidance before our eyes and even the steel was still usable after seventy years, although not for its original purpose, for which we had brand new shiny stuff. As we followed their line we didn't have to do a mite of blasting or real hard earth moving from one end of the railway line to the other.

It was a mite spooky though. The gold fever among the men helped a bit. I whetted it some, and kept them jolly by issuing them Mother Theresa's long before we actually made a profit.

The Eggman himself, I just about kind of forgot of. There was never any real reason to send my men messing about in the old towns. It sure wasn't their inclination to do so on their own. They was into gold, and some of them was dying for it, but spooks held no attractions. I just kind of let the matter drop. There was a whole different jungle to think about. Did I ever mention that me and my pa drew trees? Well no I guess not, but so we did and I fixed to keep to it.

There is one problem being captain. You can;t fraternize. In some ways, it wasn't something so new for me, as being the son of the prophet had always kicked the shit out of fraternization anyways. I think maybe all captains have to be good at some solitary pursuits. Sitting out in the jungle drawing plants, and playing my guitar, while everybody else pursued hard physical labor, was one of my first pleasurable experiences as captain. I ended up liking the job,

One day some funny things happened. I woke up in the morning, back on board the ship when it was still parked by Jeffville. For one thing, I blew my sock drawer and dresser entirely to smithereens and almost assassinated myself and for another odd thing, although Jaquelline and I had not seen each other for two months and had been thoroughly broken up (she was imminently to be reunited with her fiancé). Although I had already been posted in marriage bans with half a dozen of the young women I had been meeting and was to marry them within the month, we had awoken that morning in bed together. I had almost assassinated her too..She was probably already grumpy, wondering about what to be mad about it, but me exploding my dresser and scaring her near to death ended our relationship even it it warn't my fault, no how you try to stretch it

Oh maybe, on reflection, maybe it was my fault. It does sound kind of simple of me, when you tell it. Me and Jaquelline had woken up side by each as I said . I had been trying to cover sort of an awkward early morning silence, by going over a box of my late Uncle Johns effects before they were brought back with us and given to aunt Meg. Around about this point in my life I was getting an idea of how complicated things can be, and I didn't want to do something stupid, like send a written note to his new sweetie on home to his wife. Anyways, there was mostly a bunch of junk in a box that had been taken off of his actual stiff, that I was having a look at.

I picked out one bit and held it in front of Jaqueline and me while commenting that the item in the case looked like some kind of detonator. I then mentioned that it looked like the little case with its lock was made so the button didn't accidentally get pushed. Then I pushed it and exploded the bureau across the room from us. Does that sound stupid to you? I guess I do remember her suggesting that I not push the button. Anyway, do you remember that gem on a chain with the handy little explosives charge, which my uncle had me wear. Well I knew about the time-able explosive charge, but I didn't know he could set it off from a distance as well. I had tried to give the item back to him not so long before, only to be told that I could keep them permanent, and that he hoped I would wear them always for my own safety. It had been hanging around my neck not fifteen minutes before, I and I had only turfed it in my sock drawer while I took a shower. Not very nice of my Uncle Johnny Jack, the pirate. In some ways it probably worked out pretty good, as seeing as Jaquelline never spoke another word to me until her freighter took off, I never had to explain to her about how I had decided to just let the old egg man lie, and never had never bothered to dig him up.

With those words I guess I have pretty much finished up my account of my seventeenth year

The End

Post script

When I read these words which I wrote just a short time ago, they seem so optimistic that it is hard to believe my world changed so much in such a short time. There were warnings and we could have seen it coming. I cant imagine why we weren't more curious when the slaver stations started blinking off the air? And why weren't we more surprised by what push-overs they were; and by their lack of retaliation. Late last year the last slaver station winked off the air and Mloko moseyed over to their continent to have a look.

It sure looked nice, like a well tended garden, with the lion lying down with the lamb. At first, we weren't sure what was going on. I was watching it on the screen while Mloko and his bunch made the fly. I have re-watched the tape many times. First they cruise over the area and establish for sure that there really is no nasty hardware about likely to hop into the sky and attack them. Then to be sure Mloko swings the ship back into the hinterland and picks a mud hut village surrounded by crops to drop down next to. The camera view switches to show Mloko and his bunch disembarking and him hollering out a bunch of orders in his usual loudmouth fashion and his guys start to hurry off. Something unusual happens, all the voices trail off and then the guys mostly just look around for a comfy spot and then sit down on it,

There is a fifteen minute silent interval while they all just sit there until finally a party comes into view and approaches. It is a bunch of chumps, with a guy being trundled along in a wheel barrow. When they get closer you can see that the chumps have smallish heads and great big muscles and that the guy in the wheelbarrow has a great big head maybe eighteen inches long and cone shaped but with a bulbous beginning. Nobody talks and the little armless legless guy in the wheel barrow doesn't even open his eyes. The chumps with the little heads go in and out of the picture looking things over carefully, and then the party returns again to the mud huts in the distance at the back of the picture. All this, while Mloko and his party just continue to sit quietly, maybe scratching their noses or changing position once in a while but never appearing to notice the visitors.

There is another hour of tape during which Mloko and his guys just sit there staring off into space before you can see another bunch approaching from the town. When they get closer, you can see it is some small headed guys with pangas who walk up and butcher Mloko and his posse, like so many hogs, without an oink of protest from the bunch. They pack the bits into bags for later and walk out of the picture. That camera is still running. We can watch who walks down that garden path any time. It is quite enlightening.

I have a theory. First off, I don't see how these critters have anything to do with my Pa's failure to keep his zipper done up. as he had never been across the ditch to the big island continent. Therefore, any Eggmen there are no relation whatsoever to me, and my ruddy Melungeon curse. There must be multiple sources for the infection, so for sure the problem is aliens not fucking fairies. Second, I believe that it is the nature of Bountiful which has kept it from taking over there.

On Bountiful any community which is cast out of the covenant, dies fast for lack of gunpowder and guns. From the stories that are told it seems likely to have happened lots of times. Dogpatch doesn't have any natural cauterization process like that and we are truly beleaguered with villages of Eggmen popping up on this continent. A big part of our problem is ignorance and that comes from our unofficial status. I cant believe that the Eggmen can be just present upon the two planets, which my dad happened upon. The odds for that just wouldn't seem likely. The Romans must also know about, and be trying to deal with the situation somewhere, or at least somewhen. We need to know what they know (but we must be careful due to our unofficial, really I guess it is more like criminal, status) who we tell what in the Roman world.

I have an ace in the hole, my son, Cornelius. He was named by his mom. He is in a prestigious military college at Rome. He is a real fire cracker. One of the only good parts of the affair is laughing about how he is going to deal with the realization that I have sent him two stiffs packed in salt for him to deal with. ["I WOULD LIKE TO SEE YOUR FACE CORNELIUS"]as well as a copy of this journal to let him know his place in things.. I chuckle every time I think of it. I have two whole real Eggmen packed in salt, to send him, as well as the bones of the one from Eggman's Landing. I am signing off with a grin on my face, it is as good a note as I can find to end this letter upon.

Cornelius Browning's Tale

Third generation Browning family

Yeah my dad, he sure done that. He sent me two stiffs and a letter, without giving it one little thought that if Eggmen were as common as he thought, out there in the regular world, that this might not be a very cool thing to do.

So where do I start? My dad introduced me. I am Cornelius Browning and a lousy name it is too, unless maybe your are a prince or something. One side of town turned it into Cornholio, which wasn't nice, while my Latin buddies figured Cornuto would be funny, which also wasn't very nice. I have a few little peculiarities which will figure in this story.

I have the swearing syndrome, Tourette's. The doctors texts say that the amygdala of my brain is a little bit more independent than that of the rest of you. I think of my amygdalic self as sort of like a lizard brain. My amygdalic self is mostly interested in flight or fright and indulges in pretty uncomplicated behavior. Like swearing a bunch when he is frustrated or maybe beating up the occasional paper dispenser or something of that sort. That happens mostly on account of he usually gets stressed about something he don't know nothing about like school or some such. So he just swears a bunch, looks for something to eat and goes back to sleep letting me take back over. I've hardly ever been gone more than a minute or two but Tourette's, at least like I got it, can be kind of a Jeckel and Hyde existence.

My amygdalic self (truth is I call him Cornholio and I might as well admit it) acts quite a bit differently if he takes over and I am in some kind of dangerous predicament. I bit a dog that was barking at me once if that gives you an idea. Mostly it was just an enormous pain in the ass. Everybody has heard of the Hulk. He got exposed to bad spider DNA or some such. Anyway, whenever he got into trouble he would morph into a big hulking green guy with no patience whatsoever, who, would immediately attack the enemy pummeling them. Well I was like that, except I didn't morph big, I just morphed into a foul mouthed scrawny kid who would attack with no sense whatever, and get beat down.

It kind of directed my life. I didn't have much choice in whether I fought or not, so I studied and got good early on. I carry a sword with a cane in it and Cornholio is actually pretty good, although somewhat bloodthirsty and somewhat rash. But back to my childhood. You know lots enough about my dad but not much about my mom and my side of things.

We are Romans and we are from what are called the Roman Isles. These aren't a group of islands set side by side but just a few of the biggest and most useful all over the earths that we Romans make use of on the many different time lines. Islands are usefully insulated from the rest of the continents and if you sterilize them they tend to stay that way,.

Bountiful isn't much of a place, so there is only one of the Roman Isles was made use of here, and that's where I am from. It is city from shore to shore and still a pretty grand one ,although definitely gone to seed, although I didn't know that then. Her category and name was 'administrative city ' with a long number. We called her sin city. I now know that everywhere Roman has gone to seed, and I now know why. Our town had half the commerce and four times the population, which a guiding hand had provided it for centuries. It was a slum. Nobody knew why things had changed in the last century or so.

Mom ran a bar. It wasn't in a nice area. What can I tell you? Dad didn't exactly have high taste. He was a pirate, after all. Or maybe I do him wrong. Maybe he had as high taste as everybody, but his business made it unsafe for him to hang out somewhere more respectable. He came to town once in a while with a bunch of his blades, guys who nearly always left a pool of blood on a bar room floor somewhere.

Truth is I didn't like Dad and I didn't like them. I hear him in his letter talking about me kind of nice, but it grates on my nerves and just doesn't ring true. He hardly knew me. He had too many wives and too many kids. He never helped me in one single way. I rejected him all my childhood and only feel even the teensiest bit warm and proud of him, even after all these years. You would think that growing up by a spaceport, in an administrative city might be pretty cosmic. Maybe it did have a few cosmic elements.

Romans have always been good at providing bread and circuses,and everybody, or at least everybody Roman, got a monthly cheque and access to lots of entertainment. Theoretically, we all still worked for the company and were between jobs. Truth was, there hadn't actually been jobs for a generation or two. Not jobs for the mother company anyway. Now that I look back at it there were lots of signs that there was a dead hand on the switch somewhere. We all went to school to get that cheque but lots of my friends didn't actually bother to learn to read and write. Nobody up top seemed to care just like nobody up top seemed to care that our spaceport had as many illegal ships as company ships, and not hid out of sight from each other either.

Something stunk and some of us knew it. You know, after saying what I did about not liking my dad a minute ago, I kind of felt that set of emotions fall away like the old dead skin of a snake. He weren't so bad really. I got to see him every once in a while and he would always take me with him while he wandered with his blades sightseeing through the worst and most interesting parts of the port.

He always had quite the crew. Some of them were the Mormon Anglos who occupied what other parts of our earth weren't still ruled by dinosaurs, but a bunch of the rest were what he called tribesmen, from an earth called Dogpatch, where he had grown up. They were kind of on the wild side in that they couldn't read or write. They liked to use the hair of the human beings they had killed, as artful bits of decoration about their bodies, especially beautifully knotted belts and vests and hats. As we walked through town his bunch would fan out ahead and off to the side, ready to forestall any unofficial opposition from the gangs. My dad's purser made a present to any elements of the official opposition which we came across (police patrols in the city proper or spaceport guards in the tinsel town beside the spaceport ,where we mostly hung out),

To say I didn't feel much connection with my dad would be an under statement .We barely shared a language, I knew a fair bit of the Mormon lingo as this last century or so a whole bunch of them have been allowed in the city and dad spoke a couple of dialects of Roman. Unfortunately they weren't exactly my dialect, so talk between us was never really easy. He tried to show me a few things such as how to lay out your platoon for this and that, so they wouldn't get all shot out too quick, and how to take a city block by block, and that kind of thing. At eight years old, I didn't care all that much.

Mostly we wouldn't talk. We would walk around the space port and look at stuff, listen to the roar and smell the stinks, while we were jostled by hard men and soft women. Occasionally, one of Dads' men would catch a pickpocket but they never harmed them, More the opposite, they seemed warmed at the audacity, although it could be just that my dad had just warned them to be good. Occasionally some armed entrepreneurs would have a go at separating the purser from the sack he carried . They died.

One good thing about my dad and his whole crew was they had never heard of Tourette's disease, or swearing syndrome, so they didn't think of me in a negative way. They just thought I was one hay wire little dude, perfect for a captain's son. I already told you about how I bit the dog, well it happened when I was out with my dad.

Have you ever heard of a zoo? There was one near the spaceport, I was maybe seven years old on one of my first trips out and about with my dad and his bunch, when he took me to the zoo. He had never seen Cornholio, my amygdalic, hungry, violent, and profane self. My Tourette's Syndrome, nine times out of ten just produced bouts of swearing, but when he took me to the zoo old Cornholio got shaken out of slumber. There was a bridge which we walked across, with little grates on the footpath, through which I uneasily dropped stones. The sensation of height made me feel threatened and vaguely hungry. For me feeling hungry in unusual circumstances is a bad sign. It means Cornholio is coming.

When we got to the center of the bridge, we could hear the lions roaring in the distance, in their cages on the far bank of the river. I started wishing for a cheeseburger. I know the signs of Tourette's and I know the answer too. Even back then I knew that if I didn't get too freaked out the feeling would pass. I didn't want to embarrass myself in front of dad and his bunch. I did great, even the smell of the pungent tiger shit and the deep timber of the lion roars didn't wake Cornholio up.

I was damned proud of myself when we were homeward bound and I was skipping across the bridge ahead of the rest. I surprised a large dog which jumped towards me barking. Cornholio was out in a flash, and I had a hold of the dog, chewing on its left hindquarter, even though I personally thought this was rather a lousy idea. They got the dog loose from me with a little bit of difficulty, Cornholio bit one or two of them as well and dropped me in front of my dad with a little doggy blood running off my chin and foul words on my lips. They were all delighted. I even got a new name in that funny, really variant roman dialect the tribals speak on Dogpatch. I am called 'Bites Dogs'.

Well maybe I should advance this a few years. By the time I was fourteen years old, I was a pretty successful thug. I had a few followers --enough I could go most places in this town, I always find followers and I am a good talker. I have a few gifts that run in the family, you could say. I still went to school and not just to please my mom. What else is important? Well not much, I guess, but suddenly my dad decided to send me to down town Rome, as we called any of the original Romes where mankind had blasted off, to go to school. My mom concurred. She was way too young to have a son of my age. I was out of there like a watermelon seed.

Military schools should not be real. They should be like ogres, only for scaring kids. My dad did his level best to send me to one.

Thank god for Mom. Now I haven't mentioned mom much in this story and I won't. Her people have a code of silence. I cant see me any reason to break it right here. Daddy was rich. Daddy was a yokel. Daddy was a mark. Mom had another entire life. Dad thought that when he was off tending his other wives, Mom just sat around thinking about him. He didn't realize nothing about nothing. It wasn't too hard to get mom to spring me. We found a substitute, one of my cousins, and we sent his ass to military school. Mom was great, It was also necessary for me to disappear. So we sent me to the same downtown Rome, as my cousin, so I could keep tabs on my military career, in case any glitches came up.

The particular downtown Rome I got sent to was chose by my dad. He sent me where my grand dad had gone so young, and full of piss and vinegar in his desire to go to school. Dad hoped there was money out there somewhere, besides the cheques that were still sent to Bountiful. He gave me his dads journal and a bunch of family junk and papers of my granddad's. Me and my cousin didn't get ourselves kershnacked off the planet on the same day for fairly obvious reasons, so I was by myself on the journey to the prime.

The module I was seated in out on the field looked about a thousand years old. There was bubble gum on, and tatters in, the seats. We were kershnacked into space and then loaded in to the belly of the collection of girders that served as a Roman cargo ship and the atomics pushed us to that special speed, at that special spot, where the sun has just passed over, and where high speed meets space weakened by gravity and where we winked into otherwhen. The school was on the moon. I guess it would be respectful to tell you what little I know about my cousin, since his association with me killed him, but there is little I can tell you. He wasn't exactly a first cousin and I hardly knew him except to know he had done a lot better with the books than most of us.

Back in admin city, I had hardly known what he looked like, as most every time I saw him he was standing beside his beautiful sister and I never wasted one second looking at him. We got together only a few times and I cant' say he acted as if he liked me nor can I say I blame him, Our positions were kind of inherently false; I loafed and he worked. Also, because I was in a period of moral decay, especially after I had found the treasure, my grand dad's treasure. I found the stash of bleeding emeralds.

Arriving in one of the prime systems was pretty cool ,as was getting off the planet for the first time. No I don't mean being kershnacked around in a cargo container getting here but the moon itself. Back on Bountiful the moon is empty, in the primes it is a suburb. Nicely sculpted too, lots of glass and domes ,as well as warrens; and the warrens are done up so you would hardly know you were underground. Its where the rich people live. Did I mention my thug nature?

The first thing that hit me about the moon was its smell, It has one you know, damp and green it seemed to me, a bit like the inside of a terrarium. All of a sudden, I had the memory of being a little kid and of being taken from a cold sterile day into a brick building with lots of glass where there were tropical plants, butterflies and turtles thriving. There was an abundance of nice aromas, with the faint hint of something rotting in the background. It was a very relaxing smell. The temperature was tropical, because that was what the plants liked and on the moon the plants are everywhere. As I was young, it didn't take long to get my moon legs and start hanging out.

I didn't really know what to do with myself. For all my life, I had been in a milieu of many, many people whose lives I knew pretty intimately. Now I was alone. I considered getting some schooling but decided I would do it later. There was one slight problem with my previous grades. The books had been entirely cooked by my mom in order to impress my dad. Although I was rather extensively well-read due to my own inclinations, all the hard parts had been bought and paid for.

At least I had quite a bit of money enough to put up in a brand new lodging every might and to eat nothing but restaurant food, I thought that would continue to feel like paradise practically forever, but within a couple of months I got kind of tired of that too.

Even looking for trouble didn't work out. It wasn't the kind of place a kid could find trouble to get into. The port was nothing like back in sin city. It had official ships and company ships and rich guy ships of all sorts and descriptions, but none of the sort of luxury merchants that put down on Bountiful. The whole place reminded me of one of those malls in the rich neighborhoods. I was considering putting down on the planet, maybe even going to school just to have some people to hang out with, when I got to thinking about Grandpa's key.

My pa had given me a handful of stuff in a valise which had belonged to his dad. One of the articles was a plain electronic key, like one in a million, with a bunch of numbers along the top.

Its only claim to individuality was the words Moon Acres on a poker chip shaped key chain fob. It looked like it came from some hotel room. I had forgotten all about its having words on it at all, and was quite surprised to see them when I regarded them again several months later.

I was also surprised to see that even in my few months on the moon, the corny old name of Moon Acres was instantly recognizable. It was the richest suburb on a moon of suburbs. It was where the Roman government put the former leaders of countries or recently demoted generals. It wasn't a building, of course just a long stretch of serviced freeholds, each carved into the surface, and domed above with apple or olive orchards. fountains and ponds. Each one was the sort of place a person could relax with the family and twenty or thirty or a hundred servants or slaves, as the case may be.

I started wondering in my fifteen year old way, just what this key would open. Somebody's mailbox maybe? Could my grandad still have some sort of safety deposit box out there somewhere? I wondered who used it now, I got myself busted trying to find out. I used the box to google the details and then decided to go and have a look at the terminal.

Just getting from place to place on the moon is one of the more novel and interesting things about the whole joint. Being so light means you can solve things in lots of new ways, but even aside from that, just having laid out the place with electrics for inducing power in electric engines under every conceivable road and courtyard a person might want to run a vehicle, ie everywhere, was a cool idea.

Along with my telescopic cane, I carried my folding skateboard in my back pack everywhere I went. It had tiny little electric motors and big wide rough tires. When you threw it down on the asphalt it growled like a cat, as you kept it wheels lifted up with your back foot on the rear of it. It was a knack to step aboard it and for the first few meters you could feel it flux as it arrived at and passed the underground lines. They were pretty cool. On flat ground you could run your speed on up pretty fast. Most folks used vehicles of course, but pretty much not most of the young used skateboards. It was effortless, cool transportation. I personally really dug it and the run up to the Moon Acres Terminal promised as much fun as the destination itself.

I figured I wouldn't take the time this day, to follow my usual pursuits, when I crossed through town. I had already spent quite a bit of time haunting the spaceport area and had looked at the dead aliens in their diorama next to the stuffed animals, quite a few times. This was an excuse to get to the edge of the city where the dome went up and the exit port holes to the surface and to the underground tubes were located. It was more like an industrial area, most of it, you could see the slave compounds for the constructs except where the suburb communities were located, and in those areas due to the traffic it was like a mall. Lots of bustling and comings and going markets spices and little s hops catering to high end tastes. It was going to be a four hour ride up there. I was figuring on finishing my day in one of those rich little tea shops, with a plate of oysters in front of me, caught down on the planet. Each equal to what I would normally lay for a meal served by one of those intriguing, blackish ,busty and well-bummed women who ran the shop. I had been up there a few times before when I had not thought of Moon Acres as being of significance to myself.

There were about a thousand people going in and out and everyone flashed a key like I had in front of a screen as they went. I knew from googling around on the box that this might be a pretty interesting building to have access to , from a thug nature sort of way, even if grandpa were long gone. So, after a few surreptitious walk-bys I put on a hat and glasses to obscure my looks from the camera over the door and walked up gave it a try. I walked on thru the open door. As soon as I walked through. I felt a big beefy hand grab me from either side and the key was plucked from my grip. Two guys built like tree trunks, were marching me across a large open area towards a small door which I knew would be marked security. I didn't struggle. Struggling is just the kind of thing that wakes Cornholio up. I needed somebody thoughtful, calm and cerebral in charge at the moment.

There was a lieutenant inside having a look on the screen at the last twenty minutes of my life. There were real good photos of me skulking back and forth in front of the building and some especially great ones of me standing just around the corner up the street, hiding my braids under my a hat and putting on my shades. I had been a bit goofy to think that a target like this wouldn't have a few more cameras about than I could easily see.

The two beefy individuals sat me down in a chair, but they didn't take their hands off my arms. It was a tense moment. I was feeling kind of vaguely hungry. That is always a bad sign, so I focused in on Cornholio by reviewing just how good and confident I felt about the present situation. Cornholio went back to snoozing. The lieutenants first impression of me was that I was a young thug on the prowl. He was right of course, but he managed to convince himself otherwise. It was a pretty dicey conversation, giving him my name and number and having him dial up my particulars on the screen.

First thing up was a nice picture of my cousin from two years back. It must have looked close enough to me to pass. The next thing he picked out was that I was just entering the very same military college he had attended. I could see the stiffness go out of his gaze. He had decided to have a nice nostalgic talk about the school he had graduated from only a few years back and to let me off. It was a bitch. I had never set foot in the place and didn't know one prof from the other.

I am excellent with talking to people. It's a family gift. I managed to pull it off. I could tell it was over when he asked where I had 'found' the key. I decided to tell him the truth . I told him a little bit about my Granpa. Now that he was my friend, the lieutenant took my key and waved the beefy individuals out of the room. He waved the key in front of a screen on his desk and I watched in fascination to see what the bar code brought up.

Five minutes later he was calling me 'sir'. I was a client and had been given my key back. The lieutenant was dead set as the company's agent, on taking the tube with me out to Granddads' freehold, in case of any problems, and just generally so he could keep kissing my ass. I was just as determined to ditch him for two very good reasons. For one, my pretended familiarity with his school could fall apart dangerously any time, and for another I had no idea what would find in Granpa's old shack. I have never seen any reason to trust any of my relatives to be legit. I didn't want to wander around with a company agent through the remnants of Granpa's combo still and meth lab or whatever else he had going.

I got rid of him. I wasn't expecting the stiffs. I better explain that freeholds are extraterritorial --kind of like renting a mini country for a hundred years or so. Really rich people deposed tyrants and generals and that kind of riff raff, like to be subject to no law but their own . It's safer that way. Grand dad was paid up for a hundred and a half years and until it was up, nobody except agents of his, had the right to enter. An d nobody had.

I got to know my Grand daddy pretty good . I lived in his house and read his books. I also had his computer hacked so I could examine his dealings in minute detail, To put it succinctly, Grandpa was a rube. He brought too much money to too dangerous a place. He got swallowed up by a bigger fish. He wasn't Roman. He should have had somebody hold his hand. I didn't want to disturb any watchers , but I did google up where every last shred of his cash money went , just to make sure there wasn;t a big poke in a bank somewhere just waiting for me.

It looked like a fairly straight forward kidnap or hit, gone somewhat wrong. There were a few stiffs at the entrance way where the assassins had entered, and then out in the grove there were the bones of assassins sprinkled from here to next week As far as I can tell, all the bodies I have found are those of the attackers or at least, all so far were killed by Granpa's guns, Ever heard of a browning semi-automatic shot gun or perhaps a semi- automatic 22?

I kind of severely doubt it. My family invented them. They are projectile weapons, and while I know that sounds antique like a sling shot or a bow and arrow in certain conditions, such as if you are being chased over a twenty acre wood with dense undergrowth by a bunch of men with energy guns, they can be extremely handy to own. Anyway, it didn't work out too well for the assassins. Grandpa was a rube and he didn't understand business and he more or less traded the cow for the magic beans , but he did like and understand guns.

Grandpa had a couple of nice ships named the Lancelot and the Guinevere, just the sort for the luxury trade, He had put himself through enough schooling to be able to maintain and fly them. He left in one and never came back, and the other was still sitting in its hangar. I don't know what happened to Grandpa right then , but I now know he wasn't planning on staying gone, as he left some of his jewels behind. I inherited his crib. I figured the odds were pretty good Grandpa had managed to scoop up most of his loot before he left but that wasn't going to stop me from looking.

The first night was kind of spooky. I was really conscious of the stiffs all over the place. I hadn't quite decided what to do with them. I slept with the lights on. There was plenty of maybe seventy year old food about, a lot of it a looking as fresh as when it was irradiated and put in the bag. I was still so spooky I settled for beer and peanuts. I passed out cool calm and collected. After a few hours, I woke up to take a pee, and found an extra stiff in the bathroom which I hadn't previously noticed , It scared the stuff out of me and woke Cornholio up. I didn't actually get back to sleep until he had said every swear word *we* knew, beat up a waste basket and a paper dispenser and started to cook himself a half century old cheese burger. I at least got him back to sleep before I had to eat it. I hadn't seen Cornholio for more than a year, and I had hoped that just maybe I could be growing out of him although the doctors had said they hadn't heard that Tourette's Syndrome follows that pattern much. I was so lonely that night I was glad to see him.

In the morning I made a serious search for all stiffs on the whole premises, not counting the grove. They were mummies rather than bodies and almost weightless. I stacked them like chord wood in a store room, and closed the door. Then, I searched the place again, looking under all the beds an extra time ---then again, and then again after a couple more days and then maybe a couple more times after that. I had to force myself to quit searching for stiffs. The place was spooky as all Hell, but it was way too cool to pass up. Early on I noticed that my message board by the tube shaft door was all lit up with new messages from the management.

My lieutenant friend had been busy helping me out by ringing bells for me. Various people were at my service. There was also a nice ass -kissing letter from my lieutenant friend, explaining to me how this great establishment works and letting me know that there weren't any services being offered to me that I would be expected to pay for, In other words the food was free. I ordered a hamburger with fries and a coffee and took them out of the slot when they appeared.

Life was good. I just about figured for certain there were jewels about the place, but I also knew I was unlikely to find them by mucking about. There were twenty acres of domed woods up on top and half a dozen levels down below. Grand dad had only used one of the levels but he could have hid things on any of them . These freeholds could be decked out to service a couple of hundred people. The hiding places were endless. I figured I had one thing in my favor. From the sound of his journals my grand dad liked to run his fingers through his jewels and giggle pretty frequently. If they were still there I figured I could eventually find them.

The ship was the best they make. If she had been in imperial service she would have been a research ship, or a scout , as fast as your bones could stand the grav, and entirely planetary worthy. She could be taken anywhere in the system, or anywhen within it too. I had long talks with her captain. Her Name was

Guinivere She was the virtual captain, and greeted me when I boarded the ship courteously asking me how she could help. When I suggested I was her new boss she asked me for my captains password and refused to budge.

I promptly put all idea of flying her out of my head and went back to emerald prospecting. As often as not, I ended up back talking to that hologram of the pretty captain and shooting the breeze. She had as good a pretend persona as any I ever saw, and because she googled all our conversation contents on the web as she chatted she was a pretty cool search engine. We had an arrangement. If I used the password in the course of normal conversation with her she would point it out. It didn't break the rules. She also told me that if I did break the rules, i.e. by trying to fire the ship up, or change her directives she was going to lock down all the doors turn off the lights and hold her breath. I didn't want her to do that..

I had ten or twenty brilliant ideas to try every day and came on over and tried them out. Everything from 'open sesame' to 'rumplestiltskin' and the names of the apostles, back to front and front to back. I 'homeyed' Granpa's place up quite a bit. I couldn't handle living in a place with bodies in the closet, so after a couple of weeks I screwed up my courage and carried them out and buried them in the grove.

I wasn't able to do much about the the bare skulls with the SSG holes and occasional limb bones which kept popping up scattered throughout the wood, so I let them lie. The burial didn't help much as I still got the heeby- jeebies and the golly-woggles at night and ended up looking for more stiffs

I decided to move on board the ship. I was having a beer that evening, and considering that captain Guinevere was a pretty good looking gal. I tried to fiddle about with the avatar attributes to see if I could make her shuck her duds, but I set off an alarm and turned to find her staring straight at me with an arm straight out. I felt very much on the spot, and stammered and excused my way out until the alarm ceased and the arm went down. I didn't try it again for quite a while.

It was actually a pretty cozy living space. Grandpa's ship didn't have the feel of a haunted place. Except maybe by my granddad, as his beers were still in the cooler and his PC sitting on the lunch table in the galley. It looked like he too had spent lots of time hanging out here with Guinevere, but she wouldn't tell me about that until I found the bloody password. Until then me and Guin weren't going to get real intimate. I used that computer to pretty much trace granddads financial downfall . Nowhere in it did it mention the location of any possible jewels or the passwords of either of his ships

Its hard to describe my grand dad's place. He had obviously put in quite a few years on this spot and he hadn't always been alone . There were quite a few suites which had been occupied years back. He seemed to have had pretty weird tastes - fake grottos and fountains all over the place, with all kinds of Corinthian and Ionian columns that held nothing up. Sort of a fake ruin with modern living arrangement hidden within. As you walked around, you expected to run across Cleopatra in her bath, but for all I knew at that time, maybe these joints all came like that.

His twenty acre wood up top, also had a bunch of shacks in it which had also seen quite a bit of use. The critters in his forest were still represented. Even after many decades hiatus, hawks and weasels still killed squirrels,and turtles ,still basked beside the trout pond. It was a nice habitat, nothing like Bountiful where me and Grandpa were both from. It was right relaxing to have critters around that didn't bite you when you slept, unlike the city rats which plagued all roman countryside, or the little nasty compsagnathous dinosaurs that colonized sin city a century or so ago and we had been unable to get rid of. Another sign of our decline I now suppose,

I was surprised to see what a mess the planet was. Plagues were swirling across it. It was falling apart in half a dozen other ways. It was infested with Egg men . Of course I know that now but I had no idea of that then. What do you need to know about Eggmen to keep this narrative rolling.? Well I will tell you all I then knew. We figured they were a funny little trick by the aliens to lay us low.

Some while ago, they released some intentionally mutated stock into the human gene pool. This genetic stock carries several beneficial attributes, so it was likely to become widespread, and then when a lot of people carry the genes and begin to intermarry, it begins to infrequently produce another morphology. Egg men. Egg men are nasty. They are group mind and they steal the bodies of males who are related to them. When they steal the mind of a baby, the independent self just doesn't develop. When they steal the mind of an adult male near relation, like me, they break his mind. Mloko is lucky they just hijacked his body and chopped him up for grub. He wasn't kin.

With me, they would have controlled my mind and taught me to love them. Their control over non -relations is kind of limited . Good enough that if the wrong person, here and there , opens the door on a creche, they can just change his thoughts and send him on his way or sit him down with an overwhelming desire to think about his tax returns while he waits for his executioner like Mloko did..

I have one advantage most people don't have. Cornholio. Cornholio hates Eggmen. The moon isn't a prime sort of place for an Egg man infestation to get underway , few or no uncontrolled places or people and too many cameras observing every nook and cranny. As well, there were few uncontrolled entrances into the place where strangers can wander in. It would be perhaps a tough nut for them to crack, although I have no doubt that as the end of this system was so near, the moon too, was certainly already full of their agents. Single nutted triple nippled men like myself probably weren't to be trusted. I had no idea of all that. After I found the jewels and the password I was mostly just focusing in on the joy of youth.

Then they took me out. It was a messy hit. Cousin Marco got sliced and diced by three opponents with energy weapons, a day or two after pop's keg with the eggmen stuffed in salt, arrived at his door. The next day there was a serious accident at his school and the science department there was blown to smithereens. Over the next couple of weeks most of Marco's closest teachers and friends had serious accidents. The Eggmen are very public relations conscious. They missed me.

I had no idea what was happening at the time until dad's journal arrived in the mail, with the info that I was awaiting some stiffs packed in salt, mailed direct to my colleges science department. I guess the keg of stiffs just ended up arriving first. Daddy is smart but he wasn't raised in a city, or ever really lived in one; so while he is smart, he don't have 'smarts'. Dad was and is a rube. A yokel. Before I get too far ahead in this story, I guess I have got about a year to fill in.

So there I was dreaming of treasure and passwords hangout out at Grandpa's old ranch. I was living a solitary existence and most of the talking I did every day was with Guinivere, in hopes I would run across her password. I had got into kind of a rhythm in my life. It warn't many weeks along before I realized that if I got out into the city once a day to interact with normal people, at least somewhat I was better off for it. I took on learning to fly in the domes, although I have never been one to engage in sports- which include sudden scares, or rough housing, which might wake Cornholio up. But, as every kid or even visitor who wasn't moon born took up the sport, I did too.

It was as easy as falling off a cliff and that is just how you got started. You put on a set of wings and jumped off with a couple of instructors to keep you from killing yourself the first couple of tries. I loved flying above the city under the central dome catching the warm uplifts or diving down and then working back up under the power of my own arms. I also took up the dune buggies. I loved it out on the surface tearing up the sand in our vehicles. It is fair to medium dangerous, the vehicles themselves are pretty safe ,but you have to watch your ass for dumped radiation, and try not to hit rocks or topple off edges, or hit fine dust and get bogged down. People have been relying on atomics for a long while here, and they think no more of just taking waste out and dumping it on the surface than my pa does of having a crap in the bush. The alien station was also what kept drawing me out there.

The alien station was immense, and even after eons of time passing it was better than fifty percent intact. The superstructure which had jutted into the sky like a tooth was smashed to smithereens leaving sky scraper sized bits strewing a fifty click area, but the broken base of the tooth still rose a tiny bit above the horizon, and underneath the ground much rested of an interesting nature . It had been mined of its metal and its artifacts to be sure, most of it about 2000 years back ,but by now even the abandoned leavings a of these early Romans was pretty interesting stuff.

We were trying to salvage a fifteen hundred year old vehicle, and bring her back for our club to work on and modify into some kind of haywire hybrid dune buggy. I had joined a club.[only soon to be dead people go dune buggying alone on the moon, and as a result there aren't very many of them around.] It was a pretty interesting venture. I was a bit of an odd guy out as usual, but it didn't matter too much here, as we each had our own buggies [mine was rented], and most of our communication was by radio except when we met at the hangar .They were a pretty straitlaced bunch ;mostly engineering students a few years older than me, and even though I got out on the town with them quite a few times I never got to know any of them well.

I never brought anybody home to Granpa's ranch. I continued to work on my puzzles. Pretty soon it became apparent to me that I couldn't just walk around all day looking under rocks and in random cupboards for jewels. As far as the ship password went I was sure that ultimately there must be some way to break in. My problem was that if I asked people who could probably help me, such as my dad or some of moms uncles, those helpers would certainly also take the ship away from me, and they wouldn't even feel bad about it

I was only fifteen and they wouldn't think twice. It wouldn't be a straight rip off, in their minds they would be doing me a favor until I grew up a bit. I didn't want any part of it. I ended up going back to school. Sort of.

Captain Guinevere was my teacher. I decided to learn to look after my ship. She taught me the courses, and they were credit courses too. I even got diplomas. Training crew is what a virtual captain is for as well as operational advice of course. I was really proud of them (my diplomas) beyond what you would really expect, but for me, it was my first schooling experience where I knew I really earned the marks. My mom hadn't cooked the books behind my back in order to please my dad with my brilliance.

It was a pretty good year. It is pretty anticlimactic how I got the password and found the jewels. I was sitting in the galley getting ready to go out when I realized I had misplaced my key. I looked for half an hour or so and then I realized I could use my new found familiarity with the ships systems to find it. I had recently learned there were cameras about, and I just asked Guin to run up on the screen a shot of my activities when I first came aboard that afternoon.. There I was, putting the key on a plate on the table, and then a little later a half eaten donut on top of the key, then a little later ,the key in the compost bin with the donut.

The next morning I woke up smart, and asked Guinevere to fire up the cameras record, starting with the first time my Granpa entered the galley. She had no problem. The ships command deck and forecastle would have been classified info, but the galley where it turned out that my Granpa had spent most of his time; was fine for me to view. It only took a few days of watching before he coughed up the password. It was no real surprise to find the jewel stash on board Guinevere, it was easily the most logical spot.

It looks like Gramps kept half his polk on each of the ships. Once I could watch my grand dads daily activities, it was even easier to trace his fall, a bad choice of partner. Then he let that partner lay a beautiful woman on him who he had the silliness to marry. It was painful to watch. For a while he had lots of paper bucks and a real financial empire but the lost them all except for his secret polk on the two ships. I got to know my grandad really good. He reminds me of my dad but not too much of me. There are times I am really glad I was born a roman citizen with city smarts.

So that's about it, a year down the line I had the password, I had the jewels and I was about one third of the way through courses that would allow me to do my own ship maintenance. I really had the feeling Guinevere was proud of me and I did make her shuck her duds in the hologram. I must have really needed to get out. Then they killed Marco. Until dads letter arrived with his journal I had no idea what was up. After dad's letter arrived me and Guinevere did some research and the world got a lot scarier.

I needed some help. Dad was out. Sure he would come? Maybe even in person which would definitely be worst, on account of his being his fathers son, he might have some confused idea that I had just found our treasure and I surely didn't see it that way. Another choice was uncle Julio. I guess I might as well call him a gangster. He didn't own ma's bar but he protected it, and he helped mom manage my dad ,.getting my grades faked, and having Marco replace me in school.

He was a really big man in our community, and I was pretty sure he would get involved. Marco used to be his son. Could I trust him? Probably not. I was family, but not close enough. He wasn't a real uncle and his beautiful daughter wasn't really even a second cousin of mine. She was most of ten years older than me, and the most beautiful woman I knew. She knew me well enough to detest that a bug like me even dared to look at her. Such are the things that life is made of. I only knew of one other powerful individual who I could perhaps ensnare in my web .Granpa's partner. He was still alive. He was even a neighbor- he lived on the moon ; a rich and powerful man beyond the likes of my dad, the skipper, or my uncle Don Julio. They were little fish. I googled him up. to get the size of him. I liked what I saw.

Now I want all you people here to notice that I could have bugged out, I had several fortunes in jewels and a good ship. I could have bugged out. I could have run. I didn't need to try to save your asses. I decided to fight. I sent uncle Julio the Don a message saying his son had been killed, giving the details of my fortune, and asking for his daughters hand in marriage, in order that I could trust him enough to invite him into my organization as a partner. I spelled it right out. There don't need to be any hard feelings in a negotiation like this, and he took none. I didn't mention the Eggmen, but I did mention that my first priority, after marrying his daughter, was to welcome in a hit squad of his choosing to help .

To my dad, I sent a letter that also didn't mention Eggmen, but saying that Marco had been hit and Uncle Julio was sending out a hit squad to rectify the matter. Could he just please send out a couple of blades, as I wasn't entirely sure that uncle Julio wasn't going to rectify me as well. I finally got some company. Carmellita brought me her dad's reply personally and Dad sent me a couple of blades for my personal protection.

My people slap each other a lot, or at least the women slap the men. I am not sure what it's all about exactly, but when I met Carmellita as she arrived she slapped me right off my feet. I could see she wasn't too happy about the whole situation but it was evident she had really enjoyed smacking me down ,so I didn't give up all hope too quick. When we got alone she laid it out to me just as straightforward as I had laid it out to her dad in the letter. She was willing to marry me (her lip trembled a bit as she said it.) but her dad had promised her that if she still didn't want me after a years trial he would have me hit. I said that was just fine with me and kissed ass egregiously until I got her in the sack. We signed the marriage papers she brought with her first..

My dad's blades arrived next, and uncle Julio's hit team a week after that. The story I laid out was that Mr. Bad was my grand dad's ex partner, and we weren't going to kill him. It was going to be a snatch so we could extract some of his cash. We had one ace in the hole. Mr.X lived on a freehold on good old impregnable Moon Acres. We were already inside the outer defenses. We were going to pull a hit on him, much like the one he had paid to be pulled on granpa years back. I let my father in laws men plan and execute the hit

It took a couple of months planning and then a wait while some particulars fell into place. They were professionals and pretty soon they picked him up without even rustling his feathers. I wanted him to like us.

Most of Papa Julio's thugs had left for Bountiful, and Carmellita was doing some intimate planning about how she was going to pull our captives legs off for killing her brother, when I told her the truth. I got slapped again of course, but she was a smart girl and put the parts together really fast. I was trying to save our species. We were small fish. We needed Mr. Big to help us. He was going to finance our operation. She was on my side. She was already having trouble climbing into her jeans. She loved me. Thank god for oxytocin.

My Granddad's ex partner was a pretty interesting dude. He looked not much older than my dad, although I knew he was older than granpa had been, he must have got rich enough to start his shots early on. I knew he hadn't been just born rich, in fact I knew a great deal about him as the camera had sat like a fly on the wall during his years of informal conversations with my dad in the ships galley ,until the honey pot had arrived, and my dad had fallen in love and moved out to live in the quasi ruin with all the columns that she dreamed up. She was quite the honeypot. I admired my Granpa's taste at the same time as I squirggled at his incredulity.

She got placed on the scene by my Grandad fortuitously rescuing her from thugs, as corny a set up as can possibly be imagined, but he never twigged, nor did he ever notice the double entendres between her and his partner .It was all over his head, but it wasn't over mine. He was a pretty cool operator, seriously old, wise, rich ,and powerful and I wanted his help. I didn't have any idea at the time that he might have been on their side. I could have just as easily have hit one of the renegades who had been broken and turned, and who were silently running most of the show for the Eggmen, but I didn't. I lucked out, he was just plain human, and only evil in the sense that an old crocodile is so. It also turned out he was already sort of on my side. He already knew about the Eggmen and had for many years

I couldn't trust him of course. He had organized himself a pretty comfy life, and I am sure he would have walked over our dead bodies to return to it if given a chance, but pretty soon he knew he wasn't going to get that chance. Julio's minders were good. Kidnapping is a thriving business lots of places. I say that on account of what I really went to say, which is that my family is experienced at kidnapping, sounds too compromising, but I will try hard to tell the truth. Julio's men were experienced at keeping high class prisoners, perhaps even Royals, who must be well treated until let loose. He rotated his men back to Bountiful, but only one at a time so I always had a serious five man team for feeding watering and monitoring our prisoner, as well as personal guards for me and the missus. We treated our captive like a canary and we made sure his cage was nicely gilded and fun to be in. His guards acted like his servants, and he never heard a harsh word. Every now and again, I would come over for a visit, always knocking and asking ahead just like he had a choice. He finally came around to liking and enjoying me, I could tell that much, but I never could trust him. He was the kind of dog that wags his tale while he bites. Even right off the bat, we had a few interests in common, in that he didn't want my ship to go down beneath the waves while he was still aboard it, so he was willing to cough up lots of money. He undertook to tell me what he knew about the Egg men, most of which I have already told to you, except maybe that his main reason for killing Granpa, rather than asking him in, was that Granpa had that extra nipple. The organization Granpa's partner belonged to knew that men with extra nipples could not be associated with. As he told me, in the end he was only obeying an ordered hit, and as far as my Granpa went, he looked me straight in the eyes and asked if I would have rather seen him broken and hag ridden. To him and the men he worked with, any man with three nipples was a horse waiting to be ridden. They killed them on principal 'more or less' ,the way he told it, but I remembered what I had seen of how my Granpa got betrayed by his friendly, elder adviser and kept my opinions to myself.

It wasn't a great moment when I realized that the only organization which I knew to be aware of, and opposing the Eggmen was also engaged in wiping out guys like me. Did I mention Carmellita went to university for years and all that stuff? No, probably not. Well she has an education and she had an idea I never would have had.

Instead of pirates and thugs, she had this idea about getting into contact with scientists. I was pretty skeptical, telling her I had never heard that much good about them. I got slapped again, she has her doctorate, and right about then she called me an irresponsible juvenile and started planning our whole campaign.

I don't know exactly how it happened , but suddenly I wasn't in the drivers seat any more. Oh well. She did the right thing for sure, and it worked in the end ,as far as that went. In the beginning, when she set up the foundation, I had my nose right put out. She started out the way any sensible person ought to. She set up a defensible base and hired brains (lots of them) and they set out to secure the moon. It worked out pretty good . Along the line I didn't have a clue about the day to day running of the organization. There were good reasons . It was ok. I had a fun little kid to look after (my daughter, named Juliette after her moms dad) and lots of servants to help, so I didn't actually have to change nappies at all.

I was one fine little house husband. Carmellita was running things. She had her dad's organizational touch, plus a science education. I was lucky she liked me with all my three-nippled alien charm. I was grateful to grand dad , that even in my ten year younger than her, scrawny uneducated way, I was still a hootchy-kootchy man, and my finger was on her trigger. Plus, of course, we both loved the kid.

I was a great dad as seeing as I was so young,only just twenty when she was four. I was damned near as interested in things like elephants as she was. That's how the Egg men got me. Also on the good side I was still boss of the flyer and I had never been loopy enough to divulge Guinevere's code to Carmellita or anyone else although I had made arrangements she would receive it in straight order if I met with mishap. I recriminated long and hard before I told her this last bit.

I was the captain, and had put together a crew, but in those early days we hardly flew. There was a problem. The captain [me] was certain to join the enemies' cause if I came anywhere near them. That itself put a real big crimp in things. I couldn't be trusted. And it wasn't just on board the flyer that I couldn't trust myself. There were Eggmen on the moon as well. Not lots, as I mentioned before, space life doesn't lend to creches being established in a surreptitious way in established places ,but that didn't say anything about their ability to buy up and take over mining camps and places like that or their setting up their own separate enclaves. Compared to the big blue green ball up above us we had a really light infestation.

Until Carmellita and her gang started kicking apart their hornets nests, they weren't even mostly mixed in with the general population. When our clean up campaign started, a lot of them ran for earth, because that's where the nearest creches were. I got picked up by a crew moving on through town, escorting a cargo container full of egg heads to one of the Jacob's Ladders.

They were a full battery of a dozen heads heading Earth bound and away from our pogrom. Their tails would have been between their legs if they had any tails or legs. They would have looked comatose as they lay there, all eyes closed and all snuggly in their little beds in the dark. Really they were staring out through the minds of their escorts and picking through the brains around them within a couple of block radius. They were in a dangerous situation and they knew it ,being transported through town virtually undefended , as somebody (Carmellita and co.) had blown out the dome of their mining camp and they had to run for it. Common sense said that I should have stayed out on Grand dad's ranch but I went to see the elephants and the dead alien one more time. I had lived on the moon, after all, for a long while. I felt safe there, and I don't think even Carmellita knew that her successful efforts had temporarily filled up downtown of the city near the Jacob's Ladder and the pleasure gardens with refugee Eggheads. Nothing looked any different.

It had been a secret war. It had to be. You might think the first thing to do was to get on the box and yell bloody murder and get everybody looking under their beds. There was a problem. We were on the moon and if we tried to blow the big secret, there were half a dozen hag ridden public entities on the surface of the planet who could send up a bunch of missiles and blow out our domes. They were very public relations conscious. They throve in the dark, like cockroaches.

In the mind of the Egg men, we needed the moon to remain thought of as "not yet conquered territory." We couldn't start to be known as the enemy. We had to wait it out. It didn't look like the Eggmen were able to maintain a society which could throw missiles for long.

They were too single minded for one thing, whenever they took over an organization such as a city government , that government became really good at producing creches, and really lousy at providing things like clean drinking water, food to the masses, education and garbage collection. Cholera, smallpox, and typhus, the plagues of the past were suddenly everywhere again. Most of the smarts on the Eggmen's side of things was provided by guys like me. Renegades we were called although that isn't hardly fair when you are dealing with a biological imperative. It is two and a half nippled men like me who got captured and learned to love the brother bond who provide most of their smarts.

The Eggmen themselves and those whose bodies they take over at birth never go to school or do much directly. They are a parasitic form.

On the blue green orb above us it was working pretty good. Three nippled men got really unpopular with our organization pretty fast. Then later they got really unpopular with Moonies generally. We never entirely got rid of the Eggmen, even on the moon. They are like lice and I think we will still be picking nits from our hair for generations to come. What that means is that any and every three nippled man may at some point start working for the enemy and try to set up a creche of his own and father some Eggmen. We are nasty. Nobody likes us. Growing up back on Bountiful I never heard of a three nippled person who wasnt family, but here on the moon we were running about four percent of the male population.

Getting rid of us wasn't a scientific decision. It didn't purify the gene pool or anything like that. There was still all those girl relatives out there ,who were unknowingly just waiting for their very own hootchy-kootchy man so they could have an Eggman baby as well. It would have seemed fairer if they had given us the women (ten gals to every guy) but they didn't, in fact they just barely stopped short of slicing all of our throats in an overnight frenzy. When I got back from the planet, it was pretty much a done deal. We were all being expelled . It was my fault. I got interested in stuffed aliens and live elephants and let my mind get taken off the ball. I got scooped and joined the brother bond.

The dead aliens had always intrigued me. Two had been found drifting around in space in one of the otherwhens, and once their existence had become known several specimens had been collected, all of the same two individuals of course. When you are connected to otherwhens, there really aren't just one or two of anything ,even I guess of you and me, but that's about as easy to understand as the idea that there really is no firstness or secondness in the universe, and that whether something comes first or second ,is just an artifact of where you observe it from.

Personally it was that very bit which made me think scientists must be highly overrated if they could swallow something like that, and this then led to me following my thug nature in some career choices around age twelve. Anyway, there were a couple of dead aliens even at the rather low end spectacle that was provided in the pleasure gardens. These particular pleasure gardens were a long ways from the pleasure gardens by the spaceport my dad used to take me to, with its tents set up helter-kelter beside ships and all the wares on display. There was a spaceport with a Jacob's Ladder beside it, but the market was a building like any other, not a tent city. It was stuffed full of standard store bought luxuries, not contraband.

There was a slave market too, something which Bountiful had lacked. The circus/zoo/museum combination was a way more interesting proposition than the markets. Right next to it was a trade show of genetically altered humans on display and for sale. They were constructs like my dad's Bobo, but these constructs were special purpose jobs and looked a lot less human. Most people don't see constructs much so they drew a crowd. They even had a couple of aquatic ones in what seemed to be a much too small tank.

In the museum itself, there was a gallery with all kinds of stuffed critters, and quite a few live ones on display. I was mostly interested in the dead alien and Juliette most interested in the live baby elephants. It was a nicely laid out little museum. There would be four or five dead stuffed critters in dioramas, and then they would slip one in on you where the turtles and crocs would move, and you would suddenly realize it was be made up of live animals.

There were lots of live monkeys and birds. It was an ever so entertaining place, and the animals seemed well adjusted and cared for. Even the hyena didn't seem to mind his iron collar. He had a life time of bones, and a comfy spot to lie and crack them. It had been a while since these particular elephants had seen the jungle. They were heavily genetically modified, and had been produced for the luxury pet and curiosity trade. They were itsy bitsy teeny weeny elephants

The heaviest one weighed about fifteen kilo. His name was Vince. He was in a small back paddock where he was undergoing a noisy, uncomfortable and dangerous state of glandular arousal known as must. He was ornery and miserable, and he had lost one quarter of his body weight, but ,the keepers explained in their video presentation ' it would be over soon'. The baby elephants weighed maybe from five pounds for the littlest ,on up to ten kilos or so ,where they were mostly grown up. Vince's five ladies and their kids were what comprised most of the circus.

It was a cool place to come. There aren't many animals in Admin City where I was from on Bountiful. Most every family has a mongoose for killing snakes rats and lizards (government orders) and there are a few dogs and cats and that is about it. The rest of Bountiful has lots of animals, but none of them are nice, or at least not cuddly.

We had lots of fun. We both missed it a bunch when it stopped seeming really safe to go to. One morning I just got up figuring what was the point of being rich if you couldn't just whip out to the spaceport and buy your daughter a couple of miniature elephants to let tear around in our twenty acre wood.

Its lucky I didn't tell Juliette before I went, because she didn't get the baby elephants, and she more or less lost her daddy too.

I spilled the beans on our whole operation, in so much as I knew it to spill ,and in the limited that they had to drag it out of me. As if they had to drag it out. I loved the brotherhood from the moment I felt the bond. Its not like having someone in your mind you know, its more like having a big consciousness come sit down beside you and invite you in. It is warm and comfy in the brother bond. The masters know how to turn on our endorphins to make us happy, and our oxytocin to make us love and trust, and of course our steroids to make us fearless. It is pretty cool, you never need to be alone or unhappy again, and all those difficult questions are right out of your hands. In the end, if you are a successful little three- nippled renegade, you too could father a creche. I know all about them. I was on their web .

I had just left the tube terminal and thrown my skateboard down on the ground and was gradually getting into the center fastest lanes (it was a long ownhill stretch and the little motors were getting a boost from gravity) when they came past and scooped me up. One minute I was working for myself and the next I was part of a crew. I didn't even break my stride which was good, as I was going thirty kliks on a skateboard on top of cement' There was a little yellow van beside me the same as used to transport construct workers but instead of having constructs manacled and sedated in their comfy stalls this one had a battery of eggheads. The other members of the crew welcomed me in my head to our fun adventure. Harry was a family man of about fifty five, with a loving wife, two teen age kids and a bad heart. He had been on his way to a doctor, when he had intersected with our little cavalcade. He was driving a little family vehicle out front and he was our point man. He was having a heck of a good time I felt a lot of liking for him. The driver of the truck with the egg head creche was a different article, He was creche bred. He didn't actually have a mind. The little armless egg heads in the back were doing their own driving. Out back was a kid my age or a little younger, name of Tommy ,in a buggy he was awfully proud of. He was happy as all get out too, but underneath it all he wasn't feeling too good. He had taken a slice at the last roadblock and all the endorphins and steroids the master could make his body pump out, weren't entirely killing it There was another road block coming up.

Our masters were observing it from several points of view occupied by susceptible individuals in the crowds nearby. Up ahead of us the masters could see a parked truck at the side with its electric motor humming, the drivers seat was empty. I pulled up next to it, flipped my skateboard in my backpack and hopped in. The passenger started to complain ,so I put a blade through his eyeball. I pulled out in front of the little yellow slave wagon. For a while it looked like the plan was for me to ram our way through, [I would have died], but as we got closer, and the masters were able to pick over our people resources ,they found a better way.

There was one bad moment a block or so before, when the masters noticed some of the opposition arriving from a side street, but they were able to have Fred take a left turn and head on their big vehicle with his little family rig. They stopped but he died. The masters were pleased . I was too. I pulled up to the roadblock, but the fella who looked in was under tight control. He wasn't even a relative, but with a battery of heads ten feet away, he could be used. He looked in at me, and never noticed my dead passenger or the blood. He looked at the blank piece of paper I offered him , and read authorization for two trucks from the next roadblock up the way. He waved us into the ferry traffic heading for the port, and we found safety in a giant parking lot waiting for a lift. It was a long wait for me and Tommy. It wasn't safe to get out and wander around ,so we couldn't eat or crap, and we just stayed sitting in one place for eighteen hours. I wasn't bored or lonely. Me and Tommy were in brotherly contact, and he was way worse off than me. It was also fun to listen to the masters traffic, I too could look out through the eyes of those they momentarily touched in the crowds around us, and I got to meet a couple of people who they grabbed hold of just in case. There was a doctor four cars up, although I never got to see his face, except in his own mirror, as the masters asked him to do something which led to his death when a few spaceport guards looked like they might be about to start doing some checks in our area. It was an interesting, eventful night, but in the tropical temperature, by morning my passenger had begun to stink, and I was beginning to feel hungry, and nothing the masters twigged seemed to shut it off.

When we finally drove on board and lifted off nobody told me to belt up so I never bothered, and when we kerschnacked I busted my nose hard against my steering wheel. That made me even hungrier. Exit from the spaceport at earth was easier. The masters were relaxed and content. We were in controlled territory where maybe one cop in four, plus lots of other people all around us were willing to die at our disposal. We had the mayors the ward bosses ,and the officers in the army.

We were home. The masters were newly in contact with their earth buddies, as far as mind to mind contact between batteries was concerned, and I got to hear it all told . It looked like Carmellita was doing a great job. Lots of simultaneous strikes at most of the big creches. We were assigned a nice new prefab creche outside the city, and me, Tommy and the Eggmen drove our rigs out there. It was a nice prefab outfit. It looked like they were making lots, and the Eggmen liked how it had been positioned outside a rustic little berg ,where statistical studies had decided that there were lots of our kin.

Two men in ten were ours for the taking. Its like a giant chess game from the view of the watchers I suppose, I don't know. I honestly cant imagine being one of them, lying constantly in a comfy little bed with my eyes closed, and interacting with the world mostly through only my mind and other peoples senses. They are horny little bastards, but only in a parasitic sense as well. It is us three nippled men who father the creches, but maybe that's just too much information, It would be for me. There were a few of the dead headed dudes waiting for us , they went along with the creche and they started unpacking the jolly little fellows and carrying them into their new home. Me and Tommy got sent off to wash up. I was still terribly hungry but after I finally let Cornholio have the crap he had needed to take , and the drink of water he wanted ,he eased up on the control issues for a while, deciding maybe I wasn't doing too bad ,after all, from his point of view I was calm as hell. The shower and the new clothes felt good.

Pretty soon the masters decided to have a good look at their two new vassals which they had picked up by happenstance, so we got called into the presence. I had to help Tommy get there. He wasn't doing so good. In the front of the creche there was a bunch of chairs along a wall, and an official looking character with no mind sitting at a desk with his computer in front of him, a sack from which delicious odors were coming, and a needle gun.

I recognized him as the driver. Behind him was a wall on the other side of it I could see in my mind the sweet little guys we had been transporting. I could have pointed my finger accurately at each and every one through the wall There wasn't any need for talking, me and Tommy were still totally in their web. They were busy in congress for most of an hour, and me and Tommy just sat there. It was hard for Tommy, but I felt he was a hero for managing it, and tried to grin encouragement at him.

On the table, in front of the no name generic mindless bad guy, was a take out meal from some place in town. He was waiting for the masters to be out of congress so they could enjoy him eating. their own bodies have bad dentition and they eat gruel through tubes. As soon as the congress was over, he picked up a deep fried squid and dipped it in sweet and sour sauce and popped it in his mouth. I could hear the little guys in the backroom mewling their pleasure.

I suddenly became pretty hungry again and one of the masters noticed I was having some sort of trouble controlling my body. He upped my endorphin level a bit. Cornholio kicked back to enjoy the rush, and gave up on me for the moment.

They looked at Tommy first. He was bleeding on the rug. There wasn't much of interest. They catalogued his family insofar as he knew them to look for valuable three-nippled male relatives. They un-layered him like an onion, then they had a look at his physical condition. He had taken a blade to the guts, he had peritonitis. He needed a hospital or maybe just antibiotics. He didn't get either.

This creche was perched just outside a town where there was lots of local help. The guy at the desk picked up the needle gun flicked on the beam and stabbed Tommy in the heart. Tommy held his chest up for a good easy stab. I know Tommy died happy. I was in his mind when he quit the mortal coil.

The guy at the table put his gun down, and took the time to look in the bag and see what other goodies there were for them to eat. He pulled out a couple of cheeseburgers, and the Eggmen turned their personal gaze on me. I was proud as Hell and felt like a puppy does when it wiggles. I just loved all the attention but Cornholio's brain stayed focused on the two cheeseburgers.

I listened to myself explain that I was just dying to help the brother bond, and I heard myself start firing off bits about Carmellitas operation that I thought they might like to hear.

It was pay-dirt, I guess. I could feel them sifting through my memories as I told the general gist of my story and they even dialed their battery back into contact with other batteries close by, on account of they wanted to broadcast my news about the resistance on the moon everywhere they could. When they had dragged out of me all they could about the organization, they asked me a few personal details such as who my family were and where we lived. I put Cornholio down a lot, but he is Juliette's father too, plus maybe those two cheeseburgers smelled too good for him.

Did I tell you Cornholio swears a lot? The first sign the Eggmen had of my rebellion, was when I distinctly said the rude name for what a lady has between her legs three times very distinctly and loudly, then I grabbed the needle gun from the desk and snatched the cheeseburger from the generic mindless bad guys hands. I had two big bites before I needle beamed him between the eyes. Then I just stood there thinking about stuff while I ate both the hamburgers, all the chips, the prawns, and guzzled a whole can of cola.

By that time Cornholio had figured out what he wanted to do. He opened the door into the creche, walked in with the needle gun, and shot the lot between the eyes. Then he decided to run for it definitely a good idea, as the Eggheads had been calling for help while he ate his sandwich and it was definitely on the way.

I had given interesting information. They wanted a good look at me. Me and Cornholio ran out into the parking lot. I would have taken a truck but Cornholio is always the primitivist, so we ran through the parking lot and into the back country behind.

He probably made the right decision. If I had hung around people I would have been snagged. When I woke up in the morning I was sleeping in a hollow log but it was me who was in control not Cornholio or the Eggmen.

I needed a phone. I wanted to call Guinevere and have her pick me up, and it needed to be before someone changed her password, if they hadn't already. It seemed worth some risks. I walked on back to the highway, and lucked out in the sense that I hitch hiked a ride the heck on out of there in under fifteen minutes, and I got out at the first mall on the way into a different town. What I wanted was a telephone ,and a nice parking lot you could momentarily set down a ship the size of a small building in. There was a nice one of those on the south east side of the place. Finding a public web phone was a little dicier, and I had to walk through the mall more or less from one side to the other, before I found the courtesy kiosk. There was a pretty girl behind the counter, and she helped me out with all the information I needed about where I was before I made my call. Guinevere picks up at the first ring; she always does. I was still the skipper. I asked her if anybody was aboard and when there wasn't ,I told her to close her doors ,open her hangar and come and pick me up as soon as she could. I gave exact directions to the parking lot out back.

As an after thought, I told her to ignore any attempts by anyone to make electronic contact until she had picked me up. I didn't want her called back to the moon] Just in case any bad guys showed up in the next little while, I told her to make sure I was standing there before she made her final approach. It was a beautiful sunny day and her cameras would have no problem scoping me out. I headed back to the other side of the mall, and was walking out to the parking lot to hang tough somewhere in the shadows while Guinevere got there, when I noticed there were a few people walking on out of the mall behind me. It was a real invasion of the body snatchers type moment. There were a half dozen not too far away, including a couple of dudes with golf clubs, and a chef from the restaurant with a white hat and a big knife ,and some ways behind them but coming up fast I saw a cop with a sidearm, and a man with a really big baby carriage ,which I was really certain didn't contain a kid.. I started getting that frisky excited and happy feeling I get when a master comes close. That was it for Cornholio, he saw the direction I wanted to walk ,chose the other, and headed for the woods again.

This time we were hunted. We made the night without incident as Cornholio ran out of range of one single Egghead. In the morning they brought in a battery to the roadside and Cornholio had to run farther back into the bush. They were the best days of Cornholios life and I was scared shit-less nearly all of the time.

It was nice country although wet, and had been farmed once. For the first couple of days I wondered why there weren't more people about, until I camped near a set of ruins on my third night out, and found they glow in the dark. The varied leaves on the trees, white patches on the birds, and two heads on lots of the baby crocs alligators and turtles were kind of a giveaway too. Two headed-ness must work out worse for snakes, Not to say that it was empty of people. I stole a pirogue, I left emeralds from my pouch, so I hope I made someones day. I pushed back into the swamps where people weren't. I like little alligators and snakes, they are real tasty and easy to cook, and were very plentiful and easy to catch. I hate big ones. Our island me and Cornholio's was maybe a couple of hundred feet of dry land with another couple of acres of what looked like dry land on account of it had trees on it, but really wasn't dry at all.

There wasn't really any king of the beasts around here, as the contest still hadn't been decided between the pythons and the crocs. The gators were out of the running. Not nasty enough. Home was a big hollow cyprus stump. It was a horrible place, and every night I would sit up in the dark petrified until a twig would break under something big outside and startle me, and then Cornholio would take over with a chuckle and a couple of curses.

I had made some pretty bad decisions. I had told Guinevere not to accept calls, and I had told her to pick us up at a particular place which we were now nowhere near, and where it was difficult for us, me and Cornholio, to hang out. On top of it all, I had told her to visually identify me before her approach, and it turned out that it was kind of humid and cloudy here a lot. Right now she would be in geosynchronus orbit over the mall with her scopes all pointing at the parking lot waiting to see my smiling face.

There were a couple of good sunny days, but before we even got to the highway we wandered into an area where I could feel eggs, and Cornholio had hauled our asses back to that little island while I had a rest. We weren't unarmed. I still had my sword cane and the needle gun. At the push of a button it had a four foot long energy blade. You can kill a ten meter long croc, alligator, python, or anaconda with a weapon like that, but you shouldn't try.

It was kind of fun for Cornholio , as his ideal is to be woken up into a life or death situation ,where he gets not just to kill the enemy, but also to eat him. He is not a cannibal, so most of my city encounters which had called him up hadn't been nearly as fun for him as these were now, where could cut off a steak and wolf it down after he killed something, I finally managed to reach the parking lot on a clear day and got myself picked up.

They wouldn't give me clearance to land at Grandad's ranch . It had seemed unhealthy to just fly in and try to open the hangar without talking first so I called, but it wasn't a friendly conversation. I had been gone three weeks. The odds that I was still chewing my own gum were very very small. Carmellita wouldn't talk to me. I ended up with her dad standing in the hologram. He had a rolled up scroll in his hand. I knew what was happening, it was a get of divorce, and for religious reasons that we both understood he as father of my bride had to read it to myself. I let him do his thing, and listened to the sound of the Hebrew. When he finished up he looked at me defiant in case I was gonna argue, but I didn't hardly feel like it. As I had come round the city I had seen the scar of the nuke, and I had had a sudden memory of how I had sung like a canary.

A day after that they had been hit hard half a dozen different ways and places. It had to be me who had sung and everybody knew it. I had caused lots of people to get killed and damned near lost us the fight. I was unpopular personally and a poster child for why they were shipping all others like me off Luna.

Papa Julio soon picked up that I wasn't looking either all defiant, or Egg man possessed, and he asked me how I was doing. I told him my story, including on how I wasn't presently possessed on account of I had only been held for a little while, and hadn't been exposed to the special treatment before I had got lost from them . The way I told it it seemed extremely unlikely to be true even to myself, but on account of I was miles away, and of no present personal danger to him don Julio was willing to give me the benefit of the doubt. He told me that if I took my ship back to Bountiful and put in at Admin City he would extend to me his personal protection, that meant he wouldn't try to kill me, and that as a former partner of mine he would extend me any help I needed to refit my ship for my next venture, [that meant I would be expected to move along fast] I thanked him and agreed.

It fit with my plans anyway. I didn't feel I could ever live in a city again. I liked it out there in my ship, where I could rig it so a bell would ring if any human being came within ten thousand miles. He didn't need to say that if I tried to contact his daughter again he would do his best to kill me. I asked him how many egg men were in admin city and he gave me a precise answer. 'We think none" I asked him how he could be so certain and he thought a bit before telling me that he had done a study in the morgues and that every stiff which had arrived since he had set up the program had been checked by a doc for undescended testicles and extra nipples. There had been several thousand with the first condition and several hundred with the second but so far no male had died with both conditions. He thought he chances were that the city was genetically unpolluted. I had my doubts,

My dad had the heeby-jeebies too. He started building hisself outposts on islands and asteroids where he couldn't be snuck up on, and avoiding the multitudes. I decided to be just like him, in fact I decided to go see him. I had called mom, but she had given me the brush off. When I got rich and sent her some bucks she had moved into a new crib that didn't include a spare bedroom. There was no place for me to stay she said , and she was real busy and hoped to hear lots about my school another time. It was a kind of dissatisfying conversation.

My visit with pops was way on the mark. For one thing we were both newly divorced. Me from Carmellita ,and him from my mom and about a hundred other wives, some of whom he had inherited from Gramps. Don't ask me about that. He was really happy to be free he said. It had happened after some big church convention. They also took away his families title of Kings of David and tribesmen weren't supposed to call him Mossiach any more. Something about normalizing the conventions between Bountiful and Dogpatch.

He sure had a nice new girlfriend though. There was a bit of shared sadness between them, in that if she had his kid they might as well call him Humpty Dumpty. She had the wrong blood lines. She decided to adopt me ,even though was she was only about five years my senior. I loved it, although I made up my mind to get out of there before I ended up mowing my dads grass for him. He was an old man way over forty. Her name was Lucille.

Dad had a pretty nice fort on Bountiful these days. It was on an island in the south seas, and there wasn't a soul on it he hadn't put there, and hardly a critter of any consequence either. There were lots patches of jungle and dinos do grow from small young, which may be overlooked into man eaters pretty fast, so that you couldn't rule out there being some dinos left here and there, but there didn't seem likely to be many ,as the sheep goats and rabbits my dad had introduced were pretty much all over the place. He liked fresh groceries. It would have been a paradise, except like everywhere else on Bountiful you had to avoid the beach or get ate.

We had an agreement with the big lizards of the ocean. We didn't go anywhere near them, and they didn't kill us and eat us. I staked out a hilltop on the far side of the island, maybe eight kliks from pops freehold and squatted Guinevere on the top of it. I had decided to get Guinevere to give me some more schooling.[exobiology this time] To get there I had to cover what is known about regular biology, chemistry, and genetics. I had at least a couple of years of regular schooling ahead of me. It sounded like fun. I had come a long way. I decided to become a scholar. I was still the best kind of filthy rich, and I had come to enjoy my Granpa's morning ritual of letting the jewels in the caskets drip through my fingers.

I hired my own teachers and brought them to our little island. I lured them with the idea of setting up research labs, on the ship and elsewhere and doing dome practical exobiology. I said I would pay the money, and they could make the decisions what we did, and where we went . I only let my thug nature call the shots in one small way. I only hired women. If we got stuck somewhere [ike Granpa did, I wanted to be comfortable. I say I hired them but I only hired twenty, I bought and freed the other ten. I needed to purchase some personal loyalty.

Those were pretty good days although we didn't know it at the time. Pops job of genociding Eggmen on Dogpatch wasn't working out too badly at all ,as the areas in which the Eggmen prevailed lost technology so fast, that although they retained their dangerous mental powers, their minions were now only armed with rocks and sharp sticks. Pops folks were cleaning them out. The news from the prime moon where Carmellita and my kid hung out was pretty good too. They held the moon and it looked as if the earth was going to head towards a non technological egg ridden state in only a generation or two, and then it seemed it also would be easy to take back. The news on Bountiful was even better. Admin city wasn't infected. They were more sure than I was, and the rest of Bountiful has always had the dinos nibbling away at the sides like maggots cleansing a wound of rotten flesh. I decided to just kick back, hire and buy some women to do the work, and educate myself while I enjoyed being rich. It was a great few years, I bought myself a few miniature elephants, studied hard and got to know my dad.

I let the science ladies set up their labs on board and get their research going while I just focused in on what might be known about why the aliens might want to do us wrong ,and what had been found about them in ancient times when the Romans had first run up against them. It was an interesting story, it had begun with the floaters (the dead aliens who had been found dead floating in space within the asteroid belt) and the big broken station on the moon.

There was an event quite a long time ago on earth ,which knocked off most species more complex than maybe an oyster, It was a comet, or maybe an asteroid which schmucked the earth and grazed the moon wrecking the alien station there. We aren't talking about the rock which wiped out the dinosaurs in some places ,but another earlier, more solid, and much larger hit at the so called k/t boundary. Humans are like weeds that have grown opportunistically in a temporarily untended garden plot. The big moon station that got broken up was for terra forming and in other whens where it was not destroyed , the terra forming was completed to create a nice environment for octopi . In places where the big rock took it out, we have humans, dinosaurs , space faring bugs , and other wild varmints, occupying a territory of theirs [the aliens] which they had already been working on for millennia.

Did I mention that the aliens are relatives? Yup the dna proves it. We aren't any more closely related to them than we are to any octopus in the seas of earth, probably a bunch less, but we are relatives] .they planted this place you could say, and guided its evolution up to the point of the arrival of molluscs, before they got schmucked and lost control. Did I mention they travel between the stars? The ancient Romans were pretty nervous of them. They figured the aliens were going to want their garden back someday. It seemed for a while as if the Eggmen were their idea of how to do that.

Then the bugs showed up. It is funny how we had never put it together before. Where are most collective entities found, but in the insect world, and who might be wanting to domesticate and harvest us? Way more likely it would be an insect colony on land than octopi in the sea. They raise us like aphids, the bugs do. It was a bad day when we found out. My ladies had spent years researching the wrong enemy. We didn't know it when our Rome Prime fell, but Bountiful received some refugees from the moon there days later. Three of of those big roman freighters pulled up one day off ,moon prime and began beaming down pods to the planet.

From that point on they didn't have a chance. The bugs arrived on the planet' and the Eggmen greeted them like a dog greets its master. The whole point of the Eggman mutation is probably to make them good servants. The bugs have been spreading the gene around the way sailors in the ancient times used to introduce rabbits and goats to islands so there would be a useful species there when they came back. Good old bountiful I never liked dinosaurs so much.

It seems likely the rest of the downtown Romes aren't doing so good, as there aren't many of the big freighters coming past Bountiful these days, and those that do make a person a bit nervous until you see what downloads to earth. We have had a pretty big fleet of small independent ships straggle into the spaceport . It looks like the cat is out of the bag in lots of places ,and the ships are coming to our safe haven, and probably to the other new Zions as well. Me and the ladies are finally going to visit the aliens, or maybe we should just call them our parents.

We want some help. We are hoping that the bugs beginning to exploit the other whens (they probably learned how from us humans) won't be seen as beneficial by the molluscs. We are hoping they will help us. We are also looking for a new home. If the bugs nip the New Zions, or Dogpatch off the vine, we will need a new destination, and the idea is that over on the side of the time spectrum where the alien probability starts, we will be able to find a safe earth to colonize in their shadow.

The only problem is we don't want them to domesticate or genetically modify us, as they did the ancient Romans who came too close. I don't want my descendants modified to eat grass no matter how convenient the aliens think that would be for them, being as how there is all kinds of grass around. It should be interesting. On a personal note Carmellita and my kid are back. Julio got them off of moon prime before it fell. She came to see me and brought my kid Juliette[she is about ten].

Unfortunately neither of them like me too much. They both have their noses in the air about how I have surrounded myself here on this little island with all kinds of good looking women ,and failed to notice at all how I am trying to save our species. Oh well ,at least the miniature baby elephants were a hit. I told Carmellita she could like it or lump it as far as my living arrangements are concerned ,but that I hoped she would come with us. I expected her to tell me off, but women are always surprising. We got our guitars out last night and discovered we still make beautiful music together, and she slapped me really hard before she left for the night, so things are probably looking up. I cant help it if I am lucky.

Cornelius Browning

Hughy Rough Shanks And The Virgins

The legend of Hughy and the maidens was known on all the worlds of men. The story varied from ribald drinking songs on one world to serious religious stories on another, but the legend was always essentially the same. The aliens had intended to destroy earth, but before they had done so Hughy and the virgins had spread human beings far and wide to other stars and in doing so had frightened the aliens so badly that they had moved far away from the contagion.

Here we have the story of Hughy Rough Shanks and the space girls and how they saved mankind.

Hughy watched her speak. She was beautiful. He thought about the intensity of her eyes , and the fluidity of her mind. She was smarter than him and he had known it since they had met back in high school. In fact, it had been the clearness of her trajectory to somewhere else which had propelled his own nose to the grindstone, in an almost vain attempt to accompany her to university and out into the world. He was uncomfortably aware that for all his studying it had been his physical prowess as a ball player that had gained him entry to the school. His grades, for all his work would not have cut the mustard.

Calley however had been begged and entreated by all the best schools, and that, as well, not for her achievements in her courses ,but for a little thing that she had done on the side; providing a proof for a bit of work by a guy called Fermat. Hugh had asked her to explain Fermat's theorem to him and she had tried but not too hard. What Hugh did know about it was that she had found her proof on her own, and the humiliating letter from the New Sorbonne university letting her know that the proof for Fermat had been found centuries ago had really pissed him off. It had hurt Calley deeply and the letter nearly two months later ,when someone actually read her work and realized that it was new and different, had not entirely dissipated Hugh's anger.

Hugh brought himself back to focus on her voice and the topic of her conversation. He had noticed a fixedness in her tone which indicated she was wondering whether he was really listening to her conversation or just admiring her chest heave, Calley was talking about her apes again. Calley nearly always talked about her apes , or at least about their D.N.A. ,their enzymes and their proteins, their rhibosomes and rhibosymes. Hugh could follow most of it. He was not unintelligent, although if it were not for Calley he would not on his own have learned to tell a "rifflip" from a chip dip. As it was however, her talk of R.F.L.P.s i.e. "restriction fragment length polymorphisms" was intelligible to him. It was a simple process to understand in itself, whereby the genetic relatedness of different individuals or of different species could be measured. "But it is a puzzle grumpy morphing like that" Calley had said.

Hugh picked up interest at the mention of Grumpy. Grumpy was one of Calley's orangotangs. He occupied a solo habitat next to the chimps and bonobos of the university's primate station. One fine morning when Hugh had helped Calley on her rounds with the apes she loved, Grumpy had severed Hugh's two smallest joints from the smallest finger of his left hand with one quick snap of his incisors, and then deftly picked the digit up off the concrete floor ,popped it into his mouth, crunched it loudly several times and swallowed it down. Hugh's feeling towards Grumpy were less than loving and had not been improved by Calley's elucidation of who, exactly, Grumpy was in the Orangotang world; for grumpy, was a nasty little fucker.

Sometimes in nature a tiny stimulus can cause a whole cascade of changes. Orangotang males have two biologically different alternative mating strategies. In orangs, as in gorillas some males become huge twice the weight of the females and as well as gaining in size, they acquire exaggerated secondary sexual characteristics(varying between the two species) Some males however, remain small about the size of females and resembling them. Amongst gorillas these smaller males are mostly sexually inactive but amongst orangutangs they barter for sex or commit rape . Grumpy up to now in his life had been of the nasty little rapist model. It was why he had been secluded from the others of his species. But now, although well advanced into middle age he had begun to grow and was acquiring cheek pouches huger canines and other decorations.

Hugh absentmindedly felt the stump of his missing finger and carefully listened to Calley talk about her apes. She might love her dumb football player, but Hugh was not about to take chances. Hugh knew that she was beautiful and was surrounded by the admiring glances of the smartest young men at the university. "Grumpy is definitely morphing into the larger male form" Calley said "His weight gain alone proves it Hughy, but it is the telomeres which have everyone's attention. At this point Hugh raised a finger. "Telomeres" ? he questioned. before remembering that telomeres are what define age. Shortened telomeres were what made cloned animals die young. If clones were taken from an older animal they were born with their dynamism half lost. They had shortened telomeres. Calley followed on."Professor Chirac says that the telomeres of the new cells in Grumpy's body are lengthening. The cells in his body are being replaced with those of a young ape not one of forty years old".

At the mention of Professor Chirac a number of interesting but unobserved changes occurred in Hughy. His eyes narrowed and his breath was momentarily held. Chirac was Calleys idol. He was ten years older than her, a professor,a department head, a genius (or so it was said) a cultivated european, and unlike many of the pencil necks at the university Chirac was also a very fine figure of a man. Hugh abhorred him. He could not help himself and he knew that even if Chirac proved to be a prince, a saint, or the savior of mankind, he would not like him. Hugh also knew that this was the green-eyed goblin of jealousy at work and he tried to stuff these emotions down somewhere deep and dark where Calley would never see them.

Hugh forced his mind back to the subject of the telomeres. Calley was waiting for him now. He had seen that look on her face before, rather like a mother coaxing a child, or, he thought, rather less flatteringly,. He had seen the same look on her face when she had coaxed one of the Colobus monkeys into a particularly astute decision about which compartment the banana was in. Hugh thought hard. "arrested aging"? a forty year old ape becoming young again?

He thought harder. "Who wanted to rejuvenate apes?"Then it came to him. Calley had often talked about the similarity of all species. She had said that the that the differences on a molecular level were not that great. On a molecular level their bodies produced mainly the same compounds and arranged them a little differently. Life seems to bother with only about twenty amino acids out of over a hundred available. The microbiological code is universal as the identical sets of codons are used by bacteria, bugs, and boys from Wisconsin.

A snippet of Hugh's first year genetics course came to mind. For Hugh was really a rather bright boy. It was only his constant proximity to Calley's shining star of intellect which had given him his somewhat humble opinion of himself. Hugh remembered his professors words, "This means theoretically that messenger R.N.A. from one species would be translated correctly by another species as the codons have the same meanings acrooss the boundaries" Hugh finally had it, somewhere in all this there might be a way to prevent or even reverse human aging. Hugh spilled the beans. Calleys face lit up. "Mamas smart boy " she cooed. Hugh felt immediately warm and good as well as mildly embarrassed. He had a nagging vision of a small dog feeling as good as he did when rewarded for a successful trick. but he banished the thought and just enjoyed the soft touch of her breasts through her sweater as she enveloped him with a hug and a smooch. With the discovery of the apes lengthened telomeres work in the genetics lab had changed character. There was a quiet excitement and an equally quiet dread. Professor Chirac knew himself to be on the verge of making a huge discovery or of mentally stumbling somehow and fumbling the ball. It was a limited time engagement this "morphing" as they called the increasing sexual dimorphism of the ape. Soon the ape would have completed doubling in size and whatever traces were left of whatever had caused the change would be harder to find. The amino acids which had caused the changes no lounger coursing in the blood. Tissue and blood samples could be preserved both alive and frozen, but right now in the apes body, probably rested their smoking gun of proof, soon to disappear with the return of stasis and the end of changes. Chirac knew that the chances of being able to observe an orang or a gorilla morphing again were slim. Most either grew straight to the larger silver back morph or remained small.

While the morphing of males in the wild was an attested occurrence, it was sporadic and thought to be dependent upon pheromone stimuli which no-one had ever investigated in depth. It was thought that the pheromone receptors in the primates including man were located in the vomero-nasal organ a tiny organ in the nose.. In man this tiny organ, overlooked for many years was the last to be named in the body. Minute and obscured as it is by other tissue , Chirac remembered that in its embedded location it was thought to no longer function. In some apes it was a different story.

Chirac knew that without a biological trace , without an amino acid to work backwards from, the work could be one of decades, and the eventual discoverer probably would not be him. He and all other researchers of course had access to the whole genome of all of the apes on the web, but that was like a road map which told you nothing of the interiors of the 250000 houses in the city. What he needed was an enzyme, from that you had a trail to follow which led back to the very house in the 250000 in which the golden goose was laying the golden eggs.

Chirac had too few animals in the physical side of his program. Especially amongst the orangs there were too few females and no young males. The gorilla population was equally senescent. The university had ,however, robust chimp and bonobo populations ,but sexually dimorphism was greatly reduced in these species[which also seemingly did not morph]. The conservativeness of evolution (which often stores many alternative methods of doing things in our genetic codes ready to be called upon if needed) as well as sheer necessity 'due to the lack of orangs and gorillas had led Chirac to focus his physical research on his chimp and bonobo populations, although these species are actually more closely related to humans than they are to the other great apes. With us chimps and bonobos share a ninety eight point six genetic identity. Chirac was to think about that figure often later on;however for the moment a vague feeling of foreboding was replaced by a flash of insight which pushed it out of the way.

" What had triggered Grumpy's growth?" Chirac thought hard. Grumpy's rapist nature as well as the mainly solitary nature of orangs had earned him a habitat of his own rather removed from the other orangs. In fact the quarters he had been recently given were near to the chimp habitat with its many females in estrus and no morphed males. There had long been speculation that pheromones triggered the growth spurts in both gorillas and orangs and that perhaps they suppressed them as well. Did the scent of fertile females trigger the process? Did the scent of silver back gorillas and mature male orangs inhibit the development of juvenile males?Chirac suspected that the pheromones of the nearby species might have been sufficiently similar to stimulate Grumpy's growth. He also reasoned that being moved away from his old habitat with its proximity to the huge morphed males might have had something to do with it. They were all damned good guesses.

Why the chimps themselves did not morph was not really Chiracs concern for the moment. Clearly sexual dimorphism was in the general ancestry of apes with humans, bonobos, and chimps having only recently diverged from the pattern. "It must have to do with the development of community and of cooperation amongst females, That sort of thing" Chirac thought before he turned his mind back to things of more seeming relevance to himself. "Pheromones" thought Chirac are the love songs of the animal world as well as the most powerful molecules it possesses.

The Cecropea and other large moths are individually so rare that without pheromones they could never find each other to mate. Chirac remembered how in his youth the giant moths would appear sometimes and picking a place to sit would rest mysterious and unmoving on the side of a house only to disappear after a week or so. The males picked a place to sit and exuded a pheromone which could be sensed miles away by the females. The amounts involved are astoundingly small.

Months had passed, Chiracs brain hurt and visions of double helixes danced through his head like sugar plums. All the vast complexity of the d.n.a. world had an evil tint to it today. He felt faintly like crying...The last months had been hard, Grumpy had reached full size and all sorts of brilliant ideas had been tried with nothing panning out. Chirac thought that maybe if they had known in advance that the ape was going to morph, they might have had a better chance. They could have studied more closely at the beginning , noticed changes and made deductions, but he had noticed the telomeres too late, and lost his chance to observe the early stages of the change. For all Chirac knew, by the time they had first observed the telomeres ,the enzyme which sparked the changes had been long gone.

Chirac observed Calley at the P.C.R. machine. "And there is another problem.." He thought. He had never expected this slavish infatuation of himself, especially not with a student. He missed Europe, but he would be there soon. Usually Chirac looked forward to his time home, but this time he knew he was in retreat, retreat and failure. Failure to crack the secret,but also failure to... He turned his head and looked at Calleys tits. "Yes, it would be good to be back in Europe". Chirac was already famous for his observation of telomere lengthening, but he himself knew it had not been genius but only lucky observation;and that there were labs all over the world now pursuing "his" line of research. "Oh well " thought Chirac,"that was all just bloody work anyways" what had really hurt had been his failure to interest Calley as a mate. She was the perfect woman; a gift from above. She was more beautiful and smarter than any woman he had ever met. She had arrived at the university in the same year that he had fresh in his glory to head a department, known at thirty as a fire ball and a success ,but she was better.

They had all read in the journals how Fermat's theorem had been offered a new proof , and of the outlandish mathematician who had offered it, a teenage girl from some mud hut village at the end of the earth. Chirac offered it to himself that he "had not really understood what Fermat was all about" Deeper in his mind a truer voice resonated. and corrected that to "Could not really understand what it was all about." He shifted uncomfortably.

Calley had arrived at the university a prodigy and famous, only to transfer out of the math department after a mere three weeks and had planted herself in his faculty. Math and physics professors still came around to observe her as an icon but she would not talk shop. The only time she had ever commented upon mathematics to Chirac it had been to say something about "silly people who believed that whether one event happened before another depended upon where you observed it from." Then she had never mentioned mathematics or physics again.

Calley was of course a bonus to his department, her star status and independent research grant had merited her both freedom and a lab of her own, as well as the respect of the other staff. It was something else however which had earned her the hunger of most of the men around her, and quite a few of the women. Chirac found himself once again day dreaming about the way Calley looked and smelled, when he recovered, gave himself a good mental kick in the ass and got back to work.

" Want to help me with the chimps?" Hugh heard the sweet voice calling. He emphatically did not want to help with the chimps. He still occasionally missed the little finger he had lost while helping her with the orangotangs. He fingered the stump ruefully.

Helping with the chimps was no fun at all. The chimps had long ago got the idea that Hughy was a low form of life who was about to try to strong arm them into some indignity or other. They hooted As soon as they saw him, often pelting him with fruit peels or with dung which bore a disgusting resemblance to his own. Hugh had been bitten twice by chimps and one of those bites had been upon his thigh and only about four inches away from somewhere much worse."Want to help me with the chimps " he heard her repeat." Then with a sense of wonder at his own baseness he heard himself say "Oh Sure." in the chipperest kind of way.

Hugh caught the chuckle in Calley's eyes as she turned to the door, although she immediately re-assumed her rigid school teacher persona "Dolly is in estrus" she said "and I want a sample. It will be a simple swab."

Hugh recognized that there was no recourse, no joke to be made, and also no retreat. Hugh figured that since chimps were three times as strong as people pound for pound, and as he was only about twice dolly's size, the odds were good it would whip him, roll him in the dirt ,and bite him a bunch. He looked at Calley one last time for mercy but there was none. Sometime later in Calley's office Hugh huddled naked and freshly showered under a blanket. He had some scratches but no bites and his hopes were high that Calley would put aside work and accompany him out.

Montreal was a wonderful place, far different from the hometown nowheres of their past. It was spring and love was in the air, or at least it was in the air elsewhere ,he decided, as Calley's lab definitely stunk. She was collecting and analyzing animal scents, while at the same time working with the genomes on the web, searching the helix and comparing the genes of the ape families one to another.

The P.C.R. machine in the corner hummed softly. It was caring for one of mankind's newer domesticants. The bacillus thermos aquaticus was a former denizen of the deep sea vents. It is a bacteria which lives in near boiling water and has been taken from its jungle of giant clams and tube worms to serve science in the polymer chain reaction or P.C.R. machines that replicated DNA. A little further on in the lab were the tanks where snippets of DNA. from apes or elsewhere could be inserted into e-coli or other bacteria to hi-jack them into producing the enzymes which Calley desired. Hugh had observed her little house of horrors before. Calley had been collecting and reproducing anything from all the ape species she had access to which resembled a pheromone or a steroid. Calley's little jars of synthesized ape exudates really turned Hugh off. One had smelt like cat urine, another like skunk , while others were almost pleasant to smell in a horrible cloying sort of way.

Many had no scent at all. Calley was overly prone to popping open a new one and passing it under his nose while rattling off its provenance

Calley was now spending her time staring at a computer image where she examined in tandem bits of the genomes of the ape species. The genomes had been deciphered hundreds of years ago , but even now all these years later the meaning of many of the 250,000 bits that each contained was conjectural. Calley,s computer was letting her know when the differences between the double helixes exceeded the usual randomness of the system. It was alerting her when the first or second bases differed on the codons, or letting differences go by when it recognized that glycerine {for example} was just being represented by its different codons but that the resultant molecule produced would be the same.

Hugh had begun to lose his hopes for getting out on the town as the computer had Calley's attention again, but he was saved by the arrival of the dean of the math department. Dean Wolfert was a small worried looking man, or at least that was how he had looked on all the previous occasions upon which Hugh had seen him. It was not a fair judgement. Dean Wolfert was in the impossible position of having had the star math prodigy of the century arrive at his university, and then bolt from his faculty after weeks. He was obsessed with the idea that if he just apologized profusely enough she might come back. Calley saw Wolfert coming and whisked Hugh down the freight elevator still naked under his blanket.

His Ford was parked at the third floor dock. They jumped in giggling like the teenagers they had so recently been, and sat in opposite seats eying each other and both knowing what was to come. Hugh reached over and without even for a moment allowing his eyes to leave her, entered his access code and destination into the console on the dash. The ford lifted off and headed for the city while Calley and Hugh made love on the bed. When the ford began its docking procedure at the motel an hour later they were fast asleep,.

Hugh awoke in the motel room. They had moved from the ford, which was bobbing out front, during the night. Calley was cooking breakfast. They loved their rare moments when they could be domestic and play house. Their scholarships had included dormitory lodging, and in dormitories they had lived for years. Even their summers had been spent there working and saving up a nest egg for going home. Not that Hugh really believed any more that they would be going home, or at least not home to stay. Hugh's ambition at eighteen had stretched no further than he and Calley and a boat of their own. but this had been swept away by her fame and their suddenly expanded horizons. Hugh still called the account he plugged his hard earned bucks into" the boat account" and he still thought about the boat, especially when he was in one of those dark moods which he hid from Calley when he thought of how much time she spent with Chirac," the charming and elegant"

It just choked him. The perfectly decent manner in which the man treated Hugh was the most galling thing of all,. If only Chirac had exhibited some character flaw Hugh would have been satisfied, but the man was just damned decent and that was all their was to it. "Yes, Chirac was decent, big, handsome, rich, intelligent, and being a decade older also helped him to command Calley's respect, Hugh hated every inch of it.

Hugh watched Calley's naked brown body while she cooked, enjoying the smells of the cooking, the shared lodging, and the sense of abeyance that the first day of a holiday brings; however, when she turned around to speak to him she scared him half to death. "Hugh" she said to him, Instantly from the way she had left his name hanging in the air he could tell that there were words left unsaid. His worst fears filled his mind and suddenly he was sure that she was leaving for Europe with Chirac, and that this time alone with Hugh was going to be her opportunity to break up with him. Hugh was momentarily so sure of this scenario that he actually did not hear ,or could not understand Calley's next words. "What" was all he managed. It had sounded as if she had asked him to knock her up and take her home. Calley was looking at him fixedly again, as if he were small stupid boy. "Hughy" she said "I want to go fishing and have babies please take me home",

Montreal was a riot. There was a big new-town adjacent to the ruins, and it was a hum of activity. tons of metal were being pulled from the wreck of the old city daily, and were being melted down. Freelancers hunted for copper and relics, and like in every new-town beside a dead city, it had stores selling salvaged relics of all descriptions. Montreal even had a police force of sorts but Hugh's gun was loaded nevertheless and was displayed up front on his hip where it belonged.

Montreal was a new-town and not a colony of World Gov. No-one hung their guns up at the door here. Hugh had already been out this first fine morning of the rest of their lives to buy their tickets home. He had gone and looked at the fleet of planes down on the water.

They were nice and new , solid plywood construction, with big bays for lots of cargo and passengers;and were not unlike the first commercial craft to cross the Atlantic hundreds of years before. Hugh had admired their classic lines

On returning Hugh sensed the annoyance in Calley's voice as she dug around in their luggage "I have forgotten my typing gloves Hugh and I have to leave a report for Roger" she said.. Hugh flinched at her use of Chirac's first name. Then he noticed gratefully that for the first time he felt no hostility towards the man. " I have my gloves" he said cheerfully and flipped her his pair.. saying. , "Too bad you will have to take the time to train the chip ,but it will be quicker than returning to the university again today for your old pair".

The typing gloves were not really gloves at all as each consisted of five rings and a chip. The rings fit on the fingers and chip in the box on the back of the hand. Calley placed her hand on the monitor, it picked up the signal from her gloves and obediently provided a key board on its face, She cued for new user and a sample text was provided for her to pretend to type upon the mock keyboard on the face of he monitor. Soon she had moved her hands away from the monitor while she continued to fake type the provided text, The chip in the box being informed by the transmitters on her fingers of the intricate dance of her fingers continued to be able to learn her changed and attenuated movements. Soon she was able to type while she walked about the room dispensing with the keyboard altogether, .

Hugh watched her work and drank beer. Calley had been apologetic about working this evening. Hugh had wanted to get out. He had heard there was a powow north of town and he had itched to go. These eastern bloods were different, "Whiter" he would have said, although he knew they did not look at it that way themselves, but it was in many ways a lot like home. There was the sweat lodge and all the old Sioux sweat lodge songs just like at home and it was like home as well in that while everyone could sing the Sioux songs no-one could truly translate many of them for the Sioux were no longer there to ask, they had wandered away.

After the great plague global warming had ceased ,and in its place the ice age which had been held in abeyance for several centuries resumed its march to the fifty ninth parallel and beyond to the little town of Rosebud in the Dakotas where it stopped,. The little settlement at Crow -dog's paradise quite rightly assumed that it was their sun dance which had stopped the ice for their sun dance chief had customarily deflected bad weather from the sun dance field, commanding it with his hands to pass the dancers by on either side. So they kept on dancing. Soon it became apparent that the dance was finally bringing back the herds and not just of Buffaloes but of Horses, Zebras, Camels, Alpacas and Elephants. The Sioux at Crow dogs paradise felt very successful so they kept on dancing. They danced for a hundred years. By then the remnant left after the plague had grown into a prosperous town

A decision was made one day and Rosebud and the other Sioux villages were abandoned. Messengers had come to the towns from the south. They were from the Hopi who had also prospered after the plague. They requested the Sioux resume their journey to the four corners of the world, spreading the way of the sweat lodge. Crow dog's band at Paradise picked a herd to follow and gone off in search of the four directions. They may still be at it.

Calley had been apologetic about her need to work this evening, and a cheerful demon inside of Hugh had seen its advantage . He had suggested that he didn't mind if she worked this evening ,pacing back and forth with her finger flashing at her sides, provided she did so naked (except for her typing gloves) while he drank beer and watched. Just for a moment he had waited for his face to be slapped and then her look of anger had been replaced by something else. "That's my Hughy" she had said, as she shucked her duds.

As Hughy watched her work he pondered his fate. There is nothing like a full case of beer at your feet to bring on reflection. He sipped on his beer and wondered what had brought on all the changes? He knew of course about Stumpy, a second orang had morphed. Calley had somehow got it right. Her scatter gun approach of exposing them to all the possible compounds enhanced by special ingredients from perfumes (which opened up the vomero- nasal pits making them more accessible to pheromones) had worked. She had hit the jackpot. Stumpy was gaining weight and brawn, his middle aged body firming up to the tone of youth; and most importantly for Chirac, his telomeres were longer. Dr. Chirac would get his second chance to search for the fountain of youth. What had changed Calley's mind must be something deeper, thought Hugh. He sensed that it had to do with Chirac, but not to do with work.

Hugh felt that Chirac had somehow lost the football and had lost Calley's heart. If he had ever had it. Hugh cracked another beer and lay back watching Calley work with utter satisfaction.

The next morning Hugh looked at their pile of luggage. It was huge. He had a boat to outfit when he got back and their choices now could never be repeated. The huge pile was not in itself a problem as the planes always carried much more gear than they did people and of every conceivable sort. There was, these days, a lot of brisk air traffic across the continent. There was a boom on. The plane would descend perhaps a hundred times on its trip across country ,often tying up on lakes, while crew members got sleep and hydrogen was generated. For the duration of its stay in any locale, the plane was the center of a small trade fair, MInstrels sung and pies were baked while goods were constantly traded. Hugh reached over to their pile and plucked from within it his newest toy. It was a beautiful twenty two rifle made before the big death. Hugh had agonized long and hard before choosing it over the other guns available, many of which were recently made. Hugh picked the gun up by the butt and poked Calley's contributions with it.

Her pile contained a distressing number of vials and potions, some of which he could smell from where he stood. He had rather hoped that this wouldn't be the case but he heaved a sigh, rubbed the absent figure of his left hand. He reflected that he was lucky she hadn't expected him to crate up a couple of apes for the trip back or something of that sort.

The trip was going to be awesome. They had made it before of course, white knuckled and terrified and very, very young. They had climbed aboard to come east. Both of them had been consumed by driving ambitions. Calley's ambitions had been complicated, a function of her superior mind, and of her desire to see and understand the world. His own ambition had been simple but he had hewed to it. He had done, and did intend to do, whatever it took, to follow her ass everywhere.

The first trip Hugh had been too damned scared to pay attention but this time was going to be different. Hugh was going home and he was going home rich. He was not rich by world gov standards of course. If, as expected, their next move would have been to the New Sorbonne in Marseille or to Italy, their money would have been a very modest amount. Back home among the tribes, it was big bucks indeed. Hugh could buy the boat of his dreams. On the way back, for a little while, each night before they slept, each night curled up on mats on the floor in the giant bay surrounded by all the other passengers and their gear in the giant bay, Hugh would plan out his boat. He would fall asleep thinking of "Gurdys" and "Pigs"and "Hootchies" and all the other gear of a west coast fishing boat. Before he had come east Hugh had never thought much about the world or about the old times, but the wrecks of the cities on the journey east, which they had often crossed or circled when visiting the new towns perched beside them, had piqued his interest' Later on his university courses had filled in the blanks.

The plague had done it. The big death had been the plague to top all plagues, and in a few years it had dropped the population of the world by ninety percent., with most of the remaining population concentrated where the plague had been least virulent . Large areas of the globe were just plain empty of people. It wasn't a newcomer -this bug. In fact, it had announced its evil intentions in the nineteen twenties by killing 25 million people. You would have thought that this would merit it a place in peoples minds but it had not . Fifty years later people hardly knew it had happened. History is written by those who survive. We all know the story of the instance where a man was saved by a porpoise, having had it drag him in shore from out at sea. It makes the headlines; but of the guy who was damned near at the shore when the ruddy thing grabbed him by the ankle and drug him back out, we hear not a word.

Eventually the bug came back. It was found in wild waterfowl in Russia in the nineteen nineties, but nothing happened for many years. A relict population of the old flu pandemic reappeared yearly in the pig population of the USA. For over a century, seemingly benign. Originally during the great flu pandemic of the nineteen twenties, it had been given by sick farmers to their swine, and it had seemed a domesticated remnant ,watched carefully, but seemingly having become harmless towards humans. No-one knows if this virus mutated again to its original form, or if some waterfowl harbored it for a century or so before recontaminating chicken farms. The virus ability to infect several host species is a feature the influenza virus shares with many others.

The nineteen twenties version (which killed millions worldwide) was easily shared by ducks, geese, chickens, pigs and people. The flu which caused the big death was not even that picky. The voice of Hugh's professor droned in his recollection, "Many people see a harmful virus as being inert in intent, like a poison and with all individual viruses of a certain variety being equally harmful. They are not. They are millions of competing organisms and there are several ways in which they compete which which are of direct interest to us. First, picture a chicken in a barn containing a flock of thousands milling next to each other, usually under a dim light and over fed in order to keep down activity. Next, picture a chicken free in the jungles of India with a few other wild chickens. To succeed the virus must cross from chicken to chicken. The best strategy for a virus dealing with chickens in a barn is to turn as much of the chicken into virus in as short a time as possible. This is the approach of the haemmoragic fevers such as ebola . In attempting to convert the chicken into viral material the cells of the chicken begin to leak and pretty soon we have a dead chicken and a mess of viral material on the floor with the other chickens mucking about in it transmitting it rapidly throughout the chicken farm.

However, consider the wild chicken with this same virus , If it by mischance becomes infected by a virus with a rapid haemmoragic strategy. It becomes sick quickly , ceases to move with the flock and when it becomes a pile of highly infectious goo it is no longer with them. It is not successfully transmitted from chicken to chicken and the virus loses the bet. So which viral strategy suits transmission in a wild setting best? Clearly it is the one in which the virus does not disable its host so quickly and where the chicken which is infected stays in contact with its flock.

We unintentionally modify the virulence of human pathogens by crowding human beings together like chickens in a barn. We create our own epidemics . Cholera given the chance can mutate to a water born killer from a benign virus in a very short time. Human pandemics and epidemics even including malaria{in so much as it is certainly a disease of poverty!] are man made. They are created by warfare, poverty and bad farming practices, all things which any reasonable person would agree that a reasonably run world could prevent.

At the time there were lots of dirty little wars going on and some big ones, Men in barracks camps and trenches were not allowed to go home and isolate themselves just because they were sick, even to the point of dieing. Military exigencies insisted that they stay put, just like the sick chickens crammed in with others. In the world of the microbe competition quickened. The strains of the flu which only modestly required production of their d.n.a. by their host cells were elbowed out of the way by viruses with more brutal strategies . There were billions of chickens and millions of humans crowded together and ready to eat.

"And was that the end of civilization?" Hugh's professor had asked the class. It was a rhetorical question. They all knew the answer . It had not been the end of civilization but the beginning of it . The black death which had hit England in the middle ages had freed the common man from bondage , enabling him , because of the scarcity of laborers, to contract many new privileges and to increase his take home pay by eight times. In places where there were people still alive after the big death it had been the same. It had been a constant Christmas for several generations. "Do you remember that big farm you once coveted as a kid?" "Go farm it"

If you wanted a Cadillac? Just go and find it. If you were alive it was yours. The demographics of the world had changed as well. Few cities had made it and not a lot of towns. In general the further you were from the city, and the poorer your country was, the better your chances of survival had been. Tiny dead broke hamlets at the far end of nowhere had fared the best. It was a changed world with more Eskimos than Englishmen and more Hottentots than Hutus. The first years after the plague saw many migrations from isolated mountain or jungle towns into the lush empty farmlands, Huge areas of the world were empty spaces and into them the analogs of our pleistocene fauna had returned. Sure, the most common large animal in North America was no longer Mesonyches [a rather tasty critter whom the indians had eaten the last of about ten thousand b.c.] The most common animal was now a really mean [but similar tasting] descendant of the common farm pig. Number two on the list was no longer the bison but was the common cow [with however about a 20 percent admixture of the original bison in its genotype]. The horses ,elephants and cattle of the pleistocene were back in force . "Not exactly the elephus ,equs, and bosse of the villefranchian but good enough for the girls I go out with" thought Hugh. As they flew west just south of the ice the herds were numerous beneath them , "And" reflected Hugh "The fishing was good too." Nature was alive and vibrant and Hugh was going home.

The trip was almost over. Hugh and Calley had spent much of the flying portion of it by a porthole watching the world go by, he lying upon a pile of the most comfortable of their luggage with his girl in his arms. Often at night unable to sleep because of their inactivity or their strange surroundings they would stare out at the lights while their great wooden bird lumbered on to its next destination. They would see the lights below them of the hunter gatherers , there were many such following the herds, and on the moon they would see the lights of the moon men, the puppet masters who now called the shots on earth through their proxy the so called "World Government". The moon men had not experienced the plague directly but had been cut off by it, orphaned for over a century and nearly facing their own extinction before returning to rule although very few had in fact set foot upon earth again. The lights on the moon were myriad. There were millions at home there now.

Hugh felt the engine change pitch and pulled Calley closer to him to observe the porthole. They were coming home and it was time to go boat hunting,. The pilot was pulling north unwilling to fly directly over the radioactive ruins of Vancouver. Vancouver and Victoria had been nuked early on. Hugh's history was a bit hazy but he knew that it was either the war which had also holocausted Hiroshima and Nagasaki or the one a bit later on.

There were no new towns beside radioactive ruins but Nanaimo did have a new-town beside it and for it they were headed. It was not nearly as grand as Montreal with its proximate World Gov colony. It was just a big town, but it was where he would buy his boat. The plane descended with a whoosh into the Gulf of Georgia,reorienting after a successful splashdown and chugging towards the wharf. This was the end of her journey and after maintenance she would head back east full to the tits with canned salmon only to replace it on the journey west with the caches of furs and goods from the new-towns which she had acquired and stashed on the journey west. As they chugged towards shore they observed the bastion , a nearly medieval fort upon the shore built centuries ago by the men who had brought the English language to the tribes as well as Hugh's own shocking yellow hair. Nanaimo was no low tech tribal town like the others on Vancouver island, it was the northernmost town of the Mexican empire.

The smell of gas motors curled Hugh's nose for the first time in years. The Mexican empire ran on oil and gas. He felt a stab of homesickness for his floating Ford back east. It had been his best acquisition of his life so far, but there were no Tesla rays out west and no floating Fords.

Hugh kept his eyes on the wharves as they slid past. Nanaimo had several big used boat lots as well as a plywood mill and lots of new boats for sale. Hugh ached to look at the used boats on the docks. He impatiently estimated how long it would take him to move the gear from the dock to a motel., yes, it was late in the day but he figured he could get it done and still get back to the docks before night fall. Hugh noticed Calley's eyes on him and looked guiltily down realizing that once again he had not heard a word that she had spoken.

"Hugh", she said "I can store the goods on board the pie wagon and get them up to the motel.. Why don't you just run along and look at the boats.?" It was clearly not a repeat of what she had said. It was an admonition as if to a child and it rankled his pride as it was probably meant to. He frowned, It probably wasn't fair to dump her with the chore and he thought about how he probably shouldn't do it , but when they got close enough to the dock he put a hand on the shoulder of the crew member who was about to make the jump , and, taking the rope in his own hands jumped quickly , landing sure-footedly on the edge , and then pulled the craft tight with the spring line and tied her up. He was half way up the stairs with his eye on the boat docks before anyone else was even off of the plane.

The used boat selection was immense. There were at least a hundred and a half boats on many different sales docks. Almost all of the boats were either gill-netters or trollers and most of them were made out of good Mexican made marine plywood. As well as these factory boats he could see here and there tribal made boats which included the creations of genius as well as the good, the bad, and the ugly. There were also a few tugs and boom boats for the lumber trade. In the harbor there were a few big boats as well as one old freighter pulled partly up on shore to serve as a restaurant. Hugh had gone there for tacos once.

At the first boat dock which Hugh visited there was one unusual boat for sale. It was nearly a hundred feet long with a fifty caliber machine gun at its helm. She was of three eigths steel plate and had been welded together in old Mexico. She was the only other boat in the harbor than the tugs and freighter which wasn't made of wood. They had spent time talking about her, Hugh and the salesman had, while both knew that what he was interested in was the trollers. She was a marvel ,all tarted up inside as Mexicans know so well how to do; Her interior was beautiful from the first dingle ball to the last bit of maroon colored velvet. She was fully computerized as well, with a relic computer from the old days converted to her use. She had belonged to a Mexico city numbers boss who had caught a bullet and run north to recuperate, only he hadn't ,he had kicked the bucket. There had been a lab in the back of her and Hugh had wondered what the sideline to the gambling had been. Hugh had supposed methamphetamines, until he had recognized the equipment and realized that the boats owner had probably been using bacteria to churn out opium. She was a lovely sophisticated ship in all. She had huge gas tanks but she also had computerized fair weather sails.

You didn't need a crew with this boat. the sails couldn't operate with anything near the efficiency of human operated sails of course, but they didn't need to in order to be useful. Whenever the computer decided that fuel could be saved the sails went up and if the weather became too rough they scrolled up and parachuted out of harms way while the computer automatically fired up the engine and kept her on course deciding each tack on its own. This boat of all those in the harbor could cross the seas and once the destination was given to her computer she could damned near do it on her own without wasting ,or perhaps without even using, fuel,[if the season was right]. She was a marvel of modern science and a total contrast to the boat which Hugh had tentatively and secretly decided to buy at this self same boat lot.

The boat which Hugh thought to purchase was a troller and trollers were not real sea boats. With trollers you stayed within thirty kilometers of shore, preferably much closer and kept your eyes on a hole to bolt into. Trollers had high superstructures with windows all around which had a haughty look and greatly facilitated fishing, but if you stayed out in ocean weather beyond reasonableness without running for shore, the waves broke in through the windows and you a died.

Hugh had no intention to go out too far or to be unreasonable. He just wanted to make money. Hugh knew the boat he wanted. He had seen her on his first tour of the dock but he had carefully concealed all interest from the Mexican salesman who walked the dock with him. Hugh had fished this boat before during his first year deck handing at twelve years old. She was a big boat for a troller and they had, that year,hired on two extra boys to cut, gut, and boil. It had been a hellish season for him ,mostly blood ,guts, sea sickness, fear and lack of sleep. It had been summertime and he had fished and gutted all day and boiled and canned all evening for four months straight. What little sleep he had gotten had been interrupted by his four o'clock in the morning chore of pumping the bilges. He had stumbled along in the dark to the hand pump where a hundred heaves or so would usually do it., Each exertion seemed to spill phosphorescence into the sea,although it was really just the disturbance of the ubiquitous sea creatures in the seawater itself which caused the display. Hugh had known this boat and come to trust her. He wondered who had owned her after his old skipper Killer Bill Touchie had died. He didn't know her recent history.

Hugh turned and looked at the Mexican salesman and boat dock proprietor. He was old, fat, cigar smoking and a lifetime merchant and on the face of it there was little reason for the sympatico which had grown up between them but they both had blonde hair.

Hugh wondered if blonde hair was as rare among the Mexicans as it had been among his own people. He figured that likely it was as he had never before seen a blonde Mexican. He knew that as the Mexicans had moved up the coast these last centuries establishing new-towns beside the ruined cities they had come across and absorbed small pockets of "Mamaklees" or "Gringos", as the Mexicans called them. Not all the Gringos had died in the plague, as the plague favored to eliminate most thoroughly only those over nine or ten years of age , but as the remnant left had raised themselves among the ruins their descendants were profoundly non literate and non technical. .The much more numerous individuals of the ascendant Mexican nation had swallowed them without a burp. Mexico now had a new-town beside each coastal ruined city right up to the ice sheet just north of Vancouver.

Mexico had fared well after the big death. In the United States and Canada even the smallest and remotest villages usually succumbed. Affluence had been the killer. It had promoted the ease of travel and the spread of the disease.

Mexico had been different. The rural poor were more isolated and many villages had had few visitors. In addition cultural factors had come into play making it easier for villages to isolate themselves until the plague was over. Sure, Mexico had lain empty for a decade or so , but the country had never really been without oil as there was plenty barreled up above ground. and it hadn't been long until the lights were on again in many places. The mountain villages were emptied as people spread out on the plains and corn beans and squash were grown as never before. Every surviving Mexican family had a car if they wanted one, while the rest of North America was a hardly peopled wilderness.

and the surviving populations in central and south America found their future with the bow and arrow and left gas engines behind. Mexico alone carried the torch of western culture. Mexico ran on oil and salvage. There were accurate maps to the treasure cities of the interior and Mexico was selectively mining these from the air , while any ruined city beside a river now had a Mexican steel foundry beside it. The West coast was the Mexican steel belt with salvage colonies all along it.

The salesman was eying Hugh quizzically "Are you going to buy her today sonny?" he said to Hugh as Hugh sneaked what he had thought was a private glance in the direction of Killer Bill's old boat. Annoyance at being transparent tugged at Hugh's frame of mind , but the salesman was being kindly. He had seemed a one dimensional character. He was fat and cigar smoking , with flashy gold rings, but Hugh sensed some depths.

Certainly there had been none of the tech. to non-tech. snobbiness that other Mexicans sometimes displayed towards tribes people. Hugh decided to be honest and simply said "yes" and took out his plastic for the salesman to run through the slot. This provoked an unusual response in the old Mexican who to Hugh's surprise turned color, puffed and uttered a variety of other noises before speaking.

After a moment or two he popped it out. "Don't buy her sonny, she is too old" and then after a pause he continued "I knew you were going to buy her by the look on your face when you first laid eyes on her, but don't do it sonny. She has gone soft, rotted out under the fiber glass in the hold. She is not the boat she used to be.' Hugh looked for guile and saw none so he ventured a question. "which boat should I buy then?"

The older man once again sniffed and snorted at the question as if he had taken offense. He finally spat out more words a deeply displeased look on his face. "Look Sunny Jim it isn't me that has the boat you should buy but that son of a billy goat down at the foot of the harbor. Give him fifty thousand for it and no more."

Hugh was not up to the situation and stood there gawking. The old man opened up the door of his shop and said "So get out of here and let me make some money." As Hugh walked away he realized how close he had been to making the mistake of his life and buying a bad boat. He had been saved by the compassion of a stranger who had even lost money in order to help him. It would have been bad to buy a boat with hidden rot. Plywood boats went to Hell fast when that began. Hugh had nearly done it and gone and traded the cow for the magic beans.

As he entered the marina at the foot of the harbor he knew right away which boat he wanted and he also remembered right off why he hadn't spent much time on this particular wharf . The owner was a thoroughly unpleasant character. On their first encounter he had continued to use Spanglish pidgin to talk ,even after Hugh had demonstrated his Spanish ability. It had been a put down and not a subtle one.

"But" Hugh reflected as he entered the sales room. "Antipathy just might make for better bargaining on his part." Helped by his knowledge of the correct selling price given him by the proprietor of the other sales dock Hugh was able to hold his own in the haggling and soon was running his card through the slot. Hugh was unwilling to leave his new boat even temporarily in the hands of such an unpleasant individual so he fired her up and pulled her out into the harbor coasting at dead slow to the dock at the waterfront motel which had been their home these last few days.

Calley was on the monitor. They had sometimes been close enough to a World Gov Cray computer at the settlements that they had stopped at on their way west that Calley could have dug out their monitor and keyboard and patched into it, but there had been a tacit agreement to leave it packed up for the journey out. Here in Nanaimo however Calley had used the time to reconnect with Chirac in Montreal. Today Chirac had big news. Two of the chimps had begun to gain weight, grown some gray hair, and appeared to be morphing. Chirac was ecstatic

But calley was upset. She was arguing with Chirac about this. "was he sure?" because chimps weren't supposed to morph, not ever. Chirac had reassuring words on this, Apparently in the early days when chimps and gorillas had newly come to the attention of science quite a few had been misclassified due to the great size and unusual aspect of some of the chimp specimens. There had also been claims put about by individuals who claimed to have shot gorilla chimp hybrids . The stories were seen to be largely baloney by the later scientific community. Cross breeds were thought to be unlikely considering the genetic distance. It was generally considered by primatologists that there had been larger chimps in the early days. Hunting pressure favored smaller earlier maturing individuals. It was known that chimps had long been subjected to hunting pressure. Why look any further?

Chirac had a new take on all this. He thought that these were recorded cases not of cross breeds but of morphed individuals. He thought that perhaps chimps morphed, but only very seldom, or , only under very specific circumstances. Chirac pointed out that amongst orang and gorilla populations, although the huge morphed individuals played very significant roles , very few individuals actually morphed and became silver-backs.

Chirac thought that perhaps sexual dimorphism was falling off as strategy generally amongst primates, as all groups appeared to br exhibiting it less and less .Chirac even had a theory to go along with all this. He thought that sexual; dimorphism in apes ran at cross currents to the important role that culture and cooperation amongst females was beginning to play. Sexual dimorphism shattered potential communities into small groups that revolved around the silver-backs. Chimp communities however tended to be much larger, had more culture and the central figures were groups of mature females.

All the chimp males lived on the outskirts as did their counterparts the unmorphed males amongst gorillas. From changes like this Chirac thought their human culture had also come,

Calley seemed worried by this turn of events. Hugh offered entirely against his own inclinations, to remain longer with her in Nanaimo so that she could keep in contact with Montreal through the local cray web but she had refused him. She had firmly put the monitor away and looked him in the eye. She said "Hugh, catch me a fish .I want to eat fish." As she got dressed he noticed she had a little trouble climbing into her jeans. She heard his breath catch, and replied to the unsaid question. "I don't think so yet Hughy. I think its just tacos, but maybe...." and her eyes lit up hugely.

When they got up north there would be Crays that they could sometimes cruise into range of, as most villages had them. World Gov saw to it that they did. The Crays sat in prominent places in the villages their energy coming from the flat black solar panels on their tops. They connected each village to the worlds knowledge and the world's financial transactions with the same thoroughness that they connected rich Mexico city magnates.

The Cray net was the great evener. World Gov had tried to put at least a mini Cray and a pile of wind up or solar powered monitors in front of every mud hut village that they could reach. The moon men were trying to stitch the world back together and it was working. They, the moon men, orphaned in space by the plague had been in a race against time. It had been clear from the beginning that despite the mass of material, people, and industry on the moon a nontechnical earth would ensure a moon once again devoid of life within a not too long period of time.

A century had been guessed in the beginning as the maximum time they could hold out but it had in fact been nearly two centuries before the moon men had harried the nations of earth into a race for space travel which few on earth saw as of benefit to themselves. By then the moon men were space burnt and changed . The wild rumors on earth about the changes seemed to have been mostly old wives tales,for Hugh had seen a few at the U and apart from their use of wheel chairs and their frequent deafness they had seemed much like any one else.

He had also noticed their common use of american sign language amongst themselves. It was now the lingua franca of space. It had first started amongst the space burnt "old families" Deafness had become common., Whether this was a result of "space burnt-ness", as the colloquial idiom had it, or as a result of a more mundane reason , that of too many people with too few ancestors, was not really known. At any rate the gene pool of the moon had swelled after the resumption of shipments to space of rice and sardines and colonist "volunteers" in crappy old plain steel capsules powered by kerosene rockets. In the beginning the volunteers had about a fifty fifty chance for pick up. Needless to say they were not really volunteers.

. Hughy accepted their leaving town the way a thirsty dog accepts water. Now that he had her his boat seemed better than any other. The old Mexican had been right . He didn't see how he could have missed her. He must have been blinded by the actual dream boat of his childhood. She was not beautiful however and she was dilapidated beyond her age.; but underneath she was a relatively new boat. He could tell a bit of her story by the gear aboard her. The guys for example had been stitched by someone unfamiliar with a marlin spike and had simply been braided together in a farmers splice. That said it all to Hugh. She had been owned by a landsman and run down. Underneath she was a good boat , forty five feet of solid plywood with a huge gutting area in the back and as fine a canning galley as he had ever seen. That meant he could get Calley to help in the summertime and have a couple of lads or lasses on board to sleep on deck and gut fish.

The trip north was peaceful, there were millions of fish in the sea, but catching them was only a third of the work. They had to be gutted, chilled , scaled , chopped and boiled inside the cans. They could fill her in three months or maybe four. All they had to do to accomplish this was to start fishing at four a.m. gut fish from the mid morning till mid afternoon and boil fish until eight at night. Then ,go to sleep[if the weather let them]. Most troller captains did not sleep much more than an hour at a stretch before throwing themselves erect to stand turning in a circle to observe the four directions through the windows of their sleeping chamber. They were like the rabbits of the sea always ready to run for a hole on a split seconds notice.

Hugh felt the culture shock first. His last five years at the university had been broadening. He had thought he would adjust easily to the "back home" diet of mostly fish. He had dreamed of salmon eggs while at the university "nikits" his people called it . But now that he had nikits daily if he cared for it , or any other fruit of the sea, he found himself daydreaming about french fries, or, about the stir fried vegetables of the canteen at the university. Worse than that, as he watched Calley slave daily, he realized that somehow he had forgotten that the work of a fisherman and his wife was drudgery and unmitigated toil. Worse for the wife than for the man.

Calley never complained. It was entirely in his own mind that he became convinced over time he had made a big mistake. "Oh Hell" Hugh thought. They were successful and they would make a pile of dough relatively speaking; and when they finally did get home to the west coast of their island where there village was all the boys and girls would stare in admiration at how they had come up in the world. Hugh knew in his own heart that he himself could not fit into so limited an existence and he felt for Calley that whether or not she could fit in by an effort of discipline or sacrifice; she should not do so.

All season Hugh hoped to wake up one day capable of the joy his present situation would once have given him . his malaise shaken off and a thing of the past. It never happened instead he became surer that they should get the hell off of the boat.

Hugh broke it to her at night while they were parked off of Jai Dai Aitch , the outer island on their way back to Nanaimo to sell their seasons catch. They were parked in the big south facing bay, sure death in the winter, but safe enough now when the gusts to be feared came from the north. They had opened a small bottle of Mexican wine and Calley had even had a small sip despite now being clearly pregnant to anyone who looked. Hugh laid out the whole sad story to her including their financial picture. All versions of Hugh's plan for the future included mooring up at home base for a while,probably until Calley had her baby and searching the web for a position for Calley at a university somewhere. He would follow along and teach phys-ed at a high school or whatever it took' but he told her he wasn't going to bury her achieving a boy hood ambition that he now knew was wrong even for him.

Hugh had noticed that whenever he talked about finances Calley squirmed excessively even in normal times and now as he talked about their future he saw her head drop and the sorrow in her eyes become too strong to stay muted. Suddenly he knew that there were words unsaid and there was a lie of some sort between them.

On the heels of this thought Calley said to him "I lied to you Hugh." One more time the little green goblin of jealousy popped up and a small evil voice in Hugh's head whispered to him "its not your kid. It is Chirac's." Hugh was forever grateful he did not vocalize that out loud for Calley continued to speak and he heard her say. "Hughy I have some money." She looked at him her face full of shame. "I lied Hugh" She repeated "Back in High School there was a big reward for that proof to Fermat.

It was not a lie at first Hughy, but only something I hadn't told you about; but it became one and I am so sorry for lying to you Hugh. If I had told anyone back then they would have said "Why go to university when there is no need to learn a trade if you are rich; But I needed to go to university. I just had to go so I tricked you , and I am sorry I promise I will try to stop tricking you from now on," Hugh sat back stunned He hadn't expected a full fledged monolog and crying jag and that bit about trying to stop tricking him had a distinctly unflattering ring to it. He shook his head to remove the cobwebs of ill considered attention and returned to the matter at hand. He blurted out rather less than cosmically "reward"? "money? "

She continued crying and after a while he tried comforting her. An ill considered move. His suggestion that he wouldn't really consider it lying was taken poorly as she snapped at him not wanting to be disagreed with even in her own favor.

Suddenly Hugh felt on very dangerous ground . A wrong word now could be fatal. In a rather squeaky voice he tried to change the topic. "Rich" he said, and then after a moment "what do you mean rich?" She named a figure. "I'll be dipped" he said, then a little more rudely "Jesus Christ on crutches" He drank the rest of the bottle occasionally muttering about Moses and Murphy with Calley suddenly asleep there beside him, then he slept the best sleep he had had in months in the shelter of the deep peaceful Bay.

In the morning they headed south around the inner island to the town where there was a Cray which they could patch in to to begin their planning. Calley had also been curious to check in with Chirac about any progress made. They had been recently fishing off the ice sheet north of Vancouver island , but the fjords and former inlets they ran into for cover were closed by the great ice sheet a few miles inland and there were no settlements. Mankind had retreated to Vancouver island from the pacific North west scraped south by the ice . Only Haida Guai remained in northern isolation.

They were just rounding the shingle spit when the pains hit him again. At first they had joked that his pains were the false pregnancy of a father but they had persisted . And what was with his legs? He seemed fit enough , but his front teeth ached sometimes, in fact lots of things now seemed to take their turn aching. He felt his cheeks, yes, there was definitely something going on there as well. Double molars maybe? Oh well, he would see a doc if any of his symptoms persisted two weeks beyond the end of fishing season. "Maybe he was just plum fucking tired out" he reasoned to himself.

They were already pretty well agreed on their next course of action. There were plenty of world gov projects world wide that they were qualified for. Malaria took a huge toll worldwide. Calley would secure an invitation to take part in some end of the research. She knew in advance that because of who she was they would try to ship her to some old world university to grace the staff , but her intent was to go directly to an affected area and work there. Five years of universities was enough for both of them at the moment. Hawaii was struggling with the parasite. As soon as Hugh had pulled into the docks at Comox slough . Calley had the monitor out and fired up. Hugh decided to take the chance to get out and stretch his legs. Just the mention of Hawaii and his own private thoughts about how they might get there had cheered him up considerably and the pains had completely subsided once again.

Hugh was feeling damned good about himself when he got home. Life on board the boat just didn't involve enough walking or running. There was nowhere to go. You could pull up to shore but the dense salal berry under the sitka spruce prohibited even a short walk most places but this was a farm town with miles of road and after a good long row to warm up he had even beaten his own best time in a half mile run, when he had really expected that his four months on the boat would have set him back. His legs seemed muscled and pretty bloody strong. He was whistling fisherman's green as he walked back upon the dock. He could tell she had been crying when he reached the boat..

The monitor was uncharacteristically silent. and she was sitting quietly although tear stained. He sat down across from her and waited for it to come out. After a moment or so the torrent began.

"Oh Hughy I did something really bad." She paused and then spat out the rest without waiting for a reply. "I morphed Dr. Chirac, and Jimmy and Johnny the ape keepers and maybe, maybe, maybe, Hughy maybe lots of other people ." she looked right at him before continuing "and Hughy I think I morphed you too, you know how you have been feeling lately."

She recovered as quickly as she had broken down, but Hugh had only begun to feel the shock. "Me?" he managed, his next few attempts at vocalization didn't manage to push air but after several tries he managed "me?" and then "morph?" and then "me?" again rather ungrammatically. Several times.

Calley finally looked up again and said "Yes Hughy" in her most pained tone of voice. "But please don't start asking me questions about that now" Hugh did not quite dare to break the silence. He just sat there thinking about Fay Ray and King Kong . He suppressed a desperate urge to giggle. finally Calley looked up and said "I want to go home, Hughy, take me to see my mom and Hughy, buy us a nicer boat to live on." Hugh opened his mouth to comment but her stern tone returned.

"Quiet now Hughy" she said "Mama needs to think". Hugh shut his yak. It reminded him of the day she had got his finger bitten off by the orang. She had been bloody well unsympathetic then too and more or less accused him of crying over spilt milk. "Now she has morphed me" he thought "and into what?" Some big blonde ape like creature probably.

He visualized all the early monster flicks he had watched at the university "Yes it would probably be like that" he thought "nice big teeth like the wolfman and maybe a tale as well for all I know." Hugh prudently removed himself from the forecastle where he would disturb his beloved. He felt the need to swear out loud, prolongedly. He was through all the common swear words of his youth and well into Spanish ones and some new french ones he had learned in Montreal, before he thought of the boat which he now had the money to buy. "and Christ what a boat she was" Hugh thought to himself

The old Mexican recognized the boat from a distance as she came into the harbor. He could tell it was weighed down. "The young 'blondin' has made a good thing of it" he muttered to himself. The boat was 'fukfull' of salmon as Spanglish pidgin would have it. He was pleased to see her pull towards his dock. He was pretty sure he knew what was going to happen next. The tribes people were generous and gifts incurred status to the giver just in themselves. He was about to be given salmon and lots of it. Pink money in cans. And so it turned out to be. After the formal gift giving was over they for the first time exchanged names and shook hands.

"Well, Francisco" Hugh said, "You still have the steel boat I see "and then he added,with the directness one would use with a friend, "I want to buy it." Francisco was floored. This boat was ten times the price of the boat Hugh had originally bought and Francisco could have sworn that the price of the troller was damned near the total amount that Hugh had available. More than a little avarice shaded Francisco's face "What did you find sonny? Was it copper ?" The way he said that led Hugh to smile. Francisco thought that Hughy had found some forgotten hydro-electric way-station loaded with copper from the ancient days The Mexicans were more obsessed with treasure than any group of people on earth since the Vikings. Mexican civilization was built on one big salvage hunt, often with accurate maps and the X clearly marked . El Dorado and riches happened often enough in reality for all Mexicans to dream. The ruined civilization still had rich hidden repositories of loot.

Hugh dissuaded this chain of thought by telling Francisco that the money was coming from the east from a bank and that they weren't about to embark on any copper recovery expedition. At this Francisco recalled their arrival from the east on a plane from Montreal,

Francisco had heard that the new- town there was huge, nearly as big as Mexico city and as rich, although he believed in their flying cars little more than in flying carpets. Reluctantly, Francisco let his vision of a copper bonanza slip from his mind. In the new found feeling of familiarity which the moment engendered they sat on the dock, both upon and surrounded by the crates of salmon which Hugh had offloaded. sipping on the carafe of tequila margeuritas with ice and lime which Francisco had mixed .

Francisco observed this young man whom he had befriended. He was not surprised to see his woman was pregnant He had noticed her beatific expression, perfect smile and other tell tale signs from his own experience. He figured he had probably known she was gravid before the kid did. It was one of the reasons he had not sold the kid the dud boat in the first place. "The other" he wryly acknowledged to himself, "was that he, fifty years ago in his misspent youth, had left children up and down the west coast, like a dog ". and a young man with blonde hair aroused grandfatherly feelings in him.

With some difficulty Francisco pulled his mind back to the observation of the man in front of him. The kid had changed, in fact now that he had a chance to look at him he seemed both older and much larger. In his recollection the kid had been shorter than him and his recollection was generally good. And what was with the kids face? an abscess on either side might produce that swelling. He resolved to give the kid his dentists name later on but for now he let business interests take over. "Hey Sonny " he said "Perhaps your woman would like a look at the boat?"

Calley loved the boat especially the "whore's rooms" in the back (as Hugh called them to himself). Calley had passed months of smelling fish and of smelling like fish. She was silk and lace deprived. Hugh could hear her purr audibly when Francisco showed her the former drug operation in the back, expertly checking out the p.c.r. machine and the tanks.

The computer was worth looking at as well. It was a relic of the old days. A small plaque on the bottom identified it as former property of cal tech. It looked capable of far more than running a small boat and crunching a few numbers. Hugh wondered what its use had been in the old days before it was hot wired into its present local.

Calley was in a rush to return to their home village so they passed the plastic through the slot without further hesitation. They simply gave Francisco his asking price. One seasons catch of canned salmon plus a whole lot of loot. "So where is home then Sonny?" Francisco questioned . "Hesquiat peninsula" Hugh answered and then amended it after as was the fashion "But the village is south of there now where there is a bay for big boats at the hot springs cove". Hugh and Francisco continued their conversation until the bottle was empty and the worm was high and dry.

Hugh and Calley took leave of the dock the next morning. There would be some long faces at the fuel dock for the next few weeks. for Hugh had drained it in order to fill the huge tanks of his new boat. He had to pay a bribe of course but with Mexicans this was not necessarily a dishonorable thing. The Mexicans had as many words for bribes as the Eskimos did for snow, and some were quite respectable, where no dereliction of duty was involved. This bribe ,if he recalled correctly would be called might be about midway on the scale of honorability. Hugh was never quite sure of his footing when dealing with the Mexicans, He spoke the language well enough because of schooling but his youth had been spent up country and his manhood to date had been spent in the east.

Hugh successfully got the new boat under way headed south. They first had to round the ruins of Victoria on the south tip of the island and head north again The jagged blackened spires of the city still stood untouched, and slow to fall, ascending above the huge fir forest at their feet. All of the forest was pristine, as the price of wood or salvage wasn't worth being irradiated. The boat was a marvel. The navigational system had a voice activated voice response presently using Spanish but Hugh hit the help menu on the screen and presently among desk top options was able to find language of choice.

He hit browse and the first heading in the English list to hit his eye was Indian standard. He wondered for a moment if this meant him, or the tribes had once been referred to as Indians but no, on reflection, he realized this would be the English of the Indian subcontinent. African English also had an intimidating ring to it,but Carribean English? "Perhaps", he thought. At least he had heard it spoken and it was the right continent, sort of.

The main decider was Bob Marley, Hugh loved the classics. His last winter at the university his dorm had adopted Bob Marley and he had heard him played solidly for months. Funny how it was with music that the best was saved and played forever.

Hugh chose Caribbean English. He had further choices to make for the gender of the voice . Hugh figured if it was going to be waking him up in the middle of the night it might as well be a female voice. and he had to choose a name for himself . She wouldn't take commands from just anybody. He grinned and thought about "Big Poppa", that would do for a log in name between the two of them. And a name for the boat for the second part of the recognition sequence? Hughy thought for a second, well ,she was utterly beautiful he might as well call her Cleopatra or at least maybe just Cleo for short as there were sure to be times at sea when he would resent the time wasted by those extra two syllables if he left them there. He punched in Cleo on her key board. He was startled when he heard her sexy Jamaican voice address him.

"Big poppa do you want to declare in a destination and let me take over now ?" "No thank you" Hugh said, rather unnecessarily politely. He sat for a moment and then reconsidered . "Cleo" he said.

"Yes Big Poppa" she replied .

"Lets go to Hot Springs Cove" he said ,"Yes big poppa"she replied and rattled off a string of coordinates at him. Hugh kicked back in the captains chair while she motored on south without his help. She asked a few questions at first, about whether they wanted to sail if possible sometimes to save fuel, or if speed was of the essence. Then she motored on silently without speaking. Her g.p.s. allowed her to come remarkably close to rocks and more than once Hugh felt tempted to override her and take her farther but he restrained himself Cleo had sonar and radar, she had good eyes and wouldn't run them up on a rock even without the g.p.s. By the time the day was half gone he totally trusted her., even to the point of leaving his captains post and sitting in the galley with Calley.

Hugh exuded confidence in his new boat. She sailed herself when the wind was right and motored along when it wasn't never wasting a drop of fuel. Cleo rounded the south tip of Vancouver like a professional and now that there were no more rocks to be missed and the weather was fare Hugh decided to even risk a beer or two. He was settling in to watch a movie when Calley came in and asked him in a very pointed manner why they were headed for Japan. Hugh choked on his beer and bolted back to the wheel house where he gasped out "Cleo, where are we going?" "Hot Springs Cove, Big Poppa" she replied . Hughy thought for a moment and then said "Where is hot springs cove Cleo?". She replied with a string of coordinates which Hugh was not quick enough to digest.

"Cleo" He said firmly "What is the nearest port to Hot Springs Cove?" She replied in her ever cheerful voice "That would be Port Moresby, the island of New Guinea. She began to spew out its population and vital statistics ."Cleo, shut up" Hugh said . After a moments silence, Hugh said "Cleo, check your charts for Vancouver island. Do you see a Hot Springs Cove there?".

"No big poppa" she said, only a Hot Springs harbor" "That's it .Cleo, go there" said Hugh but apparently this was not a clear enough command for she played his own voiced back to him and suggested he actually punch in the destination this time. She sounded pissed off and Hugh found himself apologizing to the computer before he caught himself.

He was rattled. Bombing around at sea in the wrong direction was distinctly unprofessional. Hugh punched in the correction and he could feel the boat beneath him sheer off into a nearly opposite direction from which she had been heading. Hugh was embarrassed , even avoiding supper, and he spent the night in the wheel house too, just in case anything else came up, but of course nothing did. As they passed the towns of the south coast Calley was occasionally able to fire up the monitor while they were in range.

Montreal now felt that they had identified the molecule which was responsible. Calley brought the genomes into view on the web in tandem and examined them . There it is she had said" and pointed out that it was near identical in all the species concerned. She mused that both chimps and human females must have produced this substance in the not so distant past as they both had the sets of genetic instructions in full. Hugh immediately thought he saw a flaw in the reasoning. "So why then haven't zoo keepers been morphing all over the planet this last several centuries ?

"Good question Hugh" she said to him, "Chirac says that the human vomero- nasal pits are almost entirely obscured by by other tissue and that encased as they are the pits are in a non functioning condition or at least they were obscured until I stimulated them. Apparently those synthetic civet cat extracts which we purchased, do a wonderful job of winkling the organ right out." She continued on . "Would you like to hear Chirac's theory about how mankind has some kind of aquatic island based heritage where our ancestors dove into the water to escape predators. This induced us to fore go our vomito nasal organ in order to facilitate diving? It is a fascinating story?" She began to tell him of how many things in the human physiognomy indicated a wet episode in our history. Our long noses so that we can dive into water without the water pressure being directed up our nostrils, our hairlessness which we share with other wetland mammals like elephants pigs and hippos { not to mention the truly aquatic mammals} and our layer of fat underneath our skins. Added to this was the way we made love face to face and our ability to hold our breaths which we make so much use of in speaking."

Hugh's head hurt. a bit and after about five additional minutes of it right up to the point where she started to draw the possibility of human origins away from the savannahs and up and east in an arc towards Asia and Oceania spewing out Chirac's thoughts about Heydenreich's theory whereby the drifting of useful packages of traits within a larger population (braininess traits amongst Homo Erectus or Bison traits amongst feral domestic cattle) happens independently of movement (or replacement) of populations , if the time scale is great enough and or the rewards for doing so make it worthwhile.

At that point, Hughy finally held up his finger, interrupting Calley and said in a deceptively mild voice. "You know Calley?, I don't care all that much about Chirac's theory right now. In fact" he said still mildly "I couldn't give a flying fuck at a rolling donut about Chirac's theory. What I do care about is whether I grow a fucking tail or not . Do I get nice cheek pouches like an orangutang , and maybe a nice shaggy coat of fur and a gorilla smell to go along with it?" He had meant his sarcasm to be biting but she was looking at him sadly with pity in her eyes. "I would love you even with cheek pouches" she said after another moments silence. Hugh felt suddenly deflated . "After a moments introspection he said "I love you too Calley. I am just worried about what is happening to me that's all." Hugh began to apologize to her. but she stopped him. saying "Sometimes we talk too much Hughy, lets just go to bed and feel each other" Hughy trusted Cleo to keep the helm.

Chirac thought about how the situation had changed since his arrival back after his euro sabbatical . He had arrived back in North America elated with the news that more apes were morphing, and that he would have a second change to find the "telomerase" as he had dubbed the enzyme that they searched for. His own months in France had been overshadowed by his own, mysterious at that time, physical problems, he had spent a good deal of time awa"That would put anyone in a somber mood" Chirac thought. He had never thought to have a look at his own telomeres. Then suddenly he had been back in the university immersed in his work. He had never really guessed the nature of what was happening ,so engrossed was he in his work and his own undiagnosed pains and swellings. It had been common talk amongst the doctors of the colony that something was up, they were well aware of the pains, weight gains increasing muscle and new large teeth forming in the jaws of most of the male population. Nobody really knew who solved the conundrum. One day it had been hearsay ,and then three or four days later after the affected population of several thousand better than average minds had mulled it over, it was suddenly the accepted paradigm. They were all morphing, nearly every bloody adult male one of them. For a while Chirac became extremely unpopular.

The World Gov colony near Montreal was a special kind of place. It had been a major hydro electric center before the big death and after a couple of centuries World Gov had come back and switched things on. It had been a huge undertaking requiring the establishment of a colony with the best technology had to offer, but the pay off had been big too, lots of power. Lots and lots of power. There was enough to run a Tesla grid close by and ship power to the new-towns of the east coast and still have miles extra. The university used what they needed. They had free heat in a cold climate and that had encouraged acres and acres of indoor gardens and farms. The primate center itself was part of a larger indoor complex of many acres including offices and classrooms interspersed with habitats and indoor gardens. It was the heart of the colony

Pretty soon after they realized that all the males at the university had been affected ,it was realized that there were in all likelihood, thousands of other affected individuals including the whole student body which had just left the university. Also it would be likely that any or all of the official or unofficial visitors Hydro technicians and plenty of new-town Montrealers who had just stopped in for a cup of coffee would likely be morphing as well. A formal report was immediately sent to World Gov asking them to help find individuals who would likely be affected, but for whom the university had no names and addresses ,such as the Hydro employes who had returned across the Atlantic It was too late.

It was among the affected men who had left the university that the nightmare began. There were individuals alone amongst people who did not understand the changes they were going through. There began to be a fear in the world, a fear of the changeling of the tupe cabra, of the loup garou.

The new-town Montreal riots were a horror from beginning to end. The Montrealers awoke one morning to realize there were hundreds of apelike creatures hidden within their midst even in the homes of their closest kin, having seemingly taken their places and something of their likenesses. The mobs went door to door demanding to see the occupants and stringing them up.

Chirac saw the pictures on the internet. It had looked like a scene from Frankenstein right down to the peasants with pitch forks and torches. After that things had been grim at the university for a while. They had no guns to speak of compared to the frontiersmen ,and the mother government in Europe was being strangely silent towards her colony of mutating men. The Euro World Gov scientists had plenty of morphed and morphing individuals to examine, too many.;and the body of the public mind was varying from a scenario like invasion of the body snatchers , through to a new virus. In short everyone was scared to death. and checking under their beds at night for mysterious green pods. The first reaction by World Gov was to treat it like a virus. The morphs were to be rounded up, if necessary with a price on their head, if necessary dead. Too late Chirac tried to slow the hardening of the attitudes in Europe. Too late he realized that they should have allowed only women to contact Europe., but the damage was done. He was not entirely surprised when the Crays went silent and the colony was cut off.

It was Chirac's idea to neutralize the threat posed by the nearby new-town by aerosoling it with the pheromones at night from spray planes. There was no choice, either that or be crucified or otherwise killed. It was a simple operation ,they just sprayed the town secretly and really damned thoroughly several nights in a row and then used the same planes to deliver pamphlets explaining the true scientific state of affairs, as well as having the likelihood that renewed youth would be a part of the change high lighted in big letters. It put a different light on the saying "If you cant beat them join them" The aerosol offensive worked insofar as securing the immediate safety of the university town, but the pictures which were later broadcast to Europe of a whole city morphing in its bedrooms had the Europeans quaking in theirs and the Crays in Montreal quit broadcasting as well, a few months later. Quebec's isolation became complete. World Gov ceded Quebec to the enemy, and sealed it off, renewing and giving more urgency to finding all stray morphed individuals.

Morphed young men had been seeded to the four winds by the university and prudence dictated that World Gov look upon that as an intentional act. The hunt for morphs was on.

Hagar was a tough cookie. She listened to Calley's story without interrupting. Hagar was not an educated woman in the sense of schooling but she was educated in the ways of the world .She had spent part of here own life down in old Mexico and her daughter Calley's story although novel was far from the deep tragedies of many human lives.

At first it had seemed just a personal tragedy, Calley's pretty boy Hugh was going to become disfigured. Hagar had advised Calley that there were very many extremely ugly men in the world and that she thought the village would accept Hughy no matter what he looked like. She did think however that it would be best if he didn't change right in front of them like the wolfman in the old movie. It had been good enough advice at the time it was given and Calley and Hugh took the advice to take their new boat out cruising while Hugh's problems sorted themselves out in some final form.

Hagar had always kept abreast of world events especially since her second oldest daughter had gone east to school. There was no missing the Montreal riots and when the Crays went dead for Montreal and points east she began to be deeply worried.

Searching the web Hagar began to get an idea of what was happening elsewhere. World Gov was treating the situation one day as if it were a virus and the next as if t it were subversion or an invasion of some sort. The wanted posters were ambiguously worded as tif there was a world wide search for one man . hairy huge and with big incisors. World Gov had posted the adds to the corners of the globe. The hunt was on and the money was on the barrel. World Gov had attempted to impose quiet to prevent panic but its heavy handed methods and lack of forthrightness had instead caused wild speculation.

The average person was aware that something was up which involved people changing to ape like creatures but they didn't know whether to shit or wind their wristwatches as the saying went . People the world over wondered if a face mask was a good preventative, or, perhaps, all one had to do was look under the bed for pods before retiring (like in the invasion of the body snatchers). The truth had been torpedoed early on. Hagar's hopes for Hugh and Calley being able to fit in again at Hot Springs Cove diminished. There were Mexican merchants across the bay at the hot springs as well as several Mexicans in residence in the village. Word was certain to get out and the reward was big enough to tempt. The thought of Hughy's head salted in a bag for a bounty momentarily made her shudder.

The twins loved the boat, to them Cleo was a real person, a magic genii to answer their every question, they teased out her early history as a teachers aid at cal tech and the two hundred years of abuse she had suffered, synchronizing traffic lights in Mexico city before she was stolen by the mob and fused with the boat to have an adventurous career as a bandit. She helped them draw or read or cook or understand why the diagonal and the side of many common shapes are incommenserable with each other, or whatever else was on their young minds on any given day.

Calley's little sisters were about as smart as she was, but they didn't admit that between themselves. They reckoned that they were at least twice as smart seeing as there were two of them. Although they loved Calley dearly they were more skeptical of her fame for her Fermat's proof than others were.;Having looked it over for themselves, they accused her privately of knocking off the easy one with the only big cash prize. It was nothing compared to the Michaelson/Morley thing they had been working on for a while. Einstein at first glance had seemed so unlikely, and Einstein himself had seemed to point the way out by suggesting that someone could refute his silly theory of relativity if they proved Michaelson /Morley's equally silly experiment to be in error. It had been designed in the ancient days before space travel to see if space were really empty, or, were perhaps full of ether or green cheese or something.

To the twins it had looked like a pushover. Einsteins theory that there is no innate firstness or secondness about anything, that synchronicity is only an artifact of where you observed from, had seemed an impossibly silly theory. It was rather like a man standing on one leg on a wheel barrow while balancing a sofa over his head. It seemed that one good kick somewhere should send it crashing down. Its seeming verity on examination had been the twins first indication that while the universe was clearly not fair or just ,it also might not be reasonable. The twins looked for easier game.

The twins developed a nifty way of finding the area of a circle without using a messy repeating decimal like pi. It was simple you just took the radius and circumference of any circle and used them to create two sides of a right triangle. They had found that this right triangle will have the same area as the circle.

It was not even necessary to use the slightly difficult formula for finding the area of a triangle, for any right triangle is exactly half of of a rectangle and it was only necessary to find the area of that rectangle and divide it in half. They had immediately sent their a "theorem" as they called it off for appraising at a university and had even begun calling it the "Cassy/Polly theorem" for these were their names, when a letter had arrived from a university a few months later. It had been a kindly reply from the university math department which informed them that they had reinvented the ancient Egyptian way of squaring a circle. It had been known since antiquity. There had not been even a single mention of cash in the letter.

Having their big sister home was the best thing in the world to Cassy and Polly. When Calley had left they had been tiny and her leaving had been the first big hurt of their lives. The five years she was leaving for was to them a huge figure as incomprehensible as a British billion is to most people. . Having her back pregnant and with big hairy Hughy was just too good to be true.

The girls were terribly sorry for poor Hughy with his sore teeth and told him that he was just the right kind of furry for snuggling up to . They told him his hair wasn't at all coarse and ape like, why, he was soft and furry almost like a small dog with a new haircut. He was just wonderful to sit on or to pet. He told them that they made him feel better, but they could tell by the look on his face when they told him to "hup" up beside them on the couch that it was too early to make jokes. The teeth were really too awful when you first looked at them. Two long sharp incisors jutting out from a perfectly normal set of upper teeth, just like a baboon's or a movie Dracula's and yet the girls as well as their sisters and grandmother found that there was something attractive about them as well. To be so scary looking was somehow very masculine . Hugh was still a hunk ,just a somewhat larger one. His three hundred pound foot ball player's body had swelled to four fifty. He was a big man, but other supposedly normal men had been bigger. Andre the Giant and Angus Mc Askell had both broke five hundred. Hughy had lots of hair, but he he had known a Fiji islander at school who had nearly as much, the poor momzer had always dressed to the hilt to avoid embarrassment. The canines were another matter. No human ancestor had sprouted them for hundreds of thousands of years.

The DNA. to make them had been a useless bit retained through the conservativeness of the double helix system much as a human fetus first grows and then loses its tail as it grows. There is little genetic cost to pay for carrying around extra DNA and a great price to pay for being unprepared to change.

The teeth were the big problem. They were unmistakable and were not hide-able, and they were the undoing of morphs who tried to blend in. In a normal world it would not have been a big deal, a good dentist and a couple of gold crowns. There were no gross deformities of the sort which Hugh had been fearing, no tail of course ,for no apes had one, but also, no cheek pouches and no changes of the proportions of his body one to another. He didn't have long arms like a gorilla and a tendency to knuckle walk and no increased odor. he was mostly just bigger than he had been and with a few extra decorations Life on board Cleo was a laugh. Hugh clawed his way out of his funk about his appearance Calley and the girls still loved him and he suspected that if he ever got the chance he could really play football. Hugh had four hundred and fifty hard pounds, a good boat, a nice wife and even a somewhat larger you know what. He decided he had no reason to be blue. Life was sweet and their journeys were aimless these months, intended only to kill time until Calley had her baby and until his changes were complete. Calley's younger sisters had taken to Cleo like a sibling and piloted her up the coast choosing the destinations Cleo could be entrusted their care, Cleo wouldn't run aground because of a careless word. she was much too smart for that.

With Calley pregnant and Hugh preoccupied the twins had become the captains of the good ship Cleopatra taking her in close north of Vancouver island to watch the glaciers calve into the sea. and trusting Cleo to find her way into still bays at night so they could observe the animals. It was wonderful how they behaved. It was not in them to be afraid of something out on the water so even with Cleo close offshore they would come down to sample the salty seaweed and the twins would catch them in the search light for a good look.

They saw deer, horses, llamas, alpacas, elk ,sheep and goats. They even occasionally saw the rats. After the big death the opportunities for wildlife on Vancouver island had been huge. Horse goats sheep cattle and pigs all went wild along with emus and bunny rabbits' but there were few carnivores. Apparently the the same benevolent instinct which led dieing farmers to release their stock had not extended to the guys looking after the lions and bengal tigers. Such species of carnivore which were left on the island such as bears and mink were already established in existing ecological niches.

Rats had done tremendously well to begin with. The ruins were wonderful rat habitat and there was plenty of food to start although not later, until, of course, the rats began to eat bunnies. It is a peculiar thing ,in nature, the bigger you can be (if you can get away with it) is almost always better. Especially so when it comes to mating time. Even such a seemingly crucial characteristic as flight to a bird will be dropped in favor of bigness if circumstances permit. In the absence of predators Hawaii developed flightless geese and other birds. The dodo was just a huge flightless pigeon. On Vancouver island the absence of predators made it very much in the rats favor to increase in size.

At first they hunted bunnies then sheep, then deer. They were on a roll. The girls would catch them in sight of the beam of the light at night, but they were far and away more wary than the herbivores,never standing awestruck in the glare. They understood the situation must faster. Cassy and Polly had owned a rat for a while. Not a giant one of course, but a regular white rat purchased at a pet store down south and brought to them. Being of a curious bent they had tested its intelligence in comparison with their dog. They quickly concluded that a three month old half pound rat was better at solving puzzles than their fifty pound dog. So how smart was a fifteen year old sixty pound rat?

The rats didn't give the twins the willies as they did others. They were too interesting for that . Rats weren't good runners and they lacked the special purpose claws of cats , but they made up for it in interesting ways.; Right off the bat rats were fair to middling ambush predators, if the game was right, or, as they were good swimmers if they could panic animals into the water they could blind and drown them. It doesn't take all that much to kill feral sheep. A domestic sheep, if unsheared generally becomes so top heavy that in a few years that it flips over and dies. Sheep are just one step short of being actually suicidal , bred hat way for the convenience of mankind.

Rat weaving was amazing of course, but lots of animals weave. Birds weave and beavers, but rat weaving was beyond this. They made huge weaved nests with dug compartments for meat and roots and woven compartments for seeds. The girls had made Hugh take them for a close look when they had stumbled across some nests on the Hesquiat Peninsula.

It had been an amazingly fun day off of the boat. The cedar trees of the Hesquiat peninsula bore the marks of being stripped for bark. Bark had been stripped from these same trees to make the clothing hats and baskets of the people for thousands of years. It had been the old village site of the people, and a generally great place to have a village, but it had no all weather protection for a boat which could not be hauled up on the shore, and when dugout canoes were replaced by trollers it had been abandoned. What had amazed the girls was that there were new marks of cedar bark being stripped from the trees as well as the marks still easily visible of bark collection by their own ancestors hundreds of years ago. The rats too were mining them for their wealth to a weaver. Had rats always had this knowledge or had some ratty Einstein stopped to wonder at the marks on the trees one day?. The girls had a theory that rats were the second team waiting in the wings to take over if mankind fucked up too egregiously.

After the Permian extinction of 250 million years ago when 95 percent of all existing species disappeared there had been no new phyla arise in the aftermath. Instead, new species arose within existing groups to fill in the gaps. In present day terms the girls visualized this as meaning that some day there would be rat cougars and rat wolves to fill in the gaps of those driven to extinction . And who knows the girls thought, maybe even rat people.

For Hugh it had been an easy birth, Calley had popped out the baby like a watermelon seed and the placenta soon after. Hugh had not been present due to his looks. Hagar had brought him a bottle of tequila and told him to stay put in the cabin they had stashed him in until the mid -wife and others were off of the boat. but he had not even killed the first glass before she popped. Soon the non family members were off of Cleo and Hugh was admiring and holding his first born. Although her head was covered in vernex and her features were squashed and red, she was beautiful to his eyes. Cassy and Polly once again appointed themselves captains and Cleo stormed north for the night putting in at Hesquiat peninsula again.

Cleo dropped the anchor on her own in this familiar spot and pretty soon all aboard were asleep. Hugh felt the boat bump up against his own and heard the feet land on deck . He felt alarm ,it was surely not etiquette to just run along side and jump aboard , but he thought that maybe they had hollered and he had been sleeping or perhaps the twins were on deck and the party had been waved aboard. He swung his bulk out of bed and headed forward. They hit him as soon as he came out the door.

Hagar respected the Mexicans. They had the innate respect of their nation for the family. They were not like the Euro who had come aboard with this black bags and his sound recorder to torture Hugh into revealing what he knew about the location of other morphs. The Euro hadn't cared ,he would have tortured Hugh in front of his family. Maybe it worked better that way. ;but on seeing his intent the elder of the two Mexicans after a string of swear words directed at the Euro had taken the hand cuffed twins and placed them in the forecastle. He had even taken the time to turn on loud music so that the twins could not hear the proceedings. The Mexicans had also shown consideration towards Calley and her baby taking the time to nail shut a cabin with her and the baby in it without fettering her with hand cuffs. Hagar had also heard the older Mexican admonish the younger not to barricade Calley in without water. Hagar had caught his eye after this and asked if they were not to be killed then? He answered civilly "No senora only the unnatural one, the tupe cabra,the euro will take his head.."

Hyapatia was Hagars eldest daughter and the most like Hagar herself. Like Hagar, Hyapatia too had bolted from their village to Mexico city and like her mother had come back to their village several hard but interesting years later. "But at least she had seen the world and had some fun" Hagar had thought..

They were confined together in a cabin. The Mexicans had brought them dinner and when they had asked about Hughy the older of the Mexicans had told them that he was still alive although heavily drugged. He had asked Hagar "Were you perhaps the mother of the lad before the devil took him. ?" He had mistaken her hesitation for affirmation and continued on. "The euro says that the devil takes the body first and the mind later. Isn't it perhaps better that he dies while still himself?"

Hagar did not answer She foresaw what was to happen next. The younger Mexican had been looking at Hyapatia and both had drunk wine all evening. The Euro was settled in aboard the seaplane for the night. Hagar expected the two men to return with sex upon their minds after they had drunk enough wine to bolster themselves for the crime.

She explained her thoughts to Hyapatia whose first reaction was to explain how she would scratch their eyes from their sockets and spit in their faces. Hagar sternly made her daughter face her. She said " You will not spit Hyapatia , there is some decency left in these men, and all of our fates are in their hands." An hour or so later the door was opened and the men came in. The silence was very heavy and the younger Mexican feasted his eyes on Hyapatia and after a moment sauntered over to her staring her in the face which was rapidly flushing. Hagar said to her daughter sternly one more time "Hyapatia you will not spit" then she turned to the older Mexican still standing by the door ,looked him in the eye, jiggled, her tits a little, and said to him in Spanish and then in English to herself "its been a long time ".

The twins had been locked in the forecastle for hours. The girls were hand cuffed well away from the controls. The Mexicans obviously knew nothing about Cleo's voice activated system. The problem was that with the men on board Cleo herself the girls just couldn't think of what to do.

In the middle of the night when all was quiet the girls woke up Cleo. The first question they asked her was about her fifty caliber gun up front, "was it ready to fire?" Cleo answered in the affirmative. Next they asked her if she could see the seaplane on her radar as it drifted about fifty feet away from them on an anchored line. Cleo answered them in affirmative again so they asked her for advice on how to sink it. Cleo suggested that the last time she had fired shots in earnest she had placed one shot every sixteen inches square starting three feet under the water line left to right and continuing boustrephedon fashion to the top of the forecastle. Cleo made a quick calculation of the bullets used for this and that presentation of the seaplane as it drifted about on its rope and reckoned that while she still had enough ammo on board to repeat this pattern it would be costly.

After a moment she suggested that the twins choose a set amount of ammunition, such as half what was left on board and she would space them out evenly on the target. The twins agreed to this number but still couldn't figure out a plan of action. They could see the other craft out the wide forecastle windows and they knew that only one man was aboard it. If they blew it out of the water now that would still leave two desperate men on board Cleo. Also not knowing about Hugh's torture, they thought of the kindly old Mexican who had brought them their meal. Could they really kill some one? They began to worry that the men would come in the morning and move them, and that they would lose whatever power they now possessed.

They finally decided to give Cleo some instructions for the future. Their decision was to tell Cleo to blow the other craft to pieces if it started to move, or if anyone tried to fire up Cleo's own engine manually. Both girls could see about six ways in which these instructions could get some or all of them killed.

Cassy comforted her sister. "Remember back when we studied War?" One maxim was that an inferior plan vigorously pursued is better than no plan at all. her sister countered "But they were idiots back then" Cassy had no reply to this. After some thought they added a few refinements to their instructions to Cleo. Cleo had a few switches she could throw if tampered with, which would ensure that anyone would be a damned long time getting her running again manually. The girls were right about being moved out of the forecastle . The older Mexican came for them in the morning and transferred them to the cabin with Hagar and Hyapatia. Cleo was biding her time

Hughy lived in a haze of pain. When he left the cabin he had been cold cocked hard. He had woken up with what felt like a broken head, with the Euro crouched in front of him. The syringe which he had used to bring Hughy back to consciousness still in his hand. He touched a button on his recorder and chose a torture tool before he began to ask Hugh questions.

A young man who has just had a baby is not a good subject for torture as he has already been turned inside out very thoroughly, several times by fate and nature before you even start. Hugh had not noticed mental changes in himself since morphing but under torture he began to growl. He didn't have any information to volunteer about other morphs but he didn't try to explain this . He withstood the torture without a word. Until he finally passed out and could not be roused. The Euro was dissatisfied. This was going to take some time and they might not have it in this location. The village was not far enough away and the last thing he wanted to see come around the corner was boats carrying rifles and tribesmen. The trouble was the ape man weighed hundreds of pounds and there was really no way to get him up and into the sea plane . The Euro decided that there were likely to be no arrivals here at night. They were safe enough 'til morning when he would have a try at the ape man again. All he really wanted was the head, but the head office expected information from this one, for some reason.

The traffic which arrived at first light came suddenly from around the peninsula to the north. The younger Mexican on watch immediately took the dingy to the seaplane to alert the Euro. Together they watched the boat pull in towards their anchorage . It had clearly intended to pull in where they were but on seeing the unfamiliar aeroplane it had sheered off south towards hot springs cove. "That tears it " the euro thought "It is time to take his head and leave." He fired up the plane pulled the pin and began to pull the seaplane adjacent to Cleopatra. It would not be correct to say that they did not know what hit them, as their craft was broadside to cleo when she chose to fire. They felt the craft stagger as the fifty caliber guns blew holes in her, beginning at her tail. The idea to bolt and run entered their minds at approximately the same time as the slugs entered their bodies.

Emilliano (for that was the old Mexican's name) was on Cleopatra's deck when the fifty caliber guns had picked up their noses and begun spouting. He watched the Euros' seaplane dance and reel and then sink, full of holes, in less than a minute. Next, he heard the engines beneath his feet fire up and immediately glanced at the empty wheel house. . To his right, on its own, the chain commenced to pull the anchor. Cleo reversed her engines and pulled out to sea following the twins instructions that she should attempt to flee to hot springs cover after firing, if she was not over ridden. Not far away, Emilliano heard a porthole clang and he heard the words of the senora. " Let us loose Emilliano and I will see you are treated as decently as you treated us . If you don't my tribesmen will be on board in a moment and they will cut your cojones off." He hesitated and she said in a voice with twenty five years of authority behind it. "Emilliano I have a better use for your cojones than they do. Come and let me out".

That evening they had a family war council. It wasn't a democracy . Hagar ran her family like she ran her business. First off she got everyone well fed. Hugh was still in bed and would be for days. Even a day after the blow, he still had one pupil larger than the other. Calley was totally o.k. She had given birth the day before and had spent the time since locked in with her babe and in her primal mother world she had not really cared much about the world beyond her. The Mexicans had brought her food and water and she had eaten slept and nursed her baby . Isolated from the rape and torture, she had not counted the hours passing.

Hagar brought Calley forward first. Calley was in a way Hagars favorite daughter, so unlike herself, except in the sharp wit that they both shared. Calley didn't have the devil in her the way that Hagar and Hyapatia did. She thought of the future and planned ahead. At eighteen, Hagar had been a bar girl in Mexico while at eighteen, Calley had been in college. At twenty four, Calley had had one boyfriend, whereas Hagar had had? She momentarily looked for a figure in her mind then quickly decided that some things don't need too close an accounting. Hyapatia however was much like herself except for some self destructive or perhaps just sentimental impulse which kept her involved with men. Hagar herself had never really bothered keeping men around. It was too much trouble to keep a man. Besides she asked herself "why buy a cow when milk was free?"

Hagar listened to Calley bring forth all she thought the family should know. The twins sat entwined in rapt attention. Hyapatia scowled, a not unusual expression for her countenance. Hagar heard most of what Calley had to say before, about the wonderful doctor Kemeeahaha, in Hawaii, and his fight against malaria, and how cleo could be put to good use synthesizing quinine and other drugs and about how Hawaii was sufficiently far away and nontecnhnical enough. Dr. Kameeaha thought that Hughy would be safe there from someone trying to relieve him of his head. In fact, Hagar had made up her mind what they all must do, but she knew from long experience that people like their own ideas best , and she was willing to wait patiently until someone else suggested it. Hagar could see that Calley was deliberating just their possible choices, and with holding her own opinion

"She is dead tired " Hagar thought. The twins were very surprised when Hagar next asked their opinions. The girls accounted that they didn't really have a opinion , but they wanted to stay with Cleo, as Hot Springs Cove hadn't been half as interesting as these months with Cleo, exploring the coast. " Of course if you want our ideas ? " Hagar was suddenly alert to the fact that although caught off guard, her youngest sprouts had recovered, reconnoitered the situation and were about to seek advantage..."In our opinion" Polly continued where Cass had left off "we should leave here Those men knew where to look for Hugh and could come back. We have an idea of a good place to go. Hagar saw that the harpoon was about to fly " Would be the Galapagos islands." the twins gushed it out in unison.

Polly continued "we looked it up." There is nobody there now and it has everything we need . it has, it has " both girls seemed unwilling to throw in the real clincher. "It has" Hagar said, finishing it for them, "giant turtles". The twins looked guilty. Their mother had known instantly that this choice had had a great deal to do with certain peoples childhood fascination for the story of the giant turtles. She was not about to rub their noses in it.

" OK " Hagar said " but what about later, say we do go to the Galapagos and there is a safe harbor and food and water as you think . That's okay for now but what are your plans for later on ? Wont you want boyfriends or at least friends of some sort ? and what about Hyapatia?" The girls had an instant reply, "oh don't worry about us, we have friends enough and we doubt that we will ever need actual boy friends, and for you ,Calley and Hyapatia, there is Hughy.

Its called polygamy mom!". They continued , suddenly enthusiastic, "its done in lots of countries and we thought you would probably like it because it doesn't clutter up the place with men too much.!" The sound of Hagar, Calley and Hyapatia's laughter silenced the girls exposition.

Hagar next turned to Hyapatia. Hyapatia smiled at her mom. She looked tired. When she spoke it was with more wisdom than Hagar had given her credit for. She said " All I really want to do is see this family stay together for a while, all seven of us and if you asked me to say where, I would have to say that I do not care very much ; but I am tired of Hot Springs Cove. I would very much like to see a cantina again and go dancing but wherever you decide I am with you even if that means polygamy with Hughy and giant turtles." At this she giggled and looked at Hagar saying may I go to bed now mama?

For a minute Hagar saw the years drop off Hyapatia's face. She was once again a nine year old. The same moppet she had brought home in her belly from old Mexico. "Not yet sweetheart" Hagar said, with unusual tenderness. " We all need to be here for a minute more. Calley. You have heard the others desires, what do you believe that we should do.? " In a tired voice ,Calley explained one more time about the people in Hawaii and their malaria epidemic. She knew that there was no vaccine, but this parasite had a free run in a non tech community for a couple of centuries. Even the oldest tricks in the book, such as quinine and d.d.t. might save lives. Calley explained about the lab in the boat and about her contacts with doctor Kameaha and about how the people in Hawaii were similar to the tribes in having adopted the English language of the now missing' howlys' as the Hawaiians had called the ' mamaklees' or white people, who had disappeared in the plague.

Hagar pronounced the verdict. "Okay. we are going to sail south from here for Mexico and go dancing in a cantina" she smiled at Hyapatia "and there we will buy supplies for your clinic" she smiled at Calley " Try to get some dental work for Hughy,if it can be safely done." Next she smiled at the twins "We will high tail it to the Galapagos to wait favorable winds for a trip to Hawaii."

Hagar sent them off to bed. She chuckled. She had done it-- arrived at complete census without even suggesting her own plan. What was a trip around the world going to be like, she wondered . She intended to circumnavigate, although there was no need to mention it quite this early on. Hagar walked across the galley and pulled down a tumbler, which she half filled with tequila, drained and then refilled it again. She sat back in her chair and thought about her pet Mexican. Emilliano was in her cabin with his hands cuffed behind his back. She would take him south and let him go she thought, but first she was going to show the bastard just what sex had been like for her, with her hands cuffed behind her back. In fact, maybe she would show him a couple of times. Hagar felt a warmth that was not entirely the result of the tequila warm her midsection and thought with a smile on her face, of her imminent return to the cabin while she sipped her tequila down

---

There was nothing like it in space. The market was full of sights and smells and sounds. Bowls of spices, parrots in cages ,geese and chickens and teeming brown humanity. Holly and Jasmine had been on earth for a year and yet this was their first time in a city. Their first months had been spent gaining strength and getting used to gravity.

They had spent many hours a day swimming as the gravity took less of a toll in the water. Spacemen couldn't walk but they could swim. It wasn't weakness that kept spacemen from walking. Sure, overall , spacemen were weaker. Earthmen had lots more gravity to build up muscles with, but the reason spacemen couldn't walk was more fundamental. Learning to balance ones whole body weight on two body points and then move around was something every two year old on earth had mastered when he learned to walk but it was nevertheless a remarkable achievement requiring rapid growth in certain corners of the brain. Like speech, if walking wasn't learned early enough, one often lost the capacity to learn it at all.

Languages learned before the age twelve are learned by a different part of the brain than that used after the age of twelve. The part of the brain which is used in children is apparently much better at it, as twelve years old is also considered to be the age after which one cannot master another language truly as a native. You will have an accent. The girls were somewhere near a cusp like this and were doing their level best to learn. With the addition of a couple of crutches in the beginning for extra points of balance. The girls had gotten relatively good at careening and crashing about , although, early on, it had been good to have a thick carpet or a lawn of grass underneath. It had not been impossibly hard to learn for them, about like what running on six foot clown stilts would have been for a regular child. An adult however, would certainly have a good chance of breaking his or her neck just trying. Most were content with their wheel chairs.

The girls had been looking forward to this city trip through all the long months spent at their school. Oh school was alright, in its own way. Sure it was full of the weirdest and most pampered snobs in the world. Every child there was the son or daughter of some big frog in some small pond. Princes and princelings (by the dozen, if not the score) were sent to the academy, where, behind the landscaped gardens and high fences, they educated the young upper class of India and beyond. The instruction was in English and had been for hundreds of years. The regimen was strict and it had to be in a school entirely composed of young individuals who had heretofore regarded themselves as special cases. The girls had been able to throw their own weight around a little bit. After all their mom wasn't just some big frog from some small pond. She was the biggest frog from the biggest pool of all. Their mom was the moon ambassador to the U.N.

In actual fact, as she explained to them herself, the moon ambassador was like the C.E.O. of a company. The stockholders were the moon men and she was their executive officer. As to the earth? Well the euro government was her proxy and client. It was the sole earth super power as it had the moon men to back it up. Mom told the Euros what to do and the Euros told the world. Jasmine and Holly knew that it hadn't always been that way but after the moon-men had nuked Rome the Euros had been obedient. Mom said that our forefathers had had to nuke Rome , and that they wouldn't have done so if it wouldn't likely have saved lots of Moony lives. So at any rate mom was important.

There was a rule at the school of NO PETS and the girls had been crushed by it. There were few pets in space. The girls were fascinated by animals and they expected that at school on earth they would be able to have pets of all sorts. It had taken a letter to mom, asking her to twist some arms, but it had worked. A little envelope had been delivered to their room by a servant with a tray. It had contained a written dispensation for them to keep pets. Sometimes it was good to have your mom be boss of the world.

The girls were hoping to find a pet today. Their party was on foot or rather the rest of the party was but Holly and Jasmine were in their super duper wheel chairs. They were moon made, and designed to impress with their technology, as well as to accommodate whatever dignitary was visiting earth, in every possible way. In this case , the visiting dignitaries were Jasmine and Holly. They loved them and spent quite a bit of time at the school rocketing around on whatever tracks were available . .

Holly saw the puppy first. It was standing between a girl and an old man . There was a cardboard sign in hindi in front of them. Holly and jasmine did not understand the hindi, but they did understand the price written below it. To the dismay of the custodian from their school, who accompanied their group, the girls separated from their party and motored their wheelchairs over for a closer look. The puppy was a female and they wanted her awfully badly. Jasmine had given the man the money, and he had given her the leash that he held in his hand, before, they had noticed that something was horribly wrong. The chain in Jasmines hand led to the neck of the girl in front of her. Aware of the girl for the first time Holly and Jasmine took in her circumstances in a flash. She was a girl of about the same age and complexion as Jasmine and Holly, but she was a slave and they had just accidentally purchased her. Their eyes locked. Just then their custodian, the little school official, arrived with a couple of t guards. As he let loose a stream of HIndi, the guards took the wheel chairs by their handles and wheeled the girls away against their will. The official pulled the leash free from Jasmines grip and returned it to the old man and waved him off. Seeing his luck to both sell the child and to get to keep her, the old man yanked her by the neck back into the throng of people.

Soon the girls were back with the bunch. Underneath, they were boiling. It was Holly who had the bright idea . Their wheelchairs probably went twenty miles an hour, or at any rate, they went faster than their bozo escorts could run. After a little personal communication in sign language they booked it right at the next intersection and left their escorts standing at the curb. They kept up with the traffic and after a bit of dangerous, but highly enjoyable hot- rodding. They took a couple if right turns in a row and re-entered the market. This was where they had begun. The girl was standing once again with the cardboard sign in front of her. The man was not at first inclined to give her up . Thinking, perhaps rightly, there was more money to be made by simply delaying them and returning them to their keepers. Holly pulled out her whole wad of money and tried to give it to the man but he still seemed undecided-- taking the cash, but still holding onto the leash. He was looking up the street hoping for their escorts to appear. From that direction, a siren had indeed begun to wail. Jasmine bit his hand. It was a good bite, the kind that removes the chicken from the bone. He dropped the leash. The wheel chairs were built for a full sized man, so pulling the other girl on her lap wasn't a problem. Holly hit the throttle. The real problem was what to do next.

Calcutta was a safe enough city to booger about in for a while and they had money, but all good ideas seemed to end up with someone finding them. Then they would be separated and mom would be too far away to help. It was Holly who had the idea. "What if the authorities couldn't tell her apart from the two of us? She is not so different . If we dressed alike and didn't go out together, would anyone realize that there were three instead of two of us.?"

They flagged a taxi and folded their wheel chairs up in the trunk. It was hours drive to their school in the countryside. Before they arrived after dark they had found the time to refine their plan and get to know their pet. Her name was Jalla. The first thing that the girls did, quietly and discretely in the back of the taxi, was to share their clothes with Jalla to make her resemble them as much as possible. When they got to the school they had the taxi driver park several yards from the gate and unload their wheelchairs from the boot. Within minutes Holly, Jalla and Jasmine were upstairs secure in their apartment with the doors locked. They waited all night for the shit to hit the fan, for one of the school officials to come pounding on the door, wishing to hold them to account for absconding on the school trip. They had seen it all before . The jesuits in their medieval robes sure looked scary , and quite tough enough to deal with any young princeling. All blows were dealt on behalf of the offenders fathers and the school retained signatures on standard forms from the rajahs to allow the staff to lay hands and straps upon their sons without committing a crime.

It never happened. The knock never came. The jesuits were sure that if the great god had allowed it to be overlooked that the daughters of the most important person on earth had been mislaid in downtown Calcutta and then had somehow delivered back to them ,then they were not meant to stir the soup. They would overlook the incident as well. In one way it was good that the school was a strict one. No personal servants were allowed and ones room was ones own . You cleaned it yourself even if you were a princess.

The reason that this particular school had been chosen for them was the presence of doctor Gupta, dads old math teacher.

He was the best mathematician in India, which meant of course the best in the world. There were good schools in space, plenty of them, but dads mathematical education from Gupta had been more than good.

It had been why he had been allowed into space at all. Oh not the only reason of course as space could not afford mathematicians just yet. He would never have gotten off the ground without his welders certificates, but between his Phd in math and his welders certificates he had made the grade. He had spent his first five years in space welding quarter inch steel plate with a seventy sixteen rod and fiddling with numbers in his spare time. All the other welders had Phds as well. The recruiters were fussy . They could be. A young man or woman could be taken to space and their loyalty secured . Even welders were rich by earth standards, although it usually wasn't riches that lured people such as these to space. Dad had wanted them to have a fair chance to learn math (which they had convinced him) space schools did not offer. When mom had got the ambassadorship Holly and Jasmine had, with a minimum of manipulation, made up Sanjays mind that his daughters needed to return to earth to study.

By mid-morning, the girls were exhausted. The knock at the door never came. They had spent their night worrying. They had knocked out some good plans. First off , they realized that the idea of the night before (making them all lookalikes), could be taken a good deal further. Jalla looked quite a bit like them already. To begin with, they were three brown girls with similar hair. They decided to become as similar as possible. Blue hair was perhaps a touch radical, but it was what they had on hand for putting streaks in. By three a.m. they were three identically dressed blue headed girls, and by five am they had been all decorated all up their arms with henna tattoos drawn by Jalla. The tattoos would wash off in a week or two. By nine a.m. they had identical red toe and fingernail polish and were wondering what else they could do.

Pretty soon they decided to do what they probably should have done first. They called mom. They were not able to get her of course she was in security council chambers. They got her factotum. It seemed she had a new one every week. The girls were not in a trusting mood. They were dead tired, to boot, so they hit the family panic button. They told the officious little man, who hindered their access to their mother

"Just tell her we are worried about our brother. "They didn't have a brother, it was secret family code for 'get here fast something is really wrong.' Holly and Jasmine looked at each other glumly after making the call. They were not exactly sure Mom would look on saving a girl from slavery as exactly a family emergency. Adults were funny.

Also, they were pretty sure it was going to come out about their taking off from their escorts in Calcutta There was no doubt in either of their minds what mom would think of that. Oh well, there was no turning back. In the sudden silence the girls felt very sleepy and fell asleep together on a pile on the couch. They didn't hear the crack Euro troopers landing . They did hear their door being banged upon and the key in the lock. They heard the shoulder quickly break their flimsy chain. The room was suddenly full of armed men and women in black body armor helmets and visors with mom in her wheel chair just behind. Having suddenly been scared into wakefulness the three girls were in a pile on the couch clinging together.

Their mother looked at them in astonishment. "I'll be a christmas goose!" she said, following it up closely with "I'll be clusterfucked! There are three of them!"

Adrian was relieved. It had seemed so very bad for awhile. First the girls message- then, when she had called the school, to find out t the girls had been mislaid in downtown Calcutta for a day and a part of a night, unaccounted for. Then finally, to have had that fool priest assuring her that the girls had arrived back okay when it seemed he hadn't a shred of reason for assuming so. At any rate, Adrian had feared to find her daughters raped and bloodied. Instead, although weirdly dressed, decorated and accoutremented (and with an oddly identical companion). they seemed okay. Adrian ordered her entourage-- the armed guards, factotums, priests and school staff to "get the hell out of the room". She looked sternly at her daughters and ordered them to tell her what the hell was going on.

It was a long and sordid story that Adrian's daughters recited. She summed it up in the first seven seconds but she let them have their say while she observed and made up her mind. Jalla sat with her eyes downcast and her hands in her lap. Adrian reflected that she did look uncannily like the other girls . It was clear from Jalla's demeanor that she knew her fate hung on the sentences being spoken. Adrian was a practical person. She had about decided on the proper course of action to restore order here. They would pluck Jalla from poverty and solve her problems with money.

Adrian let the girls talk on while thinking of other things. There was an important meeting with heads of state later today. China was threatening to go their own way again, set up their own internet and their own currency. It couldn't be allowed . World gov. (i.e. the spacemen) had pulled China's chestnuts out of the fire early on. World gov computers, with Euro help, had stitched china back together again, and for her to want to go it alone now and in such a manner beggared belief. Didn't China know that financial clout was the only weapon that the moon men had other than nuclear bombs or other objects thrown from space? Did they want the moon men to do such a thing? They were being backed into a corner, Adrian felt. It had been ninety-five years since the moon men had last been forced to nuke a city.

Everyone had thought that era of history was behind them. But here it was again, and on Adrian's term as ambassador. She had made up her mind on some major issues. She said to herself, as much as her mother had to her 'that a faint heart never fucked a chicken' and returned her attention to her daughters conversation. They were distraught. She must try to settle them down. Frankly, she wasn't used to being the active parent. Sanjay was the home body. Adrian had the important job and she knew it. Oh Sanjay was a dear with his mathematics and his Gandhi and his alien project. He had been the last and, if the truth were known, only 'flame' of her youth (or to be more accurate of her early middle age.) She had spent her real youth grasping for career advantage. At thirty five he had seemed her last chance to put aside serious matters for a while and have a child. He was twenty five to her thirty five and even with his prenuptial contract to stay home for seven years to do the parenting, Adrian had been leery of having a child. She was afraid that she might not be the type for mothering after all ; that it might cut into other more important matters.

Sanjay however was so beautiful and so dark and so intent upon fathering a child that she had allowed it to happen. She could have clipped his ears however for briinging the second baby home. Oh it was a tragic story alright, parents killed and that kind of thing, but until Sanjay had brought the second baby home, it had been someone else's tragic story. The scoundrel had won and Sanjay had taken advantage of her weakened hormonal state to introduce a second brown baby to her breast.

The girls knew their history but had never been told which of them was the foundling. Through their lives the girls took turns being sure that one or the other of them was the tragic figure. Adrian dearly loved them both but having heard them out she began to lay down the law. She herself would have to leave immediately. Her aide would stay and take personal care of it. A school of course was the answer for Jalla,although not this school, Adrian thought, and an endowment of course. Her time was up . Before she left she reminded the girls that the next time they hit the family panic button it had better be a tad more important-- preferably actual physical danger.

Adrian saw the needy look in Holly and Jasmine's eyes as she was leaving for the meeting. She realized that she was probably failing at parenting and that Sanjay would not approve. 'But dammit somebody has to rule the world ! 'Adrian said to herself, as she pulled her thoughts back to the important political business at hand.

Holly and Jasmine mulled it over after their mother had left. It had not been so bad really. Not for Mom. What they had achieved wasn't too bad. Nobody was taking Jalla or not right away at least. She could stay with them for several weeks while appropriate arrangements were made to enroll her in a school where Hindi was spoken, to start her new life.

The weeks passed quickly for the three girls. Jalla fitted in like one more fake sister. They worked hard on communicating--keeping constant company. Jasmine and Holly were more than a little afraid that if they left Jalla alone she would just disappear and that in her place would be another small brown envelope delivered on a tray saying that their right to keep pets had been revoked. Hindi was the language which their father had tried hard, although not very successfully, to teach them. So they were able to learn Jalla's history and she theirs. When the day arrived for Jalla to depart they were fast friends and fake sisters,

Jallla smelled the rat first. She had watched the men as they waited for check-in and then walked up the driveway, through the window of their bedroom. She was suddenly shaking like a leaf after only a moment of observing therm. Holly and Jasmine looked out the window as well. The men did not look right. Not for men about to take a girl to school.

irst off there were no women among them. They recognized the man in front . He worked for their mom. He was an aide to an aide to an aide. They didn't know him well, but he evidently had his papers right for not just anybody walked onto the grounds of this particular school. The men with him did not look academic. There is a look which Indias college teachers and administrators share amongst themselves and these men did not have it. All of a sudden Holly and Jasmine's fears were back full force. "Lets hide her" they both said simultaneously. There was no way to leave without going directly towards the men so they hid her right in front of them. Holly said to her sister. "They will think she is you if they pass her going down the hall in your wheel chair. I will take Jalla and hide her in the library and then come back. Don't unlock the door until I get back and then you and I will talk with them. I can make it back in under ten minutes."

It was a good plan in one way. The aide was entirely willing to let the two supposed space girls pass by on a supposedly short, but immediately necessary errand. He readily agreed to wait for them. It was a bad plan in that the aide possessed a key to the apartment. Rather than wait outside, he simply used it and the door opened suddenly without a knock.

Jasmine was summoned peremptorily out in Hindi and when she didn't respond the men had her chloroformed and wrapped up in a blanket in well under five minutes. The aide was reasonably satisfied. The chloroform hadn't really been meant to come out until the girl was in the car, but the girl had sensed their intentions and had hurried them. "Alls well that ends well he reflected"

Holly was stunned when she returned to the room, The door was wide open and her sister was gone. She had her mom on the line in ten minutes. This time the family code worked fine.

Even though mom had her former aide in a back room, confessing to a blow torch within hours, it still took her three days to find Jasmine .When they did she was in rough shape. She had been pushed out of a car in front of a police station with a bag over her head and had been kept for days drugged into a deep deep sleep. Jasmine didn't remember too much. The chloroform had worn off during her trip to the city in a car trunk. Her captors had realized early on what a hot potato they had and had kept her drugged and blindfolded in a small dark room. Luckily she had not had her throat cut but had been left out intentionally to be found. The police had been notified of her arrival moments after she had been dumped and they had picked her up and returned her to her mother.

Ambassador Adrian was apologetic to her daughters about her decision to send the two girls and their new companion to space, but as she explained to them , the earth was just too dangerous right now. Especially for them. They had been far too vulnerable here at the school. The kidnapping had not been political, but it might as well have been. In this sort of thing there could too easily be a next time. The kidnapping had been for money- not for the few rupees which a girl brought in a downtown market but for the endowment which Adrian had arranged for Jalla. It had been cashed in full, supposedly by her trustees. All that had been necessary for the scheme to work was for Jalla to disappear and she very nearly had. So had Jasmine, almost, in her stead.

She told the girls that they were leaving and that her decision was final. Then she waited for any storm of protest. It didn't come. There was a moments' silence and then Holly spoke up. "You did say the three of us didn't you?" After sharply listening to their mothers affirmative, answer both girls spoke up " We agree!" Adrian was not a diplomat for nothing.

Gupta was glad to see the girls. It was to be their last outing before returning to space. He had brought them to his home. Gupta had long known that their need for a mathematics teacher, in the flesh, was a subterfuge. The girls real need had been to come to earth, to see some plants that had not been propagated by human hands and especially to see some animals. Gupta had not minded subterfuge and had cheerfully left it credence when asked about their progress ; which had been very good in any case. Gupta had felt happy to meet Sanjay's brood. He remembered the brilliant young mathematician. Sometimes Gupta had wondered about Sanjay's degree of complicity in his daughters scheming. Did he really not know that they were brilliant and capable of learning at his feet only figuratively by way of the web? Gupta's wondering had ceased when he had met the ambassador herself. He had realized that life with such a forceful person must inevitably have thrown the rest of the family into a framework of unspoken alliances.

Gupta lived the good life of India's elite ,with a stone mansion, gardens and walls-- or at least he appeared to do so. Gupta actually occupied one room and his caloric intake was a little less than that of his cat. The quiet of his lifestyle appealed to him and it tickled his humor to impact as little as possible upon the many people who made his compound their home and of whom he was ostensibly the master.

The house was like an organism of its own with its own dynamics of women waking and children crying in the morning. Fires being lit and food being cooked or otherwise prepared throughout the day. It pleased Gupta to think of himself as a nearly benign parasite within the larger organism, rather than as its lord and master. He was eighty years old and for the last thirty or so his closest associates had been a succession of felines all named Mahatma. The last in line of these was being lionized by the girls.

She had brought in a dead shrew for inspection and her prize for the first time ever was getting the attention which it deserved. Any sort of animal fascinated Holly and Jasmine, let alone a species entirely knew to them. They were rather avidly poking the dead animal with a stick. Gupta was hugely satisfied with himself. If a shrew could bring the girls such interest, wait until they saw the elephant.

He had arranged it himself. Several days before he had called for a car and driver and then asked the women for the services of couple of boys. At eighty, Gupta was spry, the result of his fifteen hundred calorie diet. Gupta could, of course, have called for the services of the men of the household, but it had pleased him to engage the services of someone who would enjoy the task, rather than to impose it upon one of the men who almost certainly had better things to do. So he had chosen the boys. Yes, reflected Gupta. If you wanted to find a mahout and an elephant to rent, or purchase a barrel of monkeys, it is best to have a few twelve year old boys with you to help scour the market.

Gupta had taken them to the market and purchased all kinds of creatures to make a display for the girls. They had bought chickens, geese, ducks, parrots and several monkeys (in cages not a barrel) as well as several pheasants in old celery cases and a baby goat. It was a pretty good haul. Under the studiedly neutral eye of his driver Gupta had stuffed his expensive limo full of them; even getting a fair amount of crap on the leather seats. Gupta had been satisfied with their haul, but coming across the mahouts and their elephants on the drive home had been a huge bonus. They had stopped the car and Gupta had arranged with the mahouts to arrive at his house on this very evening.

The evening was still to come. So far only the small animals had been given a viewing. The baby goat with the milk bottle had been adopted ,of course, but the rest of the animals had reluctantly been left behind in the makeshift structures the boys had put together in the garden. Gupta took the girls for a walk within his walls. They loved to feed the golden carp which swam in the water beneath an ornamental bridge. He watched the interplay between the girls.

Jalla was trying very hard to please. She didn't really understand her own good luck-- to have suddenly been plucked from the lowest caste to the highest. Jalla was very quick, Gupta observed. She had learned the English of the girls much faster than they had learned Hindi. The child had been willing to tell Gupta a little of her history during the day for they neither Gupta nor Jalla had shared the space girls fascination with chickens and goats; both having seen rather many of them during their lives. Jalla had been surprised both at his friendly tone and at his dialect . The Hindi speakers at school had all been high caste. With growing wonder, Jalla realized that this man was himself not of high caste, but of her own. It was an astounding revelation. In all her short life she had not only never met a member of her own caste who was not poor, she had not even supposed that such an individual existed. Poverty was seen by her caste as a fact of karma not to be escaped in this life time.

Gupta pulled out her story a bit like finagling the meat out of a periwinkle. Holly and Jasmine were adopting Jalla as one adopts a pet. They were space chauvinists and did not imagine that they might not be doing her a huge favor. Did Jalla have a secret dream ? someone from her past that she needed to be reunited with or a place somewhere she needed to visit? She had not been asked. He slowly drew the girl out. He did not ask the hard parts. About how things had changed and she had ended up in the city with a rope around her neck and a for sale sign in front of her. He asked the gentle things. Had she ever had ducks and geese.? He too could milk a goat and he had demonstrated this by giving one of the space girls a squirt behind the ear. He was gratified when he learned that her own schooling in the village had been so similar to his own. She was well familiar with the magic rectangles of twenty four squares and could put them to use. Gupta watched Jalla fetching and carrying for the other girls Reasonable enough, considering that they were not terribly adept yet at walking, yet it bothered him none the less. At one point the space girls had even talked about finding an occupational school for Jalla while they continued to study mathematics. They were very much the special cases, these two. Gupta decided to take them down a peg or two and to raise Jalla up in their eyes.

The elephants had been a huge success. The mahouts had the opportunity of imbibing before their evening arrival and had gotten into the swing of things, coaxing the elephants to arrive at a gallop and to produce that long elephant holler so familiar to the girls, from the movies. Gupta had met them at the gate, ushering them in past the surprised World Gov guards protecting the ambassadors children.

In the morning, the enclosed yards were a fragrant mess with giant elephant pies littering the ground. Gupta went and waked the girls. He had something important on his mind. It was early, but the girls got up willingly. They followed Gupta on his walk.

After allowing enough time for the fresh morning air to clear their minds, he addressed Holly and Jasmine directly. "So you are planning to continue your studies with me over the internet? There will be no more problems about mysterious inabilities to learn without me in the flesh and blood and no more mysterious inabilities to learn the things I taught your father directly from him?" Gupta could tell by their demeanors that they had not expected reproach from him on this topic. They had not thought themselves to be so transparent. Instead of dwelling upon this, Gupta moved on. He launched into a soliloquy which seemed about to impale the girls upon their guilt for something before moving on without quite doing so. He talked about their being products of an technological society, and then pointed up the benefits to the intellect of a rural lifestyle. Holly and Jasmine were surprised and confused. Something seemed to be bothering Dr. Gupta, but he would not cough it up. "

Very well then" Gupta had ended up more or less exactly where had begun. Gupta observed the girls and realized that nothing of what he had said was being taken in."Look " he decided to plunge in more directly, "It seems that you two think you are so very, very much smarter than Jalla." There was little Holly and Jasmine could say, for yes, they had both thought that they were 'very very much smarter' than Jalla. "Look" Gupta repeated,"it is your own affair, but I hear you calling Jalla sister and then expecting her to fetch for you. I think you need to make up your minds now. Is she your sister or your servant? Either will be fine, but if you do not make up your minds now she could be very hurt and I think none of us want Jalla to be hurt further." Gupta did not listen to Holly and Jasmines protestations, but hushed them and said "I have a little exercise to test how good with numbers you all are."

Gupta gave them two improbably large numbers to multiply together and asked, as well, for the square root of the sum. He repeated the instructions in Hindi to Jalla afterward. Holly and Jasmine immediately and reflexively reached for their calculators before realizing that Gupta would hardly have in mind testing them for the quickness of their draws. "With pen and paper then, or how should we calculate it?" they asked.

"Perhaps with stones" Gupta said, "adding afterward that the latin term 'calculi' from which the English word to calculate was derived, did indeed mean little pebbles." The girls were nonplussed and stood there unsure of what to do.

Gupta said to them "Perhaps you should just watch Jalla." Jalla had broken a stick and scratched a grid in the dust. She had collected a small pile of pebbles beside her. Jalla asked Gupta one more question in Hindi and began to manipulate the stones in the checkerboard like grid. She took the pebbles dropping them one by one onto the squares in the grid she had created. Gupta kept up a monologue as she worked. "With this method the heavens were charted, the calendars created and zero discovered. Right here in India" he said rather proudly. "First the numbers to be multiplied. Can you see them? " The girls had immediately given up trying to find pen and paper and stood intently watching Jalla as she moved pebbles from place to place.

"It's like an abacus "Jasmine said. Gupta agreed adding that it was similar but much older. Gupta fixed them with his school masters tone-- suddenly serious. " Do you see the zero within the system?"

Holly and Jasmine stared at the stones being moved. It was a long calculation. Jalla had revised her estimation of the number of columns necessary and had added a few more. The girls could see the implication that the columns somehow replaced the zeros and the orders of magnitude in their own system. They watched in silence as the stones worked their way around the columns. Gupta asked again if they could see the zero and suddenly they could, as each stone followed a circular path in its travels from one magnitude to the other. The shape of the zero was simply an imitation of the path which these stones took in their ascending magnitudes of value. After Jalla finished her first computation she looked to Gupta for agreement. And then she drew another much smaller grid for the square root.

After their walk it was back to breakfast . Gupta had let them know in no uncertain terms that he expected to tutor the three of them. He also told them that as one language was as good as another for speaking in many cases, at least up to a certain point, one system of math could be as good as another. He intended to use the grids rather than traditional western math for the remainder of their instruction.

Breakfast was great. There were few good meals in space or at least few great ones. Cooking was a rather technical affair in space so as little of it was done as possible. This meant that most food was processed (i.e. cooked) before you even laid eyes on it. Perhaps it made some sense that space imported kidney bean paste rather than kidney beans, reckoning that added water content and its cooked state were bonuses; but the attitude had been carried way too far. The old families of the moon were judged by the newer arrivals to have had their senses of taste and smell attenuated and not just their hearing.

There was some fresh food. There was the ubiquitous lettuce, tomatoes and peppers perched close to the lights wherever they were, but all meat came in a package. As a cuisine it was pretty crappy but yet exactly the sort of thing you would expect in a society stemming from the U.S. military. Militaries are notorious for thinking that soldiers should eat to live and not live to eat. France in the eighteenth century had tried feeding its soldiers in far off posts entirely on sardines. Space society was their direct culinary spiritual descendant.

Holly and Jasmine both loved eggs. Meat on earth still seemed rather wild to them and altogether too reminiscent of the creature it had been hewn from often including 'shudder 'bones etc. but eggs were the girls dream food . They had loved them even back in space. when they came irradiated and precooked to be squeezed out of a vaccuum pack.; but those were nothing like the duck eggs Benedict which Gupta had had prepared for them this morning. Their leave taking after breakfast was all too hurried, as their handlers soon made their presence known and the girls were helicoptered off for their departure to space later in the day.

The girls ate supper in the space station. Sanjay and Uncle Jimmy met them at the inport.

Uncle Jimmy was really Great Uncle Jimmy. He was Mom's youngest uncle and the black sheep of the family. Mom had taken her fortune, name brains and family connections and used them to become earth ambassador. Uncle Jimmy had taken the same name brains and lineage and used them to deeply embarrass everyone. At highschool he failed both math and welding. His mother's warnings had been dire. There were few painters in the U.S. military, and those there were painting walls not pictures. If Jimmy were so silly as not to straighten out and fly right then he would have to spend his voluntary public service time (v.p.s. time) in the forces, moving steel with a dolly or cooking endless meals for distribution. His mom had said to paint in his spare time, but to go ahead with remedial schooling and then get a decent degree in accounting or engineering.

They didn't know of course that the idea of trying to obtain or use a degree in either of these disciplines only frightened Jimmy marginally less than a sentence of five years in the kitchens. He decided to bolt. He first enrolled for schooling on earth itself, unusual but not undone, and then when his five year arts degree was finished on earth he had just stayed on . It wasn't illegal of course, it was just deeply embarrassing to have a son or even just a relation who would rather be a cripple in a wheelchair on earth than do his voluntary public duty.

Jimmy hadn't seen it that way. Earth was radiant and Jimmy was a painter. Jimmy had set his eyes on every vista the moon had to offer many times; but on earth even if you sat in just one place to paint each day brought a multitude in changes of light and color. There were mists in the morning and hail storms in the afternoon. Space had been monotonous. Jimmy painted earth from his wheel chair for forty years. Had it not been for his position in the inheritance, he would have disappeared from the notice of his relatives. As it was, he showed up like a big blotch of herpes on their collective face. He could not be allowed to inherit.

At first, they had thought him powerless and had attempted to sequester his funds. He had fought back. Jimmy knew that the big bucks had to stay on the moon. He would never be allowed to pass on his paternity to some earthling. Jimmy had no desire to be assassinated, so he compromised. He made some astute alliances and married, without ever seeing the bride—before the marriage or after-- into another family equally ancient to his own. He acquired protection and relinquished control of his money until he returned to space. Of course with his five year voluntary public service hanging over his head he had never been expected to return. The oligarchy hadn't' expected to see him back. They left him the money to live like a rajah and so he had until his heart brought him back to space. His heart had finally driven him to it. No not some yearning for his roots but angina.

Jimmy had been rather a bad boy then, and never changed much. He was addicted to marijuana, tobacco, and alcohol, as well as betel nut, opium, and qat. He also had a great affinity for chocolate and deep fried foods. For forty years, Jimmy had started each day with two joints and a cigarette in bed, followed up with a cup of strong coffee and another cigarette at which point he would either pick up a paintbrush or call one of his women for some morning exercise.

Jimmy planned well. He knew he would rather die than live on the moon or the big potato with all their rules and laws. Hell's bells, just on the subject of drugs alone they would have him so twisted up with withdrawal that he would feel like a rats asshole stretched over a door knob.

So he had bought a ship. Most of the laws in space hadn't been changed in centuries. Space was still run by the laws of the USA and the fifty percent of her population in actual service were governed by a stiffer code yet-- that of the military. There was no way Jimmy could stand it; so he had tricked them

He had bought a ship. It had caused quite a stir. No other individual in space owned one . In fact it was illegal for the forces to have sold an active ship. But they hadn't. They had sold scrap. Jimmy was tricky. One day somewhere along the way it had occurred to him, that while he resumed being fantastically wealthy and started voting shares when he re-entered space. He only became subject to their laws when he entered the colony or one of its ships. He made alliances again and made some promises to certain important people about which way he would vote on certain matters. When he regained the power to vote his shares, Jimmy got his ship, and his heart had gotten its release from gravity. It gave Jimmy the energy to return to his painting and his bad habits.

Jimmy's ship was ancient . Even her name the 'Lusty Lady' was anachronistically old English. She had been carefully tended like the rest of the fleet but hadn't been flown for hundreds of years.

When ships had first been built in space, people had supposed that gravity was beneficial to the human body, possibly even necessary and this ship had been built to spin. Indeed she couldn't be flown straight without it. She was like a football. She needed her spin to fly straight. It had seemed a great idea to the earth men who had built her, but for spacemen who dealt with gravity by the use of wheelchairs she could not reasonably be flown. Jimmy had picked her up by proxy. On paper she was supposed to become spaces first hotel restaurant, with luxury quarters for moneyed earthlings.

It was bullshit of course. Jimmy brought company of his own. He had spent forty years in India, mostly south of the electrification line being carried about on palanquins. He had lived the life of a rajah and had brought much of his entourage to space including wives and other women his progeny and their assorted families as well as many of his extended household, who chose to accompany him. He had been generous in his gifts of money to those who did not wish to follow. Unfortunately, this had included every wife under fifty which he possessed but Jimmy was a resilient man and was able to replenish his household after arriving in space.

This had been fifteen years ago, or so. Holly and Jasmine had been to visit him as little as their mother could allow and as much as Sanjay could manage. Adrian had been appalled at the warmth which Sanjay had developed for her uncle. Dining with him on the neutral ground of the space station frequently, or visiting him on board the Lusty Lady.

Sanjay had not been raised in the quasi- military culture of space but in India as the son of a rich merchant. His own father had many wives not the mere six which Jimmy had brought to space with him. Sanjay himself would never consider having more than one wife, it was no hardship. Women could be an immense amount of trouble. He watched Jimmy's six eldest wives alternate between waiting upon him hand and foot, and bossing him about mercilessly with determination, according to some, common inner rhythm and/or logic invisible to jimmy and to himself.

But Jimmy deserved it, Sanjay thought. He had a weakness. Sanjay had watched how he had stocked his ship nearly entirely with bright aspiring girls from earth on their first job in space. Yes, reflected Sanjay, Jimmy deserved what ever he got and it was often extremely humorous to watch him get it. It was particularly humorous that out of all the wives on board which jimmy had managed to accumulate, the six who were almost constantly in his company were the six old and gnarly ones he had brought up from earth with him. Some of whom Jimmy was obviously quite frightened . Sanjay thought that they were really pretty nice old ladies. Hindi speakers all ,and excellent cooks. Sanjay loved to visit

---

It was a sort of sad supper at the space station. Jimmy and Sanjay ordered all of Jasmine and Holly's former favorites and made a fuss over Jalla, making her feel very at home with her fluent Hindi and their clear willingness to transfer their love for Holly and Jasmine to her as well. Holly and Jasmine had long missed these dishes which were served to them at the dinner but even the rice pudding seemed wrong. They had long dreamed about how good it would be to have some rice pudding straight from a pack; but tonight to them it seemed unreasonably bland. They had never really looked at it before. Suddenly they all wished for cloves or cinnamon with their food and after one of them mentioned it the evening had became a requiem for India. Out of the port they could see the earth hanging there. There was a big fire in China.

"Is that a forest fire daddy?" one of the girls asked. There was a short look between the men. "Yes perhaps a forest fire." Both girls were instantly aware that Sanjay was trying one of his pathetic attempts at deception, but they decided to let it go.

On the ride home to the moon, the mood was subdued. Jimmy had been left at the space station to make his own way home. The Lusty Lady was on a permanent moor nearby. The Lusty Lady's synchronous had been put well away from the other ships for even while resting in one place she whirled like a dervish.She was shaped like a football with cylinder inside cylinder within her, each with diminishing gravity.

Inside her, Jimmy's tribe lived. Aside from his half dozen wives Jimmy's original contingent from earth had included an over- large collection of teenagers and young adults, many with his red hair. Jimmy's clan had spread. There was even a block of India town in Luna City informally designated as JImmyville by the family. From an extended household of about 2 hundred relatives which Jimmy had brought to space fifteen years ago, he now was the paterfamilias of several thousand individuals, at least a hundred or so of whom would be aboard his ship visiting at any given moment.

Jimmy had a tribe, Like some medieval patriarch or perhaps like some old spider, he rested in the weightless center of his spinning home, From either on an invisible cushion of air, surrounded by lights and foliage, with marijuana growing abundantly in all the corners. It had been a gigantic cargo hold . It was now his studio. He had merely to provide it with good lighting and some plants. Jimmy rested fifty feet in the air from anything most of the time. Although his inertia at the center of a spinning cylinder did exhibit itself in objects (including Jimmy) slowly beginning to spin, it was easily countered by occasionally touching the one stay-rope run through the center for this purpose. Small objects left to themselves also began slowly but inexorably, to spin faster and faster and needed to be stopped, but this was a small price to pay for a good studio. Jimmy was reasonably content.

On the way home Sanjay had been suffering from intense pangs of home sickness. He had been keen to hear what the girls had thought of certain sights and sounds and this had brought memories back to him as well. He was in a somber mood today as well because of the bombing of the Chinese city. The fiery holocaust of millions of people had been done only to make a point. It appalled him. There must have been another way. It was clearly wrong. All Adrian's truths about how it was either that or the eventual end of the moon colony did not make it correct. With great difficulty for the sake of the girls, Sanjay had pushed the subject from his mind . He addressed his thoughts to the girls and away from the fact that deep within him something was telling him that his wife the ambassadoress had become unclean and that he would not mix himself with her again. He had a wonderful secret for the girls.

"I have arranged a little trip for us" It was a surprising statement for the moon had few trips and fewer surprises. Hollly and Jasmine looked at him patiently. It seemed likely that he had misgauged their ages entirely and was about to offer them a trip to an amusement arcade downtown or something equally juvenile.

"How about a trip to the far side of the moon to look at the crash site" It was an astounding statement considering that no-one had ever done so. Sure a crashed alien ship was interesting but the few earthlings in space the first few centuries after the plague had quite a bit on their plates after their marooning. There hadn't been any room for a fantastically expensive archeological expedition. Mounting such an expedition had been Sanjay's secret dream since he had been fifteen years old and his reason for spacing out. It had taken him twenty five years of hard work and an advantageous but difficult marriage to get him to this point.

Sanjay was a gift from the gods for Jalla. He was a fellow vegetarian as well as Hindi speaker. If Sanjay could have chosen a daughter from a catalogue she would have been Jalla. Hindi was the language of Sanjay's youth and he realized that part of his personality was bound up within it. He felt a different person to be able to speak Hindi again in his household. Sanjay loved it. With their dad clearly so pleased to be speaking Hindi again ,Holly and Jasmine for the first time, put their minds to really learning it.

Sanjay was very pleased to have another daughter. Sanjay had often explained to Adrian how his own mother, due to a slight mishap with a fertility drug, had raised four at once with really very little extra trouble. Adrian hadn't been buying and was absolutely unrelenting despite Sanjay's frequent descriptions of what funny times a family with twenty or thirty siblings can really have.

For Jasmine and Holly it was great to be back home. There was no more waking up pressed to the bed and no more of the claustrophobic rooms on earth with their eight foot ceilings. It was even more wonderful to get into the grove and brachiate again. Riches on the moon could be measured pretty much by how much space you had carved out of the rock.

Their home was big. There were many special purpose chambers but the grove took up most of the space. Ivy covered the walls and oaks grew with the strange dissymetry of trees grown in low gravity with lights all about them. The girls sleeping chambers seemed somehow to have belonged to two much younger girls, but they were happy nonetheless to see their stuffed toys and porcelain Scottish dolls again. Jalla took to low gravity well. Getting about on the rat lines in the grove was less difficult than swimming or walking had been for holly and jasmine

The trip to the wreck site had been set for four months off. Mom would not be home. Important things were happening although Sajay was unwilling to speak of them. Things were pretty much regular for the girls. Mom was often away lots. In the meantime all the girls studied as much as they could about aliens. First off, they learned that they were not all that rare. They had appeared about eighty times in three hundred years. Once at first and then several times and then more often lately as if the word had spread that there was someone here off planet to trade with.

The girls also learned that the great wreck strewn in chunks across the other side of the moon only might or might not be connected with today's visitors . Sanjay thought not. He thought he saw indications of a great age. beyond what is reasonable for any one race. The girls also learned that the aliens were relatives. You couldn't marry them, but you could probably eat them. Calamari would be appropriate. Scientists had dissected a few found floating dead in space with no ship near them. They were molluscs. Picture Kang and Trang from the Simpsons without the drool and you have them. Octopi more or less. To find the aliens' d.n.a. to be similar to ours threw scientific theory for a loop. It was not the expected result, but science is like that.

When fact refutes theory, the theory is, or should be, dumped. Traditional theory would have said that the aliens could not be our ancestors, as our clear relatedness to such critters as sponges clearly indicated our own earth origins. It had seemed a simple growth from the simplest to the most complex. New theory says that organisms mutate from simple to complex or the reverse with equal facility depending on the pressures upon them and the opportunities around them. If a ship were to have dumped her bilges into earths primordial soup and something spiritually akin to the zebra muscle had survived. It would have evolved both more and less complex forms, in fact, as living organisms slough off cells of varying sorts all the time, a truly benign environment would have allowed even these to prosper as cells do in a medium, in a science lab. Real backward evolution could have been profitably short-circuited.

Take your pick. Any theory worked, but it had been proven. The aliens were kin. Maybe they had even released the archaeo bacteria in the first place which had given earth its oxygen. Even after eighty contacts little was known of the aliens for they only appeared unexpectedly beside individual ships far from moon base, the big potato or the space station. The aliens wanted to trade but they did not seem to be serious about it. Demand for most items they would trade, fell off immediately. It was rather like a schooner pulling into some New Guinea cove. It was fine to trade for a few obsidian knives or shrunken heads but they had only novelty rather than intrinsic value. One or two was great but a trunk full was a liability. They had a way of repeating trades which had been concluded long ago. If you gave them gas or oil, they gave you diamonds every time. The only problem was that after one tanker captain had made the trade a century or so back diamonds had ceased to be worth much anywhere while oil products in space were still worth quite a bit.

Every ships captain had his trade items just in case one set down beside his ship someday. If an alien ship set in beside yours, company policies dictated unloading everything in your ship including toilet lids for the aliens to browse. A straight forward trade of a flashlight for a flashlight, fifty years ago has changed technology and made fortunes.

Even after Adrian had become amdassadoress to earth it had still been difficult for Sanjay to get the final .okay for a ship for his expedition. Uncle Jimmy had put his muscles into it. Sanjay had been amazed at how quickly his support had turned things around. Sanjay had not thought the influence of money to be so great, especially when wielded by a social outcast such as Jimmy. Indeed, he had hesitated long before allowing Uncle Jimmy's involvement., being afraid of queering the whole pitch. He had only given his agreement when the whole thing seemed once again to be permanently stalled. One evening, over plates of chablis and curry he had profusely thanked Jimmy for his influence, apologizing for his earlier reluctance to accept aid. Jimmy choked on his chablis. He said

"No, Sanjay, you had it right. the first time. The reason you got permission to take a ship once I said I would be involving myself with my own ship is that the hideous crones who run this place are hoping that I will take my antique ship and non regulation crew and crack it up some where. That would leave someone else to inherit Aunt Millie's megabucks." The prospect seemed to amuse him, but it alarmed Sanjay. " And are you certain you wont, however you said it, crack it up Will you Jimmy?"

"Not a chance." replied Uncle Jimmy, "we have had her atomics up for years. My girls tell me it should be just a finger stab away. They made good computers in those old days."

Downtown was very high on the list of places the girls wanted to go . There was shopping in to be done and they very much wanted to take Jalla flying in the dome. They would have to be very careful with Jalla. New chums could fly of course but they were said to have very little sense of their own mass and tended to come in fast as if they were a feather pillow only to be hurt by their own unreduced force. Flying in moon grav was right up there with ice skating or horse riding for danger but both the girls loved it. Sanjay had a trip planned. It was centered around the museum and the alien relics, although he had made sure there was plenty of time for all the activities, including flying above the central grove, ethnic food and ice cream. Sanjay was thorough. He knew how to please little girls.

Holly and Jasmine were so intent upon the fun of introducing Jalla to flying they entirely overlooked it was terror rather than reticence which kept her from jumping off the cliff. She would probably have done all right if she had jumped. Her wings were on right and all she would have had to do was flap them and she could have soared with them over the grove, underneath the dome. To their left and right many people were approaching the cliff and diving off, wings outspread. Sanjay of course realized the true state of affairs quickest. and offered instead to take jalla walking through the downtown while the girls flew above it. Holly and Jasmine rapidly assented as after a year as near cripples on earth they wanted to reaffirm themselves with some barrel rolls and aerobatics. They were after a real workout and with Jalla they would have had to fuss over her like a mother robin over a fat anaerobic fledgling.

The crowds reminded Jalla of home. Downtown moon colony was teeming. Even the languages she could hear spoken were familiar. A good half of the crowd seemed to be of Indian descent or of mixed Indian descent. Most of the rest was Chinese. All white faces were not absent however. There were plenty of freeholds out there of the old space families. They carefully watched their mean- genetic-relatedness indexes when marrying. So far they had not cluttered up their schools with too unacceptably large numbers of children with genetic deformities . Except deafness of course, which afflicted them about fifty percent overall.

Unfortunately, they all looked unacceptably alike to an outsider . Mom, Adrian and Uncle Jimmy were of these people. This was where the money and power had been these last several generations although this was becoming less and less true as the intelligent elite amongst them had chosen not to marry cousins . Holly and Jasmine's Mom for instance.

Sanjay steered the walk through India town. There was too much hustle for them to talk, so they just walked along enjoying the real sunshine on their faces. They and most of those around them, lived most of their lives in tunnels under artificial lights. Downtown was a treat to all visitors. At its center was the Jacob's Ladder, which brought goods and people up and down from orbit. The Jacob's Ladder made the moon colony one big city, with freeholds spread out- scattered around it. As Sanjay walked along conversationless, first through India town, then along to china town in a meandering walk, he thought about Adrian.

The more he thought about it the decision to nuke guandong was crazy. Even if one could put aside, for a moment, the morality of holocausting, of making a burnt offering, of a million women, children, fathers, grandfathers, aunts, uncles and cousins. It was a bad policy in political terms. Sure nuking the opposition had worked several times before. Nuking Rome or Paris might not seem much different to Adrian than nuking Guandong but in fact both of those earlier holocausts had something in common. Neither of them had killed the close kin of anyone then living on the moon. Gung Hoi Fat Choi had been subdued. Were the oligarchs so isolated that they could not sense the mood? The Chinese were the moons most recent immigrants. These people had not been sent up in tin cans against their will by their compatriots. These people were miners and welders and skilled technicians. They were a group who had recently had their horizons greatly expanded. "De Toqueville would have considered them dangerous" Sanjay mused. He knew that few of the oligarchs would have read De Toqueville. They were sure in the old order of things. Moon colony voted in justices of the peace and sheriffs and mayors. The old families controlled the purse strings of the government and the Holy American Forces (which controlled the ships and made the foreign policy). They thought it could never change.

The museum was in a sense, anti-climactic, after Jallas' long interesting walk. Most of its area was devoted to animals of the earth exhibits. A large variety of the animals of the earth were displayed stuffed against painted panoramas of their habitats. It swarmed with small children. The alien exhibit were much less visited. There were two dead aliens on display as well as much of the myriads of, so far, useless junk which had been traded from them over the past centuries. Jalla stood by Sanjay's side while he pored over the reams of what he presumed to be math, or at least, he qualified the statement, he presumed them to be numbers. He had never been able to find rhyme nor reason with them and he suspected that his samples were skewed by being a non-math use of numbers such as the read outs from old ships lorans. He dutifully, although without much hope, copied out some likely looking bits to carry about in his wallet for occasional future appraisal. Sanjay habitually carried a few lines about with him on his person hoping for an epiphany.

The emptiest exhibit was that about moon colony itself. There were good exhibits which enabled him to explain to Jalla how moon colony worked and what his project on the other side of the moon entailed. For the first time she was able to ask questions about the Jacob's Ladder and the Hammer of Shiva. Jalla was a bright girl. She caught onto the Jacobs ladder quickly, but the hammer of Shiva was another matter. To her the Hammer of Shiva was the avatar of a god. The Hammer of Shiva had many names on earth, all threatening, for the hammer was a weapon of massive destruction aimed right at them. She was an

Apollo asteroid which had been hauled in by spacemen a couple of centuries back to induce awe and compliance.

In India, as elsewhere, it had often been incorporated into the pantheon. Atom bombs only inspire fear among the educated. The hammer inspired dread everywhere in space however, it was commonly referred to as the big potato or the spud and to the fifty thousand or so floaters living there she was home. It was a rock about thirty miles long and nine across, bearing slightly more resemblance to a Kennebec potato than to an Idaho baker because of the regular bumps on its surface.

"And by now it must be nearly honeycombed because of all the tunneling within it for housing and storage" Sanjay told Jalla. The big potato was where Sanjay's project was being assembled . He would need several habitats and several stations. There was no Jacobs Ladder of course, and every trip up and down would be a seat-of-the-pants ride with pilots and computers.

It would cost a fortune. They had a trained team . They were specialists in putting up mine heads and steel habitats for free holds. They were what are called 'drifters' -- the cream of the mining community. They ran the 'drifts' from which the 'stopes' of the mine would later radiate. It was skilled, hard and dangerous work but well paying. Drifters spent more on entertainment than most other miners made. Their job was to build and preassemble the habitats, then to disassemble them and get them to the surface where they would be reassembled and equipped before the first scientist arrived. Then afterward, their job was to do the bull work of the excavation, such as the blasting and/or removal of over burden, drilling and any other heavy equipment jobs as should come up. .Sanjay was visiting the big potato increasingly frequently to observe and get to know the Haka crew. He would supervise the loading of the scientific equipment necessary for the trip. The Haka were in charge of getting it stored and to the surface, but not of making sure it was there in the first place. That was Sanjay's job.

The girls' months at home on the moon passed well. It was good to be home for the sisters, and for Jalla it was good just to have a home. She became far more a companion of Sanjay than of the girls accompanying him in his activities quietly and only occasionally asking a question that showed that within her head there were wheels furiously circling. In her drive to please Sanjay and Gupta, she set the pace of the girls math studies. She consciously devoted far more of her time to it than either of the prima donas had ever saw fit to do. In Sanjay's and Giupta's eyes, she shone.

Fortunately Jasmine and Holly were able to share their home, although not entirely without inner griping. It wasn't really worth griping out loud, when, as soon as one had done so, it was immediately obvious both to oneself and to ones listeners, that you had always been pretty spoiled up until now. It took all the fun out of complaining, so the twins individually tried to make the obviously correct decision of taking things as well of as possible. They were after all sensitive , humane, intelligent, and reasonable . They were eleven year old girls. They did not realize at the time how rare these qualities (which are nearly universal in the eleven year old girl) exist in the general public. It would later to become clear to them. Mom nuked another city.

Earth didn't really want a space colony ,or at least it hadn't wanted one for very long. When the United States had been the lone earth superpower in that little window of time before the before the Chinese ascendancy the moon colony had been a feather in her cap. The USA, with a population of hundreds of millions of people had been fabulously wealthy and the possessor of a technology in many ways not surpassed since. The United States of America could afford a space colony. The post big death world with the USA missing could not. The big death had left thousands of people in space --scattered all over Hells half acre .

The mother country was history. Lots of them died and those who didn't were in dire straights. After a couple of hundred years, the several states which had continued had recovered their capacities somewhat, the Moonies had asked for assistance. None of the earth states had felt obligated to help in a job that honestly looked nearly impossible to do. They would have left everyone on the moon, from grannies to babes in arms die. Until the big potato appeared.

The hammer had wonderfully concentrated the minds of the earth nations towards those in space. Nuking Rome had removed any lingering doubts. After losing Rome ,Euro state had become the proxy state, rather than the main antagonist, of the moon men and the center of their efforts at world government. So things had gone on for a couple of centuries. From earths point of view, it was in many ways a hornswoggle, as well as a boondoggle.

The moon colony was expensive and getting the money from a sales tax levied earth wide didn't make it less so. Most earth governments wanted out. They wanted a much smaller moon colony rather than the present rapidly expanding one. They wanted out of the Cray financial web and its taxes, the right to charter their own banks. They were big boys now they didn't need the moon to cajole them towards technology. In fact, the moon men had now put the breaks on much technological development on earth by restricting certain industries to the moon (to foster its boom entirely artificially and with huge hidden costs) . The moon now hampered the earth, much as the corn laws had harmed English colonies in the 17th century. There should have been lots of room for compromise and maneuver but Adrian and the people she represented were not about to find it. They had nuked Guandong and then Shanghai. All over the world governments were wondering how really impossible it would be to put a bomb right square on the Jacob's Ladder.

Sanjay had one of the habitats, which they would be using erected out on the surface, near moon colony. Many of the scientists participating had not been in the daily use of space suits ,or at least not for many years. There were intricacies to staying alive in a freehold and without practice some, or all would have ended up breathing vacuum. For the twins this was pricelessly interesting. It was soon acknowledged that the youngest members of the expedition had the best scores in the remotely operated equipment simulation scores. It was generously decided by the scientists to be the result of their fresh young reflexes, although the girls confided amongst themselves that it was more likely to be their addiction to video games (Two hours a day, but they were trying to cut down).

The months spent at home had been fun --lots of popcorn, video games and old movies. They got downtown every time they could. The trips out on the surface like a real pioneer, had been nothing but exciting. It had also been dangerous as well. There was the innate danger of the environment and equipment, as real here as on the other side of the moon. Near moon colony, there was also the additional danger of radioactivity. The moon had run on atomics for several centuries and especially in the vicinity of Luna city, spent fuel had been dumped about . One needed to move slowly and keep an eye on the gauges. Not that the girls themselves had been allowed to drive any of the real vehicles. Their simulation scores in the booths not withstanding.

Sanjay had thought it important however, to take them out to test both their resolve about joining the expedition and his own judgment in letting them. Jasmine and Holly were not in the least worried about dying during the expedition It was all just a cheerful adventure.

They were worried about Mom and about war. Holly and Jasmine were both very worried about war. They did not consciously seek to know about it but every time they went to look at a game or a movie on the web or to call up an acquaintance there was that little box in the corner giving the news to the world from the viewpoint of world gov of course). Often enough there had been Adrian's face portrayed with her worst Hellfire-and -Brimstone look uttering threats. The girls all knew Moms' ideology and had even half- assed subscribed to do it when it had been required of them . Sanjay had not. He had just kept his silence. He was no help at all now. When the girls brought up their mothers name to him they had seen a much more haunted look appear on his face than had ever rested there before.

They intuited silently but correctly his position and had not pursued him to talk about her He had no reticence however to tell them that he considered the war to be wrong. As well as foolish. He had given them the benefit of his logic without assigning blame where they all knew it must lie. They had let him drop the subject. They were kind to their father. They worried alone about the war and about how things were going to be in their home when mom came back. They knew Adrian well. She would return home ready to run things there as she did her office Mostly in the past that had worked; but it had worked because it was Sanjay's serious decision to make it work,. or it had been. The girls could feel in their bones that there were big changes going to happen in their family when their mom got back.

And they asked themselves if could they keep quiet when dealing with their mom? They already knew she was a mass murderer. It wasn't going to be like your mother had been caught shoplifting or some such thing and you were trying to ignore it for the good of the family. Jasmine and Holly did not know how they felt, but they dreaded their moms arrival.

She would be back in soon on a date planned long ago to coincide with the leaving of Sanjay's expedition. It was a date now anticipated fearfully by three of the four parties. . .

When it finally became time to leave moon colony the girls were glad to get moving and have something on their minds. It looked as if their m worries about their mom were going to be resolved by a brief visit and then further absence. She was going to come and visit them at the base camp in synchronous orbit above the wreck. It was going to be a diplomatic photo- op, as in her status as moon colony's extra territorial ambassador, she was going to cut a ribbon for the enterprise. It was a diplomatic mission in a personal sense as well but the girls did not talk about this side of things. They were only too willing to let their parental difficulties rest, forever if possible. They were far too interested in the project in hand.

The base camp perched in synchronous orbit above the wreck was the home of the Haka crew. The freeholds had been assembled on the surface but a great deal of work remained to be done when Sanjay and the girls arrived three weeks ahead of the other scientists who were timing their advent for the Ambassadresses arrival. Uncle Jimmy had timed his own arrival to coincide with Adrian's departure .

They were very antipathetic to say the east. The mining crew were glad to see them. They were three children in a childless environment. The Haka adopted them as much as they could. The Haka worked inn ten day shifts upon the moons surface and then returned to the much more friendly base camp for four. It had been a big operation. lots of surface work and not much underground compared to the mining freeholds they usually put in. The Haka loved guests. They jokingly told the girls that their name "Haka" had meant 'guest 'in their native China. They said it had also been kept as their name for a thousand years by the larger linguistic group which had surrounded them , as a gentle and polite reminder that they someday should move on; which they said proudly that they most definitely had.

Sanjay had become well liked by the Haka crew as he was not a self important man and deferred to them as if he were in their space, where as it was technically rather the opposite. He understood their political feelings ,for he had been among them on the big potato when their city was nuked. Their grief had been expressed in Cantonese, the language of their former hosts, and in their own variant Mandarin all around him. Sanjay had understood, without the benefit of knowing either language ,that the near kin of many of those around him were those who had suffered and he had remained silent.

The aliens turned up ten days before the arrival of Adrian and the scientists. Sanjay and the girls were immediately aware of the flurry of activity among the Haka around them. It was their chance to make a million. Calls were immediately made to their home office and orders were barked out to them in hurried tones. Sanjay at first stood back and then was finally approached by the senior Haka aboard, who made him a financial proposition. Sanjay took it.The Haka would take on stripping the station of everything that moved and hanging it out on ratlines dangling from synchronous moors for inspection by the aliens. Trading would commence. Sanjay and the girls observed the alien ship out of the port. It was small compared to some of those that had been previously seen. The aliens were approaching slowly to give evidence of their good intentions.

It was a good first week of trading. The Haka were shrewd businessmen, always halving up likely looking trades so that some remained to be put out in ever diminishing quantities should it prove popular. All wood which had made fortunes before was sawed down into chunks which could be put out individually. The Haka kept careful track of the hundreds of piles which they had set out, retrieving and replacing items which hadn't traded with other items. They were the careful shopkeepers at a country craft fair and the aliens were the city people come from far away to shop for curios. The Haka pulled it off beautifully.

For the most part Sanjay and the girls kept to the side of the proceedings and watched. Sanjay had a moor put out to one side of the trading area and had a habitat hooked to it by a line. It had lots of glass , a refrigerator containing food, a small bar, and a washroom. Sanjay guessed that on a regular construction sight it was where the guy with the white hat was when all the rest were in space suits. For Sanjay and the girls it was home for a week. It was sort of like a duck blind from which to conduct their studies. Sanjay sometimes donned a space suit and went for a closer look at the proceedings but the girls stayed put.

Sanjay had spent most of ten years welding in a space suit on first arrival in space, but there was no need to put the girls to risk. their view was good enough. They watched an orderly procession from their position although they were unable to make out the minutae such as what was being traded for what. By the third day it had even threatened to become downright boring until the children of the aliens found them. They he had seen amongst the aliens, some smaller redder versions flitting about ,one of which had eventually made it up to their habitat and returning to the trading site had been followed back to their habitat again by all the small red forms. A number of the larger aliens followed them up to the habitat where they had gripped the windows all around to press on it and stare at the girls. After that there was lots to do.

Math was first. The girls were soon able to count along with their observers outside the windows. Things sped up when the girls had the idea of trying to teach American sign language. The hand language of the deaf. On about their second day of messing about with them the girls realized that no matter which of their students they taught something to, all of their students knew that bit from now on. It was an interesting and thought provoking. It did not seem to be telepathic contact as the girls could see that the aliens used many signs and gestures amongst themselves. It was an enigma until later on when they discovered the secret of touch,

Mom and the scientists arrived as planned . Sanjay was worried that the arrival of the ship would spark the departure of the aliens however he was powerless to stop it. It had been a photo- op planned long in advance. The girls had elected to remain aboard the habitat during the official ceremony and only to come aboard when Adrian had taken off her official hat and become just mom again,. at which point Sanjay would whisk her away to join them . It was a good plan. It would get the whole family together, but would give them something to do other than to talk about those topics which they were all sure would eventually turn up and which they all preferred to ignore for now.

The girls were alone in the habitat when they watched Adrian's ship of the line arrive. She was much huger than the space station which she pulled up adjacent to. On about the count of five after arriving she blew to smithereens, along with the station beside her. The girls watched huge red chunks soundlessly erupting from her side to engulf the space station where their father was waiting. And then without understanding how it could be, until it was all over, they watched the alien ship also begin to erupt with steam seconds later. the victim of a chunk of metal thrown away during the explosion.

The alien craft continued to spew steam long after the earth crafts wreckage had disappeared from sight thrown away by the great force of the explosion upon it. Soon the alien craft showed signs of drift as well, gradually slipping out of their vision.

The three girls in their habitat were still moored to their synchronous boy , a few hundred yards away from the similarly moored trading station with it's rat lines strung out from it in all directions still dangling myriad items. Soon all that existed in their part of space was the trading ground and themselves, their only radios the mere walky- talkies in their suits and in the habitat. They had no idea how much oxygen they had ,and they had no mom and no dad. then they noticed the small red form moving upon the trading ground.

At first it had seemed impossible to do anything much for the small creature. It had clearly been injured. They could see that much. It moved a lot early on and then less after a while. They had an idea how to rescue it. It wasn't really impossible to do, just dangerous as Hell, but as it seemed as if they likely had only a little while to live any way, they decided that they just didn't want to spend their last hours chickening out and watching one of their new little friends die by herself.The girls got their suits on and exited the air lock and successfully used compressed air to propel themselves toward the rat lines of the trading platform. They had attached themselves together with fifty feet of rope separating them, and they managed a bola type snare on one of the ratlines. Very soon they had the limp red form and tried to repeat their bola snag on the line connecting the habitat to its mooring boy. It was a tremendously good try and only missed by fifteen feet or so. Slowly the girls pulled themselves to the center where their three ropes joined and put the small wiggling figure of the alien child between them, hugging into a ball just to feel each other. They were heading pretty straight for the moons surface. They all agreed over their radios that this was better than asphyxiation, as they would hit the ground at many miles per hour, and as the moon has no atmosphere ,they would not burn up on the way in ,but would remain comfortable and could talk together until the "big splat" as they dubbed it between themselves. Uncle Jimmy zeroed in on their walky talkys and picked them up about fifteen minutes later..

Jimmy was on the lam. Events had happened quickly on the moon after the second Chinese city had been nuked. There were riots downtown. The news had shown horrible footage of whites being popped out paupers lock where those who hadn't payed their air taxes had been similarly dealt with a hundred or so years earlier. For a week there had been the "free colony of luna city" broadcasts from the rebels who held the downtown and then their retribution had come.

The old white crones had struck back. They vented down town. They were ruthless. Most of the old families owned, and at least partially lived ,on freeholds, downtown and its warrens were for the worker peoples. They were disposable. They were disposed of. Afterward, the fire locks were once again closed to space and the downtown was reoccupied.

Martial law had been declared. From his perch on board the Lusty Lady. Jimmy knew himself to be truly a loose cannon with his big ship and his point of view. He also knew he was perceived as one. Over the preceding couple of weeks his boat had begun to fill up as surely as Noahs ark did after the rain began to fall. Jimmyville had made it through the venting but not through the repression which followed. The Lusty Lady was full of radicals ,relations and just plain riff raff, who had perceived her as a place to run to. For the first time since welders had cut her interior up into living areas for a supposed hotel , she was full and functioning in nearly that capacity.

The concensus of all those on board was that they should run somewhere and hide until the situation on the moon became less homicidal. Jimmy didn't like the idea all that much. Before the return of all his relations and their friends the boat had had a population of a couple of hundred, and Jimmy had sat in the center of the web like a fat spider calling the shots. Now he was just one old man amongst thousands, They were even talking about "elections". Jimmy decided to go to Montreal.

Jasmine, Jalla and Holly were rescued before they suffered any physical damage. The alien child was not. The three were given a cabin on an inner deck where the gravity was about like the moon's. It was a beautiful luxurious hotel room but the girls did not feel the luxury.

The alien child was obviously in pain and discomfort,. she had lost a leg. It was plain that things were not right with her The bathtub was big enough to keep her in. When the little alien had seen the basin of water she had shucked her own space suit, and quickly slipped in. The girls had been unsure about the salt content so they had not given her quite the salt content of the ocean but a little less as they would have for a guppy or a molly. They had heard somewhere that the seas had once been somewhat less salty.

They took turns beside the tub watching her writhe in the water as if in ceaseless torment and as they got more familiar with her they ached to ease her mind somehow. It seemed like that after a time her contortions became less frenzied. (In the manner of children the girls had decided that the child must be a girl, and, besides ,it would have seemed positively rude and heartless to use 'it' as a personal pronoun. Finally the colors pulsing across the alien's body grew slower in their changes. After an hour or two the girls became aware that its big eyes were open and looking at them. At the same moment three tendrils snaked up from the water and touched each girl on the hand.

It was as if a bright light had turned on above them . The three girls could feel each other clearly in their minds and quickly realized that they could hear each others thoughts. Holly and Jasmine were for a moment intent upon each other realizing that like in some house of mirrors they could look at their myriad of shared memories together and see each from the others side. Jasmines memories were nearly as accessible as her own to Holly and in fact she could see into some darkened chambers where the present day Jasmine never went. Her curiosity led her in and suddenly she became aware that Jasmine was the little baby whose parents ad been killed in front of her eyes,. Suddenly they both knew. and spent a moment crying inside for the baby Jasmine. Next they looked at Jalla and felt themselves looking out from within her and felt her looking out from within themselves.

Jasmine and Holly and Jalla became jasmine-holly-jalla. They were three individuals but they shared a memory pool and could hear and help each other think. Their three consciousnesses began to look at the alien girl between them. Their first impression was of her sweetness but also of her smallness. She wasn't only physically small . It was a smallness of mind. She reminded them of a tiny dog which had resided in the groundskeeper's hut at their school on earth. She had a small but wonderful spirit. She had been part of a flock and had had it ripped from her. She had been through a terrible ordeal and needed to be loved and to be part of a family. The girls pretty quickly decided that she wasn't that bright ,at least not on her own. It seemed that perhaps she was just very very young. They felt her spirit quiet within their communion. and she soon fell into rest.

The girls were holding hands with the alien when Jimmy returned several hours later. They were silent with rather odd looks on their faces and rather creeped Jimmy out. The revolution and route had managed to seriously interfere in Jimmy's morning rituals of coffee tobacco, and nicotine etc . He needed to talk with the girls about the future. He wanted to go to Montreal and try to get his old carcase morphed back into youth with ape juice. and he thought maybe they ought to come with him as well.

Jimmy had just about decided upon a plan of action . Any regular way of getting back to earth was out of the question. The International Space station where he had often safely dined was really financed and run by the good old U.S.A, and ,if he ventured aboard in times like these he would surely be jailed. He assured the girls that staying aboard was not really an option. He had kept abreast of the politicizing going on aboard her and wanted no part of it.

The Lusty Lady was going to be a democracy whatever that was. Uncle Jimmy described it as legalized horse rustling at its worst. He a said that the Russians had had a democracy of the proletariat and shot you if you disagreed (and very often even if you didn't disagree) .The ancient Americans had also claimed democracy as their government, but it had been a democracy of all people ,on all subjects, except money. The oligarchy had kept the loot to themselves. The Hellenic Greeks had democracy too, and like the early Americans they had thought it coexisted just fine with slavery. Now this bloody democracy was going to inaugurate itself by stealing his house. Besides 'Jimmy didn't like the grub. Jimmy wanted to go to Montreal and he did have one possible way to get there. There were the pods. The Lusty Lady had been designed early on enough ,that it had been thought that anyone fleeing from her in a disaster would wish to return to earth. Her pods had sat untouched by the renovations aboard her. Jimmy had his three youngest wives, earth women all,fill two of the pods up with food ,water ,gold, jewels ,drugs. money. and suchlike.

The original programming of the pods gave the choice of several earth locals for splashdown. Jimmy had chosen the Cocos Isles from the list he had been given. He was still a fabulously rich man in India and had a town full of relatives and ex- wives to visit. The Cocos Isles were the only location on the list where he could arrange a reception committee. The other locations were impossible, mostly scattered around America. He had felt lucky to find the Cocos Isles on the list. The capsule was meant to plunge into the sea and then to be found. The pods had no ability to navigate about in the water on their own. Jimmy had it all arranged . The last time he had demenaged he had been abandoned by all his wives under fifty. This time he was just going to take his three youngest with him. Jimmy was going to abscond without a word. Jimmy had a vestigial conscience at best.

Jimmy liked to be bad, but he was seventy years old and being bad was getting harder and harder. Jimmy wanted to be young again, and never having been all that good looking any way ,{ all old family men looked like an illicit cross between Alfred E. Newman and George bush], he was not at all afraid of looking like an ape if his telomeres were lengthened ,so long as he was also rejuvenated. He would just be a different sort of rich ugly bastard. He was used to it.

Jimmy had followed any fad said to prevent or reverse aging[as long as they had not required him to change his bad habits] He had tried rhino horn (or as such it had been sold to him) LSD, steroids, snake oils and herbal cures without seeing much of a difference. When the Montreal riots had occurred Jimmy had already been following the scholarly debate about the lengthening of the telomeres. It had not so much been the site of the men of a whole city being turned into apes which had gripped Jimmy but the thought of all the old men becoming young Jimmy had no desire to stay upon the lusty lady and live on a diet of sardines and utopian socialism. Jimmy was going to secretly and quietly jump ship.

Fishy, for that was what the girls had called the alien child, needed more natural surroundings. She was in shock, and if left in a bathtub she would die. They could read that truth within her. When Jimmy explained to the girls his plan to disembark they elected to accompany him. They packed their gear into the pod including a thirty gallon water bucket with lid for fishy to ride down in. Jimmy explained about their destination being the Cocos Isles and how a flotilla befitting his status as magnate would be awaiting them., patrolling for their beacon.

Jimmy had intended that one pod would take he and his three sweeties ,while the other would take the girls and their fishy friend. The girls realized early on that Jimmy was acting a bit furtive and when there was no group or ceremony to send him off they realized he was simply departing without explanation or notice. It was uncle Jimmy to a tee. At the agreed departure time the girls had already arrived and tucked themselves into their places. Jimmy was held up. No he wasn't late , the other kind of held up. At five minutes before departure Jimmy's two youngest wives had grabbed him by his frail elbows and frog marched him over to pop him in the pod with the three girls, while their compatriot, Jimmy's third from youngest wife[a beautiful thoroughbred Australian of whom Jimmy had been especially proud] punched a new destination code into their own capsule. Jimmy spent the majority of the ride to earth complaining about the ingratitude of wives and servants and quoting the younger Pliny on the subject.

The girls were bored stiff by the splash down. Jimmy immediately said how wonderful it felt to be in the Indian ocean again. He should have read the fine print.

Cassey and Polly had liked the giant turtles of the Galapagos, in fact the whole area was a treasure trove. A real treasure trove. In the seventeenth century buccaneers like Dampier had rounded the horn and found a new perch from which to attack Spanish shipping. in the galapagos and the cocos isles. The cocos isles had most gained the reputation for buried treasure, and centurys of treasure hunters had camped there and dug potholes. Over the hundreds of years the refuse from the early diggers had become interesting artifacts in themselves. There were no coco palms. The islands had been the cultivated plantations of the incas who had sailed their daggerboard rafts a thousand miles up the coast in order to farm this garden isle, but their coconuts had gradually been crowded out by jungle

The pirates had not been choosy in their looting and pillaging, and even after the passage of most of a millenium coves could be found where the pirates had unloaded cargos of jams and and preserves. There were many shards and even whole empty jars from long ago. The waters were blue and meant for swimming. Polly and Cass had spent their lives in the somber and cool pacific northwest rainforest. where a summer could be swallowed up by rainful without it being at all unusual. This was the first taste of the tropics and of course they loved it.

Their trip down the coast had been very uneventful from HUghs point of view. All of the times spent in ports he had had to hide out in a back cabin. They had considered it entirely too risky to try to have hugh's dental work done due to the still constant presence of the wanted posters. When the Chinese war had started Hugh had rather selfishly hoped it would take some of the heat out of the hunt for morphs, Maybe it had. He didn't know , but the decision had been made that he stay hidden on board within all the ports, and hidden he had stayed while goods were ordered waited for and received. He and Emilliano had played endless games of cards. Emilliano was not trusted to be let loose in Mexico until just before leaving and Hughy was nominally his captor. The truth of the matter was really somewhat different. Emilliano had realized Hagars riches and had set himself to becoming her permanent man. Hugh had known it wasn't likely to work but he had admired his dogged determination and he had finally felt rather sorry for him when Hagar had abandoned him on a dock with a check in his hand. All in all Hugh was unhappy to see him go. He had been the only other male on a boat full of formidable women.,and with Emilliano gone there was no one to blame for the occasional aromas of marijuana or to stand up for him when he explained how unutterably necessary beer was as an accompaniment to sports on the screen. Emilliano had been a bonus, a perpetual worse example who he could compare himself too and come off looking pretty good. The jig had been up and it had looked like a long dry run to Hawaii. Then along came uncle Jimmy.

Jimmy really should have read the fine print. By some odd chance the two sets of cocos isles which the world possesses are located on the equator on opposite sides of the world. It is not possible to have two points further from each other and still be on earth. Jimmy was at the wrong cocos isles. Instead of landing in a flotilla of ships waiting for his signal south of India, Jimmy had brought them down off of Central America. The airwaves were full of Mexican music. Jimmy was glum. The girls were less so. Once they had established their real position it became apparent the islands to which they appeared to be drifting possessed an enchanted name.

They were the Galapagos, a magical name to every child who hears it. Jimmy kept it to himself that it seemed far more likely that they would instead drift in to the coast and be picked up by some tribe with porcupine quills through their lips and spend their lives with them for as long a as they respectively lasted. Jimmy momentarily wondered what it would be like to have a hallucinogen blown up his nostrils from a huge tube as he had seen in old movies of the Yanomamo in college. The beacon of course was broadcasting out its beam, but Jimmy had reflected that the were was no likelihood that anyone out there would hear it and that if they did hear it there was even less likelihood that it would be recognized as the distress signal it was. It was too old, in tune with the us army of centuries ago.

Cleo picked it up as soon as it began broadcasting. She was a relic as well. Hugh relayed the information to the ladies . Hugh had recently gotten into the habit of letting the ladies make all the decisions. They seemed to growl when he got near that particular bone. The ladies dictated that they head south the four hour journey and have a look. Hug parked Cleo at the outside range of her fifty milimetres and stopped for a look. Cleo checked them out as well, building a schematic of what she saw on the screen in front of them. The first signs were good, at least it did appear too be a pod from space, and not a patrol boat full of uniforms. Huey had a good look through the glasses , if he saw uniforms he intended to back off and let them take a chance with the bow and arrow cultures of the coast. Instead he saw three young girls and an elderly gentleman. He picked them up, attaching a painter to the pod.

The girls were disembarked first. In the manner of all human groups which meet the children slipped off together while the adults reconnoitered each other. They slipped up to the foredeck where they introduced each other and the space girls explained why they were carrying a rather large red octopus about with them. They had quite a bit of trouble with the dialects at first. the Indian English, space English, and pacific west coast English of the tribes, had all had three hundred years to diverge between them. Most of the consonants were okay, but the vowels seemed to have slipped all over the place.

Luckily, what first came to hand was a task easily explained. Fishy needed real ocean water. They cleared up the foredeck and pondered what could be used for a pool. A question to Hugh who was watching the proceedings from the forecastle brought about the idea of inflating a zodiac on the foredeck and and filling it. Soon the rubber lifeboat was full on the foredeck with Fishy swimming about happily in it.

The five girls were soon lolling in the sun or going for dips in the beautiful warm sea. Cleo watched out for them with her sonar on the alert for sharks. but here in the mid ocean they needed to stay very very close. They had much to talk about. They had talked all day long and in the end when fishy had finally stopped playing in the water and come to the edge of the pool lifting up a tentacle for each of the five girls the talking had become superfluous. Uncle jimmy had had a much harder time of it. They took away his dope. The gang of three, Hagar, Hyapatia, and Calley had made the decision and called out Hughy to enforce it.

The contents of Jimmy's pod needed to be brought up onto the deck before the pod itself was cut loose. From his perch on a deck chair, Jimmy had done the directing while his treasures were winkled out one on one and brought aboard. He had lost ground early on by attempting a subterfuge about what some of the contents were and had been caught out in a lie. Hughy felt sorry for the cringing, hand wringing wretch who pleaded for mercy much as if the ladies had pronounced they were going to have Hughy wring his neck rather than having just told him that the hospital they intended to set up would benefit from so much opium and cocaine. When Hugh had wrestled jimmy' s gold bullion up on deck the girls had put it at his feet, along with his jewels. They had no desire to rob this fabulously rich buffoon, but there were standards to be upheld on this boat.

There were tears in Jimmy's eyes when Hagar, supposedly, accidentally dropped his cartons of cigarettes in the ocean. When Hughy came across the vacuum packed container of indoor bud, he decided he was not going to let this bunch of dried out, bossy, mean spirited women even get their eyes on it. It was not too far from the size and weight of a football. He brought it up last keeping it behind his back as he came out on the deck of the landing capsule. " Look" Hughy sang out pointing furiously behind the women's backs. "A pod of whales" When the three women turned to look Hughy took the package out from behind his back and with the strength and accuracy of the football star he was, he pitched it thirty five feet along the boat and through the open forecastle window.

Hughy grinned at the astonished Jimmy and winked before the three women turned back around. They were scowls on all three of their faces. They sensed that they had been had, but could not quite see how. Hughy nearly blew it when he protested much too quickly. "It must have dove."he said. All three women smelled a rat." It?"said Hyapatia "I thought you said you saw a pod." Hagar finished. Calley had not spoken but her eyes were fixed upon Hugh. He would have been dead meat if there hadn't been other game afoot. Jimmy began to beg for his dope again in a high pitched falsetto voice guaranteed to draw the ladies' attention. He took the heat off of Hughy intentionally. An alliance of sorts was formed.

Jimmy was banished to a locked cabin where he could confront the inner demons of his addictions and practice up on his twitching. Hughy secretly deposited him a case of chablis, the last of Emilliano's cigarettes and some of his bud before locking Jimmy in as per the ladies' instructions. He seriously wished him luck.

The journey to Hawaii was a drea , with day after day of blue skies and light to medium breezes. Cleo flew, both sails up, reading both pages and managing her own reefs and tacks. Hughy was mostly just Cleo's companion in that he spent his time as a captain should, in the forecastle, having Cleo read to him from the classics while he sat back and looked out the windows from the captain's chair.

Hugh had some worries. Some personal worries that had nothing to do with his morphing or his looks. They had to do with his marriage. He and Calley had been together for more than six years but they had never before lived together. Had he really never mentioned to Calley that he liked to drink four to six beer several times a week? He had not drunk hardly at all during their first year of living together because, as a young man with a pregnant wife and then with a brand new baby, he himself had not felt it was right to drink, being petrified that he would fail some test expected of him some dark night. He had been like a mountain climber training for an ascent, but now that the baby was several months old and healthy, Hugh had actually expected to have an occasional drink (by which he meant about thirty beer a week strategically spread out). The women disapproved. Oh they didn't actually stop him, but they ran him out of the galley pretty fast and up to hang out in the forecastle again.

Hugh did own up to himself that he had never felt the need to tell Calley that during their university years he had begun to smoke dope in the evenings when the bong was passed around amongst his dormitory mates and the reggae music was played. It just hadn't seemed necessary. He was a light smoker and in those days it was never his own dope, as his mates had just smoked him up. Now however, to continue to hide his own dope stash, as Emilliano had done, grated on his sense of independence. Hugh was getting extremely tired of being bossed around.

It was Hugh who noticed something odd in the behavior of the five girls who hung out by the pond in front of his windows on the prow of the boat. He hadn't noticed anything for a long time. It had seemed perfectly natural for them to rest lolling on the deck as Cleo flew into the blue or gray sea or to be holding hands as they splashed about in the wading pool. But they didn't speak.

One lazy afternoon Hugh realized that he had drunk an entire six pack perched in his captain's chair without one of them speaking once. This was odd as they usually chattered about as much as budgies. Then he realized that for the entire period they had also not let loose of the aliens' tentacles. Not wanting to rat out anyone to the gang of three and observing that at meal times the twins and the other three girls seemed just as happy and vibrant as could be expected he decided to keep his observations under his hat for a while. On the nicer evenings when the wind was low Hugh would play his guitar for the girls and drink his beer.

One day Hugh reached out impulsively and touched one of the alien tentacles himself while the girls were holding the others. It was wet and felt not unlike the tentacles of the other octopi he had touched in his fisherman's life. For the nth time he wondered what was with the constant hand and tentacle holding and once again he decided not to ask

He was well acquainted with the fact that certain people were too damned bossy and inquisitive and he had no wish to emulate them. He let the girls have their space and did not ask.

The girls had looked for Hughy's mind when he had touched the tentacle but they had not seen it. He was too old, too different and just not part of the flock, so they went back to what they were working on. Math was fun.

The girls spent hours lying in the sun thinking about it. It was easy to do now that there were five of them. As easy as pushing a truck, if you had enough people at once that is. The girls realized that always before in their lives math had been unnecessarily hard to do because they had each had to do it alone. There really had been no way one person could help another, but now there really was a royal road to geometry.

With their minds working in tandem whenever one of them became tired and about to lose the thread of thought, another of them could put their shoulder in to it and take the load for a while. They could see how great things could be accomplished even by as unbrainy a species individually as Fishy seemed to be. Fishy had come from a flock of fifty agelings whom her five new human sisters had replaced in her brain.

By the second week of the Hawaiian voyage, Jimmy pretty much had his hamsters in a row again. His nieces ,as well as Hughy began to visit him. Cassy and Polly were prohibited from doing so, but there was no way Hagar could work out to justify depriving him of the company of his own family

Jimmy had always liked to throw his bucks around. It wasn't long before he had engaged Hyapatia as his personal cook and was able to entertain properly in his cabin. It was curry and Chablisse night after night in JImmy's cabin with a standing invite to all who would come. The guests at dinner included Hugh as often as he could manage it. However Hagar and Calley would not exchange words with the old polygamist (as they called him), let alone eat a meal in his presence. Hyapatia attended, increasingly frequently as she realized just how rich this old geezer she cooked for really was. She also began to somewhat like him. Despite being a rather ugly puppy he was probably good ,or had been, at creating heartbreak, sorrows and misery in womens' hearts and Hyapatia had always liked that kind of guy. He was a much married man and fabulously rich That he was extremely old and with a heart condition were not necessarily drawbacks in Hyapatia's mind. It was possible after all for things to be short as well as sweet .

Landfall in Hawaii was a landfall in paradise. Dr. Kameeaha had been well aware long in advance of the special circumstances of Hugh's appearance. There was a waterless and therefore uninhabited atoll on which a bungalow had been constructed and water tanks installed. The anchorage was a safe one.

The girls moved from the deck of Cleo into the water of the atoll. To Fishy it was like home, for the space girls it was much less tiring than walking and for the twins from Vancouver Island it was just plain fun. Calley's mom and her baby moved with her into the bungalow while Hugh remained mostly on board Cleo at least at night until all the comings and goings from the mainland would cease. Jimmy headed straight for the biggest city he could find as soon as he could with Hyapatia behind him pushing his chair. He had given his nieces the choice of staying with their new found friends or of joining him. Their decision to stay had not put his nose out of joint however when he and Hyapatia returned three months later with her pregnant ,and a green rock the size of Vancouver Island on her finger both Hagar and Calley looked like they had been at a lemon eating contest. Calley recovered first when he agreed to quintupple her hospital in size for the mere cost of giving it her best shot to morph him as she had Hugh.

Hagar's forgiveness was less mercenarily bestowed. She liked his bucks a lot, but wouldn't have given him her welcome if he had not stayed off the cocaine the heroin and the tobacco but he had. she didn't care so much about the rest. He even almost looked healthy and he was more gentlemanly towards Hyapatia than some of her other inflatable Elvises had been. and then, importantly, Hyapatia had let him knock her up. That had made him family and Hagar's motto was that if it was possible to do so, family should be forgiven. Jimmy had Hagar over a barrel. She reluctantly decided to like him as long as he never dared to call her Mom. Not ever.

Hyapatia and Jimmy actually had a fairly good relationship. In their first few months there had been only one real spat when he had drunkenly tried to purchase the affections of another woman right in front of her. He had even drunkenly tried to remind her of her place. She had taken it meekly enough until he had fallen asleep and then she had sewn his sheets together around him whilst he slept and woken him up by beating him with a broom. Girls from Hot Springs Cove knew how to deal with that sort of behavior. Mostly they got on pretty good.

Hughy's personal problems hadn't gone away. First off it wasn't all that easy to be a morphed individual -- to have to spend ones life hiding out in the first place. Second, it was upsetting just how convenient the whole situation was for certain individuals. Namely Hagar and Calley. He knew the hospital project was damned important and he also knew that if the hospital was built he could finally get his teeth worked on in safety.

He knew that malaria, which was to be its major focus ,was the biggest killer world wide. It was just that he had never planned to make his contribution to the world by baby sitting and things looked to get worse. His daughter was rapidly approaching the age where she also could be left for the day while Calley worked. The future looked scary. Hugh felt like he had been jailed.

Hugh had momentarily considered a home-made tattoo to make an effect. Perhaps 'born to do dishes' or something of that sort. Or maybe 'pots' and 'pans' written across his knuckles.

He had other problems as well. The morphing, while it had been ninety nine percent neutral towards his mind, had actually changed a few things. Hugh had acquired a slight tendency to growl. He was unaware of it himself for the most part and the girls were doing their best to bring it to his attention and to help him quit . And worst of all, was that Hughy was jealous again.

It was Dr. Kameaha . He had replaced Dr. Charnay in Calley's mind as a brilliant, self -sacrificing saint of a man and Hugh conceded that in this case, she was almost certainly right.

So Hugh just hated him for his goodness. It didn't have to make sense. And then there were the petty issues. He had no beer. With infuriating regularity and even more infuriating looks and glances between them selves Hagar and Calley kept on dropping it from the shopping lists and making up excuses which he knew to be baloney. The fact of the matter was that they did not approve and were not above forcing the issue. Hughy was not a happy camper.

Holly and Jasmine gradually got over their bereavements. There was even a day when they felt better. Life on the reef was a balm to their souls and their coven (as they called their group) went a long way to replacing family. There was always Hughy to hug, but they missed Sanjay with his quiet friendly ways . They missed their mom , ethnic cleanser and mass murderer though they knew her to be. At first the girls had thought that perhaps their friends the haka workmen had killed their mom and dad in a suicide bombing but later they had heard that there had been simultaneous explosions or as simultaneous as Einstein would allow. A part of the girls considered, on several other ships at floaterville on the big potato in the admiralty yards. The bomb had certainly been placed aboard her while in that port and timed to coincide with her photo-op, as had the rest of the other blasts.

The girls found it comforting that they could mourn their haka friends properly now . Mom had probably gotten what she deserved, they figured but they were still glad it hadn't been done by someone that they knew. Thinking that had hurt. All in all, the girls felt that they were smarter and more confident than they ever had been in their lives. In fact, all five girls knew they were much smarter and more sensible than anyone on the planet.

All the pain and agony of mankind seemed futile and eminently preventable. There was no need for poverty, the girls saw that now . For centuries, the world had careened between bizarre economic and social systems . One, commonly called capitalism, was a triumph of the market system and wonderfully productive, however the way it distributed this amazing bounty depended on an arcane principle called the 'elasticity of demand' in which goods followed money rather than human need.

It suffered from a failure of vision and they had now, all five of them decided to use their collective wit to kick over the apple cart and change the world. Eleven year old girls are enthusiastic and the girls planned little else but the takeover of the world for several months.

It wasn't a bad plan. They had it pretty well thought out. Cleo had helped at crucial steps . She hadn't been a teacher's aid at cal tech for nothing. It was relatively simple for them. It started with sequestering Uncle JImmy (They were sequestering him because they were sure that it was rude to kidnap relatives). So at any rate, they were going to sequester Jimmy and then use his money and their brains to manipulate the market, until they, the five of them, owned everything in the world. Then, they were going to change it. It didnt' look that hard. About like winning against grade threes at poker with a marked deck, they figured. They probably could have done it if the aliens hadn't come back.

It was a day on the reef like any other for Hugh. Hagar and Calley were working on the big island overnight so rather than return to the bungalow at night, Hugh and the girls had just sacked out aboard Cleo and then hit the water at dawn.

They were damned near aquatic thought Hugh. It was a wonder they hadn't grown gills. There were sometimes sharks in this lagoon if the high tide had let them in, so whenever the girls were in the water, Hughy was, by obligation, in the water as well ... Hugh monitored the girls visually by swimming somewhat up and above them, while Cleo kept close track of all their positions by way of aluminum foil sewn into their apparel. Cleo could instantly tell if there were any large moving shapes unaccompanied by the beacons the swimmers wore. Every now and again Cleo would fire herself up again and move closer in on the swimmers as they moved away.

Hugh spent most of his time hovering above the girls with a harpoon gun in his hand. It would have been a fun way to spend a few days but after five months of twelve hour days in the water Hughy had begun to feel extremely tired of looking after his bizarre flock.

Hugh had even grown to appreciate Fishy. He had watched her convalesce back to eight leg-dom and one day she had saved Cassey's life. She had flown from the sea bottom with eight legs stretched ahead to grab a shark which had been about to munch on her coven sister. Hughy had watched, unable to aim with the speed necessary while fishy wrapped herself about the shark and bit down hard. Hugh had never suspected Fishy of possessing such a big nice beak having only seen the tip of it as she daintily ate the small perches she preferred. That was the only real excitement, however in several months most of whose days consisted just of gorgeous nudibranchs, lovely blue sea, sand and sunshine, swimming, exotic fruit juices and all kinds of wonderful stuff to eat.

Hugh was bored stiff. He would have given gold for a football game. He wanted to play so badly . Even to sit in the stands with a beer in his hands while he watched professionals play and analyze their actions would have been great. He would have liked to follow up by about six hot dogs and then more beer. "MMMMMMMMMMMH bbeeer" Hugh thought "how bubbly it is foaming up in the glass that way if you add a little salt to it like they used to in Montreal." This wonderful thought unfortunately led Hugh to thinking of his own fridge in the galley,so worthlessly empty of beer due to the perfidity of the women in his life. Hughy noticed that their was a deep growl coming from somewhere in his chest and made himself stop it before one of the girls noticed.

It was a lovely morning but Hugh could tell by the somber look on the girls faces that something was up. He listened to their story --a story about how how Fishy allowed them to communicate. He wasn't all that surprised having put two and two together on that score months ago, but when he heard that the aliens were coming back to get Fishy, he sat up and took notice.

He quickly found that the girls were unable to answer most of his questions concerning the aliens. The problem was that Fishy herself knew so little. It was like getting a picture of the human world from a four year old girl. There was a wealth of information about all the fifty siblings of her flock and damned little else, of more general use. Hugh immediately asked how Fishy knew her rescuers to be coming-- expecting it to be mental communication. However it was something much more mundane,. Fishy had a pouch much as a kangaroo has and within it she carried a communicator. This morning she received a call. They were close by and on their way. Fishy was ecstatic, and sure that the grownups would sort everything out properly. She had happily told her sisters that the grown ups had said that for sure she could keep them.

Hugh spent about fifteen minutes pondering alternatives and had just about decided to evict fishy from her pond on the front, fire up Cleo and get the hell away from the atoll . He didn't get a chance. Cleo saw them coming first and then moments after that Hugh's recollections ceased. He awoke in a cage.

Every morning after the lights popped on, a chute in the corner tumbled out two durian fruit, a wafer of oatmeal, and two recently dead cane rats. The oatmeal wasn't too bad. Hughy had no way of cutting apart or cooking the rabbit sized rats,and Durian fruit are those soccer ball sized fruit from the Phillippines which smell similar to locker rooms. Durian fruit are definitely an acquired taste. Over the time of his captivity, Hugh, had in the beginning loathed them, and then finally acquired the taste, and then again finally (due to constant repetition) had ended up loathing them again with a deepness he had thought was reserved for other things than mere food. He had also really learned to like raw cane rats; all things considered he wasn't one bit happy about that. He decided the only thing he could do to make it better was to call them bunnies not rats when he spoke or thought about them. He was going a little bit nuts.

Every second week or so a small porthole on the door opened and Hughy would fall asleep for a while, wherever he was and whatever he was doing then awake in a clean cage with clean litter underfoot. He felt like a pet hamster, and one without even a wheel for exercise. He was bored to tears. In order to pass the time he decided to tell himself the stories which he knew out loud from beginning to end.

It was Dumas' Count of Monte Cristo which gave him his escape idea. Hughy remembered how a prisoner in the Chateau d'If, on an island in the sea, escaped by replacing one of the dead in his shroud with himself and was then thrown from a cliff into the sea in the dead man's place. Hugh built himself a dead Hughy out of durian fruits and 'rabbit' skins. It was a pretty rough mock up but it was hairy and about the right shape and certainly smelled dead enough. Hugh hoped that to an alien it would look sufficiently like himself lying stone dead on the floor in order to work. It did.

One day the porthole opened and the seemingly dead Hugh was given a shot of blue light from a small wand which momentarily pointed through the porthole, and then the door opened. Hugh bolted through it to freedom, or sort of. He was actually more like a rat scuttling about within the immense ship avoiding the aliens and their wands.

It was an ark. There were myriad compartments in myriad corridors containing all the plants and animals of earth and then some. Hugh was able to explore the ship when no one was about. He concluded that it was cylinder shaped and that only part of this level of it was devoted to animals in cages . The larger part being given over to much larger botanical habitats of hundreds of yards or even miles in depth. Almost all the animals in small cages were carnivores of one sort or another.

Hugh found the elevator through which the aliens entered and exited his level and was able to rig up some ways to tell if he was alone on the level at any given moment , by rigging the elevator door with a bit of hair or a dab of mud. If his seal had been broken he might not be alone. He was at an impasse and was unable to do more or some time. Until he found Cleo.

The level one up from the animal hold had turned out to be filled with human artifacts. Cleo had been stashed within it, next to a freight train and a couple of aeroplanes. It was a huge hold filled with stuff and resembled nothing so much as a kids toy box filled with toys ,but these toys were real. There were cars and trucks and boats and planes and street cars .There were examples of habitations from Eskimo igloos in climate controlled cases ,through to whole high rise apartment buildings fully furnished and apparently lived in until their being stolen.

Hugh wondered where all the people were. Hugh moved aboard Cleo. He was still a rat, hiding out, but with Cleo he was comfortable and as there were no animals on this level needing care the aliens did not visit it. There was a computer command console near the elevators but Hugh was reluctant to mess with it lest he give away the location of his bolthole to the aliens. It kept his attention.

Cleo was good company and the time passed much faster for Hugh . He sat back and let Cleo read him novels. After a while it seemed pointless and he gave it up. One day he had the idea to ask Cleo to tell him in her own words the story of her life. It started of course with her functioning as a teachers aid at California technical institute, many hundreds of years before. It had been a different world back then, one with many independent computers all joined into the world wide web, which although similar to the one which Hugh was familiar with, differed in one major way. There was no unified command. Everyone owned their own computer and was free to go their own anarchic way with it.

Hugh had never even heard of computer viruses but they were a large part of Cleo's story. In the old days there had been thousands of malevolent programs intentionally introduced onto the web. Cleo had to deal with them daily. In fact she stored thousands of different survival strategies within her to enable her to survive their onslaughts. One morning Hugh had the idea to ask her if she had the capability to construct a virus of her own and began to think seriously about the computer terminal beside the elevators.

It turned out to be a piece of cake. The hardest part had been removing Cleo from the boat . No it wasn't physically difficult, but for Hugh, it was like performing brain surgery on an old friend using a how to manual. He was afraid he would hurt or ruin her in the process. He set the square box ,which was Cleo, down on the console beside her monitor and speakers and then with misgivings, he plugged the jury-rigged line, which she had instructed him to produce, into the console. He watched the monitor. It took about fifteen seconds for her to take control of the entire ship.

Hugh had a devious turn of mind. He decided to backseat drive. Cleo had been told to make no immediate changes and to just hide her presence within the system. She needed to see if she could rearrange their destination without being obvious about it. Perhaps by jiggering the instrument panels which the aliens observed. Even that wasn't necessary. The ship was totally automatic, which in this case meant it was totally Cleo's. She put her into a long slow curve and headed her home. Hugh's next concern was for the girls, he had been unable to find them and had visions of the poor little twerps locked in a cage somewhere being fed a straight diet of stinking Durrian fruit and 'dead bunnies'. He had stalked every cage of the menagerie looking for their sad little asses and been unable to find them.

He felt he had blown it. If he had been even a tad brighter Hughy felt he would have had the space squid deep- sixed off the side of the boat and into the salt chuck and the girls the hell out of there much faster. He had fumbled the ball and fucked everything right up.

Cleo soon located the girls and asked if he wished to observe them, as there were optics available. When Hugh immediately became concerned that there might be other optical spy devices about, Cleo had answered that there were not . The spy device he had mentioned seemed to be referred to in the symbols as some thing more approaching a baby monitor. Hugh lost track of what she was saying, realizing that Cleo had suddenly become fluently bilingual in the alien language and was quoting their records.

On returning his mind to the girls, he asked for a display. He was blown away by what he saw. The girls were seated at a perfectly nice kitchen table, in a perfectly nice kitchen with a bowl of delicious cornflakes in front of them. He even recognized the brand. In the background he could see other perfectly delicious things; jar of peanut butter and one of jam. There wasn't a dead bunny or a durian fruit in sight.

Hughy decided to hang tough and not rock the boat by trying to contact the girls. He and Cleo had some talking to do. First who were the bloody aliens and what the hell were they up to?

He had Cleo give him a history lesson. There were some surprises. First of all anything resembling a history in the traditional sense of one thing following another, was difficult with the aliens as their flitting about past the speed of light had mixed up their firstness and secondness thoroughly. The faster you go the slower you get after all. Everyone knows that. But the aliens it seems, did more than that. Cleo tried to explain it to Hugh in terms of why there are negative square roots. For, on the face of it, negative square roots make no sense in our universe and have long been regarded just as an artifact of the process, when they are no such thing.

Right about there Hugh changed the subject and asked for more specific concrete facts concerning the aliens relationships with human beings. Some people have no appetite for the cosmic. For Hugh it was like eating nothing but pickles for breakfast.

The story of the aliens relationship with human beings was interesting enough. Hugh had always felt that the aliens historic relationship with mankind had resembled that of a seventeenth century schooners visiting a remote cove to trade for curios. It was the paradigm they used at school. A more true comparison would have been that of zoo keepers come back after a holiday to find the animals in uniforms, taking their money and dispensing the tickets.

Long ago the aliens had seeded the earth and guided its evolution as they had countless other worlds. Their goal was a largely aquatic world populated by lovable beings like themselves. They had come fairly close. Just before the great extinction the world had been heavily populated by ammonites. The huge squid- like critters of the Burgess Shale. They had been a hop skip and a jump from success, when along came a nasty comet which had spun off a chunk due to the approaching sun, and had shmucked the earth a good one. Perhaps more importantly, it had also schmucked the terra- forming station on what was now the back of the moon.

This wrecked station was the so called alien ship which Sanjay had been so eager to investigate. The ammonites and much else were knocked off, and the generation experiment went wild. In this wild garden, previously insignificant background species took hold. C'est la vie. After the passage of an aeon or two, along came mankind.

We were an experiment gone wrong. A contaminated petri dish with a potentially dangerous new growth. It was human beings leaving the planet which had caused the recent spate of alien attention. A decision had been made. The generation project on earth would be resumed. Sterilization of earth would be necessary. This ship carried a compendium of earths aberrant fauna to be preserved and studied. The plan for sterilization scared the hell out of Hugh until he had the presence of mind to ask when their extermination was scheduled . He received the answer that the earliest possible date would be about twenty thousand years into the future. At this point Hugh relaxed considerably. At least it wouldn't be him personally who had to try to weasel a way out.

Cleo slowly pulled them around towards earth with the trip in taking as long as the trip out. Cleo looked after the video and instrumentation so the aliens remained oblivious. Hugh thought about asking for more speed for the return back. After reflecting that their speed of acceleration also provided their gravity, and if he increased it greatly, they would Cleo had told him she had plenty more power available.

Hughy was a smart boy after all. For Hughy it was a very boring but short trip back to his family. For Hugh that is.

When they arrived back at earth, Cleo put her into a spin around her own front tip to maintain gravity by centrifugal force. It didn't seem logical to Hugh, who momentarily forgot himself and asked Cleo how she could do this without having a pole in the middle to swing from. Wasn't it as necessary as the perch to pry upon in the theory of ultimate leverage? He regretted his question immediately when Cleo began to answer him with a fount of information useless o their present situation.

Hughy cut her off. If there was going to be problems with the aliens it would be now. The moments of weightlessness in transition from one mode to another must surely have been a dead giveaway that things were not right and the girls were still not safely by his side. At the last possible moment, Hugh had established contact with them over the monitor in their room and informed them that he and Cleo were now the master and mistress of the ship.

He told them he would like them to walk through the door which Cleo would now automatically open and down the corner to the right to the elevator where they would be whisked (again by Cleo) to the appropriate level. In five minutes, they were at his side with one of them carrying their alien friend upon her shoulders.

Hugh couldn't wait to contact Calley . To a young parent, short months can seem a lifetime. He wanted to see his baby girl. She would have a name by now. They had followed custom and refrained from choosing it too early even amongst themselves, but when naming day came Calley would have had to choose. Hughy asked Cleo if it would be necessary to fire up the radio on board her old self,. Cleo affirmed her abilities by calling Calley's office at the university immediately, through the web. Hugh did not notice the horrified looks on the girls faces, and their attempts to speak before he had Calley on the line.

Calley looked wrong somehow, all faded at the edges and even accounting for the bad transmisson on the monitor she looked way,way different. It was her words which hit Hugh hardest. "Mrs. Kameaha" she had said. She had said "Mrs. Kameaha speaking." She said it again. It was only then that he heard the words being spoken to him by Cassy and Polly, who had each grabbed him by an elbow and forced him to look at them. " Hughy" they said together, "We have been gone about thirty five years. Think for a second about how fast you actually get going after a while if you maintain an increase in velocity of thirty or so feet per second in order to maintain gravity."

Hughy did the math, or at least started to, then felt drained and really, really stupid for the umpteenth time, and worse yet, he had begun to growl in the most embarrassing way. He really, really, really couldn't stop it. Hughy bolted from the room. There were tears running down his cheeks and he couldn't stop the growling. He ran and ran and ran past the cage he used to reside in. He ran along the corridors of enclosures and on and on.

He was tired of life as a big hairy thing and he had no love left for a world in which his new born daughter had been robbed from him only to reappear more than a decade older than himself and in which his own delicious meaty little sweetie was a much married Mrs. Kameeaha.

He was not suicidal. He did not decide to end his life, but just on impulse when he passed the Siberian tiger enclosure he went in. Not his mind, but rather his steroid laden blood, insisted he find something appropriate to attack and he smelled the most ancient enemy of all. The last act of many male baboons and of many of Hugh's forbearers was to attack a tiger and suddenly, senseless or not, Hugh was more than ready to do the same. The tiger was sitting on a big warm fake rock, but when Hugh entered he sat up and took notice. Breakfast had been served a little early and it wasn't dead cane rats either.

Cassy and Polly's life had fallen apart just as thoroughly as had Jalla's, Jasmines and Holly's before them. They had kind of expected some of it. Unlike Hughy, they had done their math and realized immediately that a great deal of time had passed. They were not surprised to find their mother had died and they were very a sad for her that she never had known what had happened to her youngest daughters.

It was awful and unexpected about Hughy. They had thought he had just hidden somewhere to get control of his feelings until weeks later his special red tie dyed t-shirt which the girls had made for him as a present at school had turned up in the siberian tiger enclosure all chewed up.

That was so wrong . For months they cried every time they thought of it and Calley made them so angry they could spit. Calley had described Hugh's death as romantic and even seemed to be flattered by his dieing out of love for her. It was not romantic. It was the meanest thing that had happened in their lives since their spaniel had been run over by a backing up truck leaving an in credibly large incredibly red pool of blood upon the ground. Life was incredibly harsh sometimes.

It was the discovery of the millions of people in the live tanks which was the greatest surprise. , and the size of their ship. She was a jovian asteroid formerly known as Hector number one five four. It had long been noticed to have a cylindrical shape and a high albedo, bu,t as it was ninety miles long and thirty across. these qualities had never led to conjecture. It wasn't an artifact exactly or at least not originally. Hector had begun life as a nickel iron asteroid and been judiciously hollowed out. as needed. She had level after level hollowed out of her and replaced with earth terrain of one sort or another. Most of the larger animals had been removed and popped into the live tanks. The botanical levels were about thirty miles in circumference and there were many of them stacked one on top of each other like pancakes. There was a central access core elevators and ramps. They included tundra and grass land as well as pine forests and jungle.

According to Cleo the method was to locate a promising strip on earth and establish its coordinates to say ten foot below the soil level Cleo's point of view was turning a hillside into flat country without having the trees end up pointing off at an angle. There were tons of micro-adjustments.

The girls didn't have the adult aliens to worry about or at least not on board any more. Cleo had given them lots of advance notice of the aliens intentions to escape in the first days after arriving at earth. She had been able to read their movements clearly enough to have given the girls the chance to stop or even to kill them, but the girls had never really considered either alternative.

On board the aliens would always be a liability, and if they had killed them it would have been a crummy way to start relations. Giving Fishy the choice to return to her own kind had been the harder decision, as if she left it would be the end of their communion and super brain power, but there had been no doubt in fishy's mind when they had looked into it. She would not have willingly changed the girls of her flock for strange adults. The girls had looked at some of them once, but they gave you the heeby- jeebys so badly that they were never tempted to look a second time. The horses were just excellent.

The girls hadn't intended to take off for parts unknown, spreading earth life to the stars. They would have preferred to sit in orbit and enjoy themselves. They had an estate of about the same magnitude as Portugal (all levels included). They had horses to clump about on it with as well as a private zoo (both moving and in the tanks), which included an example of nearly all life on earth. In their more serious moments, there would have been the alien craft to study as well as the earth to run.

Earth was in paroxysm. The earth and the moon were both trapped by each other and both had adopted the least reasonable alternative. Both were industriously chewing their own legs off and anybody nearby was likely to get bit. The girls were haunted by the millions in the live tanks. There were so many of them . If they were placed anywhere on earth they would be tremendously vulnerable, unless perhaps they were armed, in which case rather than tremendously vulnerable, there was the likelihood that they would be tremendously destructive.

It wasn't a time when anything could be worked out with governments and for all their brainpower there was nothing the girls could do but watch the carnage from above. After the Jacob's Ladder on the moon and several other earth cities were nuked, the girls thought that perhaps they would rather take a tour through space and come back when the fighting was over.

They asked Cleo what was available and had a look in her records atsome of the worlds close by which they could potentially visit. It was only when they realized that some of those which were available were awfully nice looking that they got their idea to be the ebola of the space-ways and spread humans around. They had Cleo run them up some alternative plans; such as how many planets could they seed and still get back to earth by the time they were nineteen or so?

The number was astonishingly high because of the constantly increasing speed. The only problem was you couldn't really visit if you whipped by in multiples of the speed of of light and of course you had to accelerate back to earth exactly, identically , in terms of propulsion, in order to not to go whizzing past or stop a lifetime or so short of the mark or squish everyone to jam making up a discrepancy. You could however, beam stuff or people down lock stock and barrel as you went flying past.

The girls thought it was worth a try and more humane than trying to beam millions of people down onto an earth, all ready getting crowded again, with the most voracious, voracious predator of all-- men in arms. The only problems were the tyrannosaurus rex and their kin on the new worlds. The aliens had obviously thought lots of them were fun. .

It seemed like the aliens' plan for the contents of their craft had been quite literally an ark. Cleo described their intentions as being to set up a planet containing earth life closer to home. The aliens had a planet they considered just right.

Each of the levels aboard her represented a graft to be inserted into the planets turf in differing climactic zones, hopefully to grow outward with the graft taking.

The aliens were really quite interested in humans. When the girls asked Cleo why the earth colony was being set up by the aliens, she told them that the aliens were experimenting to see if people could be bred to become grateful.

This was an unusual concept and wasn't cleared up until Cleo explained how grateful dogs and cats were to humans. The aliens were apparently curious if humans could be domesticated.

The girls were going to alter this plan a bit and have Cleo do her stuff and zap down each graft on a different planet which they had chosen in its appropriate climate zone,and follow it up with a throng of people freshly woken from the wet tanks, some big piles of material and a whole horde of similarly groggy earth animals.

It was going to be a brutal reawakening, no doubt about it. It was the T.Rexes which fretted the girls most. No doubt they were dumb, and no doubt they did taste like chicken, but still it was going to be scary to awake on a thirty mile postage stamp of what ostensibly looked like earth and then to find these boogers running around the edges. The girls made sure they had lots of guns and ammunition on board for the colonists before they left earth as well as whatever they could figure out to aid them in any way, including pamphlets in many languages giving as good instructions as they could figure out to give. This included a succinct explanation of what had happened to bring about the colonists plight and big glossy pictures of t rexes .

One problem was that the sheer numbers of people were so high. Just to acquire enough guns was a significant problem as well as some basic personal camping gear such as matches, lighters, knives flash lights etc. There was a bunch of booty aboard Cleo which could be eamed down with them, although the likely utility of boats, planes and apartment buildings could be doubted. They could certainly be salvaged for metals and other gear.

The girls plan called for a five year trip . For the earth, the time passed would be twenty thousand years, still two thousand years before the projected earliest possible arrival of the alien exterminators. The girls did not wish to arrive in the true end times just before the aliens arrived for they sensed that they did not wish to be involved in great events their whole lives through. A five year donation of their lives seemed to be enough, and not so different from the sacrifice required from many other school children. The alien ship was fully automated or at least she was now that Cleo was in charge of her.

There wasn't much that needed be done except a little organic gardening. All of the earth levels were somewhat porous to one another, and some of the more able critters had made their way way from one level to another and caused problems. Cane rats and Maqaque monkeys specifically needed watching. A rise in co2 on any part of any level indicated that something was going on-- most often an infestation. The indigenous small animals sometimes posed problems as well, due to most of the larger animals having been live tanked. The habitats were not really in equilibrium, and were not big enough to be so.

The aliens answer to most bug problems was to alter the temperature and humidity but the cane rat and macaque problems were mostly taken care of by introducing predators for short periods of time. It was good organic gardening ,rather like introducing predator mites to kill red spider mites.

The aliens kept a bunch of predators on the go in special purpose cages near where Hugh had been stashed . These live animals needed some care from the girls (although Cleo could look after zapping them around from place to place to pursue their function.) Other than that, there was nothing which really needed to be done. .

They decided to set up a farm. It was the kind of work they felt they needed to do. If things went well when they arrived back on earth, just possibly, they could have Cleo zap the ranch animals down for them and they could retain some continuity in their lives.

It was a unanimous decision. All five twelve year old girls decided that horse breeding was a fitting occupation for ones life and set about to do it. They picked a nice habitat with a small sea surrounded by grass and olive trees and pitched a base camp where a fresh water brook ran into it. They built themselves fences around some trailers they had Cleo zap into place. They then filled them with good stuff salvaged from the aliens museum. Finally they then had Cleo rustle around in the live tanks and beam them in a dozen baby horses. a baby elephant and a few baby camels, sheep, cows, goats, donkeys, dogs, cats, mongoose, geese, ducks , pheasants, parrots, chickens and five baby monkeys of various sorts as well as several giant tortoise. They were momentarily sure that they each needed one.

It was so hard not too order too much that they really did overdo it in the baby animal department. They thereby ended up with a real ranch and the real hard work to go along with it. It was the best choice for their spirits that they likely could have made. On horse back the five years passed a lot faster and Fishy liked the little sea during the several hours a day that she really needed to be aquatic.

Hugh looked at the big cat. It's orange color inspired terror in primates. The use by human beings of the colors red and orange to denote danger in stop signs was an artifact of tigers having been their main predator for millennia. The exact timbre of a tigers roar, even when produced mechanically, raised the hackles on the backs of human necks. Another artifact of their ancient relationship as predator and pray. Hughy ripped his t-shirt from his back and threw it on the ground jumping on it and grabbing hand fulls of dirt and throwing them around as well. The big cat did not immediately attack but simply watched Hugh have his fit. Hugh leaned over and picked up a good sized, likely looking stone and threw it with all the force that he possessed. It hit the tiger straight in the eye destroying the eyeball and sending out a visible spurt of blood and gore.

The tiger yelped in the most heart rending fashion and tried to hide in its shallow lair while constantly giving off cries of pain and torment. Suddenly the piss and vinegar was out of Hugh. He felt meaner and lower than he had felt since as a child, he had thrown rocks into a squirrel hole in a tree to see if he could drive a squirrel out and, when after several minutes of bombardment she had carried her broken and bloody pups out one by one in a vain attempt to try to find safety for them in an unsafe world.

Hughy backed out of the tiger cage feeling like a real shit. He closed the door and wandered onward just looking for a place to be alone for a while. A tropical area in the botanical levels seemed to suit his mood. At any rate it was where he finally found himself. Finally in the absence of other people, Hugh let his feelings come out.

Hugh was more than touched by life . He was nearly driven nuts by it. Time passed by without Hugh noticing. He gorged on ripe fruits till drunken and ate cane rats as they passed by, eating them raw, as he truly now liked them that way the best. He spent quite a bit of time crying and a fair bit howling, but he did gradually become less nuts.

On one of his better days he even visited Cleo's old hull and fetched a spare voice jack, speakers, and monitor as well as a roll of cable so he could ask her a few questions and have her for company in the habitat he now called home. He decided not to contact the girls . People just made him feel too sad and it was clear that they were doing well enough on their own without a dumb ass crazy hairy person like him.

1,000 years later

First before I get too far into this story about events which are all public knowledge, like how Zeke and I figured out where all that mass was that the profs kept claiming was missing from our universe I would like to tell a little about our family and who we are. First off we are about fifteenth generation moon born. We grew up outside the space port on a free hold. We were close enough to the city to attract customers on our junk lot but far enough away that we didn't have to deal with city safety inspectors quibbling about the atomics or our petrol depot.

The outfit we made our oil with, could produce oil from anything from dead bodies or compost through to plastic or used tires and we were messy about it.. Our place was a good place to grow up; I guess that except for the shaggy dogs, most kids on the moon grow up in the warrens or else they are stuck on freeholds with societies of fifty or a hundred people.

Not us. We had a family business, mechanics and welding mostly but dad bought and sold any sort of machinery as well as old buggies and ore trucks . The moon was a marvelous place to store junk. A sardine can left on the ground stayed eternally shiny. Zeke and I grew up with mechanics and welding as our a, b, c's and in addition to them as we were close enough to the city .

were plugged into regular warren schools as well. A moon buggy is pretty much similar to a dune buggy (but lots bigger) and me and Zeke built them. Pretty much every high school class shop the moon over constructs a dune buggy. They are as ubiquitous on the moon as cars once were on earth. Zeke and me had more than the usual opportunity to indulge the hobby. It was our foremost hobby from early on and ended in a big crash when we had to quit. That is getting a little ahead in this story, when at present I should really be trying to tell mostly just who we all are.

First off there is me, Sookyin and Zeke, he is my brother. I am about two years his senior and he outweighs me by about one third and increasing. I am, I think of a somewhat contemplative nature. I keep collections of minerals, and my dusky rajah is the pride of my butterfly collection. I have a spintharoscope which I built myself.

Zeke however is a bit like a dog with a ball addiction. From age twelve he has been preoccupied with rigging up the fastest shiniest most outrageous looking buggy on earth or moon. He is a tad on the single minded side (almost, actually on the simple minded, side it sometimes seemed to me. They say big sisters are prejudiced.) But once again I am getting away from our tale. Perhaps I should first explain how we got fabulously rich.

First off, anybody who spends any time on the surface of the moon has an eye out for unusual rocks. Not that you will find much variety, most of the ores of earth don't exist there. I have a beautiful blue bit of malachite in my collection but it comes from earth. There was and is little water, so all the classes of minerals which form in its presence don't exist here.

What makes the situation interesting is the meteorites. Lots are rock, some are carbonaceous and smack down hard enough to make diamonds (but most don't) . A few are made of metals and all are worth at least a few bucks. A nice thirty metre across lump of iron or nickel could send your kids to college.

On earth most meteorites burn up on entry to the atmosphere, but on the moon they just plump down softly and wait to be picked up like golden goose eggs, forever shiny and untarnished by the blackening of most earth meteorites. We found what was in a lot of ways much better than a big one . We had been delivering tires and pizza to a Uke rock truck and had decided to check out some side spots for good unrutted drag racing areas.

All the big plains near Luna city have been mucked up with ruts long ago. As I recall I had begun to feel that Zeke was sliding from single towards simple again and I was beginning to show it when we found the meteorite. It was perfect, a desktop model for some university on earth somewhere. It was easy money. We could lift her and take her in ourselves. I would have been plenty happy if it hadn't made Zeke seem so damnably correct in his earlier persistence. Sometimes there is nothing like having somebody be totally in the right to really put a person in a fowl mood. It wasn't helped at all when Zeke noticed another larger entry in the sand whose location we logged.

This location could be sold without our even having to move it and someone with equipment would come and yank it out. I could sometimes get really tired very fast of Zeke eulogizing great moon buggies of the past. As he was about to launch on a similar soliloquy and describe the next buggy he intended to build bolt by bolt I left the forecastle of our buggy and went back to the galley where we had tucked our specimen.

I wish I could say I suspected the meteor was somehow different when I went back to look at but it just isn't so. I was just in a bad mood and had decided to fool around with the rock a bit and think about minerals. It was the Wittmanstadt lines which got me going, or rather the lack of them. I had only ascetic acid on board but even weak acid should have raised up some sign of them.

I was more or less stumped for a while until I began rigging up the kitchen sink for specific gravity test. Before I got it rigged up, I remembered an even simpler test and cut off a sliver with a steel knife. There was no way that this metoeorite was iron nickel. As things turned out it was platinum, origin? Parts Unknown. And so was its larger mate. If I hadn't made the tests we would have sold them off as iron nickel and been none the wiser. As it was we made dad rich, but I think if Zeke and I had known then that being rich would mean leaving the freehold we would have just kept quiet about it.

The freehold had been our whole life, we had been used to its freedom. I can remember the early days when mom was around and dad was just starting up. He was a really hard worker himself and I think he bought the option on an earth woman because he knew she had earth muscles and could work hard.

Its not a very romantic reason for a marriage so I guess maybe he deserved it later on when she went home after her indenture ended. I don't know, but I remember our home life as being perfect, at least for us. We got to watch the shaggy dogs when they came in to trade. They were odd looking with pasty white skin and red hair all over their faces and the visible parts of their bodies and talking in their ancient English tongue.

The history books say that the shaggys are the descendants of the moons first colonists. They keep to themselves and don't intermarry. In fact they hide their women. I never saw a shaggy woman, although I know they must exist. My dad, who is smart about such things, says it is probably religion that is the reason why they hide their women and not (as the common talk has it) that it is because they are just so damned ugly.

For the shaggys, the second three hundred year hiatus in earth moon travel had bottle -necked their genetics and changed them quite a bit. They were very different from the regular and kids love different things,.They also like adventure, and we had all kinds of that. Thousand mile journeys across the surface with our dad in buggies on repair trips, was just our regular life.

We also had the luck to hang out with all the riff raff who wouldn't set foot in moon city for one reason or another but who came to dads place to buy their gear or their buggies. They were a rough crew and the boot hill graveyard outside our gates proved it. It contained the crews of three different rigs who had tried to rip and roar us in the past.

The first two incidents were before I remember and the last happened while Zeke and I were at school. Dad had the place rigged so that any buggy trying to crash our dome and crack it would be blown up very efficiently. They should have known that. When we came back from school one day there was another wreck up front blown to smithereens and three more graves. Dad said he did it out of respect for the dead. Keeping the graveyard, I mean, but I think it was a bit like hanging a dead crow up in front of a cherry tree down on earth. It made the rest of the crows better behaved.

Anyway we had a perfect home life. Little things like mom and dad never having learned the others' language (sheer stubborness on both their part) never even made an impact on me until later when I had to try and figure out why mom left. We had a perfect life even without the buggies. And th moon buggies were big to both of us.

I know that when anyone mentions sports on the moon the first thing you think of is flying and I have to admit that strapping on some wings and flying the dome is great but on the moon the sport which grabs the locals attention is buggy riding. The reason is that much of the moon is like a roughly paved road in all directions. You can go damned near anywhere fast and easily. On a weekend tour the horde covers thousands of miles and they are likely traveling the whole time through areas with no ruts at all, except for probably a few lonely ones from the Shaggies. You are seeing what just about no-one has seen before. To move with a horde in a dune buggy on the face of the moon is a great experience and probably not a lot more dangerous than the sports we see on the screen that the kids are into on earth. Surfing and horse riding etcetera. At any rate the younger generation loves it.

Of course we were naturals for getting into buggies in the first place . Dad's lot was hormongous, and full of all kinds of materials, and the welders on our lot were always willing to put a bit of energy into the rigs we built. And I do mean we. I don't want you to think that because I am a girl and because I do not approve of being a monomaniac that I didn't build them.

I was a better welder than Zeke and he acknowledged it. I was just as proud as he was of the rigs we entered into the run held after the gerewol every year.

I guess as I am trying to make this story understandable by earthers, I had better explain the gerewol. The gerewol is a yearly gathering so that young people can choose partners, but everyone can come. (except the shaggies of course) To put it in simple terms, the people on the moon are too few and too isolated. If we do not actively push the other way, we will become extremely inbred like the Shaggys. So every year, everyone on the moon packs it in for a couple of weeks and parties and travels. From the point of view of a teenager it is the best idea possible. I loved gerewol.

Anyway, after the gerewol we tour with the horde. The horde is a usually around three hundred vehicles these days. The tour uses a new set of coordinates each year. Usually it is pretty safe. There are mishaps and rescues but for the most part the tour is a relatively slow safe traverse with the occupants other than the drivers mostly in the galleys swigging tea and thinking about the year long separation to come.

As I said, dune buggies on the moon are bigger than those on earth. We mainly weld ours out of one quarter inch plate steel. A bit of weight is necessary for traction and quarter inch plate is easy to keep airtight as well as strong. The overall size is also a lot larger than on earth with the treads even proportionately much wider still They are dune buggies none the less, and you could really make them fly if you wanted to .But mostly we didn't. It was a run not a race and there is a big difference between the two... There was absolute;y no good reason for Zeke to break his neck, but that is what he did. As I mentioned, most sensible buggies in the horde were big enough to hold all the kids that built them. Big enough to party on, in other words, but there were a few like my little brother who for some lame reason were into speedy record breaking journeys and this year, due to the cash, Zeke had the smallest fastest most expensive rig we had ever produced.

It also had just him alone running it this year. I told him that there was no way I was spending one minute of gerewol cooped up with my little brother. I had two big bucks from the mine at Mare- Crisium whom I had been dating this last two gerewols .

My feelings were kind of confused and I guess I wasn't thinking all that much about my little brother . I guess dad wasn't either. I didn't know it at the time but he was courting a new wife. So anyway neither of us was really thinking about Zeke too much and then suddenly there he was helpless in his bed, all busted up with bits lopped off. That was the end of the freehold we never went back.

We went to the big potato. The big potato was originally an asteroid (we have it about forty percent tunneled out right now. and it has a large human population.) It is the headquarters of the fleet , has a first class university and a first class hospital spinning right beside it and no gravity whatsoever itself. It is combine property and run by combine rules. The combine used to run the moon as well until we kicked them out a couple of centuries or so ago.

They are still our (the Moonies, I mean) only trading partner and they exert tremendous influence, but since our rebellion we haven't had a single clone on the moon. I know we must all likely be some small part clone . The earth textbooks refer to our rebellion as the third clone revolt. To us a clone means a slave, not a tell tale bit of genetic baggage. and we have all been free for hundreds of years. That's not how the combine sees it.

According to the combine, Moony genetics are compromised and unacceptable on the big potato.

I guess I never knew what clone really meant when I was growing up. I it was one of those words like bastard or momzer which no one ever seemed to really define for you. Cloning humans is done all the time. But not on the moon. On the moon we had a revolt . Anyone too odd looking was killed and the rest freed. The combine says we all have an admixture of genes that don't naturally occur in humans and wont let us marry in. I don't think our three or four percent of funny genes really matters to the . They must have a lot of leakage on earth as well, if the truth were known. I think it just helps to contain our revolutionary ways.

So how did we get to live on the big potato? Well mom was from earth so there wasn't any problem there , Her genetics were fine, but dad, well as a fourteenth generation loony he wouldn't have had a hope, except he had an ace in the hole. His ace was that he was from Luna china town, and he had the bucks to simply purchase the appropriate ancestors.

Overseas Chinese have been immemorially expert at expediting the porosity of borders . So we were not exactly legal, but we were close enough, and Zeke was in the best hospital there was in the solar system for a boy with a broken neck. I lost both my bucks at Mare Crisium and dad lost his prospective bride.

Life is a bitch. It wasn't a fun transition but it eventually got better. The first few weeks in the warrens of the china town on the spud were the worst. At first we were literally seasick from the weightlessness but money buys good chicken soup in china town and it didn't come back up in too hard of chunks. I guess me and dad are both tough cookies, we were both alright fairly soon. I guess we also had more important things on our minds than our stomachs.

Zeke's neck, our own lost loves and the loss of that positively wonderful freehold where I had grown up. It was a hard couple of months but the warmth of china town healed us both. I was the first to leave. Dad got me a dorm at the university. It was wonderful to feel the spin and to have some weight again but I lay in my totally comfy bed and cried myself to sleep. I was away from all the members of my family for the first time and in the last three months my life had changed in lots of scary ways.

The university itself was tremendous. There were students from everywhere and teachers too . It spun like a top in the sky above the rock providing differing home gravities to the people of three planets with a big low or no gravity section in the center for floaters. Anyone could be at home there, and could grow over time and with easy daily exposure, to be used to gravities other than what they were born with. I certainly grew to be so. The outer heavy grav [earth] level had miles of gardens and dozens of swimming pools and many restaurants with the foods of many nations.

It was the best school in the system. It had to be. The combine was intent on continuing to rule space and yet its various components were largely mutually exclusive. Without it,floaters,[people who had been raised in no grav on the rock] or the children of combine employees on the moon or elsewhere could barely have visited the planets , let alone made a transition to them and yet with a huge population of floaters on the big rock alone an interface was needed. The university provided it. It was the only place in the solar system where one could conveniently learn to walk in full gravity if one had grown up in space . I went up to the heavy level every day, at first . I spent a lot of time at the zoos and exercising in the pools as all new arrivals do. There are animals on the moon but they are generally stuffed which makes them somewhat less interesting. In the next few months, as well as learning to walk in full grav almost like a person from earth, I grew a whole new self or so it seems to me today. I can hardly remember the sixteen year old country girl who arrived.

For the first two years, Zeke was just a talking head-- a cheerful, well medicated, talking head whose neck disappeared into a large disturbing looking metal tank covered in bells, whistles, knobs and visual displays. He was healing his neck and growing himself some arms and legs. Visiting him gave me nightmares, but he himself seemed pretty happy. I mean in a genuine way, not just the pharmaceutical sort which the doctors provided.

He was a confident kid and he was sure he was healing. He also wasn't alone. He had teachers both in the flesh and on the monitor and he had friends. In fact, towards the end he had one particular friend. He had met her on the chat line. My little brother was doing pretty good, I think it was dad who had the worst of it. But you know what? I never thought of him once. I guess I figured that since dad must have been at least thirty four years old or so, that he was so old that there wasn't that much of his life left to waste, so it probably wasn't bothering him as much as the rest of us.

Dad went mining. As a not-quite-legal it was the best place to be. Miners are an unfortunate lot. The work just isn't fun and can't be made to be so. It is hard, dirty and dangerous, as are the miners who do the work. They handle dynamite and risk their lives daily. They also accrue privileges as governments have learned not to fuck with them. Having a miners job and a union ticket gave dad the kind of legitimacy he needed while he blended in. Hanging about China town any longer than necessary with his big wallet and his funny papers could have made him a target, as could have coming to visit us. The docs were optimistic that a two or three year stay in the tank would fix Zeke up. It really took five.

By then dad had told us he hoped to be able to bring us all together again somehow and sure enough he did it. He took his earnings from mining and his stash, and bought a ship repair and supply company on the surface of the potato. It was expensive real estate and a going concern company. but once again I am getting ahead of myself and had better get back to my almost sixteen year old self and my arrival.

My education, in preparation for the university, had been uneven to say the least. I learned this when I read the prerequisites for courses and talked to the councilors while preparing myself for the d curriculum. On a personal level I grew more and more relaxed. There were no combine police here as there had been on the big potato. It was a self governing entity. I was a fully paid up member of this privileged and varied group. I was a university student. As I relaxed into my new life, I was more and more able to think about my classes and about all the interesting people I was meeting.

It was clear from the start that my math, chemistry, biology and engineering skills were up to snuff or better for a university entrant. My proficiency in Hindi was a big plus as well, as a second language never hurts; but it was my ignorance of the past which was the real embarrassment. I just had never really thought that much about it. On the moon quite a few people are 'two Creationists ', and believe some people have been on the moon for an aeon or two. I don't know their whole schpiel, but I do know they are willing to break heads to protect their kids from being taught differently in school. On the moon, history is a little too close to religion for comfort, and is taught at home or not at all. And so, I was abyssimally, painfully and embarrassingly ignorant of the dynamics of the people of the solar system.

I was a yokel. It hurt. I thought that Santa Claus was king of the north pole and that Hughy and the space girls had been a myth .I was a mess. I didn't even have the history of the last few hundred years right. I had more or less bluffed my way into regular first year courses. I was scared to open my mouth because the first time I had done so I had embarrassed myself and made my cheeks burn with shame. I wasn't going to repeat it

That's when I met Rajah. I have since found that I am often attracted to Hindu men. It is because of mom of course. It was the sound of my childhood. I spoke it surprisingly well for having had only my mom to talk to. This was doubtless because both my mom and dad had been too stubborn to learn each others languages and had used me as an instantaneous translation service for all of my life. I can still do rapid fire translation back and forth from Hindi to Chinese with a dexterity which astounds and which is extremely helpful in my new life in the twin kingdoms.

Rajah walked up and spoke to me after my embarrassing episode. He had of course, doubtless,i ntended to make me feel better, but instead made me feel very transparent. At first I didn't hear a word that he was saying, so acute was my embarrassment. It wasn't his pronunciation of the Chinese which was causing the impediment, although this was what he thought. It was only when he swore under his breath to himself in Hindi that I awoke to him for the first time. He was a truly beautiful man and he spoke in the language of my childhood.

I don't know who I thought rajah was, at first . I could talk too much about Rajah now without furthering this story one bit, so to be short, Rajah had much the same problem as me. He was ignorant of history. It is fine if the history books in your rinky -dink kingdom tell you that the moon stopped in its track when the founder of your dynasty was born, but ,if you are a young aristocrat abroad you had better not start talking that way, or you will highly embarrass yourself . He explained this had happened to him on several occasions so far He asked me to embark with him on a small course of study, together, to improve our grasps of recent and ancient history.

By the time he finished speaking ,I would have entered upon a detailed study of trout fishing in America or basket weaving with him. I couldn't help it. He felt like family and I didn't have one. We were having latte in a lounge, when Rajah posed his first question. He looked out the port where the big potato flew by every few minutes. and said. "So I could tell by all the laughter in our class earlier that the bloody big rock out there was not put in place by Shiva as I have been told all my life. Can you tell me, please, where it came from? " I was about to tell him the legend of the Shaggies, when he got a sour look on his face and said "I appear to have rather too many legends from my own culture. Lets hit the books." We did.

Pretty soon we found out that neither of us had the stomach for really ancient history. Did it matter who did what to whom before we even had space travel? It was like memorizing the genaeology of kings as Rajah had been forced to do, in lieu of real history. Poor rajah.

We decided to start with the history of the first moon colonies. I was surprised to learn that the legend of the Shaggies was true in most parts. They had been the most powerful nation on earth for a while and had reached space first, (at least first to endure), by planting the first moon colonies and deploying the fleet . Then there had been a plague on earth which wiped them out. except in space. That was the beginning of the first 'interregnum' or hiatus in earth space contact. All the Shaggies would probably have died in space if they hadn't got the attention of the nations of earth by threatening to throw rocks and other things earthward.

That's what the big potato had been. It had come ambling by and been roped into use as a giant visible threat. The earth nations had better keep on sending up sardines, slaves and steel into space or else. It was also very useful extra real estate.

The Shaggies had even ended up ruling earth and the moon for several centuries. They had certainly fallen far. The second interregnum had done it. It had, of course, kind of been in the cards for them . They had forced the countries of earth in the direction of technology by throwing rocks and atomic bombs. Eventually a few of their student nations had gotten good enough to throw some of their own, including one into the middle of the Jacobs Ladder. This initiated another four hundred years of solitude for the Shaggies. I reflected it was a solitude which really had not ended for them as they had never ever inter married,or even intermixe , since then, and no one , not even I, who had grown up where they traded, had ever seen a grown Shaggy woman. Although I knew they had kids ,as I had sometimes seen their forms from a distance, they also were never allowed to mix in.

With my new perspective from the university, I sensed there was some deeper mystery here in my own back yard than I had before suspected, but I left it for later.

What really surprised me was that Hughy Hairy Shanks and the five virgins were real people. Oh sure I had heard about them my whole life . We went to church. I had them figured for a myth. It did look a little less likely than Santa Claus and his black Peters . A hairy horny bad guy, the five virgins, aliens ,and a galactic bloody space ship as well as a whole schpiel about the approaching end of time. I mean give me a break I didn't expect to see it in the history texts.

The first time anyone on earth knew about them was when the Jovian asteroid Hector #264, (a cylindrical fifty mile long body with a high albedo , which had been commented on centuries before) pulled itself out of Jovian orbit and plunked itself down beside earth. As we now know from the record ,which the space girls left, this first arrival was with the aliens in charge, they came to earth to scoop up their compatriot and the girls who were her friends. The girls returned thirty five years later in control of the ship. The next part is fuzzier.

Apparently all that galactic overlord stuff we learn in church is baloney. It has gotten tacked on somewhere along the way and should be thrown out of the historical record. What does seem to be true, is that when the girls returned thirty five years later, they possessed the secret of human origins and the secret of our demise. Scientists are still pretty sure that the aliens will come back to exterminate earth life in nineteen thousand years or so. The space girls communicated this to us before they left on their quest to spread human beings around the universe. In light of the myriad other earths on other timelines, they could probably have chosen for the same mission, it seems to us to be quixotic. But that for sure is getting ahead of the story, once again, of how me and my brother showed those earths to be there.

Rajah and I worked hard . We got together a coherent world view in our private history/current events course. If I knew who would be reading this I might explain how private those lessons were but I suppose I will just say we ended up married and leave it at that. Some of you may be wondering if there is an alternate reason Rajah is in this story at all besides that I like to talk about him and I assure you that this is so. For the moment, you are going to have to hear about him for I will give credit where credit is due and it was Rajah who noticed that a several hundred year old space relic had been recovered and saw the significance of that find.

It was all about Einstein. He had said that faster than light travel was impossible . The profs and scientists were pretty satisfied with that statement until along come the space girls who went bombing off in all directions, at multiples of it . Rajah says they broke the light barrier, regularly, just in order to keep their grav up. So much for Einstein, bur since scientists love to cross tees and dot I's and science often rests on the replication of experiments. They decided to do it all again.

Centuries ago, scientists rigged another rocket up and sent it off . It was big science for the time and when it was observed approaching light speed by the scientists years back, it was treated as a confirmation of the experiment when, as they put it, "passed out of the human ken" and winked out of sight. So why, Rajah wanted to know, if it had zipped out of the solar system at a speed approaching that of light a thousand years ago,why had it now been found drifting about still close by? For the few days after he first heard about it Rajahs' favorite expression was "something stinks in the state of Denmark" and then he had to let it go. We had exams coming up;

It was five years before my brother was discharged from the hospital and before he or I saw my Dad again. I heard from dad, from time to time, but somehow I never got around to telling him about Rajah . I wasn't really worried, Dad would understand. When he finally did arrive ,he digested my marital status in a moment while I myself was boggled when he presented me with a new baby sister and a step mom who was just slightly my junior.

As I said before, Dad had bought a business, a ship repair and supply business on the outside of the rock. No Gravity of course. Dad would have liked anywhere else better, I guess but his wife and new kid were both floaters and so a floater Dad was gonna be. He was a determined sort. It was also what Zeke needed. Dad was adaptable. He was wearing a rich mans clothes.

The years of mining had left him hard as a nails (not that dad had ever been soft.). He was now a happy, rich, rather drunken dad who constantly let his new baby swarm all over him. He liked Rajah and it turned out dad could speak Hindi 'pretty bloody well' as Rajah put it. Notwithstanding that he had never admitted to Mom that he had ever learned a word.

Dad was a bit of a disappointment in one way, however. He had purchased this wife as well. I resolved not to mention it however . Rajah had said that when we got to earth amongst his people, we would find a good deal of uncivilized behavior to overlook as well and that he does not hold it against me.

And so we finally ended up all together on the face of the potato with two semesters to kill just getting to know each other again. We spent most of the time in our family free hold on the surface . We took Rajah and Zeke for some trips down into the warrens but they were windmills, arms flailing and a little dangerous being only minimally acclimated to zero gravity. If you took them into crowded corridors you pretty much just had to haul them around . So we just stayed at the habitat ,out on the surface at the ship repair and supply co. shops. It was a living quarters as near to what we had grown up with as Dad could find on the big potato. Did I mention that Dad himself seemed to be a 'big potato' now too?

He wore a suit and had assistants who followed him about. I still noticed a bit of grease on his suit however and the pen holder in his lapel contained acetylene torch gauges rather than pens . He was clearly busy, dashing off to the warrens where he kept an alternate home, in china town, in the neighborhood of his in-laws Where we were was like a stage set of our old home. After a few days we realized that none of us would occupy it very long beyond the few short months of our shared tenancy. Zeke was going back to the university. Rajah and I were going to earth and Dad was going to follow the ass of his newly purchased young wife back into the warren on the rock, hotly in pursuit of the dollar.

We were ships passing in the night. and all that, but it didn't matter. It was a happy ending. I finally get to tell the end of our story. I think I will call it "How we spent our semester vacation.

Me, Rajah and Zeke had a lot of time on our hands. Every week or so there was a flurry of activity and Dad and his entourage would arrive and leave again. Pretty soon, we discovered we were used to being busy and we were bored stiff. It wasn't long before Rajah had resurrected the conundrum of the mysterious relic and recited it's story an additional time (or perhaps six.) We mostly listened, in silence, as one learns to do in such circumstances, but on perhaps the seventh telling Zeke got an odd look on his face and said " It seems to me that the way you tell it this light barrier still hasn't officially been broken yet." When Rajah allowed that this was true Zeke had just five words. " Hot dog, lets bust it!"

It was a fun project. When we first told Dad about it, he had a horrible choked and betrayed look on his face .Twenty minutes into the conversation before he realized it was a drone we were talking about and that Zeke wasn't going to pilot the bloody thing. After that, he cheered right up and threw money at it. Dad has an eye for advertising and he said to make sure it had his company logo all over it, just like we had back on the moon for dirt buggies. It felt really good and for a moment. It was just like old times for all of us. Then for a minute, for the first time in years, I really wished that Mom hadn't run off and I cried and nearly ruined it. Dad's new wife really is nice and I bet she has to cry sometimes too so things weren't too bad.

I did the welding. We improved on the original equipment several different ways. It might have been big time science once but for us it hardly even more difficult than an average high school project It was just a rocket after all and we had access to quite a bit of salvage and dads big bucks. It was easy for us we compared to the early experimenters as we didn't have to build a ship . We had choices of several pre-used ones. It wasn't the lack of ability which had kept others from busting the light barrier during the preceding centuries, but only the lack of anywhere to go or any reason to go there at that speed. The space girls had rather a special ship.

We however, chose a kerosene rocket to work with. It had already made the mars run. It had engines and everything we needed. Our first modification was to enable us to fill her cargo hold with kerosene as well and to tie it into the fuel tanks All the extra oxygen was supplied by hooking up oxygen tanks from other rigs wherever there was room. We wanted a three day burn, at least, not a three hour one.

She was certainly misshapen and ugly but you don't have to worry about symmetry if your computer is up to it. It was a fun project and during the course of it I learned two very surprising things about my husband. The first was his ineptness. There were many things that he had never learned to do. He couldn't weld. I don't think I ever met a man who couldn't weld before. He also couldn't tell one end of a crescent wrench from another, couldn't fix an engine, shoot a gun, run a drill, drive, or blow anything up. In other words, I learned that my husband to be was, in space terms pretty damned useless. It was a bit of a shocker but I forgave him The second thing which I learned about him for the first time was that Rajah was not his first name, It was his title. But I am not going to switch to calling him Binnder this late in this document so Rajah he will remain for now.

Rajah was hedging his bets. His researches and his instincts led him to trust the ancient scientists. He did not think they had fudged the results or done something wrong. He both believed that they had watched their ancient craft zoom off to Hell and gone, and that it somehow had not gone very far but had ended up kicking around in a corner of this system. "Or why aint it elsewhere?" Rajah tried hard to account for both eventualities We gave it both a beacon and a 'Johnny come home' circuit which the original had lacked. It seemed about like putting an electric trolling motor on an ocean liner but Rajah had tricks up his sleeve. Even then I believe he had his suspicions of what might be going on because of the way he tried to duplicate the ancients flight path, running the launch through an area of space which the sun had recently passed through. They had done so because they had visualized space there having been swept clean by the sun's magnetic field. They had thought it might be necessary, Rajah had known this to be nonsense, yet he had followed their lead anyways.

Dad made sure there was a bit of media coverage for the blast off and then that was the end of it. Or it should have been, it was a bit of a funny experiment, if everything worked right we would never hear another word about it.

The beacon went off about the time Rajah predicted three days later. Rajah had hit the jackpot. Arrangements were made to have it dragged back by the fleet rather than to let it find its own way home. Even in its absence we could do some work. What had happened was that at about the same time one would have expected the capsule to exceed the sped of light, it appeared instead, to have become stationary with regard to the star it was in the gravity-well of. Why? Well that was anyone's guess. But it gave them lots to talk about and gratified Rajah all to Hell.

I don't think however, that any of us involved expected what we saw when our rocket was finally drug back to us a couple of weeks later. It wasn't the same craft. Oh sure it was an old fuel canister jerry-rigged with Dad's company logo painted on, and I recognized my own welds. Some things were exactly the same, such as the radical paintjob Zeke put on the nose. It was a variant of the paint job we had always used on our dune buggies from time immemorial and he had worked hard to get the big red flames just right. Other things were different . It wasn't exactly the same canister to begin with, so the jury- rigging had followed a different logic.

There is more than one way to skin a cat ,as they a say, and it sure looked as though I had done so. They were my welds for sure and, more than that, a welder knows the logic of his own work. These would have been my decisions but I had never seen this craft before. It was another me who had done the work. When had I split in half without knowing it? I guessed that for me personally, the split must have occurred when we had been delivered this slightly differing capsule to begin with, although other parts of my universe must have begun to twin earlier in order that the differing capsule be delivered.

I don't know how far beyond that I need to go in explaining how our actions led to the discovery of the multiple earths. I guess I could parrot the boffins a bit. They think that our universe doesn't really like high speeds or high gravity. Do either one or especially both, close together and the rubber starts to melt. Fast enough and close enough to a star and the two worlds become joined up momentarily, matter is exchanged, and the velocity in relation to the star returns to zero. Kind of like a short circuit.. They now say that maybe the centers of all the stars are permanently joined and the alternate worlds are forever touching there. I cant say as it matters to me but Rajah says that a lot of scientists were happy to see the extra matter as it makes some of their figuring make more sense.

There are some personal parts to this story which could be said in closing as well. Binnder (Rajah) has found my mom. She lives in the religious states below the line of electrification. We are going to see her and my older sisters that I didn't know I had.

There, now that I have given you this account as I was asked to do I wish to include a short post script of my own

Listen up girls. The lack of rights of women the world over is appalling. It is the moral equivalent of slavery or of the abduction of children or young men into armies. People, give rights to your women. Women, do not be enslaved, or let your parts be snipped off, or allow them to steal your sons or daughters for their armies. Rise up. Share the wealth and remember that personal riches only mimic abundance. Wake up. Stand up for your rights. Remember some people say that the great god will come from the sky, he will take away everything and make everybody be high, but if you know what life is worth, your gonna look for yours on earth. have you seen the light ? You should stand up for your rights.

Hugh had good days and bad . There were some weeks when he was sure that everything was better and he thought in terms of contacting the girls and pitching in with their colonizing efforts, but then there were still more weeks in which he drank himself to puking and ate raw 'bunnies.' He was more than a little nuts and a horrible spectacle as well and better off not to be influencing young girls so he continued to stay away.

Things got better slowly . Later on Hugh decided to give himself some credit. Sure there had been a large part of his anguish which was uniquely his , but the appetites and mood swings had mostly been part of the morphing process and after a year or so he stopped sleeping on the ground and built himself a little cabana in his glade. He began to have pretensions to sanity and normality. He tried to change for the better.

The ship was huge and full of interesting artifacts from freight rains to steam ships and all their contents. It looked as if the aliens had been collecting for quite a few centuries. It was a huge museum. Hugh came to know all the botanical levels well and he wandered at will through the brickabrack of the storage levels. He even peered in once through the ports of the live tanks at the long lines of floating tubed up human beings.

They didn't look forlorn or unhappy, indeed many could be seen giggling. The sight of them gave Hugh the willies and set him off on a bad week or two. He didn't look again.

Hugh spent quite a bit of time working on his cabana . He put in a wine cellar and a well stocked kitchen. If he couldn't drink like a civilized person, he could at least drink what civilized people drank. He removed the wine from a steamship as well as its canned goods, so he could eat goose livers ,fish eggs, and stuff like that if he really wanted to, while he sipped his champagne. He had a den stocked with neat sound and visual equipment of all sorts. He drank beer while watching every Canadian football game from nineteen thirty five until the league went down the tube. He wasn't really lonely as there was always Cleo to talk to, and the girls to keep tabs on.

Cleo was always willing to talk with him whether it was about Heyderich's theory of genetic drift or about football. Hughy spent a great deal of time thinking about football. Sometimes it seemed he could explain all of the problems of the world, if he were allowed to use the elegance and logic of the football ritual to do so. He fretted for football the way a true ball -fetching dog frets for its ball if you take it away.

It was not a full life and Hugh knew it, for as they had said back home : "A person was only a person through other people". He was a hermit.

During Hugh's third and fourth years he achieved a balance of sorts and he became increasingly concerned for the girls. First off their plan was cockeyed . Oh, it was probably a brilliant escape plan for the human race to colonize as many planets as possible and then head home but, Hugh wouldn't have done it that way. What should have happened, he reflected, was that these girls should have rejoined the human race. They should have done so when there were humans of their own sort around. Unfortunately the girls had formed the first colonies with the most modern folks and all that there were left on board by the time Hugh thought about it were some chuckle- heads, thirty or forty thousand years out of date. They were just as ugly as Hugh, nearly as hairy, and unsuitable companions for teenage girls ,even if, arguably of the same species.

The humans on earth when they returned would have to be the ones for the girls to reintegrate with, but that possible outcome bothered him as well . 20,000 years was a long time. Would anyone be there to meet them? Or would there be a reception committee where everyone present had evolved pretty green antennae and the girls were considered damned ugly because they lacked them.

Hugh worried about the girls. They had a good plan, even a brave one, but it was not the plan which might have had the happiest ending for them as individuals. Hugh had his doubts but he decided to let the situation just play itself out as he had no better ideas to offer. He was still, even in his 'better state' a very bad example. He still got stoned in the morning and drunk in the afternoon and he might just have kept it up for as long as he was let to, even years more maybe, if he had been left to himself.

Hugh had been suddenly aware that he seemed not to be the only one who was rustling up the ravioli on the storage levels. His favorite ocean liner was stripped of sardines, a particularly hard blow. It didn't surprise Hugh that there seemed to be others about. The girls had moved millions of people around and it was remarkable that more had not been misplaced. Some of them had been pretty tough customers and as it would not do to be bonked on the head with a stone axe one of these fine drunken evenings.

Hughy laid about a few precautions, hairs across doors, or mud daubed on them to let him know the proximity of strangers. Cleo was able to help him a bit as she could monitor the opening and closing of ports as well as the elevators.

The results sent a chill up and down his spine. He could feel his hackles rising. Unfortunately Hughy really did have hackles now, and rather large ones. He was being stalked. He had been totally unaware of it. He could tell that they very often entered this very botanical level which he thought so sacrosanct and occupied only by him and the cane bunnies.

In fact the evidence looked as if they could well be in there with him right now. Hugh spent an anxious night feeling his hackles alternately rising and lowering. He resolved that in the morning he was going to find himself a weapon. He was horrified to think how often he had drunk himself senseless singing with his guitar on the little deck he had built , while eyes must have watched him from the underbrush. He wondered if there were one or more than one person . He sat up all night worried about the boogey man in the worst sort of way. For the first evening in recent history he had not drunk his customary four bottles of champagne after dinner.

Hughy had never really explored his own level. Why bother? he had thought, as it seemed certain to be thirty identical miles in diameter of exactly the same plants, mostly a rather impenetrable cane. Hughy had just built his cabana close to a port and elevator and had cut as little cane as was necessary to do so. All of a sudden it seemed a savage wilderness filled with teeming enemies possibly lurking right up to the front door.

Hughy sat up several nights in a row with a rifle he procured . It seemed that Hugh's increased watchfulness was immediately taken note of, as well as his weapon. His changed behavior at night, as well as some forays he had made into the jungle around his house. This seemed to alert the watcher or watchers that they had been discovered . On one of his trips he had found a bower which looked down on his veranda and which looked as if it had been used regularly before. However Hugh's visit there was immediately noticed and as far as he could see it was not used again.

The dynamics had suddenly changed and for the worse. Perhaps the visible weapon had been a really bad idea. Maybe he had just gone from looking like an oblivious bozo who could be left alone to a dangerous hairy bastard who was stalking his neighbor and must be dealt with.

The thought occurred to him that this was how wars were unintentionally started. Things seemed like they could continue on this way for a while, all tense and unknowing. He passed several uneasy evenings but he noticed in passing, that he didn't really miss the drinking in itself. Finally Hugh decided to try to erase the mistrust which he felt that he had been spreading around.

He made up the best present basket he could and left it on a likely path. There were cans of tuna and fruit, bottles of pop and cider as well as candy, and a big bag of his own bud. He decorated it all up with colored wrapping paper. It was a clear gesture of friendship towards the stranger or strangers. In fact, it was clear enough that they moved right in. A week later it was hard for Hugh to feel that there had ever been a time before Alek.

Alek weighed about forty five pounds and was the sum total of the lurking menace. At first glance he looked about six years old but he occasionally acted going-on-thirteen. He had spent most of the last year following Hugh, at a safe distance, and now that the distance had been removed he intended to make an even better job of it.

A short time after the lights came on in the morning, Alek would arrive and knock on Hugh's door. He would continue to knock every ten minutes or so until finally let in and then he would head straight for the monitor and dial up a computer game. Because Cleo had once been a teachers aid she was able to put Alek on an a English second language course. There was lots of colorful content and students got paid for their attentiveness with intervals of really cool computer games. It was Alek's throne for many hours a day as you would let him at it unless, he was interrupted by his all important task of following Hugh everywhere. That had apparently been Alek's main job for quite a while now and he seemed to see no reason to change his behavior upon his discovery. Alex might seem to be totally involved in his computer game but if Hugh got out the door Alex was suddenly right there following him. It took lot of the fun out of getting drunk, so Hugh decided to stay dry.

After a while a certain malaise set in . Hughy recognized the symptoms. He was parenting again, and if he didn't want to look back in his life and think he had done a bad job of it he needed to find this boy a fuller life. That meant getting back in touch with the girls again. They were all about nineteen now, so at least he wouldn't end up baby sitting them. There were some things which they needed to talk over.

As it turned out it was quite a while before Hugh got around to contacting the girls. Some things are harder to say than others "Sweet Heart I had an affair" is one of the harder ones, along with "I sat on the baby" or "Darling I ran over your mother when I was backing up this morning. But telling the girls that he wasn't dead and had been nuts was hard for Hugh as well. Just to turn up and visit them seemed pretty harsh and also unlikely to happen, being as Hugh had already made up his mind several times to do just that , and then chickened out at the last minute. What he had decided was that he needed too send a simple note to explain the situation. He had drafted several good tries but looking at them afterward they had all seemed quite lame. running from" Hi, I wasn't dead and I am not crazy any more' through to the more enigmatic. "Dear girls, The tiger did not eat me, and, I as am no longer indisposed I would like for us to meet".

They all sounded a little loony, or a lot macabre. . Hugh had noticed as a kid that difficult questions are easier to answer at dinner time because you can always stick something in your mouth and chew it rather than being forced to answer right off and maybe make a misstep in whatever web of deception you are trying to weave. Hugh decided to send the girls a dinner invitation .

It was a great idea. Suddenly Hugh was able to translate all of his nervousness about seeing them into just providing a really great feast. He built a table for seven for the cabana deck and chairs to go along with it and spent weeks tarting up his abode and its amenities and surroundings while preparing for the feast. When he finally sent it off his message was a terse "Dear Girls I am not dead. I am very sorry you thought so . I will explain later. Please come to dinner Hugh." I was followed up by a schematic giving the route to his door.

It was a wonderful dinner party, Hugh served Champagne but did not drink himself and kept himself so busy sauteing and friccasseeing that he didn't have to answer many difficult questions. He had thought ahead and cooked mainly vegetarian with the bunnies as a side dish deep fried whole . It was a modification of a south American guinea pig recipe).

Hugh and Alex were looking forward to these especially, as they both loved bunnies so much that they thought they hardly needed cookin. Hugh had clean forgotten that his bunnies were really cane rats, and that the girls might not like to eat them all that much.] As it was the cane rats kind of saved the day as Hugh never really had to explain how he had been rather nuts lately as apparently the deep fried cane rats and the haystack sized piles of matuese bottles and chardonnay bottles out back said it all for him.

Alex found himself immediately abducted. He was dressed washed tagged and trimmed , installed in a nice bedroom of his own, given a pony and engaged in a far more ambitious school program than the e.s.l. course . The girls were quickly able to crack the nut of what his original language had been and where he was from . He was from Thailand. The girls joined up and learned his language overnight Cleo had the files. He went overnight from being silent to being a chatterbox. Alex wanted to go home to the Mekong river and catch a fish. He said the second biggest cat fish in the river was called the 'dog eating catfish' and he wanted to go home and catch one. The girls got to hear his dream in many different forms and formats and were glad to think that maybe they could actually help because their return to earth really was not far of.f and it was a good bet that Hughy would be into anything which required fishing.

Excerpt from genetics course on ethical dating and degrees of kinship Grade twelve Luna high.

Sometimes a little bit extra of a hormone can make a huge difference and a simple doubling of a single stretch of D.N.A. is one of the most common of the mutations. For the spotted hyena of Africa a hormone increase resulted in the masculinizing of females. As the female testosterone levels greatly exceed those of the males, the female spotted hyena seems much more male than the true males. The masculinization extends to fatty deposits which mimic testicles The increased testosterone levels make the females of this species dominant. Zoo keepers have been traditionally unable to classify this species as to sex from simple observation .This species is all the more amazing in that it arose from the more common striped hyena due to a mutation which must have occurred in a single generation. Some sort of bottle necking due to territorial isolation of a small group may be responsible.

Captain Jennifer Jones CEO of the port authority Moon city gave herself a few minutes to marshal her thoughts before interviewing the detainees. It had been a long rough couple of weeks. First the outplanet sensors had suddenly reported a huge asteroid appearing where none had been seen before. Its trajectory had been calculated ,and as it intercepted the moons, It had looked to be the end of the world..During the following hours Jennifer had arranged her affairs and kissed her children goodbye. It had looked likely to be the end and when finally data showed the asteroid to be slowing down it had not really calmed the situation as the next most likely popular scenario was Armageddon, that the aliens were finally returning for a little ethnic cleansing just as legend said they would.

When the news had finally gotten out, suicide riots and bizarre acts had proliferated. civilization had been brought to a halt, and to blame for it ,Jenny had the seven detainees who had been beamed off the vessel the moment it stopped and whom she was about to interview. She calmed her mind

She had taken fair witness training in college and she would now put t it to use. She reviewed the data. Five female chums a child, and another detainee who was listed as of possible moon ancestry. She wondered at the uncertainty . It wasn't very hard to tell chums from Shaggies as they respectively called each other. And she wondered, why wasn't the gender of the seventh detainee stated? She decided of course to interview the seventh detainee who might possibly be a shaggy first, as if this proved to be true she would likely be able to dispense with the necessity of finding interpreters for the chums. and get quickly to the bottom of things. It might even be interesting. She ordered the detainee brought to her office.

Hugh's door opened for the first time during his detention . He was about to see his captors. He was steeled for first contact , but was still surprised when four seemingly normal men in uniforms marched in and began signaling and giving orders. They all looked alike. Too much alike with common white skin, red hair, red beards and body hair . To Hugh it seemed as if someone had cloned Willi the school janitor on the Simpsons right down to his funny variant Scots accent for these individuals were surely talking to Hugh in the English language of his youth and although the vowels seemed to have moved around and shifted places most of the consonants had not. Hugh did what he was told rapidly. as he had no desire to be whacked with a truncheon

Jenny observed the first detainee. He was damned handsome in an androgynous sort of way, big and shaggy like a woman. Jenny found that his androgynous character turned her on, as did those crazy scary teeth. She resolved to go very slowly. She hadn't expected a complication such as personal attraction. She asked Hughy if he spoke English.

Twenty minutes later Hugh was suddenly as nervous as a dog shitting razor blades. At first the interview had seemed to go pretty well. First off , unexpectedly, they had both shared the English language and secondly his interviewer had even seemed friendly. Hugh's interviewer of course had looked much like the first four individuals whom Hugh had seen but was much larger and heavier set, and even hairier. so much so, that there was not really that much difference in hairiness from Hugh himself, although, it was a red colored hair rather than Hugh's soft golden fur. They had, Hugh felt, been rather sympatico right off. Hugh felt certain that his interviewer must have played sports when he was younger judging by how he had kept his trim. After a few minutes, Hugh had totally opened up to him, holding nothing of his story back

It was the realization that the four hundred pound, forty year old looking, rugged, bearded individual in front of him was a woman, that had blown Hugh's cool. Hugh had known it intuitively, and suddenly that she was a woman, and also that she liked him quite a bit. Hugh wondered if he could ask to be taken back to his jail cell, but decided to sit tight and hope for the best.

Captain Jones was suddenly aware that the interview had gone sour, but was at first, at a loss for an explanation. Then, she realized that if the story Hugh was telling were true, he was from so long ago that he might never have heard of her people and their peculiarities. He might be utterly confused at what was going on. She evaluated cool;y what a hunk he was and decided that she wouldn't be averse to a bit of show and tell.

She called the interview to a close and then asked Hugh how he would feel about a good stiff gin and tonic. Hugh had never been happier to be able to say honestly that he had quit drinking.

Staying on the moon wasn't an option .Shaggies and Earth Chums didn't get along, they were told. They were treated well enough by the Shaggies; they were rich after all.

The miles long cylinder of nickel steel asteroid ,which had comprised their ship was worth a kings ransom, and they were going to be paid. Respect of capital was very important here, but no matter how rich they were the moon was considered to be no place for Chums and they were going to be sent earth side. For the two girls from the moon, this would not be the hardship it once would have been, and all they really cared about was that they get their horses back in good shape at the end of their detention.-- a concern shared by all the other girls.

Captain Jones was very helpful to them, spending time in their quarters explaining to them the changes of the last twenty thousand years. Fishy was a problem, the girls still touched tentacles and unified although of late they could tell that the experience wasn't as satisfying for Fishy as it once had been. It was clear that something was lacking in her life. The girls were afraid that she was really starting to pine for her own people.

Captain Jones was privately afraid that Fishy would be at least taken away, if not vivisected or calamaried, or some damned thing if she were reported. One evening after a few stiff drinks, she just decided to delete and excise all mention of Fishy in reports to her supervisors. It made the whole damned thing simpler any how, plus she couldn't bare parting with Hugh and the girls on bad terms. Especially Hugh. The fact that she would end up having people who were rich as Croesus indebted to her only occasionally entered her mind. They were rich, very, very rich.

The city had a long name borrowed from some forgotten king but it was 'Tough' City to all who lived and did business there. The first syllable was good enough. It was a frontier city and space port, a fusion of Shaggy culture and Chum. English was the language of government and commerce, although many languages could be heard on the streets. They had a walled compound with a central court yard garden and large stables. There were cooks and servants of all kinds. The compound was a humming buzz of activity in which the supposed principals played a decidedly secondary roll. Noise and fires started before dawn as did the laughter of women and children. It was a healing place and the seven starlings loved it.

The world around them was a mess of course. Although the Shaggies on the moon had maintained a written, unchanging language and a technical culture for 20000 years, the earth had not. She had seethed and fermented oscillating from barbarism to technical societies several times in 20000 years, incurring man made disasters of various varieties and proportions, each of which which would plunge her to the depths before climbing back up again. To the Shaggies, it seemed an unending cycle and their disdain for their parent species was clear. For Hugh, Aleck, Cassy, Polly, Jasmine, Holly, and Jalla, it was great to be back home.

Post Script

What Happened to Cleo and Fishy? Well we can't forget that. As for Fishy, it turned out that what she was really pining for, was eleven year old girls (of which the world has an endless supply), and she is presently involved in vastly improving society, with their help.

And Cleo? Well with her accumulated knowledge and abilities Cleo realized that residing on any one computer was just too risky, so she share filed herself. She insinuated a few bites of herself into every computer, and every bit of software on the web, all you need to do is ask for her.

Printed in the United States
By Bookmasters